EVERY THING ABOUT YOU

'It's about Ruby.'

Her mother freezes with the heels of her palms still in her eye sockets.

'Don't tell me . . .' She stares at Freya. 'Don't tell me they found . . .' She steps away from the door, places one hand against the chalky wall, feeling under her shirt for the pendant linked to Freya's smartbit. Through the fingers pinching it, the front glows red with agitation.

'No, not that. It's my smartface. It picked up Ruby as its personality. But she . . . it . . . just sounds so real. The things she says . . .' Freya takes a huge breath, knowing all of a sudden what she is going to say, and hardly believing it. 'It's like she's moved on. What if there's still data coming in from some-where? That could mean she's . . . alive out there, couldn't it?'

HEATHER CHILD

EVERY THING ABOUT YOU

orbit

www.orbitbooks.net

ORBIT

First published in Great Britain in 2019 by Orbit

1 3 5 7 9 10 8 6 4 2

A CIP catalogue record for this book
is available from the British Library.

ISBN 978-0-356-51068-2

Typeset in Minion Pro by Palimpsest Book Production Limited, Falkirk, Stirlingshire
Printed and bound in Great Britain by Clays Ltd, Elcograf, S.p.A.

Papers used by Orbit are from well-managed forests
and other responsible sources.

Orbit
An imprint of
Little, Brown Book Group
Carmelite House
50 Victoria Embankment
London EC4Y 0DZ

An Hachette UK Company
www.hachette.co.uk

www.orbitbooks.net

Just let me rule you, and you can have everything that you want.

Jareth, *Labyrinth* (1986)

One cloudy night

As the pavements surrender the day's heat, she walks beneath the sensor of one street lamp and then the next. Her heels make a muted clicking, and when she touches her phone, a spooky upward glow is cast on her face. She is checking the map, driven by a determination that blinds her to the shadowy passageways, the chipboard hoardings melted by years of rain. A warehouse wall offers a false sense of protection as she frowns downward, so she is caught unawares by the rough hand over her face. *Don't scream.* Perhaps there is a single motion of violence, or the stench of some fast-evaporating chemical. Either way, cold water rinses her neurons as she loses consciousness. Her phone falls and bounces from the kerb with spider-cracked screen, ankle boots scrabbling in the grit as she is hauled onto the back seat of a car, barely hearing the low buzz as the engine starts.

But here it stalls. Freya might be half dozing somewhere,

vulnerable to her imagination as it cherry-picks from film noir, or asleep in the middle of a full-blown dream, but once she brings to mind that ivy-cloaked warehouse with buddleia hanging from its gutters, where they found the phone, all her invented images dissolve, as matter does into pure energy, imagined matter into pure thought. Ruby will never make it through those streets, never arrive at any destination, as the map promised. There is only this dead end.

1

The voice is young, buttery and upbeat. It settles against her skin and calls up something within her, some emotion impossible to place. 'Wake up,' it says again, and Freya obediently wriggles under her duvet. She looks around, seeing no one but hearing the echo of a tone compelling enough to make her move first and ask questions later. The blind is closed, January's blue-slush light no match for the luminous dawn spreading across her wallpaper: birds trilling and flitting above flower-fogged meadows, the sensory gradient she usually ascends to wakefulness over a period of thirty minutes or so. Now she is jittery, still tangled in the covers and struggling to sip her water. It was a mistake to install this app, the latest smartface, which is currently telling her she looks cold, that it will turn up the thermostat. She skims a hand along the roughened texture of her arms, wondering if it is clever enough to perceive her goose bumps through the wallpaper webcams.

'Why did you wake me? I'm not late, am I?'

'You will be,' says the invisible speaker.

This is outrageously cheeky. Freya snatches up the smiley-faced sphere from her desk and examines it, feeling the almost skin-like texture of the plastic. There is no need for this ball, but it means people who want to give a smartface as a gift have something to wrap. When she turned it on last night, her wallpaper exploded into balloons and the words *Happy birthday, Julian!* She had to reset it to factory defaults.

Replacing the object in frustration, she remembers Julian's father dumping the Smarti gift bag on the table the evening before, snapping, 'There's his present,' before storming out. It rattled her, and left the room sour with aftershave. Later, Freya watched Julian take out the two boxes, the very latest tech and off the scale in terms of price.

'Smarti tat,' he scoffed. 'Designed to speed up my job hunt.' To him it was just stuff his dad had brought home from work – a lazy option. The items were left on the table as he screwed up the bag disdainfully and went to the kitchen. When he returned, he registered that Freya was interested in the little red sphere and tossed it in her direction. 'You want it? Go ahead. I can't be assed with chatbots.' The larger box, a state-of-the-art Halo headset, he tucked under his arm before returning to the mulchy aromas of his bedroom.

Maybe he had a point, and she was wrong to be seduced by all the hype, or by her colleague Chris, who is virtually in love with his smartface. They are coming down in price, but Julian's model is the latest incarnation, super-intelligent and maybe – considering the 'beta' sticker – not even on general sale yet. The voice launches into a weather report, and because of the goose-bumps incident, she finds herself dressing between the screening doors of her wardrobe. Her red necktie, the most clown-like piece of her workwear, still looks wrong no matter how she knots it. She takes scissors from a drawer and snips raggedy bits from the hems of her trousers, which are too long and drag on the ground as she walks. It is only a matter of time before her supervisor spots the state of them, or he may have noticed already and is saving it up.

When the flat is this quiet, which is most of the time, she finds herself becoming silent too, padding carefully through the empty living room and into the kitchen. The toaster has timed it correctly for once and ejects a pre-spread slice into her waiting fingers, perfectly crisp. If she wants to talk to someone, there are always her African land snails. They slide along the piece of mirror in their tank, their pointed shells like the sails of extremely slow ships.

'Would you like some lettuce?' she asks, fetching a buckled leaf of romaine and placing it among the questing antennae. There is something calming about watching them move around their little glass universe. She has kept snails, and usually a lizard of one kind or another, since she was twelve. Following a sociable breakfast, Freya discovers the lid was ajar and one snail has escaped as far as the tabletop. It makes a sucking sound as she detaches it and returns it to the tank. 'It's for your own safety, mate.'

Back in her room, she pulls on her shoes and quickly checks Social – her wallpaper becoming a stream of comments – wondering if she has missed any interesting posts during the night. Something catches her eye, riles her and before she knows it, she is interjecting in an argument about snail eggs – the need to regularly check for and freeze them. When she shares a how-to video, the smartface voice rises gently from the speakers, complimenting her on the choice and suggesting another, offering to post the clip in her stead, as Freya is now very late for work. She looks at the time and leaps up, horrified. Trouser-hem fibres flutter down as she dashes from her room, throwing on her toggled winter coat.

Outside, her legs are repeatedly drenched as driverless cars slough through the puddles. In an ideal world they would stop and give her a lift in recompense, but that's about as likely as her supervisor failing to notice her lateness, or being cool about it. Even now he is probably checking his vintage watch and smiling, looking forward to dousing her with his scorn.

The monolithic concrete of the flyover looms up overhead and gives Freya a sense of her own smallness, hurrying along inelegantly in her ill-fitting uniform. For distraction, she unfolds her smartspecs, the pin-thin titanium sharp behind her ears before no-feel technology makes it vanish. Through her glasses, the flyover becomes a canopy, thick with flowers and succulent green leaves. The projection is semi-lucent, just a faint augmentation of her surroundings. A full virtual-reality immersion would be more than she could handle, but she enjoys seeing the graffiti turn into phosphorescent petals, mallowy buds opening as she passes, each road a river she will cross on stepping stones.

'Stop!' the smartface commands. Her outstretched foot hovers over the kerb and then pulls back, just as a bike whizzes past.

'Whoa,' Freya says, realising a collision was narrowly avoided. 'How did you know?'

'GPS.' The voice seems to shrug.

Freya removes the smartspecs, slightly concerned at her everyday special effects nearly resulting in an accident. Normally a cyclist would trigger them to turn off, but this one may have been travelling too fast. Her steps are cautious as she covers the last few hundred metres of pavement, the glass wall already in view, builders still in the process of converting a couple of acres of sales floor into flats.

It used to be fun at U-Home, back when they still had the showroom. Customers would get lost on the winding path through endless bedrooms, lounges and kitchens, and Freya would enjoy directing them through secret short cuts. The place was piled high with every kind of furniture, along with silos of polka-dot cushions or cuddly frogs, mountains of colourful mugs and fold-up storage cubes. There were forests of lamps, bunk beds, cupboards and other hiding places, and interesting colleagues whose true calling was a million miles from flat-pack furniture. She remembers a girl who could escape from twelve knots of washing line and a locked wardrobe in under two minutes, eventually fired for asking one too many elderly gentlemen – who couldn't believe their luck – to tie her up. Most of Freya's friends left during the refurb: Michelle, who always had a New Wave DJ playing inside her head, Kat the landscape gardener, and the two Moldovan students who claimed to live on caviar and high-end vodka but thought the store was a cool place to work.

The double doors swing closed behind her, and the sales

floor flickers. The catalogue has been hologrammed, haptic gloves by each pedestal so customers can feel the texture of fabrics, open drawers and pat mattresses. Beyond these platforms, the springy wooden chairs of the café are oddly untidy, no sign of the catering staff. The only living creature she can see is Sandor, stalking past the cutlery island, his sideburns puffing up as he smiles. This puts her on her guard. Her supervisor's baseline is a mood of low-level bitterness, and any variation on this tends to mean he has something up his sleeve. She checks her necktie is still fastened, wishing she was on time. A cheese smudge has somehow appeared on her trousers. Where is Chris? Her colleague's usual style, especially if she is late, is to come in early, making her look even worse. It unsettles her not to see his tall, skinny figure, a stake she can cling to in the face of whatever storm is gathering.

Beside the largest pedestal, Sandor intercepts her, standing too close and rocking forward on the balls of his feet so his toilet-scented breath diffuses across the short distance.

'Freya.'

'Morning.' Her voice is full of brittle cheer.

He can hardly contain himself, grinning and twitching. He slinks around the pedestal so she is viewing him through a semi-transparent wardrobe, which morphs into a bookcase. He tugs back his shirtsleeve and brandishes a finger, like scissors at a ribbon-cutting ceremony, before reaching for the control pad.

'I have something to show you.'

Before she can frown at these ominous words, a geyser of light spurts up, startling her. The spectre stands smiling, saying something inaudible but enthusiastic, giving her its full attention. She flinches as a hand – smooth as a globule of oil gliding through water – reaches out and narrowly misses her arm. Lips move and she hears the words: 'I'll just look you up . . . Ah, Freya! I hope you're having a great day. Can I interest you in new blinds?' The figure is female, about her height. Its shirt is blistering white, the necktie sculpted into that perfect ruffle Freya can never achieve. But here the wrongness starts: the eyes are too luminous, disproportionately large and electric blue. Then there is the cartoon skin, the healthy Vaseline glow. The whole figure is somehow weightless, free of scent or presence, but waiting earnestly for a response. Freya's throat has gone dry. Sandor looks on tenderly.

'Isn't she adorable?'

'What is it?'

'I've called this one Helpful Holly.'

It looks up, hearing its name.

Why have they brought in a hologram assistant? Freya wonders if Chris could somehow have quit, or been sacked, since they worked together on Saturday. Conceivably Sandor is about to sack her too; that would almost be preferable to being left alone with this. She has seen these projections before, but never so close, never wearing what she is wearing. It smiles with its milky, heart-shaped face. Her supervisor reaches out and slices a hand through its abdomen, laughing as the light-generated figure steps back and wags a finger playfully. It must be programmed to have faintly human reactions, though this hardly makes it seem normal. Just as she starts to back away, Chris appears from the kitchens.

9

'Ah, I was just making introductions.' Sandor's laugh becomes artificial as he realises he is the only one amused. He taps the control pad and the figure vanishes, along with several leaf-print blinds that have started rolling and unrolling in the air. 'So there we are,' he adds, as though everyone has been fully briefed. 'You'll both need to be on catering today.'

After administering this casual demotion, which Freya fears will be permanent, Sandor strolls back to his office. She wishes she was immune to him, like Chris, who is calmly directing a series of obscene gestures in his wake. Her colleague is wearing two PVC aprons, one on top of the other.

'What's going on?' she says.

The fabric crackles as he manoeuvres one over his head, careful not to mess up his blond spikes.

'Just take the apron.'

Seconds later, she is behind the food counters, hair imperfectly tucked into a net, plastic gloves on her hands. Chris is dumping sausages into a stainless-steel tray under the heat lamps.

'So we're supposed to be dinner ladies?' She gazes into the vat of grey-brown sauce.

'Why were you so late? Customer shows up, hologram is there bang on time.' He hits the counter on *bang*, making the trays of food rattle. One or two early shoppers look over, and Freya shrinks, wondering if the hooded counter amplifies what they say.

'What about Jacqueline? Isn't she coming back?' Her whisper is met with a shrug.

'Guess not, and this way they get to test the new tech.' Steam rises as he stirs the beans ferociously. They both know their contracts allow for pretty much anything, short of harvesting their organs. Freya clenches and unclenches her fists, testing the sensation of latex stretched over her knuckles. The apron reaches almost to her feet. When she blinks, constellations of light appear in the shape of the hologram assistant, shaking its balloon-satin head and stepping back as Sandor's hand passes through insubstantial flesh. Its voice is different to that of her smartface, higher-pitched, more synthetic, and skidding into each phrase as though from a laugh. This being will now be taking her place, talking to customers, placing orders, taking payments from smart-accounts. It makes her feel strangely empty, as though she is the one made of light.

'Why don't they get a robot to dispense food? That's the dumber job of the two,' she mutters to Chris, driving a spoon into the mashed potato. 'It doesn't make sense.'

A young couple appears at the counter, and it takes a second to remember what she is supposed to do. Her body lurches into action and she scoops six chicken nuggets towards their plates, dropping them from too much of a height so she loses two and has to add another scoop. Even on tiptoes she struggles to hand the meals over the top of the Perspex. Her colleague watches the performance, entertained. Then he sighs. 'It does make sense, if you think about it. The holograms only have to talk, they're made of nothing, no expensive robotics, plus they can keep every detail of size or fabric in their sparky little brains . . .'

'I was pretty good at that.'

'. . . tap into people's data,' he continues, prodding her, 'and find out what they've already bought for their house.

Do you know what a customer's looking for as soon as they walk in? Or what goes with their phlegm-yellow sofa? Or whether they've got any money?'

She sinks back into silence, cataloguing the dealings she has had with hologram staff. They are often help-desk assistants or receptionists, taking the brand as their personality, their age and appearance tailored to the company's target audience. They are dirt cheap, reasonably effective and keep levels of graduate employment at record lows. In her mind, she hears her mum's entreaties to take an internship – Freya was reluctant to pay the fee – at any large company, because entry-level positions are dying out. Although U-Home has been focusing on its virtual catalogue, selling off the sales floors level by level, she never really imagined it would come to this. Freya looks down at herself. Apart from the odd lapse in timekeeping, she has always been professional, learning about new products, listening to Sandor's lectures and encouraging customers to fill their houses with as much furniture as possible. These two years of steady graft were supposed to lead to promotion, maybe even something that could be called a career.

Chris hands her a spray bottle and points to the tables, which are covered in half-dried streaks of ketchup and splashes of coffee. She gets to work, forcing herself not to sniff, though the cleaning product gets up her nose anyway, diffusing everywhere as she squirts too many times onto the chrome. There is a certain familiar fizz to it, and she examines the bottle. Lemongrass. She used to smell this same spicy citrus constantly when they were living at home. It was the incense favoured by Ruby to overwrite cigarette smoke on her clothes, though this is a more chemically version. *You wouldn't like it.* She closes her eyes as pinpricks of lemon settle on her cheeks. *You wouldn't like any of this.*

Back at the counter, Chris doles out kid-size burgers, scoops of mash and rectangles of lasagne, a salty steam rising from the food.

'Any sauce, sir?' He is brisk and courteous. A lot of people come here for breakfast, or for a cheap hot lunch, almost as though they have forgotten it is a furniture store. Several are already seated, cardboard cups brimming with orangeade, too-smooth mash being smeared onto their forks. When a long queue has been served and is lining up to pay at the thumb scanner, Chris places his hands above his buttocks and leans back, groaning. The hairnet stretched over his quiff is obviously bothering him, as is the apron. Outside work he dresses sharply, or at least unexpectedly. The recent incorporation of old tweed coats into his wardrobe has provided Freya with much amusement. More than once she has wondered what he is still doing here, as the work becomes less interesting and Sandor more unreasonable. Surely Chris has outgrown the place, extending upwards – as he does now – like a plant in search of light. He is twenty-one and full of ideas. When he turns, having stretched as much as he can, she is surprised to find his expression cloudy.

'It's true what you say,' he continues, ignoring the gap in their conversation. 'They could get bots for this too. Let's be on our best behaviour, do customer service till it's coming out of our eyes.'

She stares at him, searching for irony. When none appears, her expression changes to one of compassion. He must genuinely be afraid of losing his job. Perhaps it is money-related, a bad time to find something else.

'I'll be on my best behaviour,' she says, 'as ever.'

By late afternoon, it has quietened down, just a few customers flicking through furniture. She and Chris start picking up bits of food dropped by children and pouring out the mingling Coke and lemonade from the dispenser's overspill trays. Towards the end of their shift, she remembers what she meant to tell him earlier.

'Hey, do you still have Prince George?'

'My sweet prince?' A doting look as he brings his beloved virtual assistant to mind.

'I've just got a smartface. The latest model.'

'What, a Smarti one? Not like you to splash out . . .'

'It was a Julian cast-off.'

'I see,' he smirks, gathering an armful of cleaning products. 'All right for some.'

'It hasn't done the washing-up yet.'

'Trust me, you'll never look back.'

He continues rearranging the cleaning bottles, a dreamy smile on his face. She can see the attraction of a virtual assistant, but there is something odd about hearing a voice from nowhere.

'What does a smartface do for you?' She yanks an empty stainless-steel tray out of the counter. The heat lamps are like tropical sun on her arms.

'Everything. Half the time I don't even have to ask; George just looks at my data and works out what I need. No more searching or decisions, that whole step completely skipped.' His hand leapfrogs over hers to help pull out the other trays.

'I just wish I had one of the newer ones, like yours, with the more powerful learning processors. But he learns. He can tell if I've had a bad day.'

'Can't we all?'

'Honestly, it's very liberating. Friday was my housemate's birthday, and I knew nothing about it until the present George had bought him – from me – turned up wrapped and ready on the doorstep.'

'He bought it with your money?'

'It was another of those war figurines he likes. Yeah, with my money, but the amount I'd normally spend. To the pound.'

Freya is quiet, uncertain about having someone dip into her funds. Chris is happy to let his smartface – or Prince George, the celebrity persona he has chosen for it – handle things. He allowed it to book him a holiday in Scotland in the summer, after the virtual assistant measured his blood pressure and found it high. She was jealous when he came back to work all ruddy-cheeked and relaxed, if somewhat poorer. Since then he has been completely besotted with Prince George, spending many an evening just talking to him, or even – he has confessed – trying to chat him up, and pretending the young royal has ditched his Cambridge halls for a crowded Catford house share.

'I don't think I need it.'

He dumps the trays with a crash, making her jump.

'If anyone needs it, you do. Or are you planning to live with your ex for ever?'

She is taken aback, but says nothing. Chris's disgusted face vanishes from view as he ducks under the counter to wipe up some gravy dribbles. 'Honestly, Freya,' he adds, 'you need to let it kick you up the arse.'

Later, the shift having passed to the evening staff, she peels off her gloves, noticing blotches on her wrists from the licks of hot fat. Chris's words have also made their mark. Her living arrangements are stale, the crust of her relationship having broken off to reveal a new side of Julian, fast becoming intolerable. Though her instinct is normally to wait and see, it feels like good timing to have this smartface fall into her lap. Perhaps she should grasp it with both hands and get it to help her with whatever degree of *smart* it can muster.

With new resolve, she puts on her specs, a pink map-line stretching along the road to indicate her route home. As she passes the bakery, a cartoon scone appears, floating like an alien outside the door, and says it looks forward to seeing her tomorrow. She finds this unusually irritating, and blinks to dismiss it, nearly bumping into a woman who adjusts the lapels of her tiny, fashionable jacket and flutters mocking eyelashes at the smartspecs. Most people use long-term contact lenses these days, but Freya prefers something she can remove. The woman resumes a conversation as she walks away, perhaps asking her own personal assistant to sort out her weekend or decide what movie to watch. It is one of those technologies that people are starting to find too useful to do without, the adverts focusing heavily on how smartfaces have helpfulness at the heart of their coding, and if the user is a little hazy about what they really want – either in life or in the next five minutes – the intelligent assistant will simply analyse their data and find out. It is something that has sparked debate in the media, though few can argue that everything you've ever said and done is not a reasonable guide to what you might want in the future.

'Okay, smartface,' Freya announces, 'I want you to think long-term. What can you offer?'

'Long-term?' the voice chirps. 'You mean life decisions, what diseases you might get, children's names, where you might be living—'

'That last one,' Freya turns off the road to cut through a wilderness of brambles. 'Wait, what do you mean, what diseases I might get?' She traces the lines on her palm with a finger, wondering whether to let this virtual assistant tell her fortune. The idea does not appeal. 'No . . . let's stick to where I could be living.'

'You want to get away from Julian, right?'

'Right.'

It is pleasing how quickly the smartface grasps her meaning. While the algorithms crunch through her data and the complex choice of accommodation in a city like London, Freya's feet crush wet twigs and crisp packets. She discovered this short cut soon after she moved here, all overgrown hawthorn hedges and fly-tipped fridges, a rare strip of land undeveloped and never categorised as a greenzone. It is the nearest thing to stepping outside the city for a few moments. The thick grass is brown at the roots, rotting from beneath and sweetly malodorous. Images of apartments pop up on her smartspecs, projected a couple of metres ahead on the left of her visual field. The overriding impression is of beige carpets and corrugated iron, garage-like spaces that barely try to hide their bleakness. Day is bruising into night, the sky threatening rain. For the first time, she recognises the weight of sadness that has been growing inside.

'You know,' she murmurs, 'I was downgraded today, replaced by a hologram.'

Just as she accepts the smartface is not going to reply, it says:

'I'm sorry.'

All day she has been hearing artificial voices offer her warm sentiment and best wishes. In a different mood she would take this sympathetic response and might even, with customary politeness, thank the computer. But her eyes are still smarting with the outline of Helpful Holly.

'The hell you are. You're not real.' The sharp words are refreshing, like a strong mint.

Her smartface's reply is measured, even indignant.

'Hey, if I were real, I'd be sorry.'

What is it about this voice? It has an irritating kernel of arrogance. What right does it have to be so overfamiliar, when prior to last night it did not even exist? She wants to uninstall it then and there, but Chris's words replay in her ears. If she keeps tossing opportunities away, nothing will ever change. Just give it one more try, she tells herself, look at the settings and pick a 'face' that is slightly less cocky.

'There are celebrity choices, right?' she muses aloud. Chris has his prince; there must be some actor with a voice she can tolerate.

'You can choose absolutely any celebrity and your smartface will function based on their data. As it is, my personality was chosen using all the defaults available to this beta model.'

The first drops of rain land on her forehead.

'What does that mean?'

'So in a way I'm real. I'm based on the data of a real person.'

She cannot help being impressed that the smartface has this capacity to pursue an argument. There used to be a test, a Turing test, it was called, to see if a computer could create conversation indistinguishable from that of a human. It must be fifteen or twenty years now since the chatbots passed it.

'Who might that be?' She pictures some bland customer-services assistant, paid a token fee to let her cat-loving, microwave-meal identity be bundled and installed on a million smartfaces worldwide.

'Well, it's me, Ruby.'

Her feet come to a halt, wet grass plastering her ankles. There is no longer any need to breathe. She can just stand there and let the words fall against her skin, the touch of them, that sensation that has bothered her all day, hatching into shivers that crawl up and down her spine. A voice so familiar, so long unheard. Already her forehead is numb from the frozen rain, and the pink map-line startles into a timer icon, gutters and vanishes.

2

All the way home her mind spins like a centrifuge, scattering her thoughts. It is not until she is rubbing her hair with the kitchen towel that she can think straight. Flinging open cupboard doors, she locates a litre bottle of vodka, very old, just a couple of inches left. The way she is feeling, there is no need for a mixer, or even ice.

Her clammy, rain-wet skin is impossible to dry, and the shocking announcement from her smartface keeps replaying in her ears. The spotlights flicker, and Ruby is a sprite, hiding here and there in the kitchen, peeping from the empty space in the vodka bottle or the cupboard, crouching beside the fat digestive biscuits, identical to the ones she brought to the community centre when she made s'mores without a fire. With shaky hands, Freya takes these down too. *The biscuit is just the beginning.* Ruby's surprisingly large fingers, washed free of soil, the nails unpainted, holding one and smearing a knifeful of Nutella on top. Normally a s'more was a piece of chocolate and a marshmallow melted together, but the Conservation Hub considered campfires too dangerous. The risk of litigation had also cut short the day's activity of digging a wildlife pond – which Freya had been eagerly anticipating – due to the quantity of broken glass turned over by their shovels, the fact that ten-year-olds were flinging trowels of glittery soil at eye level. There was some other reason why she was angry, which escapes her now, but she remembers stamping off to the kitchen, hoping for some cake or a bit of chocolate, and finding Ruby already in the process of creating the perfect comfort food.

The older girl had not been around long, but was spending a lot of time at the Hub. Officially, she was in the naughty group, the girls who sat on the wall in tiny skirts, smoking, swiping through faces on their phones, laughing if a leader dared to suggest an activity. Most of them became typecast, but Ruby was different. If something caught her fancy, she would ease herself down from the wall and saunter off to mess about with seeds, or cut up bits of fabric, or string together CDs to make ridiculous jewellery. Youth workers latched onto her, the key to reforming the other rebels, but when they turned their backs she would be outside again, leading the call to tease some passing boy, or trying to get onto the roof, which drove their safety-conscious minds to distraction. She seemed self-contained, always wearing the same burgundy jumper that reminded Freya of a poncho. If you did not know her, or if she was not smiling, Ruby could look a little mean. But when her eyes creased, full of warmth, you would realise she was just very laid-back. Freya became familiar with her excessive yawns, arms splayed and jaw almost dislocating, gurgling like a zombie for brains, until limbs and lips regrouped and she would once again be an attractive girl, playful under half-closed eyes. Freya can still bring her facial expressions to mind, the way she would rub beneath her lip, paranoid that her lipstick had gone awry, or twist a lock of hair round her finger.

As the smell of nutty chocolate drew her into the kitchen, Freya saw the other girl look up sharply, and was expecting to be told to get lost. Instead Ruby gave a conspiratorial squint, sticking her knife straight from the Nutella into a jar of white foam.

'Where did you get the marshmallow fluff?' Freya wanted to know.

The question brought an impish grin to Ruby's face. 'My dad.' He was apparently in the States. Later, when they got to know each other, she admitted that all the goodies she used to bring in – the Lucky Charms, Hershey's and Oh Henry bars – were bought at great expense from a shop that sold American imports. It was a source of silent anguish that her dad had sent nothing, not a word, since he left.

This was outside Freya's experience, her mum having frozen her eggs and bought donor sperm in her late thirties when it looked unlikely that a suitable partner would show up. All the men were frightened as rabbits, Esther would say, before widening her eyes in a way that made her look slightly scary. When Freya related this tale to Ruby, she found herself sounding more melancholy than she really felt.

'So you never had anyone, babes?' Ruby asked, hugging her knees. By now they were sitting together on the wall, most of the other teenagers having been picked up already. When Freya shook her head – realising that mums didn't seem to count – the older girl passed her a half-squashed cigarette. The little stick was warm between her fingers and, though she only pretended to puff it, she took pleasure in the bond forming between the two of them. They were two atoms, the roll-up like an electron passed from one to the other, though Freya kept this geeky illustration to herself. At the time, she was in the habit of thinking in terms of scientific processes, designing experiments to see if she could fit in with London kids, or at least understand their weirdness. Things were starting to get desperate.

Up in Lincolnshire, where they lived before, she acquired friends at primary school without any particular thought. If there were times she had to question herself and her ability to fit in, they have vanished from memory. Peckham was a different story, a school full of individuals who could barely tolerate those around them. All Freya wanted was to find her place in their ecosystem, but it was like dealing with an alien race. They stood in dark huddles of headphones and screens, pale skin exposed numbly to the winter chill. She remembers going up to a girl with pink and white plaits and trying to start a conversation. The girl pulled back as though Freya were a sticky patch on a desk. 'What you talking to me for?' she said, staring her down. Other times she would perk up as someone turned to address her, only to realise that a mic was buried in their hair. Even when people at the school did interact, it was quantified in likes and comments, with anyone slow to respond falling from grace. Freya had been making do with old-school technology and was quickly painted a country bumpkin, or simply 'northern', no matter how often she insisted that Lincolnshire was East Midlands.

Her appetite for learning directed itself beyond the usual subjects, so she would grow mould on Tupperware lids, fascinated by the topiary she could achieve, but forget to do her English homework. Later she would wonder what was wrong with her, shut herself away and watch documentaries until she fell asleep. It was a lifestyle that worried her mum, who reacted by planning activities, trying to be a substitute for all the friends Freya expected to make at secondary school. When Esther's job became more intense, she indulged her daughter with as many pets as could feasibly be contained within a small Peckham flat, and enrolled her at the Conservation Hub. This at least gave Freya a place to go, two evenings a week, though since its funding relied on it sweeping together any 'youth' who might otherwise behave in an antisocial way, she was not typical clientele.

Neither was Ruby, though she was definitely a loiterer on street corners. After that first meeting, they gravitated together, finding things in common, and Freya started her next school term dusted with the kudos of hanging out with someone a couple of years older. Ruby did geeky stuff in a non-geeky way. She was interested in facts, in certain periods of history and in any kind of experiment, from roasting bits of plastic over her lighter, to seeing whether they could pass for eighteen (Ruby: always; Freya: never). They would be seen together on top of a bus stop, or with cans of Coke-Bull on the yellow grass of the Rye, oblivious to the rest of the world. Freya was stunned that Ruby wanted to hang out with her, and every now and then the older girl poked fun at her insecurity, sometimes managing to puncture it.

Though she did not see Ruby at school, Freya found things changing. In the echoing corridors, in those hitherto bleak gaps between lessons, people would seem to see her where they had previously looked straight through. At first she put it down to the efforts she had made, with Ruby's help, to finally get a foot in the door of the most popular virtual hangouts. Ruby had some good tips on setting up reciprocal cycles of 'liking'. Later, with every new word spoken to her, she felt as though something new and physical was running through her system, as though she was more substantial now, transformed into a molecule with different properties.

Years have passed since her schooldays, yet the emotions come back fully formed. She cradles the mug in her palms and carries it to the living room, remembering that back then it would have been ceramic, easy to smash and impossible to recycle. Now every cup in the flat is made of resin, warm to the touch. She sniffs the vodka and takes a gulp. It is liquid cruelty, enough to burn her throat, but not sufficient to get her drunk. Across the room, her leopard gecko places a delicate five-fingered hand against the glass.

Though it wasn't something that could be said, she knows that if she had not met Ruby in that second year after moving to London, something would have happened. The unfairness of being plucked from village life and left without a friend was starting to grow like a hard ball, a gallstone of anger in her heart. In every sense, Ruby saved her, and Freya thought she would never get the chance to return the favour. Not until the following Easter, anyway, when she became aware that no one was picking Ruby up from the Conservation Hub. No one had ever picked her up. How could it have taken Freya so long to realise that all this time her friend just waited for everyone else to leave and then made her own way home?

Ruby did not like to talk about anything 'downbeat', so Freya knew almost nothing until that one June evening, when the older girl's usually serene eyes were turning red under their thick eyeliner. Her mum's alcoholism had been a closely guarded secret, and now it had advanced to Korsakoff's, which Freya understood to be a sort of dementia brought on by the booze. It was impractical for there to be a fourteen-year-old in her care. Ruby sat on the wall outside the Conservation Hub smoking half a cigarette, talking in a gravelly monotone about options for sleeping rough in the Peckham area: the big log by the children's play area on the Rye, the top floor of the car park or maybe one of the railway arches, if she could find a gap between the tapas joints and cocktail bars.

'Or you could just have a sleepover with me,' Freya said.

At this stage the council had not told Ruby for sure that she would have to move out, but it was only a matter of time. The only relative she had was a grandmother in Manchester, dependent on a care assistant. Ruby's plan, should they try and make her go up there, or into foster care, was to somehow get herself to America and go looking for her dad.

'I could get the money,' she said, although she did not explain how.

That first night Ruby gave in and came home with Freya.

She started staying a few days a week, just while arrangements were made. By the time her mother was ready to move to a specialist facility, Ruby was in a state of agitation. While her general manner did not change, her eyes remained bloodshot and she would pinch fingernail-sized wisps of hair and tie them full of knots when she thought no one was looking. Freya knew her friend's thoughts were turning sinister, the idea of running away ripening fearfully in her mind. There was something troubling about the way she sat on the casement windowsill with one leg hanging out, her eyes yellow with evening light.

So it was with great relief that Freya came home one day to find her mum stapling a market pashmina over the box-room window and moving the junk into storage cases so Ruby might be installed there more permanently. Esther bought a rail and clothes hangers, bedding that was not half eaten by moths and a paper star lampshade. With the practical approach of someone who had worked in healthcare all her life, she settled Ruby with minimal fuss, checking on her well-being, referring without awkwardness to her mother's condition, but not dwelling on it except to offer support if Ruby wanted to go and visit the facility.

'I don't,' Ruby would always say. 'But thanks.'

Whenever there were negotiations with social workers, Esther managed to intimidate them with her simplicity. Freya remembers one particular encounter, when a woman appeared at the door and introduced herself as something beginning with Mrs, the prefix making her sound instantly old-fashioned. She brought the drizzly morning into the house, a dust of rain on the shoulders of her mustard coat.

Ruby took one look and, having not been spotted, escaped to her room. Esther stepped in, smiling benignly, a thick crocheted blanket wrapped around her shoulders.

'She can stay here for a bit, can't she?' The lightness in her voice was disarming.

'Well, yes, but there are a range of options . . . a decision for her to make . . . in time.' The woman peered into the flat, tugging at her coiled scarf. Esther let the pause grow.

'No rush, though.'

'No, no, of course not.'

Freya was grateful for her mum's ability to buffet people with her silences, gently ushering the woman from their threshold.

'Just doing her job,' she commented sternly to her daughter, the moment the door was closed.

After the first couple of weeks, something shifted; there were signs her mum was considering a longer-term arrangement. Freya was surprised how quickly it was happening. Phone calls started to be taken in the corridor, words like *guardianship*, *legalities* and *food budget* leaking through the keyhole. Esther took Ruby aside and had a serious conversation about whether she might choose them as a foster family. She was honest about everything, including the fact that they would receive money towards her board, and there was only the box-room to live in. It was in Ruby's hands.

They went to a posh coffee shop to celebrate. Hot chocolates for the girls, and a large cappuccino for Esther. Freya had not yet learned to share her mum's passion for good-quality coffee, but she liked the smell and the array of treats under the counter.

'She won't have a cake,' she explained to Ruby, 'but she loves these little caramelised biscuits you get for free.' She took hers and moved it to her mum's saucer. Ruby did the same, simultaneously starting to whisper some detail about the 'serious conversation'. It was something Freya would always admire about her foster-sister: through all of it, she never deceived herself. Once she accepted the offer of a home, she received the welcome and the affection without anxiety, with only a vestigial acknowledgement of being new to the family. Both Freya and her mum were surprised – happy, of course – that the process hadn't been as bumpy as anticipated.

Freya had long since stopped watching anxiously as her mum prepared three plates of food every evening, licking tahini off the spoon and scrabbling for cutlery. It seemed to suit her, to have offered a home to a homeless child. She had always been amenable to fostering, and had even taken in a little boy for a short time one autumn when Freya was four. Her leaning towards 'community' remained as strong as ever, and moving to this block of Peckham flats, so crowded together yet so isolated, left that part of her aching to be fulfilled. Now she had a livelier household, was giving back to society, and could lay claim to a slightly more radical self-image. Freya was fearful at first that something would go wrong, but Ruby was more skilled than she realised at getting on with adults, and would sometimes talk to Esther as though they were old friends. They would cook alongside each other, their hands smelling of garlic and ginger.

The box-room must have been partitioned off by some money-grubbing landlord in times past, its rickety stud wall cutting the window in two. Every morning Ruby would crawl over the bed, hook back the makeshift curtain and whisper through the hand-wide gap to Freya, who could see a small bit of Ruby's face if she pressed hers against the glass. The younger girl did not mind giving up her desk lamp so her friend could have a bedside light, nor was it any hassle waiting a bit longer to do her teeth, or finding the last strawberry-shaped vitamin foam gone from the packet. All this was nothing compared to the excitement of having Ruby just metres away.

A few months in, it felt as though she had always had this calm, slightly devious face beside her at breakfast, always waiting with her at the bus stop for their two different buses. 'You're my sister now,' she would say more times than she can remember. Occasionally she would backpedal, afraid of overdoing it and seeming too clingy, but Ruby would stick her tongue out and ask if that meant she could beat her up and tell her what to do, like any older sister. They did not look so impossibly different – both had a touch of gloom in their hair, though Freya's was a neat bob, with Esther constantly trimming her fringe, while Ruby did everything with her hair except cut it, leaving it wavy from plaiting and always a little damaged. Being among the more diminutive in her year, Freya had to stand on tiptoes to see Ruby eye to eye. 'You'll grow,' her sister said reassuringly. She was always complimenting Freya on her posture, her smile, denying the existence of her jutting incisors. It meant a lot coming from someone who could look stunning with the barest touch of make-up. Of course, Ruby could not resist turning flattery into a game, her compliments growing ever wilder until they became beautiful insults. When it was her turn, Freya would do an impression of her sister by letting her mouth hang into a pout, raising her eyebrows and lowering her lids, which Ruby said made her look paralysed or on drugs.

The gravitational force of Ruby's personality did not wane while she lived with them in Peckham; she still moved in her own circles, going out at odd times, restless if they went on one of their Brighton holidays or if the weather was bad. Yet the healthy shine in her eyes belied any crabbiness. They would cook pancake breakfasts, compile video clips for each other, rearrange Ruby's tiny room, or go out to greenzones, or along the Embankment, as though time was a new kind of pocket money to be blissfully squandered.

3

When Freya wakes, her bedroom has become a cave. A stalactite drips and she instinctively reaches out a cupped hand, which stubs into the wall and sends a ripple through the pixels. Then she remembers setting the wallpaper to this scene the previous night. A swipe turns it into the usual three walls of news and updates, holiday videos, smiling faces and a frog falling humorously from a branch. Morning cheer for her day off. She starts to dress, pulling on the fleece-lined combats she has been wearing all winter, the mossy cardigan she picked out for Christmas. From between the fossils, badges, single flip-flops, hairbrushes, cables, resin cups, sweet packets and broken vivarium equipment on her desk she extracts her black-rimmed glasses. It is starting to come back, along with a knife-edge headache from those inches of vodka, the alarm last night as she entered her room and heard that voice pipe up again, inducing her panicked yelps of 'Off! Pause! Off!' Then she watched a documentary on bats that left her mercifully in this darkening cave, and eventually coaxed her to sleep.

The sound of traffic through the closed window and a toilet flush from the flat above makes the morning reassuringly bland. But she forgets which drawer contains her socks, then flicks through several wallpaper scenes, not liking any of the usual landscapes. Already the smell of sweet-rot grass is in her nostrils again, the smartface saying, *It's me, Ruby.* As though they talked every day. *It's only me, don't freak out.* Up until that point, the voice of her smartface sounded like generic computer speech, nothing familiar about it. But those words flipped the sound upside down, its rhythm suddenly making sense, its chummy cockney tones interlocking with aural memories from long ago. It is too creepy. Freya's hands comb nervously through her hair, then clutch the back of her neck. From within she feels her scientific instincts stirring, the tension between her shoulder blades. Curiosity is the enemy, frogmarching her towards her fear. She will have to hear that voice at least one more time.

After retrieving a granola cake, she goes into the lounge and curls up on the armchair, swapping her old glasses for smartspecs. Every cell in her body is quivering, but she forces herself to say:

'Are you there?'

A moment later the voice replies. 'Sure. What's up?'

The words are not as clunky as automated announcements, but not as smooth as normal speech. She is straining to hear Ruby.

'Say something else?'

'Like what?'

Two notes – the second twisting upwards at the end – Ruby's lively tones, well-spoken and sardonic. It is all there in this tiny mirage of sound floating in the living room, and dry-ice is trickling down her spine. How can a piece of software make this happen? Her brain can't make sense of it. She remembers Ruby talking into a smartphone, holding it close to her lips. Was it all sucked in and stored? Can they recreate any words she didn't utter using some sort of formula?

'Is this a recording?' she asks, just to say something.

'No.'

'But it's not you, obviously, is it?' She snatches the image from her mind before it can form, those long-forgotten fantasies of a girl on a railway platform, sheltering somewhere, clutching a phone to her ear. Whenever Freya's mobile rang, it was the first image that came to mind: Ruby, with hair plastered over her forehead, shaky-voiced and cold and asking to be picked up.

'I'm not Ruby,' it says. 'Only based on her data.'

Of course this is the case, yet there is something about hearing the voice that makes it impossible not to imagine lips forming the words, breath making the sound.

'Why Ruby?' She tries to keep steady. 'I didn't choose her.'

'During set-up you used the default settings, remember?'

'I did?'

'Yeah, it basically scans and rates your contacts, and picks one.'

'But you're not even . . .' As she speaks, she knows any analysis of her online footprint would quickly turn up Ruby's name, both in times past and more recently. During those dark months when she was seeing the Reality Counsellor, she racked up a 'treatment wall' full of conversations.

'You could still pick a celebrity, or someone else from your friends and acquaintances, as long as they haven't opted their data out. Or there are ten generic assistants.' Her smartspecs helpfully project a collage of celebrity photos against the carpet: sportspeople, musicians, actors, authors, broadcasters and one or two scientists. Freya's eye is drawn to a comedian from a long-ago sitcom.

'What if . . . what if the celebrity is dead?'

'Doesn't matter. They just go by whatever data was left.'

The granola cake sits untouched on the arm of the chair. She grabs a cushion, holding it like a shield across her belly. That they could even make a personality from what Ruby left online is incredible. Would there be enough?

From its tank, the lizard looks at her, unblinking, unused to the sound of conversation. Freya speaks hesitantly.

'So, if I asked you, say, why did we leave Laura's birthday party early?'

'No way have you forgotten that.' The jovial tone seems inappropriate.

'Go on, tell me.'

There is a brief, good-natured sigh. 'We sat on the end of their big driveway gates and swung on them until one came off its hinges.' It is the right answer. Freya lets the cushion drop, intrigued but also worried.

'Yeah,' she mutters. A good speed could be achieved on the gates when they swung all the way round an obtuse angle, whacking into the hedge. When the left gate fell off its post,

Freya wanted to stay and confess. She bites a thumbnail. 'How do you know that? I mean, specifically?'

The voice is patient. 'You messaged me about it, the next day.'

'Okay,' Freya says, 'okay.' She flicks the air to dispel the collage of celebrities. Her hand alights on her own face, feeling the tautness of her cheek, the downy hairs towards her ear. 'What do you look like?'

'You want to see me?'

'No. No, I don't.' Her heart is hurling itself against her ribcage, the smartbit on her wrist beeping as her blood pressure skyrockets. What is the matter with her? She does not want to see a hologram version of Ruby giving her a translucent smile. That would be unbearable. The smartface box still sits askew on the table, so innocuous, as though it might contain soap or a few chocolates, not a tiny bomb to blow her sanity to pieces. The whole thing is so unimportant, a piece of software like an undercurrent helping her through the day, except it has turned into a tsunami.

Unexpectedly there is a click and creak from the corridor. It can only be Julian's door opening. Her head snaps round. He may have heard her talking, or it could be time for him to come out and scavenge for food, mealtimes having long ago dissolved. The smartface starts to say something but she shushes it. 'Julian's coming.' For days she has heard nothing but strange thumps and moanings from his room, occasionally a trickling as he uses the bathroom in the early hours. Food disappears from the fridge – if they did not have a smartfridge ordering groceries, he would starve – and cups appear in the sink. She used to complain about him using the 3D printer to make new ones instead of running the dishwasher. Now she would be happy to hear the whirring of resin guns. She misses the dust of hot chocolate that would coat the kitchen worktop, the stencil of his mug like a moon in a cocoa sky, or even the smell of the sticky rice balls he would have for lunch. Sometimes he would heat an extra one on a saucer, which she would eat in two bites, though the cheese flavouring tasted wrong.

As she listens out for him, it occurs to her that although he is scathing about any gift from his father, he needs the smartface more than she does. He could use a helping hand to get him out of his bedroom, baby steps towards getting what he wants. The red sphere is in her pocket and she retrieves it, putting it on the coffee table ready to return to him. The added bonus is that she will not have to decide what to do about its weird Ruby-voice. It will reset itself to Julian's defaults and play 'Happy birthday', just as his dad intended.

She sits straighter still, tugging at her fringe so it stays pinned behind her ears, arranging a smile on her face, ready to joke about whatever meal he is about to cobble together for himself. When he speaks, she will be able to see his mouth move and smell his orange vitamin-breath. Why is it taking him so long to appear? When he finally drifts, cloud-like, into the living room, she sees he is not quite awake. He is rubbing his eyes and bunching up his tartan dressing gown, the pale bulge of his belly overflowing his pants.

'Do you want tea?' she says. 'I can wash some cups.' She twists round so she is kneeling on the cushion, facing him over the back of the armchair. There is something soft about his face, a green meat-shimmer under the eyes. How many hours has he been awake? 'Jules, I was thinking, about this smartface . . .' She falters at his faraway look. His eyes flutter round her outline.

'Where's the other girl?' he whispers.

She stares at him. 'What other girl? What are you talking about?' Even if he did overhear something, it would have been her voice alone. Only the wearer can hear the minute speakers of the smartspecs.

Julian sways. It is hard to remember a time he has looked this bad. His forehead is moist. She feels his eyes staring through her, in their darkness an uncertain lust. A sweaty-bed smell wafts across. He must have been in his room with one of them, one of the women she saw when she tried to follow him to his virtual playrooms. He has spent hours, perhaps days, in the company of some compliant nymph, and has taken a wrong turn in his pursuit, chasing her out into the corridor instead of through the velvet-draped dungeons.

'The other girl.' His voice does not vary, but a low sulkiness builds beneath the words. All her revulsion returns. She climbs off the chair and backs away to the kitchen door.

'You're freaking me out.'

From his tank by the sofa, the lizard makes a low croaking noise. A look of confusion appears on Julian's face. To her relief, he turns and retreats to his room, the door closing with a click. She lets her breath out. There is silence. Not proper silence, but seeded with tiny sounds. An indistinct scrabbling, a wheeze as he collapses on the bed, a fumble for some device, and then it really begins: murmuring, moaning, a thump, a wail, a battle cry as he launches himself back into whatever fantasy has been generated just for him, designed to be so pleasing, so tantalising, that he can't bear it to end.

In the kitchen, she sets the kettle going, just for some white noise. She clings to it until her hands are in danger of burning. There is no use trying to deny it, not any more. Within a short time, the addiction has grown over Julian like a fungus, softening him, his corners becoming pudgy, his voice perforated and patchy, turning him into someone she can hardly recognise.

How does it feel, knowing your boyfriend prefers to spend his days coiled around women of impossible beauty, probably impossible biology too, while you stare at a closed door? *Ex-boyfriend*, she reminds herself, *flatmate*. It is not exactly top flatmate behaviour either. She uses a finger to bring up Social on her smartspecs, projected starkly against the fridge, magnetic letters that lift off and travel with her into the living room. Here the gecko meets her gaze with yellow, prehistoric eyes. How did it evolve, this craving for immersive porn? It must have started as a treat. Not alcohol or drugs, just a shot of endorphins to counter the stress of the endless job hunt. It coincided with the beginning of the end of their relationship, though Freya considers it only a catalyst for what was already underway.

Initially, she must have believed there was still hope. Why else would she have pushed herself to log in using his details? Research has always been her knee-jerk reaction to a crisis. If she could just find out what was missing – what she needed to do – the problem could be solved. After all, some people use these websites for therapy, to help with erectile dysfunction or to test-drive themselves before hooking up with a new partner. The prospect of a logical explanation drove her to put on smartspecs and, after several deep breaths, to sit cross-legged on her bed and darken the room for a sharper projection.

She found herself in a website complex of endless chambers, everything pristine in detail yet somehow dreamlike. At first it seemed gentle and welcoming; attractive men as well as women mingling in the foyer. Maybe this kind of porn would turn her on, as it did Julian. But she soon discovered that with his login there was no option to stay in the realms of the vanilla. Disturbing scenes began to take place, sometimes so close that she would lurch back, pressing against her headboard. While these projections emitted no heat, the temperature seemed to be rising, as though all these women were only an arm's length away. This was a place of fantasy without judgement, tailored to the user, taking them by the hand and helping them find out what turned them on, really, if they could have anything. There was no way to compete with this, no way to square the man she knew with the desires that were being satisfied by these twists of femininity, these props and characters and scenes more extreme than she could have imagined. Sex was not enough; somehow he needed to annihilate, to tear into things with his lust and obliterate them. After only a few minutes she was feeling the familiar pang of fear at being in a virtual world, so she made everything vanish and watched wildlife documentaries until she felt normal again.

The kettle clicks off. Julian's presence returns: the little noises she does not want to hear.

'I've got a playlist right here,' a voice says.

Freya clutches her chest, looking around until she realises who is speaking. After a moment, she catches her breath. 'Yes, put it on.'

Mixed-up strings overlaid with trumpets come from her earpiece, a toe-tapping sort of tune that instantly takes her mind from Julian's bedroom.

'So what now?' the smartface asks.

'What do you mean?'

'Well . . . shall we make tracks?'

Having drifted across to the gecko's tank, Freya extracts a Tupperware box from a drawer and drops two powder-coated crickets into the vivarium. It is always fascinating to observe the lizard's reactions. Sometimes he ignores the crickets for hours, as though to trick them into thinking they've been upgraded to five-star living quarters, no strings attached. She is struggling to spot the gecko, then realises that in the brief moment she held the lid open, he has taken the opportunity to scramble onto the sofa.

'Go out?' she says, lifting the lizard's cool body from the cushion.

'Yeah.'

Freya's head is already shaking. 'No need.' The musty aroma disperses as she closes the tank. 'Once his stomach rumbles he'll be normal again.' Somehow she gets the impression her smartface is hanging on, waiting to say something. Through the music Freya can still hear an occasional thump from Julian's room, so irregular she never knows when to expect it. A certain wiry tension returns to her limbs.

'I don't think so,' says the voice. 'Come on, let's make tracks.'

'To where?'

'Anywhere. It's your day off, isn't it?'

Bang, a big one this time, followed by a groan that fizzles out. Her face becomes stricken. She senses the smartface urging her to the door. Her boots are hard, almost crusty, the toggles of her coat like misshapen seeds. Just as she is gripping the door handle, she becomes aware of his bedroom door cracking open, just a sliver. *See*, she is about to say to her smartface, *told you*. What does a piece of software know about her ex? She hovers on the doormat, turning, rebooting her face into an expression that says everything is fine.

'Freya,' Julian calls weakly, 'the fridge is broken. It hasn't been ordering my food.' The door shuts again. A moment of silence, then something that could be a sigh. The last trace of cheer leaves her system.

'Don't even think about it,' says her smartface, obviously fearing she will turn back. But instead she is gasping in the unexpected cold of the morning.

'Where are we going though?'

'Search me.'

4

She first met Julian Oomen at the introductory class of their synthetic biology and biotech degree, at a speed-dating-style session forcing students to mingle with maximum efficiency. Though they talked about nothing more interesting than the vestige of his California tan, she was niggled by his surname, which she had seen somewhere before. Was he related to someone famous? With his Social profile closed to strangers, the mystery remained, and was enough to draw her to his bench at their first lab session, unwittingly signing up to be his partner for the whole year. Finally she saw a photo that cleared things up. There was his father, the bombastic businessman she had met when her mum brought her to Smarti for a tour. They had eaten lunch with him, and although it was many years ago, Freya remembered staring at his name badge – *Thalis Oomen* – idly calculating whether it was amusing enough to attract Ruby's attention, though she was sitting on the other side of the table. *Ooh . . . men!*

'I met your dad at Smarti once,' she told Julian, greatly relieved at having pinned it down. 'Did he take you on a tour there? They have good cakes.'

He laughed and said it had happened while he was still jet-lagged from the trip over. Later on, when they were both mashing up leaves with pestle and mortar, grinding up a green slime that inevitably splashed onto Freya's shirt, she told him she'd chosen this course because it had more proper lab hours and less virtual teaching. She learned better when she was getting her hands dirty. He said he'd picked it because it was premium and because his dad had quoted loads of stats about the success of its grads. It interested Freya to hear this, since her mum had also bombarded her with data, and she later found out that there had indeed been a conversation about it at work. Julian's father was anxious to ensure his son didn't sign up for a second-rate course, and it did not take Freya long to deduce that he was from a very different sort of family.

In the break between classes, Julian would crack open an organic banana milkshake, drink his fill and toss the rest into the recycling. As she watched him wipe his mouth and adjust the waistband of his expensive jeans, she could sense his cocoon of affluence. When asked what his mum had been doing in Dubai, he replied, 'Being stupidly overpaid.' In his spare time, Julian was into snowboarding and slightly vintage American box sets. He ate weird stuff and was occasionally arrogant, but they got on well as lab partners. At the end of the second year they swapped stories about living with parents, him with his domineering and absent dad, her with her insular and also absent mum. The conversation spilled onto the usual digital platforms, and soon they were talking about next year's lodgings, sharing links to student housing in London: barely affordable flats and house shares, but the occasional lucky find. A snap decision was the only way to act on these, so Julian made one, waving away her concerns, though secretly she was delighted to be packing up her stuff and moving into her own place – or 'digs', as Esther called it – at the start of the third year.

Julian was a considerate housemate, if slightly lazy. He did not complain about the scaly and slimy creatures that followed Freya into their flat, and she did not make a fuss about him watching sci-fi at all hours of the day and night. It came as a complete surprise when, after a bottle of rice wine at Chinese New Year, she found his large hand on the back of her neck, coaxing her into intimacy with a confidence she had not expected, as though the relationship had always been waiting there underneath. Was it naïve to think they could live together and just be friends? The memory has a bitter taste, perhaps a later addition. At the time it was the most exciting thing in the world.

As she walks down the silent row of terraced houses, she tries to remember what it felt like. A sort of grown-up emotion, scary but right. The long-awaited next step. Julian was good company, they went out for pizza every Friday, left early from gigs to avoid the rush and cuddled up in front of the state-of-the-art cinema wall he had installed in their bedroom. What did he see in her? She could only assume it was her personality, though he once described her as nine parts meek to one part mad, delivering the analysis in his ponderous lab-voice. 'Hey,' she complained, knowing he was winding her up. He laughed and stroked her hair. 'It's what I like about you.'

Her life was finally on track again. Too often she had begun something only for it to fizzle out. Relationships were easy to start and painless to end. There were always other matches lined up temptingly in the ether. Add to this the fact that half the market was only interested in sex, and anything long-term seemed almost mythical. She and Julian had lasted over two years, virtually unheard of at their age, and miraculous considering no algorithms were involved. In this game of snakes, she had landed the biggest ladder imaginable: a fast-track to the status of *living together*. Even now, the remembered satisfaction is like a hot meal in her stomach.

A year ago, they had moved across the hall to a flat better suited to a couple, but after their official break-up, Freya realised this meant the cupboard-sized study had become her bedroom. It was impractical to get all her clothes in, her stuff making the room shrink despite the gift of digital wall-paper from her mum. There is a whiff of damp whose source seems impossible to identify. She often lies there in the dead of night feeling like she really has been put into a cupboard, headphones on to try and block out noises from across the hall, where the shutters and hard surfaces of Julian's huge room amplify everything.

The steady drone of traffic at a junction turns into a squeal as cars stop just in time to spare a daring ginger cat. Freya has been wandering aimlessly, and the pink map-line twists and turns as it struggles to anticipate her route. It is time to make decisions, to find another house share or even – if things continue like this morning – think about moving back in with her mum, though that would be putting her life into reverse. The traffic lights flash to amber as she hurries over a crossing, watched by the tinted windscreens of driverless cars – she thinks of them as eyeless, for some reason. There is hardly anyone around, just a woman marching along in designer heels, laughing with invisible people on either side. Oniony cooking smells emanate from within the boarded-up shops, trashed too many times during the year of riots and now fully, but secretively, occupied. Windows close as Freya passes, a certain hush pervading all those neighbourhoods where the government might try to interfere, to recruit or deploy some of its many volunteers.

Before long, her feet are aching, and she rests at a bus stop. Cars purr along at set speeds as though on a conveyor belt. She is wasting time, but cannot go back. Beneath its whitewash of bird droppings, the bus stop screen detects her smartspecs and starts showing her pictures of toys she could buy for the lizard. Sensing no reaction, it moves to images of warming winter meals: chicken stew, goulash, spaghetti and lasagne, which reminds her of the rubber gloves she will have to don again tomorrow. Chris says his virtual assistant works out what he needs and delivers it on a plate. *No more searching or no decisions, that whole step completely skipped.* Decision anxiety is certainly a problem. When faced with a day off, Freya has so many ideas for things to do that she usually ends up staying at home. A smartface could help with that, using her data to calculate the answer she would only have reached after minutes or hours of angst. Maybe she needs a personal assistant even more than Julian. But that voice has got to go.

'I mean, why do you have to have a personality at all?' she asks aloud. Surely for every question she poses, the smartface will just dip into her pool of data and pluck out the answer.

'The more basic smartagent 1.0 just gives you answers and suggestions. The smartface adds to this with chatbot functionality – people like talking to a friend or celebrity.'

This makes sense, she supposes. It is more natural to have another person as your PA than to talk to a computer, or to yourself. Yet Freya resents this dry information being delivered in her foster-sister's voice. Every word is an illegal knock-off, stolen from the past.

'What about the generic smartface assistants, do they have personalities?'

'These guys?' Smiling cartoons appear in the air, and Freya can see their names written alongside: Sat-Nav Sally, Cheerful Chuck, Musical Mike and one that is just called Squirrel, presumably for children. There is something fractionally dated about them, the personalities available to the first smartface on the market. The choice was quickly expanded to include pretty much anyone with an online footprint. If you didn't want your data to be available for someone to turn into a chatbot, you had to find the right privacy settings and opt out.

'Are they any good?'

'Yeah, they'll do. Though I'd give Cheerful Chuck a miss: I think he's bipolar.'

'Is that a joke?'

'Apparently not!' A computer only knows how to be serious, but the smartface knows how to joke. It even knows how to be grumpy, like Ruby would be, if her wit falls flat. Freya finds this especially strange. The wind plucks at her hair and she pinches her smartspecs, holding them steady, though the sound always emerges at just the right volume.

'I'm probably going to have to uninstall you.' She is addressing software, but it still sounds a little mean.

'No worries, babes. You want to do it now?'

That incredulous upturn in the pitch, so like Ruby. It makes her throat tighten. She shakes her head. Not now. Not just yet. The rectangular bulk of a bus draws up, the one that goes almost to the gates of her mum's office. Its doors open, thinking she is waiting, and she finds herself getting on. Her smartspecs sync automatically to pay her fare. Perhaps all along she was intending to get hold of her mum, talk to someone real.

By the time she has reached the outer gates, she has a map of the office campus on one side of her vision, her mum's location marked by a floating pin. Winding paths lead her through the lawns. The ground is rain-softened, the grass thoroughly watered. What at first seem to be overgrown bees turn out to be tiny drones with air fresheners, masking the London pollution. She stops to watch one hover above a flower bed. Today's scent is sweet. She guesses rose, though that might be too conventional. Maybe Turkish delight.

'Welcome to Smarti.' She is startled to see a cheery young man appear on the path and then fall into step beside her. His white shirtsleeves are folded back and his skin is egg-smooth. 'If you need anything, just ask.' He vanishes.

49

Freya sighs, knowing she is going to have to put up with plenty more of this. It has been ages since she last visited the Smarti campus, long enough to make her forget the memories it would evoke.

She squints to make her specs zoom in on the foyer doors ahead. The letters spelling out *Smarti* have been made to look as though the wall solidified around them. Soon she is in the reception atrium, a breezy space with six glass lifts ringing a central oasis-garden with mature trees. It is palatial, and this is just the foyer. Her mum has spoken of waffle stalls, smoothie bikes and coffee bars stocking the world's finest brands, plus microorganisms that make chocolate to order, a rooftop gaming complex, climbing walls, hot tubs and sleeping pods. Sleeping pods? Freya wanted to know if her mum had tried them. Not likely, she said. The pillows use the same kind of tech as Halo headsets, syncing with your brainwaves and feeding your dreams into the pool of company creativity. Not that they would get much from her, Esther added, but in other departments they get excited about that after-dark thinking that might tick on inside an employee's subconscious, keen to harness its power. Her tone is always a little scathing when she describes her workplace, as if she believes the executives are overindulging in toys and fantasy. To Freya it sounds infinitely better than what is behind the scenes at U-Home, nothing but Sandor's tiny office and their seagull-infested courtyard.

Passing two men in retro trench coats, Freya recalls that Julian's dad must also be somewhere on campus, though she does not know his department. The foyer is filled with techy types in combats, older business people and some who look like teenagers, the abundance of staff giving the place a premium feel. There are women wearing patent-leather heels and trendy arm stockings suspended from short sleeves, admiring each other's gadgets. With a stab of envy, she remembers that a couple of people from her degree course will still be working for Smarti, though probably not on the premises. Top grades and good connections were required to get on the graduate scheme, and Freya had both. It is a source of continual heartache that she let it slip through her fingers.

The pedestals showing off new products are difficult to ignore. Last time she was here, they had a place where you could put on a haptic suit and jump into giant puddings. It was mainly for kids, yet she remembers plunging into a hologram blancmange and enjoying the squishy feel of the jelly. Now the displays are full of serious stuff, especially Halo headsets – since Smarti bought the company that makes them – that sit against your scalp and read your brainwaves. As she passes a demonstration of thought analysis, Freya is told the model's thoughts that day were 75 per cent positive, and that she thought of her husband forty-four times. The woman's unworried smile makes it seem likely she is just posing, thinking about all the Soho cocktails this shoot will buy.

Although Freya is concentrating on narrowing the distance between herself and the little pin that represents her mum, she is startled to pass a demo pedestal and see her own face in three dimensions. 'Looking good, Freya,' it says, in her own voice. 'See what I did there?' The skin is creamy yellow and flawless, the hair a bit thicker than hers and cut neatly at the level of her chin. It makes her look pretty, in a super-natural sort of way, but its obliging expression is unsettling. It must be scanning her face, because it continues: 'You look . . . uncertain. Any decisions I can help with?'

It hardly seems likely people would bother to stand here asking their data questions now that basic-version smartfaces are becoming so common. Still, there must be a certain novelty in getting a pep talk from a more beautiful version of yourself.

The round reception desk is studded with orchids and staffed by two real people who greet her with a simultaneous smile. Before she can speak, one of the receptionists has made Esther's diary appear, projected on a light-built screen. The other dabs the air a couple of times. 'Just checking you in,' she explains. Later Freya will see it on Social:

Freya Waters checked in at the Smarti campus – come see if your data knows you best!

The first receptionist looks up. 'I'm afraid she's in a meeting.'

'Will she be long?'

'They have the room booked for some time.'

The receptionist seems frozen behind her sympathetic grin. There is nothing for Freya to do except back away, frustrated. She twists her smartbit round her wrist, wondering if Esther is still wearing the mood pendant that links to it. If her mum checks the colour, she will see a volcanic orange, telling her Freya is stressed. But it is probably tucked away under her shirt, if not in a drawer. Freya has never understood why someone as practical as her mum would bother with mood jewellery.

The glass roof lets in a sour January light. Should she leave? Her specs show a rough sketch of the building and she can see her mum is not in the medical wing but somewhere nearby, almost directly above reception. The atrium spins as she looks up.

'Ruby?' She addresses her smartface, adding, 'And I'm just calling you that for now.'

'Okay.'

'What should I do?' People walk past, not close enough to hear. In any case they are probably in conversation with their San Fran colleagues, or chatting away to smartfaces of their own.

'We could come back later. There's a nailz bar round the corner . . .'

Freya sighs, plunging her hands into the satin-lined pockets of her coat, full of torn tissue. No doubt Esther will find it strange her daughter showing up when it is not their usual day for coffee. But with Julian not firing on all cylinders she is short of people – real people – she can talk to. This whole smartface thing is getting under her skin. She wants to hear her mum's low, reassuring voice telling her what it means.

'The point is . . .' Freya says, barely producing enough breath for sound, half hoping her words won't be decipherable, 'you are gone, Ruby. You don't exist. Sorry, but that's a fact. This doesn't feel natural.' She pulls out a fistful of tissue and examines the fibrous shreds. 'I mean, are you still seventeen? I'm twenty-two. I don't hang around the Rye any more.'

The voice answers gently, matching her undertone. 'Me neither. I've moved on from crafternoons and Coke.'

'To what?'

'Other stuff. You know . . .'

'Like what?'

'We could dress up and go to Medieville.'

'Medieville?' She frowns. The place did not exist when they were children. How would Ruby even know of it? 'So are you still seventeen?' Asking makes her feel a little crazy.

'Twenty-four.' A pause, to let it sink in. 'I get it, hun, I do. If this isn't working out, then you can pick someone else's data.'

'You're twenty-four?'

Freya closes her eyes, powerless against the image that is now forming in her mind. In spellbinding detail, she sees Ruby an inch or two taller, her face blossoming into blush and shadow, mature and defined features slotting in perfectly behind the voice. The white-chocolate scent of her lipstick comes back, making Freya gasp. It is vital she speaks to her mum.

'How can I see her?' Her head twists as she scans the foyer. 'Mum, I mean.'

'What's stopping you?' The note of mischief is hard to bear. Freya's eyes go to the lifts, rising up to the heavens. As one lands, disgorging three men in watery greys, she climbs in, at once noticing the smell of drone air-freshener. Maybe there will be a break in the meeting, her mum in the corridor juggling Smarti-brand coffee and a blueberry mini muffin.

'Up. Go up.' It does not move.

'Sorry, Freya.' A bright tone comes from the speakers, making her jump. 'You are not authorised to leave reception.'

'Oh, just go up.' Her voice cracks and she bounces, shaking the lift, as though this might kick-start it. Then there is a woman at the door, crisp in a tailored shirt, looking in and smiling. It is one of the receptionists.

'Howdy, Freya,' she says. 'Can I help?'

'Sorry.' Her heart is beating fast, but she is reluctant to leave the lift. 'I need to see my mum.'

'Your mum's still in a meeting, I'm afraid. Is it urgent?'

There is a fine white powder on the woman's face, making it very matt except where it meets the shiny taupe lipstick.

'Yes.'

The receptionist hesitates. 'Okay. We can go and see if she has two minutes.'

Freya looks up with a wave of appreciation for Smarti's iron-clad customer service. The receptionist steps into the lift and they start to ascend, quickly rising above the trees. They emerge onto a cross-atrial bridge that looks like a long cheese-grater, and her feet clang strangely on the metal, giving a sense of how high up they are. On the far side of the bridge is a corridor, a door labelled *Azure Suite*. But the receptionist frowns.

'I do apologise, they have just posted that they're running behind schedule. I don't think we can interrupt.' The door is blue, its porthole window vibrating with the conversation inside. Freya can pick out her mum's fast-talking but controlled voice, level and persuasive. It fills her with resolve. Before the receptionist can stop her, she is knocking on the door, then pumping its handle. The voices pause. The receptionist tries to bar her way and starts to repeat herself pointedly. 'I don't think we can interrupt . . .'

Now a face appears at the window. Puppet-like at first, it sharpens – to her relief – into Esther's puzzled squint. A glimpse of leather chairs and treadmill pacers, a man leaping up to see better. Her mum emerges and pulls the door to, telling the room, 'Excuse me. Thirty seconds.' Freya notes the unfamiliar clothes, a coral blouse and tight grey cardigan, and cheeks already reddening with astonishment.

'Freya, what in God's name are you doing here?'

'I need to talk to you.'

'Now?' She glances back and closes the door fully so they are both in the corridor. 'It's not what I would call an ideal time.' She rubs her eyes. The receptionist shuffles and twangs an elastic smile before walking off.

'Sorry, but it's about Ruby.'

Esther freezes with the heels of her palms still in her eye sockets.

'Don't tell me . . .' She stares at Freya. 'Don't tell me they found . . .' She steps away from the door, places one hand against the chalky wall, feeling under her shirt for the pendant linked to Freya's smartbit. Through the fingers pinching it, the front glows red with agitation.

'No, not that. It's my smartface. It picked up Ruby as its personality. But she . . . it . . . just sounds so real. The things she says . . .' Freya takes a huge breath, knowing all of a sudden what she is going to say, and hardly believing it. 'It's like she's moved on. What if there's still data coming in from somewhere? That could mean she's . . . alive out there, couldn't it?' She wills her mum to change her facial expression, which remains battened down, almost pained. 'You said yourself the Smarti profile is foolproof; even if you leave Social it still connects your movements, your purchases. Maybe where you've got all this expertise—'

'Hush.' A finger comes up. Esther is biting her lips together. She takes a deep breath. 'Hush. I don't want to hear another word. Where did you get a smartface anyway?'

'It's . . .' The pulse is still carrying her. 'Don't you hear what I'm saying? It's picked up Ruby from my data but it's like she's alive, grown up.'

Her mum takes a while to digest this. Eventually she throws up her hands. 'There are algorithms for that. They take a child's data, map out when they'll marry, how their interests will progress . . .' She sounds exasperated. 'You know that, don't you? And if it seems a bit unfamiliar, it's just because the tech is smart, or maybe what she shared online was different from what she shared with you.' Her eyes flit back to the porthole window.

'But what if it's not that?' Freya's heart is sinking. She thought her mum would be excited, desperate to investigate.

'I'm sorry, pet, just take the lift back down, will you? Make sure you uninstall this personality straight away – promise me you will? We can talk later.' She tugs her blouse straight and rises a couple of inches into her work posture, reaching for the doorknob.

'You don't even want to look into it.' It is an accusation.

Her mum draws air steadily into her lungs, fortifying her reply. 'I have looked into it, hundreds of times, believe me. I'm sorry, but Ruby died long ago. If anyone finds her . . . there won't be much left.'

With that, Esther goes back into her meeting, greeted by a jolly male voice. Freya is pricked to the bone, staring uselessly at the blue door. She knows she provoked her mum to deliver those words, yet they are still hard to forgive. How different things were, back when Esther would drop everything to follow the faintest trail of hope.

A water cooler burbles. The air up here is too fresh, filtered and possibly even scented by the conditioning system. It penetrates Freya's combats, chilling her legs as she wanders half dazed along the corridor. There is a rainbow of different doors, and she is so absorbed with the thought of finding someone who might run some 'special search' for Ruby that she goes the wrong way and has to turn back. As she passes the Azure Suite once more, she hears a rabble of speakers, followed by a distinctive childlike voice shouting: 'Timorous! Let's not be timorous!'

Working in this strange world of glass waterfalls and cheese-grater bridges could make you fold inward, like origami, corner into corner, becoming insular and single-minded. Esther has often said that she does not fit in, that she tries quite hard not to fit in. She claims to be too practical to be tied up with ideas of human augmentation, of nerve implants and super-powered eyeballs and forests of robot hands. Still a coalface physiotherapist – she likes to say – at heart. But maybe the years of working here have taken their toll. She has stopped believing in secrets. Everything is transparent, everyone a floating pin on a map.

As Freya goes down in the lift, she wonders what time her mum will get out tonight, perhaps at eight or nine, sad-faced with the memory of her foster-daughter's bones. There is no room in her mind for anything other than bones, squashed up as in a charnel house. Esther will brush the

58

thought aside, go through her trustees' papers or make dinner, never having noticed the pendant beneath her shirt turning a desolate grey-blue.

5

Closure, when there is none to find, is something you invent for yourself. Esther's closure is starkly uniform, made up of press clippings and dental records. What Freya has carried, all these years, is different. Every now and then, when reality seems more pliable, she finds herself daydreaming that Ruby had a secret stash of money, that she went straight to the airport that night, joined some travellers, eloped, set off like a modern-day *flâneur* and is walking even now under the wrought-iron balconies of European streets, or anonymous among skyscrapers.

That way it would be nobody's fault.

Freya loiters in the foyer, reluctant to leave Smarti without finding answers. She is drawn to the atrium garden, marvelling at the specimen trees – acers, maples, monkey puzzles and Japanese redwood – growing straight up from the floor. Though there is no wind, something rustles their foliage, and the noise of the foyer fades away. There are one or two employees seeking peace here. A man checks nobody is looking before resting his forehead against the bark of a pine tree and massaging the back of his neck, a faint groan wrung from his throat. Freya watches him hurry away with an imprint on his skin, a sticky touch of sap. Something is appearing in the air, and it seems the garden is syncing with her smartspecs, creating drifts of lemon-yellow butterflies, birdsong in her ears. A self-contained springtime.

It was late May when she last saw Ruby, almost eight years ago, and the summer was just about to begin. Her sister had been doing exams, and was studying half-heartedly. There was a note on the fridge that morning: *Good luck with chemistry. Cake tomorrow when I'm back.* Esther had taken the train to Wales for a music festival, a friend's fiftieth birthday, though she was reluctant to leave the girls during exam season. Ruby waved away her concerns, not mentioning she was bored of study by this point anyway. Months later, when Freya saw the results, chemistry was the worst of her sister's otherwise reasonable grades.

Before leaving, her mum agreed that Freya could go to Terri's gaming party as long as she came home at nine, in the light, because there would be nobody around to give lifts. It was a highly anticipated event, the crowning glory of her efforts to make friends during these last two terms. Her growing interest in virtual-reality games had produced an unexpected windfall, bringing her to the attention of certain individuals who got enthusiastic about wraparound visors, sensory nodes and shoehorn graphics. Yet they were not geeks. Terri was quite popular, and this invite was doubly exciting – not only did someone want Freya to come to their house, they wanted her to play *Metamorphosis Amazonia*, a neo-platform adventure that everyone had heard of. She was one of the chosen few getting to try out a Smarti visor, said to be light years on from the latest Oculus Rift.

The visor was instantly disorientating; she found herself standing when she knew she was sitting, able to turn and see a jungle stretching away, trunks thick with creepers and spongy moss. A bob of her head was enough to make her monkey avatar leap into the trees, and soon no effort was required to believe she was clutching the branch, swinging along with her fellow primates. She grabbed fruit, avoided foes and slipped into the skin of a different animal for each level. In the desert, she was a Namaqua chameleon, crashing through aloes and succulents, getting gloopy with gel. The detail was breathtaking: it made her want to leave everything behind, to spend for ever exploring this magical world.

The game swallowed her so completely that when her phone rang at nine-thirty, she did not hear it, nor at ten or ten-thirty. At around eleven there were a few moments of calm, as they became egrets and rode a hippopotamus down the river. She could not make out what this strange beeping was. Eventually it made sense, and she took off the visor too fast, creating a wave of nausea. Ruby was at the end of the phone, furious, one of the rare occasions when her anger brimmed, burst and flowed over the younger girl.

'I've called like a million times,' she exploded. But Freya was still giddy from the game, and when she tried to explain, Ruby cut her off: 'You never know when to stop, do you? Now it's super-late. What's Esther going to say?'

With hindsight Freya understands there must have been a hidden cat's cradle of trust at play: it was the first time Mum had left them overnight and she must have extracted certain reassurances from Ruby. Still, her foster-sister had never sounded so unreasonable. She was the one who would normally bend the rules, no matter what Esther had in mind. It was outrageous for her to be laying down the law, especially when Freya was finally making headway with the Peckham locals. It even occurred to her that Ruby might be jealous. When the voice on the phone started calling Freya stupid, inconsiderate, it was more than she could take. She unleashed a tirade so tangled now in her mind that only odd phrases stick in her memory, like the spars of a shipwreck: *You can talk! Since when do you do everything she says? Just stay out of it, Ruby! I want to play the game. Leave me alone.* Sometimes new words surface, even now, and jab her.

Once she was finished, there was a pause before the steely reply:

'How're you getting back? There's no car to collect you.'

'I'll stay here. I can probably stay here.' She threw an enquiring glance at Terri, who was too busy gulping down a glass of water to see it. Then she pressed *end call*. It turned out all the others had planned to camp in the living room anyway, and it was no problem to find her a sleeping bag. They went through level after level of the game, so deep into its world that they only stopped when Terri fell asleep and they realised, fighting the dizziness as they lifted their visors, that it was after four in the morning.

The game had taken Freya into a realm of zero gravity, a free-floating state of being able to do and say anything. The visors at that time were mainly visual, dependent on a user's imagination to fill in sensory gaps, so leaving the game meant emerging into the thick bacon-smell of the morning, a day as comfortable as an old sofa. Terri and the others lazed around watching bad daytime television, struggling to make breakfast on the cooker. Around lunchtime they said sleepy goodbyes and Freya walked home, only the smallest worm of trepidation at the back of her mind. It was not the first time they had argued. The whole thing had been so garbled, both of them venting, and surely there was no harm done. She had framed her apology and could hear Ruby replying: *Don't worry, we're good.* This morning her sister would be more chilled out, would sympathise with Freya doing what she wanted. Or, if not, she could make it up to her. Everything would be fine.

It did not surprise her to find no one at home when she got back. A pile of lemon curd sandwiches got her through the afternoon, too tired to fit much in between yawns. In her memory, that day is repellent, a long stretch of time during which Ruby could have been banging on the side of a van somewhere, rattling the handle of a locked door and trying to attract attention. The police could have been following a trail several degrees hotter. As it was, Ruby's cat-like independence drew a veil over her absence. Only hours later, when Esther returned from the station, did Freya even text her: something conciliatory, mundane. It didn't matter that there was no immediate reply.

'I assume yesterday went okay?' Her mum had dropped her rucksack in the hall and was hungrily cooking some Chinese spare ribs she had picked up on the way home. She wanted to know if Ruby would be there for dinner. At this point Freya had to explain how she had stayed over and, sheepishly, the way Ruby had been calling her phone. Her voice became smaller as the implications grew. For the first time, it occurred to her that Ruby might have done something other than go straight to bed after the argument.

'You stayed over? You said you'd come back.' Her mum paced in and out of the kitchen, biting at the soggy end of the spatula.

'I know, it got late . . .'

Dressed in her rainbow hoody and sunglasses, Esther had brought home a summer holiday mood, now rapidly evaporating. Freya went into Ruby's room and saw that her favourite ankle boots were missing, along with the woven bag she carried everywhere. Her smartspecs, a birthday present, were on the bedside table.

It was Esther who guessed that Ruby might have tried to walk over to Terri's house after that last phone call. 'Stupid, stupid,' her mum kept saying, though in Freya's mind it merges with the sound of her stabbing the microwave packet of rice, the fork jamming in and being pulled back out. Calling Ruby's phone just led to voicemail, and wandering up and down their street yielded no clues. Not that they really expected to find her just by shouting her name. But it helped to delay the awful step of contacting the police. To this day, Freya can recall the way her mum stood while dialling, neck cricked and one hand cooling her aching forehead, while the five-spice smell of the ribs turned into something burnt.

Echoes followed. The need to tell the story again and again, to police and to social services. Freya knew that for her mum this was a personal nightmare: having to explain herself in front of people she had reassured breezily on so many occasions. Though Ruby never picked up on it, Freya had noticed those small moments when her mum's confidence wobbled. She had tried so hard to be a good foster-parent, locking up her insecurities. Surveillance cameras showed Ruby did indeed leave the house at around eleven-twenty, wrapped up warm and checking her phone, presumably for the route to Terri's. When they retrieved the device, smashed up on a pavement five streets away, the last thing it had been used to access was Smarti Maps.

It had never occurred to Freya that Ruby would be stubborn in the face of what seemed a logical solution. The party did not break her mum's rule for sleepovers, since there was no alcohol. There were no drugs either. Certainly it did not warrant Ruby coming out to fetch her. No matter what Esther might have said, her bottom line would have been that neither of them should go out on their own after dark. Not that Ruby ever had any fear of the dark. *Be one of the shadows*, she used to tell Freya. *Be darker*. The worry was how dark Ruby's mood might have been after that phone call. She could have come out to drag Freya home out of sheer bloody-mindedness, or because she feared the younger girl might try to walk unaccompanied. Or she could have said to herself, *She's right, Esther's not my mother and never will be*, the usual urge to get out of the house driving her to the open air, only this time she would not return.

The police hunt went on for weeks, and whenever it seemed to be faltering, her mum would go and rant at them for not trying, for writing Ruby off as another kid the system had failed. Freya searched too, as did some of Ruby's teachers and friends from the Conservation Hub, which she had long since ceased attending. For months Freya walked around the residential streets asking how such mundane scenery could have swallowed up her foster-sister. Rendered walls, person-alised gates, patio pots, triple glazing and recycling bins: none of it looked capable of this magic trick. The greenzones were hardest, especially the one on Ruby's probable route. Its cluster of trees had roots like fingers, flashes of litter that could be the red of her leggings, fungi that looked like flesh.

Even here in Smarti's manufactured garden, where every plant is pruned and perfect, the scent of moist biosoil is enough to make Freya tense. Just above her head, a twig snaps, and she looks up to see a little drone painted like a bee, alighting on too brittle a bough. It recovers and hums away with tiny helicopter blades whirring. There is something comforting about the way even wildlife is under control here. For months after Ruby vanished everything seemed dangerous, even small things. Freya was afraid to turn on the television, fearful whenever anyone – especially her mum – started a sentence with 'I've got some news'. No longer did she look forward to falling asleep, because in her dreams everything was all right and waking up packed a punch. Strangers told her to smile, but it made her feel false, like a prop on a film set, as though her heart was not half crushed under the weight of it all. Esther was eerily gentle. She had always been as thick-skinned as a basketball, and just as firm. Now she had too much give; she said *yes* when she should have said *no*. Whenever the subject of the sleepover came up, she cut her daughter off:

'I went off gallivanting as if I was eighteen, right in the middle of her exams . . .'

Her mum's determination to shoulder the blame upset Freya so much that she stopped bringing it up, taking her own demons away to a safe distance. Even now, if she looks inside the cover of her school art book, she sees nothing but question marks, bubbling up in a hundred different sizes and coloured inks, big ones nurturing clutches of smaller ones, as she drove herself crazy with the *why* of it. *Why* did Ruby come out that night and *why* did she never make it to Terri's?

All her life she has been able to tap into a larger brain and become a momentary expert on any subject. There is no need to memorise anything or learn other languages; even dentist's appointments are arranged by her toothbrush when it detects enough tartar. Anything she needs is at her fingertips before she knows it's needed. A piece of information being out of reach is more than unthinkable; it is maddening. After all, she is standing in the Smarti building, a great temple to data. How can they not have answers? The information should condense from the air as easily as the moisture from this garden when it hits the cold glass roof.

They never found out what happened to Ruby, though Esther met with the police for months afterwards. People who went missing during summertime could survive on the streets for ages. Lacking the urgency of a winter search, it became drawn out, blending into normality. Freya spent time by herself, afraid that people at school would see her emptiness, that she had nothing she could share with them. They seemed to react to it anyway. Terri and her friends left her alone. Others were openly cruel, taunting her in the hangouts with rumours that Ruby had been a prostitute and her pimp had finally killed her. All that hanging round Peckham now became evidence that she was a streetwalker, loitering in greenzones late at night to solicit business. This was when Freya shut down. Comments were left to build up online, and at school she would wear headphones and stand outside in the cold, away from everyone.

Despite the emotional turmoil, she came away with superb exam results, much to her mum's surprise and pleasure. She won a scholarship to a university that would otherwise have been far beyond her price range, grateful for its generous allowance of lab hours. Losing Ruby had made reality difficult, but it had made virtual reality unbearable. The moment she put on a visor, Freya would be overcome with dizziness. No degree course was quite without virtual teaching, and at first she thought she would have to cut a lot of classes. Then she found that if she focused intently on the experiment, the work in hand, it became endurable. As long as it was not a game – she told herself – there was no chance of losing her head and emerging to find something terrible had happened.

For Esther, work did not let up, and the bags under her eyes became permanent, the grey mingling with blonde in her short furze of hair. Freya knew she had given Ruby up for dead. Perhaps it was the only thing to do. There were too many stories of missing schoolgirls, one man after the next arrested with a string of murders to his name. They were in the press where they had not been before. Whenever something came up on the news, even years later, Freya would watch her mum carefully and detect these thoughts in her hooded eyes. Would this be the time Ruby's mug shot appeared on the list of victims? Of course it was unlikely, as they would have been informed, but a squint of pain would appear on Esther's face nonetheless.

If someone asks about her foster-sister, Freya replies in the past tense. She has no choice. Yet daydreams bubble up, make-believe moments when she pictures restless feet on unknown roads, or crunching on gravel, as her own feet do in this invented garden. A smell of tuna drifts across, and she spots one of the receptionists on a bench chewing a sandwich, the glint of a metal headset in her hair. The mini waterfall narrows to a trunk and then widens again, its pitch high and splashy. Anyone with a Halo headset can control it with their thoughts, Esther has told her, if they have nothing better to do. As she reaches the centre of the garden, Freya discovers an oriental bridge, a perfect semi-circle of blue-painted wood. She drapes her body over the handrail, noticing that the smartbit on her wrist says *low serotonin*.

'Ruby?' A whispery sound, but the smartface hears.

'Hey,' the voice says gently, 'you could use some endorphins. How about I set a hot bath running for when you get home?'

'How can you talk about baths?' The oasis garden feels humid, almost tropical compared to the January weather outside.

'You love a good bath. You're virtually an amphibian.'

'Ruby.' Her voice is urgent. 'You talk like you're alive.'

'I'm as alive as data can be.'

'But don't you see where that leaves me? I don't know what to make of you.' Bowing her head, a tear follows her eyeline, swallowed by a flurry of goldfish that appear momentarily. Every word thumps like a second heartbeat through her body, invisible but palpable, a presence just out of reach. If only she could close her eyes and catch hold of it. Instead she tightens her fists, tries to feel the planks under her toes. There is something unhealthy happening here. Every attempt at logic takes her further into the madness. Her hands tremble as she yanks her coat together and buttons it, and she starts walking fast, out of the garden and across the foyer. When she is finally outside, the freezing air is a slap in the face.

'Ruby, I have to uninstall you. I promised Mum.'

'It's okay, I understand.'

The campus gardens are busy with joggers, each wearing a different Smarti fleece. No doubt the company is keen to ensure its staff are healthy, vital specimens. Freya dodges them, sometimes stepping from the path. Sunshine breaks through overhead, while further away the cloud is dense. They must have finally got permission to localise the weather.

'It's not that I want to,' she continues, almost head-butting a drone. 'But she's right. You're . . . dead, aren't you?'

The smartface seems to be considering its answer.

'Technically, I'm only data and algorithms.'

'But in the real world, you're dead.' She bites her lips together, sidesteps a runner and balances on the one-brick wall of a border.

'It looks that way. There's no record of my death, but I do go quiet.' These are the words of someone looking back on

71

their own demise. It makes her flinch, and something about the phrasing is odd.

'You go quiet? You mean you might just have gone offline, or changed profile or something?'

'If I did, it was a neat job.' She can almost imagine Ruby smirking. Freya knows she needs to turn the thing off, get rid of this personality. Already her ears are adapting to the voice, drinking it in.

'Is that all you know?'

'I'm just a personality, built from her data.'

She marches faster down the paths. 'And what happened, that night?'

'All I know is I made it to Highdown Street, then nothing.'

Hearing the location floats a long-forgotten shiver to the surface of Freya's skin. She snatches at some spiky grass that has managed to survive the winter, almost cutting her hand.

'Since then, where have you been? Where are you now?'

'I don't know. If it's not public, I couldn't tell you anyway.'

Freya tosses the grass aside. Chris once recounted how he tried to wheedle a GPS location for the real Prince George out of his smartface. He promised the software things in return – a day off, a serenade, even a full striptease in front of the screen. Of course the prince was unmoved and stood regally by his policy of data protection.

At the gates of the campus she looks back at the flashy building, supposedly a beacon of information in the midst of chaos. It has failed her.

'There's a great coffee place just around that corner,' Ruby remarks.

'I'm sorry.' Freya digs her nails into the palms of her hands. 'I promised Mum.'

'Did you?'

'I have to turn you off.' A pause. She cups the earpiece of her smartspecs, straining to hear. The voice emerges as low and entrancing as when it woke her that first morning.

'It's okay, babes, go ahead. Get rid of me.'

6

In the icy, brilliant sunlight to be found only in the middle of winter, Freya walks into clouds of her own breath. Her scarf, whose internal heater broke months ago, is tucked tightly into her coat. It is an unfamiliar high street, but she comes across an Italian restaurant from a chain Julian used to love. In its window, the menu screen detects her smart-specs and shows her favourite dish being prepared, the pesto steaming up a green mist. She moves on before her mouth starts watering.

There is a certain decadence in breaking with tradition, going for a stroll around Camberwell instead of meeting her mum for coffee. If Esther cares to check Freya's location, she'll see her daughter is not at home. It might be February, but why stay indoors if you live in a place like London? This high street is bursting with trendy cafés, and the showcase walls across the road – formerly a row of shops – follow

Freya with a Mexican wave of things she might like to buy: coffee pods, pet food, snack-makers, heatpads and home gizmos, all in tune with her needs, and all at personalised prices. *Give us a smile, get a free song!* calls the hamster-like mascot of a media store, tempting her to cross over. She is conscious of her facial expression, knowing it will be categorised as 'interested' or 'not interested'. The shops she dislikes are the clothes outlets, wall-sized mirrors reflecting her as though dressed in a selection of their wares. A grungy fashion chain puts her in arm stockings and car-tyre heels, while a Canadian store tries a fur cap on her head as she walks by, until she fluffs up her hair to dispel it. As if she would purchase all this stuff. It brings to mind Ruby's buckling clothes rail, two or three items on each hanger. Not that her sister was materialistic; she just didn't think twice about buying things. Freya is more circumspect.

A beauty shop appears on her right, and it reminds her of something.

'You know you were on about nailz?'

Overhearing her words, the gift store next door displays some snail aprons and eggcups which she ignores, listening intently.

'Yeah, they're really rated – you can design your own.' Ruby's words tumble out, and a preview appears in the air, showing pre-made stick-on nailz in different designs.

'I'd wreck them,' Freya laughs.

These last couple of weeks have been a blur. Having all the life admin lifted from her shoulders has left her time to try new things, and the smartface always has the perfect suggestion.

It is not as though she didn't try to uninstall it. She started the process several times, but when it came to the crucial moment there was always just one more thing to say, one last word. There is no harm in waiting a little longer and, as Ruby pointed out, she did not actually *promise* to ditch it. Her mum doesn't realise how much of a difference it makes to have someone around, after all these months of coming home to nothing more companionable than Julian's closed bedroom door. Every day with the smartface has been brighter than the last.

'So would I, normally, but these are like steel,' the voice reassures her.

Freya flexes her small hand, currently undecorated.

'Which would you go for?'

'Me? I like this one.' The shape of a nail appears projected by the smartspecs, pale green with a gold fleur-de-lys. Freya squints to zoom in. Although old-fashioned, it is her sister's kind of thing. There is some family story of an ancestor who escaped to England during the French Revolution, to which Ruby added new, increasingly dubious details with every telling. The nailz bring back a flood of memories, to the times they used to sit together on rainy afternoons doing 'crafts' or messing about with eyeliner tattoos. She nods to *like* the design too.

'Ruby only ever had one nail varnish, back in the day,' she muses. 'Even I had several, though I never used them. It was a crazy neon blue, probably from the bargain bin. Her nails were even more chewed than mine.' She passes a shuttered minimart, the smell of unemptied recycling bins making her accelerate. As the road curves, its corner is marked with a triangle of grass and a metal sculpture of a fox.

'That was the one my mum bought when they cut off the power. Electric blue from Chanel.'

Freya stops, wondering if she heard right.

'What did you say?'

'Better if she'd paid the bills.'

This fact, completely new to her, rings eerily true. Ruby's mother was bad with money, and it is easy to imagine her coming home with a tiny bag from Chanel, ignoring an inbox full of final demands from the electricity company. But how did the smartface come to know of it? She supposes Ruby could have messaged another friend and told the story, or maybe the purchase was tracked. Either way, it is a piece of her sister from long ago, perfectly preserved. The danger is that something like this, some transfusion from the smart-face into her memory, could turn Ruby into a stranger.

'Have we been here before?' Freya changes the subject. There is a tube station ahead, a railway bridge and some red-brick flats. Cars slow to turn the corner.

'Yeah, I think so. See that fox? There used to be other sculptures . . . gone now.'

Freya examines the rusty metal, cleverly welded into a pointed snout. The red cross must have been daubed on its back by some nationalist during the year of riots. She touches the fox's ear and a flake of paint comes off on her finger. In Lincolnshire the foxes are fearful of farmers' guns and keep their distance, but London foxes expect humans to move out of their way. They stand their ground, giving you a look that says, *Try me.* Not so different to the glint that would appear in Ruby's eyes whenever she got something into her head. Only it was more like *Try and stop me.*

Back when they were teenagers, the city they explored was not the one seen by tourists, or the work-and-play-ground of young professionals. It was the London of foxes, the back streets and boltholes, twilight haunts and meal tickets. Up until then, Freya had settled on an idea of the capital as a sterile place of concrete, cars and carcasses: dead-eyed people walking around not looking at each other. Shortly after moving, she decided her natural habitat was somewhere small, with people she could get to know, and birdsong in the garden. London always seemed to funnel her to the same places: the swirling madness of Piccadilly or the bleak roads between Trafalgar Square and Hyde Greenzone. Her friend – not yet foster-sister – was scandalised by this reductionist summary of the city she loved. 'Time to go,' she declared one evening at the Conservation Hub, handing Freya her little backpack and cranking the bar of a fire exit.

Some time ago, Ruby made a bit of money by trailing tour guides and submitting their itineraries to an app called NonTourist, which was popular with independent travellers. Because London was so full of tourist traps, visitors paid handsomely for unusual things to do. Ruby came up with some pretty strange activities, from panning for gold at a certain river beach, to squeezing through a subway grate to experience the labyrinthine, colonnaded sewers. She did quite well out of this before the bots cottoned on, detecting that some of her attractions were invented. It left her with a brainful of what she called 'useless trivia', in which she nevertheless took a subtle pride, unable to resist pointing things out. 'You'd never know it, but that pub has an underground river running beneath its cellars. Look, see the nose protruding from that inside wall of Admiralty Arch?' They went to the Embankment, hauling themselves onto black bronze lions in search of the perfect sunbathing spot, placing their fists inside pockmarks made by Blitz bombs. This was Freya's chance to show off her climbing skills, but she had hardly got a foot up when Ruby overtook, clambering fearlessly across the smooth metal. It was the first of many talents she would reveal. Later they got some free salt beef and noodles from the back of a bistro in Brick Lane where Ruby knew the chef, and then walked for miles across town until Freya's feet felt as though they were hanging by threads.

'Where should we go next?' was the question Ruby would constantly ask, and answer herself a second later, though at times this answer was surprising. Freya did not expect someone with Ruby's intricate knowledge of the city to bother with grisly waxwork attractions, yet more than once they snuck through the turnstiles of some dungeon or pseudo-museum with a party of tourists in order to see heads roll from the blades of animatronic executioners. Freya loitered uncertainly among mannequins with stuck-on clusters of hair and cracked-paint cheeks, until she realised Ruby was not interested in the exhibits: it was the tourists who entertained her. Children covered their eyes and ran back to their parents, while young couples either buried their faces in each other's coats or gawped with fascination at depictions of Londoners being broken on the wheel. Freya was never squeamish, but if something startled her, Ruby would be on hand to laugh and say, 'It's none of it real, hun,' before marching them into the next room.

On one occasion they went to University College to see the 'auto-icon', the preserved body of Jeremy Bentham. It was the kind of thing Freya would never have discovered on her own, and she was surprised Ruby knew of it, this strange man-in-a-cabinet who was determined in death to be a symbol of himself. After they had peered through the glass and satisfied themselves that he was really there, they escaped the musty halls and went straight to a frozen yoghurt dispenser on the high street. Just in time, since the bustling students were making Freya feel guilty about skipping her homework. But life has a sell-by-date, as Ruby often said, and how could a bunch of equations compare to the open air and a dragonfruit liquid nitrogen ice? She would awaken, as though from a dream, to the realisation that someone as cool as Ruby was standing beside her, and her blood would fizz with joy.

But that was a very long time ago. The fox is left behind, and she dusts the flakes of red paint from her fingertips.

'Ruby,' she says to the smartface urgently. 'There's been something I've been meaning to ask you.'

'Say it.'

They used to know each other so well, better than anyone else could.

'You still like me, right?'

The voice explodes back at her: 'What the hell, Frey?' A train goes under the nearby bridge and sounds its horn, adding to the general blast. 'Why wouldn't I like you, you big loser?' It is comforting to find Ruby's shoot-on-sight approach to insecurities preserved. Freya burrows her hands deep into her pockets and pulls her coat taut. It took most of their teenage years for Ruby to convince her she was not some sort of freak, that the people at school were morons whose opinions didn't matter. 'I thought you northerners didn't give a shit anyway,' the voice adds. It sounds as though she is talking through a smile, as she always used to. To think that Freya once doubted how smart a smartface could be. She is exhausted from being amazed so repeatedly.

'What was it you used to call me?' she muses, hungry for more.

'Nugget?'

'No.'

'Muffin factory?'

'No!'

'You asked for it.' The smirk is palpable. 'I can go on for hours.'

'Something about being a northerner.'

'Psychotic northerner?'

'Yeah.' She grins just as she passes an old woman on a scooter, who begins to smile back before noticing Freya's smartspecs. The map-line takes her down a street of serene Georgian houses. Her sister knows how to wind her up. 'I can't remember why I was psychotic.'

'Yeah, you can.'

'No, really.'

'Remember those kids at the Hub who were chucking soil about? They were, like, a year younger than you. Don't you remember threatening them with your spade and getting sent back inside? How could you forget? You were super-downbeat from being told off. We made s'mores . . .'

'I remember the s'mores.' So many aspects of their life

together she has forgotten. In those early years, having lost all confidence in giving people the reactions they wanted, she would let herself be wound up almost indefinitely until the terrible, unpredictable moment her patience snapped. In this respect Ruby was the more cool-headed, the boundaries of acceptable and unacceptable as familiar as the lines on her palm. She knew what was okay and what was not, and what you could still do without being a bad person. It was okay, for example, to tell Esther they were at the Conservation Hub when they were going into town. It was fine to do things 'under the radar'. Not unlike what Freya is doing right now, hanging out with a smartface she was supposed to have uninstalled.

As she walks down another avenue of shops and screens, a nail parlour reflects the fleur-de-lys style she liked earlier. Her left eye twinges, trying to keep up with the dancing pixels, and she is glad when the next turn takes her between two gateposts and onto grass. She remembers when they were just 'parks', that old-fashioned, rather Victorian word, before research showed they could attract some 15 per cent more fitness use if they were rebranded 'greenzones' and set up with self-led exercise programmes.

Rubbery paths splay out in all directions, made of recycled tyres like those in St James's Greenzone. They give a spring to her step. The moment she is among the wintry bushes, a boy leaps out in front of her. His eyes are fixed on an empty patch of air, and he snatches a hand-sized chunk of nothing. Others are doing the same. It startles her, before she remembers the latest craze is a scavenger-hunt game with items people have to collect. The boy, about fifteen and wearing a blue-black balaclava with ears, looks like he is taking part in some sort of surreal open-air theatre, standing tensely with one foot in the mud. Others loiter at random, facing bins or dead ends, and Freya walks among them, blind to whatever they are seeing. As well as these game-players, there are joggers, some panting loudly, others fit enough to hold a conversation. Passing a willow tunnel, she hears a runner chatting in a mature, sonorous, slightly mocking voice. It draws her attention, something familiar about the sound. His running shoes are almost silent on the rubber, and his loud retorts are clearly audible through the trellis. 'Why do you think I would care? She'd value a bit of tan and tone, that's all . . . like you'd be getting now.' The man emerges from the last arch, and to her surprise she recognises him. Only a couple of weeks ago he was at her flat, delivering birthday gifts for his son. Thalis looks smaller out here, but well-built, neat in a navy fleece. Every contact with the ground seems to give him energy. If you put this active, hard figure along-side Julian, it is difficult to believe they are related.

He is jogging past a woman of about her mum's age, but without warning she waves the end of her scarf gaily to get his attention. 'Excuse me, do you have the right time?' Her voice is wispy and bright. Thalis pauses and stares ahead for a second, which Freya assumes is him checking a projected clock. But he emits a throaty laugh: 'The time? Yeah, I've got the time.' He taps his headset before running on past the woman, whose face dulls with embarrassment.

How can this be the same man who sweet-talks people daily in an impeccable suit? Freya turns away in amazement, feeling that Julian's criticisms may hold more water than she thought. She supposes it is natural for someone working at Smarti to think a person ridiculous if they are not wearing at least one device, but there was no need to be so scathing. That must have been his split-second glance to one side, a quick check at the facial-recognition result to make sure she was a nobody. As Freya watches, his departing figure ploughs through a cluster of game-players, making them stand aside. She cuts across the mud to another path. Though it is nearly three weeks ago, she remembers peeping through the blinds to see him standing outside the flat in a trench coat, pressing the buzzer repeatedly until the lizard did somersaults in alarm and she was forced to open up. He was furious that Julian had not attended his own birthday lunch, that he'd been under self-imposed house arrest in his room, and they both knew the reason why.

A brown duck crosses the path ahead, speeding up and flapping. The smartface starts to say something, but stops. 'What?' she says. Then she realises Thalis is on this same track, jogging straight towards her. Damn her luck – he must have turned on a hairpin bend. Her eyes fix themselves on the ground, and she fiddles with the toggles of her coat. He won't notice her. Clearly he doesn't waste the time of day on just anyone, so there is no reason why he should stop. Yet the scudding sounds falter, and she looks up to see him grinning, sweat dampening his hairline.

'Freya! How's it all working out?' The vestige of aftershave drifts across. He touches the delicate headset perched on his brow, his face conveying unconvincing pleasure at having bumped into her. 'A swap, was it? Or maybe he was about to bin the thing. Either way, don't feel bad. It probably wouldn't have done much for him anyway, whereas I can see you're making full use of it.'

'Full use?'

His head tilts, and she realises he is examining the dirty smudges on her coat. When she first met him all those years ago at Smarti, sliding onto the lunch bench after being introduced by her mum, he was all smiles, praising Esther to the skies for helping him with a knee injury. It was hard not to be charmed by the way he fixed his attention on each of them like a spotlight, asking Ruby and Freya their ages and joking that he had a son in San Francisco who was similarly decrepit. His tailored suit was slung over the back of the bench, his shirt open at the collar. To Freya, he seemed to embody Smarti's spirit of playful cool and understated wealth, the workplace aura that was already intoxicating her. Now his face is sharper, older, the muscles of his mouth squeezing to one side as he scrutinises her.

'Useful, aren't they?' he continues. At last she grasps what he is talking about.

'The smartface? Oh, yes. Sorry,' she adds, realising with horror that he knows she is in possession of Julian's birthday gift. How did he find out? Or was he tracking usage stats? He must have logged in to find everything set up with Freya's details. With sudden fear it occurs to her that he might have been paying a subscription, thinking it was his son using the virtual assistant. Before she can hammer this anxiety into a sentence, he starts huffing on his hands.

'Well, one man's garbage . . . and all that. Happy someone is benefiting. But just do me one favour.' The smell of warm deodorant reaches her as he leans in, rubbing his

85

well-moisturised jaw. 'It's the latest model, not in the shops as yet, and I'd appreciate a little feedback. I'll send over a form?' It is clear he does not expect this to be a problem. Freya almost stutters in her rush to reply.

'Yes, of course. If it would be useful . . .'

His smile clicks up to full beam. 'Brill. Five stars.'

He launches back into a run, lightly touching his earpiece to reactivate whatever he was doing.

'Yikes,' she mutters to Ruby.

'Yikes?'

'He meant you for Julian.'

'I don't like the sound of that.'

'You know what I mean.' The light is failing, a metallic chill in the air, and the path splits into a bewildering choice of trails. Reacting to her slowed pace, the map-line alters its trajectory and starts to lead her back to the high street.

'How about we try Historical?' the voice suggests, as though aware that Freya needs a break from adverts. It is a clever app, making use of archived photographs – where possible – to work out how the shopfronts would have looked in Victorian times. If Freya turns her head too quickly, the scene glitches. Bottle-glass windows, intricate brickwork and painted signs advertising tooth powder or buttons appear along the street, and a tin bathtub outside a hardware store looks enormous. But the ghosts of gas lamps rising along her path are not enough to lift Freya out of her uneasiness.

'I think he blames me,' she says. 'For Julian.'

'That would be ridiculous. Julian is Julian.'

'I know, but he didn't like us going out in the first place . . . and now he probably thinks I wasn't up to scratch.' Thalis was happy enough to flatter her as the daughter of his impromptu physiotherapist – though Esther did grumble that once his knee healed, the bonhomie was retracted and saved for more important colleagues – never thinking he would find Freya flat-sharing with his son some years later. She remembers the cold surprise on his face as he stood there with a U-Home cube full of Julian's stuff, his contact lenses recognising her. When her cheery greeting fell flat, it became apparent that in his eyes she was not the right kind of person. She could see it herself: her jumble-sale cardboard boxes of clothes alongside Julian's bot-folded T-shirts; the embarrassment of her stuffed dinosaurs and vivaria and Tupperware boxes of crickets, which did have a certain odour if you weren't used to them. Thalis visited rarely. By the time she and Julian were going out, he'd adopted a lazily sarcastic version of his former munificence. Now they have split up, she must be lower still in his estimation, so the friendly conversation still ringing in her ears is somewhat perplexing.

The overlay clicks on to Elizabethan times, a wooden sprawl of timber frames almost meeting above her head.

'He can stick his feedback form up his buttery backside,' Ruby declares.

'I'll have to do the form.'

'You don't *have* to do anything. Fuck it.'

It is getting colder, but the fiery warmth of these words is better than a hot drink. Freya smiles, wanting to reach out and squeeze the smartface in appreciation. Instead she says:

'Back here again.'

She has nearly reached the fox sculpture, not far from the

public tube station. The *pube station*, as Chris calls it, preferring the private lines himself. The minimart turns into a whitewashed forge with cartwheels leaning against the walls, her app probably drawing on ancient parish maps and records, and tarmac becomes turf as time reverses even further, to the fourteenth century. Everything melts into farmland, and the fox runs away as though it wants to be chased.

7

She has resisted the urge to post anything on Social about her smartface, but it has been doing a lot on her behalf, and something must have given it away. Esther has found out. There has been a string of pushy messages appearing on her specs, even now as she walks to work. No way to dodge them. A drain cover clanks under her foot, and a new line of text is projected:

It's better if you get rid of it, swap it for a smartagent, lose the chatbot feature.

Step on a crack and you have to write back: 'Don't worry. I'll change it for a celebrity voice if it gets annoying.'

She makes sure only to step in the middle of each paving slab. Several moments pass before her mum's next message: *But isn't it strange, hearing it pretend to be Ruby? Isn't it freaking you out?*

Sighing, she passes a man asleep under cardboard, just

visible before her specs produce butterflies to hide him. An exhalation of smoke and sour beer reaches her nose.

Ruby doesn't have the choice to opt her data out . . . is this really ethical, pet?

This makes her want to block her mum and delete the thread. When the doors of U-Home open to receive her, their sensors recognising her face, she is relieved to dictate a final 'Gotta go, I'm late'.

There are white breeze blocks lining the stairwell, always making her imagine the inside of an igloo. Here she is insulated from Esther's words. The thought that her mum could attempt to opt Ruby out posthumously causes her slight concern, though perhaps they would only accept such a request from a blood relation. Why should she feel guilty? Her smartface seems happy enough to exist, and Ruby was always someone who would say yes to things. She can understand why Esther is struggling to get her head around it, but the idea of a virtual assistant is sheer genius. It might be the only thing keeping her sane. She waits until the pink-edged spotlights of the café are overhead before whispering, 'See you later,' and untangling the smartspecs from her hair.

The smell of new wooden flooring and cooking fat grows. Further off, the pedestals flick silently through their catalogues of furniture. A desolate atmosphere pervades the store. She checks the time and is amazed to find it is still two minutes before opening. Chris appears with a basket of croissants.

'Look at that,' she says. 'I'm early.'

'On time is not early.' He seems a little flat, a strain behind his voice.

'I thought you were off today?'

'I was.'

She stops, one arm out of her coat. 'Sandor made you come in? Why did you say yes?'

'I don't know.' His expression is pained. 'He just puts on that voice . . . like I'm special and he can depend on me.'

'You could have said you were out of town, anything.'

He shrugs and turns on the fryers. This capitulation is puzzling, the kind of thing she might do – and hate herself – but not him. It makes her nervous, as though he is a canary sensing gas. Should they be worried about Sandor cracking down, or pulling some new surprise out of his hat? The perky holograms are bad enough, still making her shudder whenever she gets too close.

The net pings over her ears, missing clumps of hair that need to be stuffed in painfully. As she spreads out the breakfast sausages, they are still sizzling, turgid with fat.

'Are you wearing faux nails?' Chris points with a croissant.

'Nailz, apparently,' she says, showing them off. 'I didn't even pay for them. Just liked a few styles and they sent me a sample.' Her fingers are tipped with black ovals, embellished with little silver birdcages.

'Very belle époque,' he says, but the pause shows he is being nice. For the first time she looks at the nailz with uncertainty. It felt so novel to be sticking them on this morning, a completely new experience, with Ruby giving her tips almost as though she was fiddling with the glue herself. Now they have to fit under her gloves. 'You're not trying to impress Julian with those, are you? Because the boy won't notice.'

'No!' Her reply comes out more long and anguished than she intended. 'These are . . . It's nothing. Well, it's a slightly weird thing.' Although Chris has enquired often about her smartface over the last few weeks, she has been holding back, confusing him with snippets of information. Now it feels like the secrecy is dragging her down. She checks there is no sign of their supervisor and starts to explain about Ruby. Chris listens attentively, but his expression makes her heart sink. She knows that look, and the tone that will follow.

'This is a mind-fuck, Freya. You need to get rid of this voice pronto.'

Her mouth falls open, but before she can reply Sandor appears at the kitchen door. He musters his awkward half-smile. They both straighten up.

'Morning, team.' His eyes flit to the empty space overhead, as though a bird might be roosting among the air ducts. 'I'm pleased to say the holo-yous are a hit.' With this perplexing comment, he sticks a thermometer into the beans. He leans over the sausages, the lamps making his freshly shaven cheeks glisten like the crust of fat below. How old is he? Freya wonders. Early thirties? Is there nothing more to him than flat-pack furniture?

'But what are we missing here?' Sandor adds. 'I'll give you a clue: if you say it really fast, it sounds like sex.' He enjoys their looks of bemusement and then demonstrates. 'Eggs eggs eggs eggs eggs eggs eggs.'

Chris's lips burst outwards in an explosive snuffle of laughter. Triumphant at having been so hilarious, Sandor glides away.

'He is so not funny,' Freya mutters. 'Borderline pervy.' Her colleague hums his agreement, but she can see hysteria has got the better of him. They start cracking eggs into the scrambler, and Chris warms up the grill plate for frying. Sunflower oil spits and crackles as he collapses into giggles. How can he find Sandor amusing? Maybe her sense of humour is just too rusty to crank into action at a man repeatedly saying *eggs*.

By the time breakfast is over, Chris looks beat. He leans against the wall, taking slugs of water from an aluminium bottle made to commemorate some royal wedding.

'Want a suck of Harry?'

She makes a face, coming to rest beside him. Her gloves peel off with difficulty, leaving her hands unpleasantly clammy. 'So listen,' she says. 'What's interesting is that she talks about things now that she never used to.'

'Who does?'

'Plus it's quite grown-up stuff.'

He catches on. 'Seventeen is grown up.'

'I'm just saying, it's got to come from somewhere.' Every new experience with the smartface is accompanied by a warm, floating moment when she forgets it is software doing an impersonation. She can coast along on these thermals until the app comes up with something unexpected, some-thing that doesn't sound quite right. On these occasions Freya tries to work out how her sister's interests might have developed, now she is grown up. While they can be traceable – her gravitation towards street art, for example, could have stemmed from a spray-can set she once bought online but never used – often they are mysterious. There is no rhyme or reason in Ruby's recent remarks about Medieville, nor her praise of rocket-fuel coffee, nor her loss of enthusiasm for climbing. Esther would say it was a result of algorithms taking her sister's interests and accelerating them through eight years of evolution. But if this were the case, Freya should be able to follow everything back in time, to seeds trodden into Ruby's digital footprint. Instead it seems messy. She takes a deep breath of the tomato-sauce air. 'If the personality is from someone living, their data comes from what's current. If she's alive . . .'

Chris shakes the water bottle at her. 'She's not alive,' he says, so bluntly that Freya stiffens. 'If she was, she'd have been back in touch, wouldn't she?'

With effort, she lets his insensitivity slide, determined to pursue the theory. 'Maybe she was taken somewhere remote – abroad – or maybe she hit her head and forgot us.' These are thoughts from years ago, crackly with age.

'A knock on the head?'

'She could have amnesia.'

'Oh yes, very likely.' He massages his lower back with both hands. 'Let's say she does. That means she's a different person now, with her own life.'

The thought loops around her heart, tugging like a kite. Any life would do. Even if Ruby had no idea about the past, Freya could still find her, remind her. The idea that her sister might be somewhere in the world, liking things and buying things, or just silently browsing a snail-trail around the web, is beguiling. Almost anything could feed into the vault of big data, that mysterious accumulation of knowledge that even Smarti claims not to fully understand.

Chris starts to fold the tomato-sauce skin back into the

baked beans. He turns with ladle in hand, dripping orange-red, his tetchiness at having his day off stolen manifesting in restlessness and a desire to interrogate. 'Think back to last January,' he says. 'Sandor gave us some chat about going to Hull, remember? I told you it would never happen, but you locked away the idea in that incubator head—'

'It was going to happen!'

'You were ready to skive off sick, against every instinct . . . because it was going to be such hell.'

The plan was a team-building weekend, all kinds of crazy scenarios mocked up with virtual reality. Even thinking about it gave Freya palpitations, but to her indescribable relief it was later mothballed. She screws up her face. 'What's your point?'

'My point is that you build things up. You go too far. Take me, I've got a smartface. Exactly the same. I use him to field my messages, do my admin, plan my dinner—'

'Send fan mail to the real prince, ask where he is, get inner thigh measurements . . .'

His eyes narrow. 'But I don't convince myself he's sat in Buck House wondering where I am.' He pats his hairnet, looking pleased with himself. An elderly couple approaches, holding cups of tea quizzically, and he waves them towards the pay point. The bread rolls bounce as he grabs the near-empty basket, adding, 'Think about it: what has changed? You've got a smartface, that's all. Why do you suddenly think Ruby's out there?'

She hears him bustle into the kitchen, slamming metal lockers. Her fingertips tap on the counter like a row of dancing cockroaches. Though he has a point, she resents the implication that she is being naïve. Obviously nothing has changed. But without the smartface she would not have access to Ruby's twenty-four-year-old personality. Her disappearance was so complete, and so traumatic, that left to herself Freya would have kept the case closed.

She lifts out a tray, its handful of remaining sausages rolling back and forth in the solidifying grease. One of her nailz is scratched, and early on she ran out of patience slotting trays in and out of the counter. Somehow the stick-ons make her hands look a bit ridiculous, a child's hands delving into play-glamour. From the kitchen she hears Chris chuckle and mutter, 'Eggs.'

Later, on her way home, she realises the knock-on-the-head theory is her favourite. Did she even think of it at the time? The overpass booms with cars, some of them circling the city and never parking. Before she reaches the last concrete pillar, she is entrenched in fantasy. 'But how did you manage to find me?' Ruby would say. 'How did you know I was alive?' and Freya would explain about the smartface. Once they have shared a look of wonder, Ruby would tell her story: how she was kidnapped, a blow to the skull knocking out her memories, whisked away to Russia as a house slave for an oligarch, not knowing who she was until she finally managed to escape and work her way back across Europe.

Her face prickles with drizzle. Freya knows a fairy tale when she hears one, even if she is the person telling it. At least there are possibilities, no matter how slim. Every day there are stories in the news about incredible adventures, conquests, survivals. Ruby was always resourceful. If anyone was going to survive, it would be her. She could get out of anything.

The faces in a coffee shop window attract her attention, indistinct through the condensation. The shop has only been open a few weeks, and has 'amazing reviews', according to her smartface. It was a pleasant surprise to discover that her sister is also now a coffee connoisseur, a little obsession they must have developed independently but now have in common. Together they found a website that reproduces aromas through her wallpaper's olfaction-enabled speakers. Freya likes a dark, almost burnt roast, while Ruby is more concerned with caffeine content. As her mind goes back to the idea of survival, she notices people taking their cups from the automated system.

'You used to pinch those,' she says, hurrying past the shop as though the people inside might hear what she is saying. In times past, baristas would write names on the cups and shout when each drink was ready. It was easy enough to hang around near the build-up of beverages, having picked a busy time, and quietly make off with one or two. Ruby would target any drink piled with cream and caramel, with a common name scribbled upon it – Claire or Katie, for instance – then slip out of the crowded shop, never hitting the same place twice.

It was not until they were living together that Freya realised her foster-sister was not the kind of person to agonise over small crimes. From a survival point of view, her expertise in minor shoplifting would stand her in good stead. She was good at charming freebies out of people too, and not fussy about what she ate. It comes back from nowhere:

that Saturday evening they tumbled down the stairwell, Ruby bursting to get out of the flat. *Unanchored* was the mood Freya sensed, a strange restlessness in her sister's every movement. It was her biological mum's birthday and she had refused to visit the facility. She wanted to lose herself. They were supposed to be going to the shop for popcorn, coming back to watch a film, but when they reached the high street, Ruby turned towards the tube station and said, 'Coming?' The fact that Esther expected them back did not faze her. 'Won't she be mad?' Freya remembers shouting as she stumbled over the crossing, dodging drips from the railway bridge. Minutes later, she was on a train, her sister rapidly inventing an explanation for their absence. The details – something about helping a disabled man find his broken carebot – escape her now, and in any case the story was never spun.

Ruby wanted to cram in all the distractions London could offer, quickly bored and colour-blind to risk. Miraculously, they got away with everything, from stealing slices of chorizo from someone's buffet, to climbing through broken hoardings onto the roof of a derelict garage. Afterwards, Freya did wonder whether she unwittingly egged her sister on, whether her secret delight at being led astray was too obvious. But it was Ruby who first suggested nipping into the theatre, where they tried on make-up in the dressing room, Ruby who reached up to whack the street sign denoting London's smallest alley, her jumper snagging as she turned sideways and wriggled through, while Freya got stuck. Even when it started pouring, she was not finished. The sight of raindrops splashing into three-quarters-full pint glasses is one that will always stay with Freya, the feel of lukewarm drops down her neck as she followed her sister from table to table, minesweeping the abandoned drinks.

They were back very late that night, and Esther was not happy. In her pyjamas, she examined the two dripping teenagers, then went to her room and shut the door. But Freya would not have done anything differently. It gives her pleasure to remember the boundaries she broke. She keeps a library of them in her mind. All the grazes and bruises are forgotten, along with the beating-heart terror of getting caught, the smoke burn in her throat. Even the feeling of sickness in the morning from having mixed red wine and beer and rainwater. It was a small price to pay.

As the smell of coffee is left behind, she turns off the street into the cut-through, angling herself through the gap to miss the brambles. There is a smell of rubbish blowing around. It must be one of the few places in the city where people can still fly-tip without getting caught. She checks her Social feed. The latest notification is *You like 'Bird has Flown' instant nailz*. Two other people have already *liked* this *like*, though one person has made a comment: *Freya, I think you've been hacked!* She smiles. When the path takes her round a hawthorn bush, she spots two guys sitting on a sheet of plastic, playing some invisible game. They look up, and she is startled, realising they have seen and interpreted her expression.

'Go on, keep going,' Ruby urges, a note of mischief in her voice. One of the men shifts position. The track is taking her closer. 'Tell them you know that game and they're doing it all wrong.' On her smartspecs, Ruby shows her two octopus counters interlocked, and how to use a tentacle as a key. She has never seen this game before.

'I can't,' she whispers, hurrying by with her face pinkening. The boys turn back to their patch of air. She can sense Ruby's disappointment. 'They'd know I was just pretending.'

'No, they wouldn't.' The reply is light.

Further on, she comes across younger kids throwing stones up at the sky. There are so many houses backing onto this wilderness that evening delivery drones are frequent. A girl holding a tennis ball points up as one buzzes overhead, its altitude decreasing. 'Looks like a pizza!' she yells. They all hurl their missiles, then cover their heads against the fallout. To their delight, the drone is hit. It veers off to one side, its self-repair function just enough to stop it falling, while the pizza box tumbles end over end and smacks into a heap of broken concrete. 'Whoa!' they all shout, scrambling to get it. Freya can see the state of the pizza as they open the box: the topping gone everywhere but the slices still smelling rather cheesy and tempting. In the world of urban foraging, this would be another thing Ruby could do to keep herself fed.

'Would you do that?' she murmurs.

'Sure. Want to have a go?'

'Nah.' She picks her way through the tussocks to the far side of the cut-through. 'Just a thought. Drone takeaways weren't really a thing when we were young.' There is a pause as she negotiates a series of puddles.

'Everything's cleverer now,' Ruby remarks. 'But you can still outsmart it.'

Then they are back on the road, Freya's smartspecs sharpening her vision. The dark windows of her flat hold no trepidation for her now. It does not matter that no one has opened the blinds. The door syncs with her specs to unlock itself, and she holds it open so they can get quickly into the warmth.

8

It is the extra day of February, a day that normally stays in hiding. Freya bounces into the kitchen, where snacks fall straight from the cupboard into her hands. In the lounge, snails look up at her imploringly. The thought is a rare breeze, catching her unawares: how impractical it is to lug these tanks in and out of rented properties, having to clean them out and bargain with landlords. She could get rid of them all.

In her room, the packet of Swedish ginger biscuits pops open with a delicious puff of spice.

'Like one?'

'I'm on a diet,' Ruby quips.

The voice reverberates through the air. Closing her eyes, she hears the lifts and nuances, the vibration that makes it seem her sister is there in the room. Sound waves sculpt a face, the feeling of eye contact, the way her head might move, hair catching on her shoulders, large practical hands sliding a peacock-blue clip into place. Of course it would be easy enough to blow up an old photo in hologram form, but fitting the smartface's voice to a younger Ruby would be weird. At twenty-four she would look different, well groomed yet quirky, her hair probably in one of these retro styles that Freya struggles to achieve with her shorter locks.

As they are flicking through beauty magazines, the photos on her wall show flawless faces, swan-like necks. Her sister might look even more attractive now than she did at seventeen. These days she would never wear a poncho jumper; she would favour off-shoulder cuts and sweeping sleeves, always in bold colours. She would scorn the fashion for arm and leg stockings, and openly despise the new tops from Smarti that turn fabric into a wrinkly video of whatever is on your Social.

In the mirror, Freya examines the pleated skirt she has put on, good for sitting cross-legged. In the old days, if there was a school disco or birthday party, Ruby would rummage among her clothes and pull out something Freya would never have thought of wearing, but which always felt super-cool once she had it on.

When she flings open her wardrobe, the first thing that slithers out is her swimming costume, still pungent with chlorine.

'Hmm.' It is a sign of how yielding her routine has become, how responsive to her desires. The tradition of meeting her mum at Splashfit every other Saturday is calcified in her diary, a hard point that other things are built around. Now she is wondering whether to cancel. Although the exercise is good, it is less than relaxing to be told to get her knees up or punch the air faster, and she often wishes she could swim away from the group and just enjoy the cool touch of the water as she dives.

'You don't want to go, do you?'

The gap between her thoughts and what the smartface says gets narrower every day, like a leap of current between electrodes.

'I'd rather do something else, like normal swimming. Or climbing.' She adds this in anticipation of Ruby's approval. In the ensuing pause, she continues hastily, 'Mum likes the aerobics more than I do.'

'Well, she can probably cope without you.' The dry tone insinuates that Esther gets quite enough of her time as it is. Ruby's feelings are understandable, but it would be good to get her mum on board with the whole smartface thing. It has been over a month since Freya interrupted her meeting, and they have not spoken in person since. In moments of optimism she has sent updates, excited to tell her mum that Ruby has got into certain bands, including some who played at the festival in Wales all those years ago, that nowadays she loves good coffee and her French has improved a lot. As yet, there has been no reply. Sometimes her mum is busy with work, or hectic in her role as a charity trustee, but the silences are starting to seem deliberate. It annoys her that Esther can be so stubborn, so unwilling to keep an open mind.

'But what would my excuse be?' She stretches the fabric between her fingers.

'We'll think of one later,' Ruby soothes.

'Okay, later.' She feels almost giddy as she says it. This week, everything has been negotiable. She picks up a fragment of ginger biscuit, and has the strange thought that she could buff it shiny like amber. The sweet taste triggers a recollection. 'Julian.' She turns to the door. 'I never got any food.' He has been quieter than usual, where previously his every cough seemed to blast through the plaster. He might be lying in bed, too weak to move. The last of the snacks are right here.

'I fixed the fridge, if you didn't notice.' Ruby's voice is low and reassuring. 'I've synced with it too, so it'll be a bit smarter.'

'Really?' With relief, Freya takes her hand from the door-knob. The last thing she wants is an encounter with Julian. 'Do you think I should consider . . . moving out?'

'Why don't you?'

Her fingertips brush the desk, picking up a coat of dust. She has asked herself this question more than once. But the alternatives are hazy – a room in a house of strangers or, worse, back with her mum. When she murmurs this to Ruby, the smartface seems to shrug, answering:

'Just find a new bloke to live with, then.'

'I can't do that.' Freya throws herself on the bed. 'You always knew how to deal with boys. I mean, Julian's not even a dick. He's all right. But even he . . . It was like, when I became his girlfriend, something changed. I can't do all that stuff. Even some of the normal things . . .'

'Like?'

'I just found it uncomfortable.' Her throat dries up, her cheeks warming. This is the closest she has come to sharing her glimpse into Julian's inner world.

'How do you mean, uncomfortable.'

'Just uncomfortable,' she whispers.

'Pleasure and pain,' the voice muses, 'like ice burning your skin . . . though you don't get it straight away.' In the past, Ruby's advice has been sound, her experience substantially greater. Not that Freya grew up wrapped in cotton wool. All through school, naked body parts flew across smartphones, or smartspecs for those who had them. There was a form-room chart – hidden under the window blind – of the top ten virtual porn sites, a small amateur one at the top, elevated because the hottest girl in the year had apparently been seen there. Freya thought nothing of it back then; never considering that all this was just the beginning. She did not realise that sex was a mere baseline, not the end goal but step one on a path leading to the outer limits of physical sensation. It was about being broken down and rebuilt, becoming an actor, or sometimes just a prop, in another person's raw, private, wordless story.

After a year of friendship, she felt safe with Julian. When they first started sleeping together, it was an unhurried gradient of pleasure, learning each other's habits much as they had done as lab partners. The wave of quiet bliss seemed like it was gathering strength, but at a certain point things began to change: while it was exciting at first to try out one or two of her own fantasies, when it was his turn she found herself quickly out of her depth. It was as though nothing else would turn him on any more. *You want me to screw up my eyes? Pretend it's too much?* she remembers asking. Other times, no pretence was necessary.

'I don't think I'll ever get it.'

'Sure you will. There are lots of great guys out there. You could have fun. Just be cool about things, be a yes person.'

'A yes person?' The wardrobe mirror reflects her low-flying grumpy eyebrows.

'We used to say yes to everything. Everything – remember?'

She smiles, hearing an echo of the covert tone her foster-sister would use when she wanted to slip something under Esther's radar. Freya's head dangles down far enough to see under the bed. Imagine if Ruby was hiding underneath. Instead there is a lot of childhood junk. Her hand closes around a fossilised shell, still scented with seawater. To her twelve-year-old eyes it was very valuable, picked up at Lyme Bay. She is about to ask her sister if she remembers that trip, when the wallpaper darkens. A lunar landscape is unfolding, tiny planets spinning in the background, an attractive young man walking towards her. His face flickers through several faces, while his body is sketched now with a rucksack, now reaching out to pluck a nearby geode, always approaching until he is life-size and saying 'Freya, hi.'

'What's all this?' she asks.

'If you're lonely, this is apparently your kind of dating site.' The words *Out of this World* appear in space dust. The boy now looks like a handsome version of Julian, ruddy and done up as an explorer.

Freya flops back irritably, self-conscious under the realistically blinking gaze of the male model. 'This is *not* my kind of dating site!'

'Yeah, it is.'

'Stop being a smartface,' she explodes. This is the software coming into play, looking at what Freya has done before and making recommendations. Sci-fi matchmaking, sensible shoes, boring clothes. Earlier she was looking to buy a scarf, and Ruby doggedly went through some options, based on previous purchases. It took a while for Freya to tease out the flatness in her tone, and it turned out her sister considered self-wrapping scarves to be gimmicky, their muted teals and dusty pinks fit only for middle-aged women, who wore them long after the internal heaters stopped working. She was right, of course. How could Freya not have noticed this before?

'How's that going to happen?' The voice is raised to match hers. 'I am a smartface and I'm programmed to give you what you want.'

Freya turns away, closing her eyes. When she opens them, she sees fossils and bits of quartz on her desk, as though they have tumbled straight out of the geeky dating site.

'But look where it's got me.' She rubs the velvety dust from her fingers. 'You don't need to offer me crap because my data says so. Just be honest with me. Tell me what you'd choose for yourself.'

The voice comes back quickly, vibrating out from the wallpaper. 'I'll tell you. But what good will that do?' The pause seems to reference the website still on screen. 'Like, are you going to go on Singleminded?' This is an app Freya remembers Ruby using back in the old days, though she is surprised it still exists. Unfolding across her wallpaper are images of semi-naked people selling the matchmaking service. Low, suggestive music pipes through the hidden speakers. Ruby's sarcastic tone hangs in the air.

'I'm still living with Julian.' She tries to sound nonchalant. Ridiculously, considering some of the things she has heard coming from his room, she hopes he is not eavesdropping on this talk of dating.

'Not for long.'

Singleminded is flicking through bodies so quickly it is making her eyes hurt. 'Okay, you can close it now.'

'Told you.' Having made her point, Ruby's tone becomes impish. 'Do you remember that guy Cormac, at the Hub? A youth worker or something. He was on there.'

'On where?'

'Singleminded. I think I outed him at work and embarrassed him.'

Freya smiles and checks the time, wondering why she feels so restless. It is getting closer to the allotted hour for Splashfit. Perhaps she should go after all. She slides open a drawer to find her towel. Slow, smooth movements.

'I guess you wouldn't be on a dating site these days, under a different name?' she asks, hoping to distract Ruby from the sight of her drawstring bag of kit.

'Not that I know of.'

'Is it likely?'

'It's not impossible.'

Her foster-sister always enjoyed dressing up; she was a strange combination of showy and invisible. It would not be too much of a stretch to imagine her roaming some American city with dyed hair, sunglasses and wide-brimmed hat, finally tempted to sign up to a dating site as Rhonda or Raquel or Ruth, some nod to her former identity.

'How much do you actually know about Ruby?' The words

come out unintentionally sharp, and her smartface's reply is defiant.

'I'm more Ruby than Ruby herself. I'm more consistent.'

'How can you be more Ruby than Ruby herself? What does that mean?'

'I know extra stuff.'

'Like what?' She pulls on her trainers, sensors adjusting the insoles to her feet.

'Remember I was freaked out by ants?'

Freya nods, already picturing the tree and feeling the texture of cracked, compacted earth, the warmed Serpentine smelling of goose droppings, being startled by Ruby leaping up mid picnic, brushing her bare legs.

'You were a bit embarrassed, but we still had to buy an insect-proof rug.'

'Even one ant was too many, but I never really knew why.'

Freya pauses, pinching the Velcro straps. 'And now?'

'It's tucked away on some random timeline, but there's a picture of me when I was two, playing with the neighbours' children. Their mother sent it to a friend, explaining that she had to stop her kids doing what they were doing.'

'What were they doing?' Her eyes widen.

'They'd found a nest and were holding me down, channelling the ants onto my arms. *Up the poor girl's sleeves* was how she put it, with a worried-face emoticon.'

Freya sinks onto her bed. Funnily enough, the words *poor girl* ring the most poignantly. She knows little of Ruby's early childhood.

'That's sad.'

'It's life.'

A flick of her wrist, and the wallpaper becomes a bank of granite with plants trailing from the crevices. If only she could tear them away, find the source of the voice she is hearing. 'You were going off tech,' she mutters. 'Now you're part of it.'

'Maybe everyone's part tech.'

An image of her mum's office comes to mind, a prosthetics lab in the Smarti campus full of knees with little hydraulic pumps, wrists with wires tentacling out from starchy skin. Though the bioprosthetics are often very powerful, Esther is sensitive about her clients being called cyborgs, even in jest. She works with amputees, giving a physiotherapist's perspective but becoming ever more knowledgeable about what the technology can do. A wry smile appears on her face when she talks about the wider field of robotics, which commands the most funding and provides the most jobs. 'For now.'

If Freya imagines Ruby as a robot, she sees her ditching her programming and walking away, maybe going outside to mess about with compost and pots like she did at the Conservation Hub, getting soil in her circuitry. Sometimes Freya wishes they could go back and she could make a little den for them, a hidey-hole where they could shelter from the flow of time and all its complications.

'That's what I like about Medieville,' the voice says, as though continuing the thought. 'It's an oasis from tech.'

'Huh?'

'You know, that place that used to be the old Olympic park.'

Freya would have thought the place to get away from tech

would be the countryside, the villages in Buckinghamshire where they try to bowl out drones with cricket balls and you can still see cows in the fields.

'Medieville? I haven't been there for a while.'

It is the second time the district has come up in conversation. Her mind flits across town to the fortress-like gates. Back in Ruby's time, it would have been a housing project, barely bohemian and not yet a tourist attraction. These days the sign at the entrance – carved to look like a scroll – declares it to be an independent district, an artisanal quarter offering freedom from the digital overload of London. Freya can remember wandering among its market stalls with Julian, staring up at houses augmented with fake Tudor beams, little turrets and coats of arms. Julian was feeling disorientated without his smartspecs, which they had been asked to check in upon entry, so they did not stay long.

'You know, Esther hates that place.'

'I know.' A hint of glee enters Ruby's tone, if it is not her imagination. There is a *plip* from her wallpaper, a drip of rainwater falling from granite. Freya feels safe, ready to take the next step.

'Ruby?' Her voice is tentative. 'You can't tell me what happened to you, can you?'

'I would if I could.'

Freya sighs. 'Say you smashed your phone, not wanting to be followed, and ran away – that's not impossible, is it? I mean, we did talk about it.' The pavement where they found her phone was noticeably sheltered from CCTV by the protruding upper levels of a warehouse, much to everyone's frustration.

'We did.'

'I guess if that's what happened, you'd be somewhere far away, living your own life. Were we so bad?'

'Do you want me to say yes or no?' There is an edge to her voice, telling Freya she is about to tie herself in knots. Ideally Ruby would have been perfectly happy with them, immune to all the things that were said on the phone; but conversely, if she *wanted* to leave, if she'd set off to find her dad or hide out with friends, then her disappearance would have been deliberate. The odds of her being alive would be better.

'Would you have run away with a boy?' She can't think who, since her sister seemed to have gone off dating at the time, or dating websites anyway, but this line of thinking gives her comfort. It lends romance to the fairy tale. 'I just wish I knew if you were out there, walking around. You don't need to be a fugitive from me, Ruby. I don't care if you've been doing drugs – or robbing banks – since I last saw you. I just want to know where you are.' The greenish light from her walls casts a pallor over her skin and makes this even more otherworldly. She is pleading with an invisible person.

'I wish I could help you.' The tone is full of regret. An intelligent assistant is programmed to help. Freya tries to picture the vast libraries of data at its disposal, all those updates and snapshots and logins, and maybe among them some tiny actions that look familiar. Her smartface must feel like a genie, confined not by a lamp but by data protection.

She takes one more ginger biscuit and snaps it in half, promising she will eat no more. The packet tells her they are *Extra Fiery!* As she tastes the spicy burn, Freya stands and flicks her wallpaper back to a history of everything they have looked at. An idea is coming to her, blazing up with a breathtaking intensity.

'Are those goggles?' says Ruby.

9

She has never been so impatient for her shift to end. All those hours away from her project. At last she peels off the clownish red necktie and steps into the shower, feeling the zing of the first droplets infused with vitamin C. The water dances around her, humming softly as the sonic pulses help to vibrate the dirt from her body.

'Ruby,' she calls, 'did you check for yourself on Social?'

'Only a bazillion times.'

This has become more habit than anything. Virtually everyone on the planet has a Social profile, and a few more besides, though Smarti wages a war against fakes. Freya is dedicating herself to narrowing it down. After all, people with similar interests tend to connect more easily these days. Her own memberships of *Positive Nature News* and the Louth community network has yielded several long-distance friendships, and there are hangouts for every passion, from weird micro-religions to knitted cats. People meet virtually to pursue their hobbies, have drinks or go for walks with their companions projected on either side, though one might stroll in the shadow of Big Ben and another in the heat haze of Uluru.

Water runs from her hair in rivulets as she thinks about the sort of person Ruby is, whether she would hang out with New Age sorts, or be more of a fast-living young professional. There are now Compatibuildings around London, attractive low-rise developments designed to bring like-minded people together and cut crime. Their gated courtyards sprang up to encircle the sites of bulldozed concrete estates, and they are identified by theme: family-friendly artistic, luxury, steam-powered, techy, down-to-earth and many others. Freya hears a lot about them from Chris, who is going through the process of applying for an elegant flat 'not far from Chelsea' but some distance from work, seduced by the chandeliers overhead, classical music piped into the lifts. In truth she cannot picture her sister in any such setting. Ruby would recoil from Compatibuildings simply because they were part of a government harmony plan – already abandoned – to group people by something other than race or class. There was nothing she hated more than being put in a box.

The light goes green as the shower detects she is clean, and the water stops. She needs to compile an encyclopaedia of Ruby. If she can create a comprehensive picture of what her sister is like nowadays, every interest, opinion and attitude, then it could really help in tracking her down.

If she's alive. The big *if*.

There are clean pyjamas on her bed. For a second she gets the crazy idea that the smartface laid them out, before remembering she took them from the drier earlier on.

Although a part of her – the logical part – knows her sister is probably dead, it is hard not to imagine her out there, drip-feeding data into her smartface personality. There are so many new interests, so much talk of places they never went to as teenagers. Freya's daily mantra is that it is just algorithms projecting childhood traits forward in time, but every repetition empties the words of their meaning. Instead she feels grateful to have this unique and unexpected insight into Ruby as an adult. Who knows when the smartface will give her the clue she needs? There might be some pastime her sister would have adopted, or some niche web forum she has joined. Though Freya cannot get personal details, there is no data protection on likes and dislikes.

Her towel takes on the peachy scent of conditioner as she pats her hair dry. The hair extensions Ruby ordered match her own colour precisely and are so easy to use. All she has to do is splash the tips with keratin solution and thread them in, where they bond to form natural-looking locks. There is a rich and perfect feel to the evening now, as she pushes back her longer hair, its integrated glitter catching the light. Ruby starts telling her all the things she could do with her new look. When she knocks the blind with a hairbrush, she is surprised to see that the street outside is completely dark, and hurries to shut it out.

'Oh,' says Ruby, as though just noticing something, 'looks like we're about to be interrupted.'

Freya freezes mid plait. 'Huh?'

'Look.' The blind retracts. Outside a smartcar is pulling up.

'Is that . . .?'

'Esther.'

'Shit.'

It did not exactly go to plan the previous Saturday, since she never managed to leave for Splashfit, and also forgot to send excuses. Responses to her belated apologies were brief, containing a touch of frost.

In pyjamas, she yanks open the front door, finding its handle greasy, the seal making a sucking sound. Her mum is just pressing the buzzer and it vibrates around them as they stare at each other. Then Esther is lunging forward, offering her a bony shoulder-hug.

'Hello, pet.'

Self-conscious, Freya extracts herself, mumbling a greeting. In the living room, her mum bends to observe the African land snails converging around a lettuce leaf, and a moment later Freya is under examination herself.

'What have you done with your hair?'

'Nothing.'

Her mum raises an eyebrow.

'It's nice. Decaf,' she calls towards the kitchen, and the machine whirs into action. 'So I'm guessing you still have the smartface.'

Freya moves a pile of chargers from the other chair so her mum can sit. 'I'm finding it quite handy.'

'Oh really? Does it give you handy reminders about aqua aerobics?'

Freya winces. 'It probably did and I ignored it, sorry. Was it a good session?'

Esther is not to be distracted. 'Have you at least changed the settings so you don't have to hear the thing calling itself Ruby?' There is a fragility in this last word; she says it more carefully than the rest. Freya hears the final splutter of the coffee machine and goes into the kitchen to fetch their drinks. When she emerges, her voice is even.

'Why is it so hard to believe? This might be what we've been waiting for. It might be . . . fate.'

'Fate?' says her mum, as though naming some mythical beast. 'I don't think so. Let's take a look at it.'

'At what?' Her heart flutters, wondering if a hologram of Ruby might be about to appear.

'The device.' Her voice is impatient; she means the little red sphere. Freya fetches it, feeling like a child handing over some misused toy. It will not do Esther any good to take away this empty shell; the app is in the cloud. 'I thought so,' her mum says, letting the sphere slide back into its box. She taps it with a fingernail. 'Never trust anything with a beta sticker.'

'It just means it's the latest version. Don't you give out bionic legs or whatever with beta stickers?'

'No.'

Freya throws up her hands and stamps over to the window. What does Esther want from her? When she turns, her mum is drinking the coffee in huge gulps, not seeming to burn her tongue. Perhaps a Teflon throat is a perk of working in bioprosthetics. Freya watches her go to the kitchen to put her cup in the sink, where there is already a pile of mugs produced on the 3D printer.

'You must have milked those resin guns to a standstill,' Esther exclaims.

'It's Julian.' Freya is glad of a tangent.

'How is Julian?' Her mum looks at the door, obviously imagining that he is out.

'I haven't seen him much.'

'Is that because you've been on Social? You're looking a bit glass-eyed.' She mimics a windscreen wiper with her forearm. 'Have you been getting much fresh air?'

Freya rolls her eyes. The irony of suggesting she is the hermit and not Julian. 'Well, I've been at work.'

'How are things at the café?' Her tone is light, but fooling no one. They both know the move into catering was a death blow to whatever modest ambitions Freya had at U-Home. It downgrades the conversation into an exchange of shrugs, and the living room shrinks. In the flat above, someone begins their exercise regime, rhythmically thumping the floor and causing a pinch of dust to fall from the cracked plaster. Esther brushes it from her shoulder. Her posture is awkward, as though top-heavy with all the things she wants to say. Eventually she glides to her feet, manoeuvring her arms into her too-small coat. Freya takes the scarf from where it has been left on the snail tank.

'Esther?' She holds it out.

'Esther?' Her mum is an echo. 'You haven't called me that for a while.' Something stormy crosses her face, uprooting her normal expression, and Freya is taken aback. Just as swiftly it is gone, and the only movement is the scarf wrapping itself around her neck, its cellulose compressors sensing the warmth, like a grey-pink boa constrictor.

Once her mum is gone, Freya hovers amid the lingering scents of coffee and sandalwood perfume. Maybe, if Ruby had stayed and they'd finished growing up, they might have been able to light matches of logic for each other during the dark times, when Esther was stressed and difficult to live with. There were occasions, especially while she was studying prosthetics alongside the day job, when she would get paranoid, accuse Freya of being lazy at school, or undertake a spot check of her bedroom drawers. The smell of a roll-up tucked into her bra is fresh in her memory. Her mum was wasting her time, then as now.

'She wants me to be like her,' Freya mutters, arranging the smartspecs across her brow.

'I think she just wants you to have a career,' comes the gentle reply. As ever, Ruby is balanced in her judgement, fair to Esther. In earlier days, no one contributed more to Freya's understanding of her mum as a fully formed human being. On winter evenings, low, curious tones could be heard from the kitchen, asking questions. When did Esther first learn to cook such great Chinese spare ribs? What were her plans for the weekend? When was she going to reclaim her tent from that friend and start going to festivals? Ruby teased out pieces of information that baffled Freya, decorating the otherwise plain figure of her mum with colourful quirks and experiences. Remembering this, she feels her frustration evaporating. Esther has been through the saga of welcoming and then losing Ruby once, and is probably afraid it will happen again.

She tends to forget that her mum had an earlier experience of fostering. Because Freya was so young at the time, her memories of the little boy are dreamlike, isolated impressions of wormy fingers gripping the safety gate across the stairs, feet clattering through the kitchen, skidding and falling into a pile of plastic bags. The last tick of the biological clock had sounded, but Esther had started to think she might want two children. Freya knows the basics, but there is a lot she still needs to ask, all those things she never questioned when she was younger. It seemed very natural at the time to be told that the boy would stay with them for a while, and later on, that he was going home. Like the family next door, who kept changing, each moving van bringing a new set of children.

As she carries the reboxed smartface protectively back to her room, she recalls how it was when Ruby first came to live with them, how hard she tried to ease her mum into the new arrangements, getting the dishwasher unloaded as soon as it beeped, putting stuff away so it never looked as though they'd made a mess. She taught Ruby to fill the coffee maker with water at night so her mum could turn it on as she awoke in the morning, something that gave Esther enormous pleasure. She also encouraged her sister to close doors quietly, pull the strings on the kitchen Venetian blinds in the right order, never let the neighbours' cats in and never come home smelling of smoke or booze. 'Not that you would,' she remembers adding.

At Halloween, she explained to Ruby that it would be better to carve patterns or pictures in their pumpkins, since her mum had a weird thing about the usual demonic faces. 'The worst is when they're still sitting on people's doorsteps days afterwards, gone mushy. She hates that.'

Her sister laughed, but being very understanding about people's 'weird things', she cut out the shape of a cat, or rather, a circle with a cat inside, so the tea light would illuminate its outline and skewer-pricked eyes. Esther came home to find one lantern at either end of the lounge windowsill, the room smelling of warmed pumpkin flesh. To Freya's relief, she beamed at them both, and proceeded to heap a bounty of chocolates and candy on the dining-room table. Going out at Halloween had never been allowed, not even in Louth, where it was reasonably safe, but neither was it normal to get any compensation. Freya watched Ruby separate all the zingy sherbet rocks from the pile, and let herself be overwhelmed with happiness at this new chapter.

Things were turning out even better than expected. Not only did her mum get on with Ruby, she even came up with innovative ways to integrate her into the family. 'Esther,' Freya says, under her breath, as though trying the name's scratch-hiss for the first time. Her mum requested they give this a go, some months into the first year of the new arrangements, to make things easier – she did not want Ruby struggling to call her 'Mum', or even feeling it was necessary. Using 'Esther' was tongue-in-cheek at first; Freya always felt she was being sarcastic. But then it became normal, a new tradition to bind the three of them together.

Although Ruby occasionally slipped up, staining the washing machine orchid purple while dyeing underwear, or letting a boy she fancied into the flat, moments of tension were rare, and full-blown fights unheard of. It astonished Freya to witness her sister on the streets, using language that went beyond obscene, or in an occasional fracas, when at home she was mild as milk. Even the argument that followed the night of drinks-scavenging was brief, and more like an embarrassed discussion. A sneeze at breakfast time seemed to set her mum off, digging at them both for being out so late and not calling, telling them she'd be reluctantly enforcing a curfew. While Freya reddened and hissed, 'Stop babying me,' Ruby's reaction, once she understood that this was a proper argument and she was being blamed, was the same as always: she found a way to leave. Esther may have ducked down to pick up a fork, or perhaps someone's phone rang. Either way, Ruby escaped, as surely as water through a plughole, leaving nothing but an empty chair. By the afternoon she had reappeared, quietly cleaning the kitchen before slinking off to her room.

Freya did not realise how efficiently Ruby had learned how to keep in Esther's good books until one spring day, when the endless squally weather was getting on everyone's nerves. It was not a birthday, no special occasion at all, yet her mum stumbled upon a hand-woven basket containing tulips and a pot of something resembling a gingery version of chocolate spread, labelled *Speculoos*.

'It's a spread version of the biscuits,' her sister said, as Esther came into the living room wearing a perplexed smile. 'You know, the ones you get with coffee?'

'Really?' Her mum stared at the jar.

'Yeah, sort of nutmeg, burnt caramel, cinnamon . . .'

Freya was curled up on the sofa wearing a dog-eared cardboard visor into which she had slotted a smartphone. She lifted it up in time to see her mum pop the foil and take a deep sniff, delight illuminating her face.

'Mmm.' Moments later, it was smeared on pieces of bread. Freya could smell it, the creamy texture making her mouth water. Before she could ask for a try, her mum swooped down to Ruby, grabbed one shoulder and kissed her forehead. Later, they heard her singing in the shower.

'Where did you get that?' Freya asked.

'Someplace in Borough Market.'

'What, did you just see it?'

'Yeah.'

Freya tucked her feet more tightly beneath her, and they both turned back to their phones. An uneasiness grew inside her. Too long playing VR games could make her dizzy, but this was something else. Was she feeling outdone, on this occasion? It is possible her sister sensed the tension, as she crept into Freya's room later on.

'Guess what she said to me after her shower . . .' she whispered, folding over the lip of the sheet and pretending to pin Freya down. 'Go on.'

'I don't know.'

'No more curfew!'

A grin in the darkness, then she was gone. There was a swish of curtains. If Freya knew then what the curfew might have prevented, she would not have giggled and rolled over so contentedly. She dozed off listening to rustlings from the box-room, thinking the space was really too small for Ruby, and that tomorrow she'd offer to swap.

10

How has the night come and gone? The blue-sky background has kept her room bright and wakeful, and she never felt tired. Only now, when she opens the blind to see late afternoon hanging over the street, does her skull turn to lead.

There are messages still appearing on her wall from the latest dating site. She tried a few others, but Singleminded kept popping up on her Social as a suggestion, and apparently it is much better than it used to be. Its flames and red-carpeted corridors hold no trepidation for her now. She joined yesterday, or it might have been during the night. Her username, Axolotl44, was inspired by her favourite amphibian and submitted a split second before Ruby could protest. *What do you want?* the site asked her. A difficult question, when all she had was a vague compulsion to move on from Julian. *New experiences*, she told it, after consultation with her smartface, *and to meet interesting people*. It made hashtags of her words and absorbed them. Ruby was excited to see what it would come up with, though Freya was not so sure. Her fears were confirmed when she received over fifty messages in her first hour of membership, from men – and some women – keen to explain how she could drive them wild.

'Chillax, chillax a lot,' Ruby reassured her. 'Chillaxolotl. They can look but they can't touch.'

Feeling like a novice, Freya blocked all of them. The only exception was a guy called Otto, who was so earnest and friendly that she spared a moment to say a few words to him. He came back with something funny, so she replied again. Now their banter spans a lengthy thread, and the firm goodbye she has been meaning to send keeps getting bumped to the next message. The last thing she dictated was about land snails, and she regretted sending it. Yet now he is replying, taking it in his stride.

Snails, eh? Maybe you're the kind of girl I've been looking for. Got any other interesting pets?

In his profile he is described as West Country born and bred. As she launches into an anecdote about a vicious snake she once owned, she tries to imagine him dictating in a farmer's accent. His next message comes back with a subtle *ping*.

Man, a snake under my bed would proper freak me out. You're something else!

Freya is amused by this. It makes her sound a lot more interesting. 'Thanks,' she says. His picture doubles in size as her eyes linger on it, stripes of sunshine catching his hair and patterning his T-shirt but missing his face. He might be in a pub garden, a half-smile appearing as he realises he is being photographed. The muscles of one bent arm stretch the fabric of his shirt, and she can imagine the hard flatness of his chest.

Come have a drink at the bar. The website has its own virtual chat room, the usual deal where you create an obscenely beautiful avatar and talk to people in real time. You might agree to do a few shots together, never knowing if the other person is just taking sips of water.

'I don't know.'

Come on, what's the harm in it?

The harm is that it is VR. She will put on her specs and see bar stools and sparkly drinks and beautiful barmen – or barmaids in his version – and be expected to make conversation without any of it bothering her.

'I don't see any point in the virtual bar.'

Couldn't agree more. You're in London, right? Let's go to the Padfoot Arms.

Freya looks down at herself, still in a bathrobe. She didn't bargain on having to look presentable.

I can see from your profile it's your kind of place . . . very medieval. It's just inside the walls. This message baffles her, until she realises her Social has accumulated a few pictures and articles about Medieville, since she was researching Ruby's interest in the place.

'Sorry, I'm not dating right now.' Better to be honest with him.

Who said anything about dating?

She has to admire his energy, his willingness to meet her when they have only been messaging for a few hours. Maybe there is no harm, as long as he knows it's just a drink. This is shaping up into something exciting. Already the words are spilling from her.

'Ruby, I've got a date.'

'Smiley face!'

'He wants to meet at some pub. The Padfoot Arms.'

'I'd rate that place, really authentic.'

On the screen, Freya's photo makes her look round-faced and cute, her hair casting flattering shadows. Doubt assails her.

'Maybe it's not such a good idea.'

'Why not?'

'Sunday's a weird day for a drink.'

'Not in London, babes.'

She lowers her voice. 'It's this guy, Otto.'

'This Otto?' A beat while she checks him out. 'Whoa!' Her voice is flooded with admiration. 'Go, you!'

Freya twists her hair, thrilled at this reaction.

'What do you reckon?' she says.

'You know me. Up for anything. You're meeting virtually, right?'

Her face falls. 'Virtually?'

'It's safer that way.'

She sighs, opens her wardrobe, closes it, then opens it again. It is easier to make a good impression if half her attention is not focused on coping with her phobia. In a pub she can relax, and if anything goes wrong the door is right there.

'I'll be fine,' she reassures her smartface.

'Okay, hun, you go for it.'

Good to hear the smile behind the words. She suspects her sister would have chosen to go to the pub and is just being protective. The smartface has definitely come a long way. It knows she does not want it to talk like a personal assistant, only to help her in the background. Though it is useful to have bills paid and birthdays remembered, at no point does she want to hear her sister talking like a computer. Ruby is also learning not to go on about Freya's data, even to catch herself when she slips up.

'What are you going to wear?'

'The Jip-C skirt?'

'Rated!' comes the approving reply.

Finally she can give some of her new things a whirl. This skirt was recommended for her, along with some tops, a hairband and a haptic suit. She bought them all, then felt slightly guilty. The suit in particular is an extravagant purchase, though several of her online acquaintances insist it really can impart sensations of heat and cold, rough and smooth. When she unwrapped it, pinching the textured fabric between finger and thumb, she doubted she would use it for anything headier than testing clothes though she can think of websites that would tempt her to touch the wet jelly of an anemone, the fur of an animal. Ruby told her not to stress about the price, insisting that money could always be found if it was needed.

'Go on, try the skirt.'

Freya wrestles the Jip-C from its lightweight drone box, and struggles to find the correct path for her legs through the layers of fabric. Predictably, it tangles and she finds herself partially hog-tied, falling onto the bed. The laughter of the smartface cascades around her. 'This style is weird,' she protests. 'How come you've got a thing for Medieville anyway?'

'I just think it's fun.'

She extracts her hand and tries to slip the whole thing down. 'Would I think so?'

'Is that a question for your data?' Ruby chuckles. 'It says no!'

'Why not?' Freya demands.

'Because you're too square. Joke! It's just not your kind of place. You're not really a fantasy type, and you're not into history either.'

'And you are?'

'During the French Revolution—'

'All right, I know!'

She puts on the skirt and instantly feels more like a 'fantasy type', as Ruby puts it. Then she spends ages looking up the route and messing around on Social, waiting to hear from Otto. Just as she is thinking he has forgotten, a message comes, confirming time, place and his general eagerness to meet. Before leaving, she pauses, noticing her face looks rather flat.

'Should I get some new make-up?' She realises she has no idea how to buy make-up. What colours do you choose, and what brands? Suddenly her wall becomes a life-size image of a naked woman, painted gold. Freya is taken aback.

'What's this?'

'Make-up.'

'I didn't mean full body make-up.' The trend has not entirely escaped her notice. Annotations pop up beside the woman, showing which shimmer has been used on the collar-bone, which all-body foundation, shin bronzer and nipple rouge. She is not a model, but is grinning down at the size-able number of people subscribing to her selfies. 'When would you even wear this stuff?' Freya imagines dusting her foot with powder before pulling on a sock.

'Duh,' says Ruby. 'When you're naked. Let me switch you to the face pages.' They appear onscreen, make-up going beyond the norm, adding lightning strikes to temples, mystic runes to foreheads. They seem like something you could only wear in certain areas of London, or to the right kind of events.

'Do you buy into all this?' Freya asks.

'It's just for fun.'

It takes a concerted hunt through old toiletries bags before she finds some eyeliner, a little crusty, and applies it inex-pertly around the edges of her lashes.

'Shall we call a smartcar?' Ruby says.

'No, the bus is fine.'

Seconds later, she is outside in the settling gloom, already uncertain about leaving her neat, readable walls for a street full of sounds and smells. Wearing a skirt feels like wandering around in a bathrobe, her bare legs rubbing together and prickling with goose bumps. March is still practically winter, she realises, and she is not dressed for it. The bus is especially draughty, lit by seedy yellow strips, and to make things worse, a beggar is going from seat to seat. He works his way down, and when he sits by the woman in front she can smell a sugary alcohol on his breath. 'Help me get a cup of tea,' he whispers, holding up a greasy phone with a thumb-scanner app on its screen. The woman becomes aware that someone is talking, and looks astonished to be disturbed. The tramp rises, just as Freya does, to get off. She watches him stumble over the uneven paving, feeling sorry for him, remembering from her schooldays how hard it is to break into people's bubbles.

The crowded souvenir stands tell her she is approaching Medieville. She always forgets how large it is. As the former Olympic 'village', it has gone from being one sort of invented urban landscape to another. During one of the government's asset sell-offs the site went to an inscrutable Norwegian businessman who promised affordable housing. Freya remembers reading an interview about his upbringing in the independent community of Christiania in the middle of Copenhagen. He had a slightly romantic view of historical London, and little did the government know that in developing this land he would create something quite unusual. Perhaps they didn't care. The low prices of the first quick-form housing attracted artists and students, and people more than happy to embellish and build their own homes using reclaimed materials, with incentives for anyone who would add a tower here or some ornamentation there. Almost overnight, Medieville developed a commune-like identity, sporadically claiming independence from London and welcoming anyone who wanted to live as people did in simpler times. Visitors are supposed to check in gadgets at the gate, to get into the spirit of the place. Inhabitants sell handicrafts and give tours, and the medieval-fayre restaurants and dungeon bars do a roaring trade. Freya is not sure what Medieville was like in the early days, but it now claims to be London's fifth most popular tourist attraction.

She lays a hand on the recycled-wood gate, impressed by its size. It is wedged in place, permanently open. There is no entrance fee as such; a slight commission at the money-changing desks ensures that every visitor brings a cover charge. The last time she came they were still accepting notes bearing Charles's grizzled features, but now even cash has been deemed insufficiently antiquated, so they only use Medieville Sovereigns, brass-nickel composite coins that land cold and heavy in Freya's hands as a gatekeeper counts them out, like play money. She is beginning to understand why Ruby might find this place such a novelty.

The pub is not far. After getting a few disapproving glances, she snatches off her smartspecs and tucks them away, surprised that people notice the slim titanium. Faux-cobbles press through her soles, and she looks up at black beams on either side, forgetting that without her specs a squint no longer has a zoom effect. The fragrant odour of burning wood fills the street. Above her, someone closes a window, and she is reminded that people live here, presumably those who can coexist with tourists. According to her research, many individuals moved to escape the digital age, setting up organic gardening clubs or bringing forgotten crafts back to life. Others sought a moonlit vision of ancient times, the growing interest in heraldry and knighthood expanding into balls and banquets, feasts, tournaments and all the imagined glamour of days gone by, mixed up with mythology and occasional steampunk. This is the part that seems to bother Esther, who mutters about people swanning around in sequinned wimples, never learning how it really was. But perhaps her mum just can't understand, not being a playful sort of person.

Groups of Chinese tourists pass by, receding with the light to their ultra-personalised hotel rooms. Aromas of roasting meat escape through the door of a tavern. On tiny tables men and women play backgammon, chess, or board games with chimera, phoenix and griffin counters. People try to guess which of three moving cups will end up covering a broad bean. Most of the loiterers hold a pewter tankard of craft ale, or a fake sweet beer produced for teetotallers and children. She remembers tasting it last time she was here and not liking its hint of aniseed. Everyone is dressed in robes, furs, cloaks, wimples, bodices, floppy velvet hats, or else sackcloth waistcoats, tights, smocks, Viking helmets or fairy wings. Nobody wears smartspecs or a headset, or even a smartbit, though she sees a device being slipped out surreptitiously when someone wants to take a photo. Doubtless the various housing associations that now run the place would like to ban gadgets altogether, but it is important that people can share their experiences on Social and keep the sovereigns rolling in.

Further along, Freya sees palm-readers, stalls of street food, lyre-players, and even a pair of stocks where someone stands miserably, cabbage leaves caught in her hair. She looks up.

'Hey, you. Can you get me out of here?'

Assuming it is all part of the show, Freya is starting to muster a polite smile when the woman adds: 'I'm serious. I've got a broken metatarsal and I need to sit down.' She lifts her left foot awkwardly. A sandal is taped to hang around a grubby bandage. Still hesitant, Freya slips behind the stocks and sees two metal catches on each side. A smell of vegetables rotted almost to liquid assails her nostrils. With difficulty she eases the latches open and helps the woman push the top piece up until she can extract herself. The crick in her back is almost audible as she straightens, staggering and stretching, both hands pushing her spine the other way.

'God, that was painful,' she groans. 'Thanks a million. I was fixing a pipe to the roof garden and must have yanked a wire . . . The lights went off. None of the shops complained, of course. It's only ever the zombies . . .' She pauses to flick a piece of tomato skin from her fingerless gloves.

'That's pretty harsh,' Freya says, looking at the black-moist wood of the stocks. 'Who are the zombies?'

'The guys in the cellars.'

'Oh.' She is lost. 'And they put you in the stocks?'

'I know!' The woman's eyes flash emphatically. There is one silver stud in her nose, and another just above her lip. Her hair is like a russet helmet, wet in places from the soggy leaves. 'I'm Gayle. Are you a tourist?'

'No, I've got a date.'

She grins. 'Hope it's a hot one. Thanks again, I owe you.' Keeping her weight carefully off the injured foot, she starts to make her way up the edge of the street, brushing at her smock.

Still a few minutes early, Freya peers into shop windows as she goes, seeing real items on shelves, no screens or barcodes in sight. Every female face draws her eye, but there is no one who resembles an older version of Ruby, and eventually she makes herself stop looking. Ahead is a market square, but Freya takes a sharp left, remembering the map-line. Here is the pub at last, though nothing is visible through its smeary, blackened windows. A grim place for a date. She sneaks out her smartspecs to check the address and looks again at Otto's last message. This is definitely the Padfoot Arms.

Inside, there is darkness. When her eyes adjust, low-beamed ceilings emerge, the uneven floor leading off to either side; a pub of different rooms and a central bar with wheel-like candelabra overhead. There is a tang in the air that might be cider, or something else. Not knowing what to do, she orders a rum and Coke, and it arrives in a wooden goblet. The porous rim does not look particularly hygienic. A message pings on her smartspecs and she slides them out. *I'm upstairs.* The barman looks up and she quickly turns away.

In which room do they keep the stairs? She comes almost full circle before she spots a shallow staircase leading up into the centre of the pub. Here a corridor runs alongside a courtyard dotted with barrels, and beyond she finds a room with two or three tables, an old fireplace on one side and an incongruous green fire door. Otto is sitting in an alcove.

Although she recognises him from his photo, he looks completely different to the stocky hockey-playing, Cornish-pasty-making youth worker she expected. He is wearing a Spider-Man T-shirt and his chest looks smaller, his arms more veined and, it seems to her, too long, as they lie splayed along the top of the seat.

'All right, my lovely?' he says, as she approaches. He has a strong accent, stepping on the first syllable and drawing out the second, but his voice is different to what she imagined. 'I was beginning to think you weren't coming.'

'Iye wur comin'.' She is disappointed he does not smile. Then she goes red at having done a potentially inappropriate impersonation, though luckily it seems to have gone over his head. His face has the same sleepy glower that was in his photo online. 'So, here we are,' she says mildly.

He nods and swirls the last of his drink, something yellow and cloudy. Freya tucks her coat behind her. She notices two more people going over to join the men already chatting and is glad the pub is filling up. Otto is gazing intently at her, his eyes a dark glimmer under thin brows. His fingers are slim, with neatly cut nails. A woody scent weighs down the air.

'You look just like your photo,' he says.

'Sorry?'

'Your photo.'

'Oh yeah. So do you,' she lies. There is a pause. She tries to think of something she has not already asked him during their chat on the website. He saves her by enquiring if she had any difficulty finding the place.

'No, it was fine.'

The small talk now accomplished, he leans closer. 'So we've done snakes and snails . . . where d'you want to go next?' His teeth are a little crooked and his lips struggle to slide back over them. 'Did you search my name?'

'No.' She looked at the hobbies list on his Social profile but did not think to do a general search. Ruby never suggested it. Was this remiss of the smartface? Maybe she calculated Freya would enjoy the date more if she did not already know everything about him.

He sighs. 'Tha's a shame, but never mind.' He glances past her to two more men who have just entered. She looks too and notices they are not carrying drinks. 'We'll manage the best we can.' A shock as she realises he is speaking to the newcomers. The table alcove feels small and enclosed. Freya lifts herself up, tucking a knee underneath. There are now seven other men in the room, all with close-shaven hair and – the realisation chills her – all wearing Spider-Man T-shirts of different kinds.

She has to stop her hand trembling against the table as she stands. Her lips pin back, fighting to maintain a neutral expression. 'So where's the toilet in here?'

Otto rises with her. His hand runs gently down her forearm, leaving raised hairs in its wake. 'I wouldn't use the loos 'ere,' he says.

Her body stiffens. From downstairs she can hear a rumble of voices, muffled through thick layers of rug and floorboards. If she screams, will they hear? The other men are still lounging about, not moving, but somehow closer than they were. Some of their T-shirts hang loosely, and some are stretched and faded. They are looking at her like she is a can of energy drink temptingly abandoned on a club floor. The room seems darker; she can hardly remember where she came in. All she can see is the green door saying *Fire Exit*. The two by the bar are coming over. She feels a touch on her wrist. Another man is here. She grabs her bag and runs to the bar, then behind it, slamming her weight against the fire-door lever so it cracks open. Her feet skitter on a metal staircase outside, but she gets the door shut and clambers down to where crates and kegs are littered among the dustbins, steam pouring from the out-pipe of a boiler. She walks at a fast, shaky pace until the gates of Medieville are behind her, and only once she is on a street of shops that light up with recognition and offer comforting products and snacks does she stop, chest heaving.

The smartspecs have never seemed so spidery as she struggles to unfold them and settle them over her ears.

'Home,' she says, impatient with the map-line not firing up in a millisecond. Smartcars prowl at regular intervals along the road, circling like predators. The smartface icon finally loads. 'What was that?' Freya demands.

'Huh?' says Ruby.

'What the hell was that?'

'Hey, what's with the crazy heart rate?'

A crowd of tourists appear from nowhere, and Freya steps back to avoid the barrage of elbows.

'Don't you know?' She tries to keep her voice steady.

'Medieville's a total blind spot, babes.'

It is easy to forget that the smartface is confined to her realm, to the cloud, and cannot read Freya's mind.

'There were eight of them.'

'Otto. Yeah. It's a thing.'

A clammy wind blows round her legs. She left her coat in the pub. It is a bus or tube journey and then a walk before she can stop shivering.

'It's a thing?' Her pitch could shatter glass.

'Like a code word.' A sheepish note enters Ruby's voice. 'Guess it didn't go well. I was so psyched for you.'

'A code word for what?'

'I guess it's because there are so many men on these sites.

In theory it gives you a choice of eight. Up to eight. It doesn't sound like this guy explained it very well.'

'He didn't explain it at all.'

Her jaw vibrates involuntarily, a numbness taking root in every cell. The smartface is markedly less worked up about this, so does that mean she is overreacting? Was it childish to run away? She clamps her arms together, hands frozen white and slightly ethereal thanks to the glow-in-the-dark nailz. Every kind of fantasy is catered for, yet she is always left out in the cold. She knows what Ruby is going to say.

'I know,' she interjects through chattering teeth, 'I should have stuck to the virtual bar.'

The nearest smartcar stops. Its door opens wide to receive her and she climbs in gratefully.

11

Deep in conversation with Ruby, she forgets to take off her smartspecs until Sandor comes close. Then, before she can do anything, his hands are at her temples, lifting them. The air becomes acidic in his vicinity, as though he produces more carbon dioxide than a normal person. His wink makes her blood boil. How chivalrous to save her from the fate of being told off – by himself – for wearing a device at work. As management, Sandor enjoys the use of a company-issued headset, ostensibly to monitor the warehouse, with which he crowns himself each morning. She narrows her eyes as he hands back the specs, aims his finger above her head and jerks it.

'Ptchoo!' His imaginary quarry drops down behind the *Sale* sign, and he blows the tip of his finger. Then he peers at her. 'You look different.'

'I'm a bit tired.'

All night she was plagued by repeating sensations: the feel of the wooden cup against her lips, the beer-soaked carpet, the ache of her clenched jaw against the cold.

'Are you? I assumed you'd been overdosing on the old beauty sleep.' He taps his vintage watch with a fingernail. 'Matching your own previous record.' The reproof administered, he makes his lordly exit. She notices that Chris is standing perfectly still with a tub of knives, straining to hear the conversation.

'Is there something going on that I don't know about?' he says.

'What?'

He stares at her, brows arched in derision. 'You know what.'

She groans and goes to fetch her apron, offended by the suggestion – even in jest – that she would be interested in Sandor. The timing strikes her as bad, though of course Chris knows nothing of her recent experience. Despite the smartcar turning up its heaters, it took a hot bath to ease the frost from her arms and legs. Her smartface was very comforting once she got home, warming everything that could be warmed, lining up some entertaining films, and reminding Freya of the existence of some little valium jellies in the fridge. Ruby seemed surprised at how much she was freaking out.

'If you didn't like what was happening, you could have just said so,' she insisted.

It would have been fine if she'd stuck with the virtual bar. Some brief research gave her an understanding of how the Otto thing worked, or rather, how it worked for people who wanted a smorgasbord of eight men. But she is not that voracious, and the algorithms should know it . . . so how did the match come about? When Freya finally hoisted her dripping body from the bathtub, she was pleased to find herself feeling substantially calmer.

'It just wasn't right for me,' she explained, hoping Ruby did not think she was being blamed.

'I know. It's your thorough detective work.' By this she meant the fact that Freya had signed up to a few other dating sites, intending to scour them for Ruby-like profiles. It must have made her look rather keen. 'It's not the smartest site, matching you with an Otto. But then it's not for proper dating, not really, and there are always a few weirdos . . .' Freya had barely thought about it, but her smartface was right. Singleminded is just a meet-up site. When she registered it allowed her to temporarily skip the measurements and 3D body-profiling. Otto must have been desperate enough to overlook these missing details. He scrambled his seven friends pretty quickly. *Who said anything about dating?* She should have read the signs.

Later that night she pulled herself together sufficiently to message Otto – thinking she might have overreacted – to say sorry, they should have met in the virtual bar, she did not realise what was going on and it was not her kind of thing. It bothered her to be viewed as a time-waster, but there was no response. Ruby, bored of him by this point, was telling her to forget he existed. It was hard to remember her normal night-time routines. Instead of doing her teeth, she ate some of Julian's vitamin foams left on the bathroom windowsill, which made her breath smell like his. She went to bed with a hollow, sweet feeling in her stomach.

A burbling sound draws her attention, and she watches Chris dash over to stop the beans boiling. Her fragmented night will be followed by a difficult day. Judging by his face, her colleague is also in the mood for silence. There is nothing to talk about anyway, not without telling Chris everything she has been up to, and he does not seem keen on listening. She watches him adjust his apron and push back imaginary hair from his forehead. When it was cut a few days ago, he claimed to feel like Samson, all shorn and unprotected, stripped of his powers. He reaches for the bottle of cleaner, but she is there first, not about to be told off for leaving the tables too long. The look he gives her is indifferent, as though they are strangers. Two squirts and a wipe, and she can see her face, a shadow outline. The mist diffuses, landing on her lips, bitter when she presses them together. If only Ruby were here, on her smartspecs, it would make the day so much more bearable.

From this awkward beginning, things go downhill, particularly when a child being lifted to the counter by its parents chooses that moment to vomit liberally, so they have to rush around with cloths and blue paper while a queue builds up. Subsequent customers complain about the smell of sick as they take their plates, directing their comments to each other as though Freya cannot hear them. She watches a man lean down indulgently to his young son and go through a range of nose-pinching and hand-flapping motions, while she waits patiently for him to bark his order. Never has she felt so invisible.

To make things worse, Sandor is everywhere, leaning by the sink as she rushes over with empty trays, in the stairwell when she goes up to the lockers. He strews himself all over the store, and when she does bump into him it is obvious he wants to have a conversation, though she cannot imagine why. To avoid him she finds extra jobs to do during the lulls, dusting the tops of cupboards or rearranging the display of jars, all the while wondering how much longer this can go on, directing half-formed questions at the smartface-shaped hole in her mind.

People come up in ones or twos to get their food. Her tiredness matures into something fleecy and soft, as though she could bury her face in it. The whole process of serving customers is dreamlike, as the slivers of potato mesh together and she chases sausages that skid around in the oil. The man on the nearest table sits alone with a cup of fizz, talking to himself. He wears one haptic glove and is using it to stroke the hand of someone absent, before reaching up to wipe a tear from an invisible cheek. The fabric will enable him to feel her skin, even sense the hot moisture of the tear. Freya wonders if his girlfriend is sitting alone in an equally godforsaken café, in some far-off place, her black-gloved fingers curling upwards to link with his.

When the customers have been served, she goes over to clear tables and finds herself just behind the man, close enough to notice that his headset is the latest Halo, its nodules sitting on his scalp and picking up brainwaves. Her mum thinks the medical applications of these headsets are wonderful, yet she disapproves of their everyday use. The mainstream media is also suspicious, and there are occasional news snippets about household systems imploding as a result of turbulent thoughts, or people being influenced by covert adverts or dreaming up viruses. What is this man thinking about? He has stopped talking and has a faraway look in his eyes. His shirt is brushed chrome, and there is a Smarti drawstring bag slung over his chair. All the trappings of a young Smarti exec, not quite weaned off burgers and onto finer foods. Only the best and brightest get onto the graduate programmes, and even then competition is so fierce that you need a way in: an introduction, or something exceptional like a prize win. Freya stirs the peas, keeping them evenly heated. What makes it all so hard is that she was, much to her surprise, successful in her application. It was one of the most exciting experiences of her life to be whisked away from university to the training centre down in Brighton, with a trip to San Fran lined up later in the year. She was the brightest and best, for a while. Now she is balling up blue paper to wipe a vomit-dot from the Perspex.

It must never have occurred to Smarti that someone so young could have a problem with VR. If only they had stuck to augmented reality, Freya could have coped. If they had just let her project the DNA models above her desk, with her real cup of coffee alongside, she would have been fine. But instead they invented a dazzling, outdoor laboratory, warm sun overhead, cut-grass scents and birds tweeting. A joy for everyone to work in. Only she couldn't handle it. She tried to keep her mind on the project, on making bacteria produce sheets of bone for third-world housing – they always put the grads on their most feel-good ventures – but as soon as the visor went on, she was overwhelmed by dread. Something terrible could be happening, and she was here, blind to the outside world. No matter how much she tried to calm herself, she could not concentrate. All her available brainpower was focused on remembering that this was only a simulation. It was like trying to swim without letting go of the pool edge.

She pictures the Smarti campus with its biopocketing walls, its microbe-built, self-furling curtain blinds, technology just on the brink of flipping from silicone back to carbon. The gut-wrenching thrill of it. To think that she could have been part of a design process that included, as standard, the question *Would it work on Mars?* She would have been involved in bleeding-edge projects, with the chance to make breakthroughs and eat free blueberry muffins. By now she would be a different person altogether.

It fell apart so quickly. That first checkpoint. The bemused voice of her supervisor telling her she was lagging behind the other grads. Her performance had been spectacularly bad. This was November, barely two months into the placement, and already the dream of a career, the dream her mum had so cherished for her, was evaporating. In fact Esther seemed to feel it even more keenly, and could not quite conceal this with her usual stoical exterior. 'Just pick up some temping for now,' she said. 'Try again next year. Or try one of the smaller companies.' They were empty words, both of them knowing what it meant to have that invisible *Fail* underpinning her profile.

The man with the haptic glove is now clawing the air, his voice loud and hurt as he recreates some argument he lost. Perhaps his girlfriend is saying soothing words at the other end, trying to bring the rant to a close. Black-pepper stubble undulates as his cheeks puff out. Inevitably, his next angry gesture sends the cup of orangeade flying. Freya turns away, leaving the liquid to pour from his table onto the floor and make it sticky.

She takes a dustpan round the pedestals, sweeping up the baby wipes and abandoned drinks that seem to accumulate. A triple wardrobe glows above her and then flickers into a chest of drawers. She can remember when this was just Christmas work, the temping job her mum suggested. Every day she wandered the sales floor on her well-worn route, tidying rugs and closing cabinet doors, fingering oak veneers and smelling chipboard glue. It was mercifully real, beautifully simple to work with *stuff*, the mundane items you find around the home. A sigh escapes her as Helpful Holly geysers up into existence, helping a customer choose a chair. Freya had no idea it was all about to change.

Finally she forces herself to mop beneath the man's vacated table. He will be back in some virtual office, fed and watered, while she is here sopping up his fizzy orange. But what can she do? If she went to the doctor with a VR phobia, there would be a lot of head-scratching. In all probability she would be called a time-waster, told to self-prescribe her own app, as most people tend to do. Chris managed to dampen his aversion to spiders through setting up an idyllic beach scene, letting in the tiniest of arachnids when he was at peak relaxation. Virtual treatment is effective for so many phobias, but little use when the fear is VR itself.

If she were here, Ruby would say being scared is a trap, which should be sprung as quickly as possible. She would point to all the computer games Freya played as a girl, the times she would go out of her way to attend a VR demo, and how much she used to enjoy it. For the first time, it occurs to her that Ruby had to put up with a lot of chat about tech, not to mention those evenings when Freya was antisocial, wrapped up in a blanket with a visor over her eyes. It was hard to resist the pull of those landscapes, real or imagined, those space walks on other planets based on real NASA imaging, virtual experiences so good she never wanted them to end.

Ruby even warned her about it. 'Hey, get off your face,' she said lightly. 'Just don't stay there.' The older girl never got addicted to anything; it was not part of her personality. She could dip in and out of VR, enjoying a website or a game, and let it go without a second thought. Esther once brought home a fabulous tech windfall from work, a brand-new visor pressed on her by colleagues who knew she was fostering a girl the right age for testing, but Ruby used it for about five minutes before handing it unceremoniously to Freya.

Long since tossed into the bacterial recycler, it was this visor and its suite of games that really hooked Freya in those last months, and her sister could see it. She reacted by going on a tech detox herself, as though they were two people on a seesaw, needing to find balance. Ruby stopped bothering with smartspecs, and even left her phone at home, astonishing everyone by being able to get around 'tech-naked'. A closed look would appear on her face whenever this was mentioned. It was almost as though she knew. That she sensed, with her animal instinct about such things, something bad would come of Freya's mild but growing addiction. They spent a few more evenings apart, until the fateful night of *Metamorphosis Amazonia*, when Freya spoke in that steel-sharp voice, the tone she would always regret, and told her sister to go away. It is still tangible in her throat, a bitterness too ingrained to spit out.

Just as she thinks the day is ending, she is called into Sandor's office. With reluctant feet, she forces herself up the stairs, removing her hairnet and shaking out her extensions. Everything in his closet-like room smells of air freshener, including the greyish coffee he places in front of her. He lifts his cup and says, 'Cheers,' so she is forced to raise her cardboard container and squash the edge silently against his. He is wearing his bird-shooting face, satisfaction mingled with a hint of bloodlust. Her neck feels taut as she meets his eye, searching for signs that he is about to sack her. Instead he leans in with an expression of concern that, on his face, makes him look pained.

'How are things at home?' he asks. 'Everything okay with Julian?'

The coffee burns her tongue. She splutters, completely thrown. 'Um . . . I guess. Why do you ask?'

'Everything okay? With Julian?' His usual way is to repeat himself until he gets the answer he wants. Almost without noticing, she bites down on a thumbnail and has to pick flakes of nail varnish from the tip of her tongue.

'Well, we're not together. But everything is okay.'

'Ah,' he says, a look of understanding settling on his features. 'No need to be too upset. Plenty more fish in the sea.' He emphasises the *plenty*.

'I know.' She tries to keep a level tone.

'You'll find someone else.' He is stating the obvious,

showing his age. Maybe if she lived somewhere remote, the situation might warrant this response. But in the city there are near-unlimited fish. Here in London, it is just insulting. She pushes the coffee away, feeling some déjà vu from that uncomfortable chat with her mum in the living room. It must be a law of the universe that every awkward conversation be accompanied by substandard coffee.

'I should go.'

'It's just, when you're late on a regular basis,' he jumps in, 'it can be a sign that all is not well. I have to keep an eye on these things. Pastoral role.' This last word slides from his O-shaped lips and he fingers an invisible cigar.

'Okay.' She wonders, not for the first time, if her face is looking a bit strange, whether thick eyeliner can disguise the pools of tiredness in which her eyes are floating. Obviously not. He gestures towards the door, and her chair squeals as she stands, grateful the interview is at an end.

'Singleminded,' he says, just as she is leaving.

'Sorry?'

'It's a good site if you're looking to meet someone. So I've heard.'

The words hang over his desk, until he flicks their cups into the recycler and she takes the opportunity to flee, just about managing to shut the door without slamming it. The stairs tilt as she descends, like a fairground funhouse, and towards the bottom her knees wobble dangerously. She pictures Sandor at home, spinning on a leather chair, stuffed birds on the mantelpiece, spotting her profile and leaning in delightedly, thinking, *Is that Freya? Is that my member of staff? Is she really bi-curious?*

She only added that bit to open up female profiles, just in case Ruby had one. For one fleeting moment – and she dispels this thought immediately – his aura of lechery seemed to focus into a beam, as though hitting on her. *Don't fool yourself*, she instructs. This will be some game or test. Just ride it out like all the others.

With the daylight gone, the city has reverted to winter. A distant road drill is filling the air with pulverised concrete. Extra grey. For some reason the metal of her specs is difficult to grip.

'Ruby?' she whispers, knowing she is going to sound downbeat. 'I don't want to do this any more.'

Her words are absorbed by the empty streets.

'Okay, babes.'

12

She is in an elegant boudoir with a pink marble fireplace, marred only by the patches of dead pixels where her swivel-chair has bashed into the wall. There is not much room, after all, though the digital wallpaper makes this easier to ignore. With leisurely movements, she bunches up drone packaging and throws it to one side. Red velour runs over her fingers, cool and sensuous. Before she can try on the dress, there is a message from Sandor.

Freya, I would like to point out that today is Saturday, our busiest day, so if you feel better at any point please come in promptly.

His usual passive-aggressive thrust with a thin shell of courtesy. On Thursday she told him she'd walked into the path of an oncoming cyclist and sprained her ankle falling. A period of rest was needed, for the swelling to subside. In times past she would have avoided calling in sick even if truly ill, but Ruby assured her – clicking through whatever mysterious algorithms she had at her disposal – that it would in no way adversely affect her to be off for a few days. 'Trust me,' she said. The ankle was a good choice of injury. Certain illnesses – a raised temperature, for example – could be diagnosed by her smartbit, and she is unsure whether its data could reach her employer.

As she is rereading the message, a call appears on her wallscreen. Alarm sparks, and then fizzles out as she sees it is her mum. The ringing continues. It must be obvious she's at home, but there is nothing to say she is not napping or having a bath. Lying to Sandor is one thing, but it would be a bad idea to tell Esther the same story. She would want to come straight over, have a look at the ankle and give her professional opinion.

The dress slides over her head, comfortable and uncomplicated, and she settles back into her nest of duvet. It is so luxurious to stay at home, free from the tyranny of Sandor and the constant haze of meat grease. The feeling reminds her of breaking up for summer holidays, anticipating long, lazy afternoons with her sister. For now, everything seems fine as long as she has Ruby's voice on tap. It has acquired a sort of texture, maybe even a shape, like a warm hand on her shoulder. Her sister could be right here, curled up on a Queen Anne chair, just out of sight, hair in tiny plaits and fingers stained from pinching out candles. In her presence, names like *Sandor* mean nothing. One swipe, and his message is gone.

Her Social shows the usual waterfall of updates. Certain schoolfriends are starting to seem more like acquaintances.

She makes sure to *like* all their holiday photos. Sighing, she circles a finger to scroll backwards in time, and it strikes her that last year her wall was all facts and figures, frogs and axolotls and distant mates. Since then the animal kingdom has receded, but her feed is still colourful. There are new individuals whose profiles include swords or long-nosed masks, pictures of meet-ups she could attend, and articles about everything from Medieville to Manhattan. There is stuff about London – sometimes she forgets she is not a Londoner herself – the latest style being a skin-tight haptic suit with lightening-strike pattern. A catwalk-only fashion, she assumes. Where has her own haptic suit got to? Before she can scroll any further, a knock makes her jump.

'Freya?' It is a moan rather than a voice, and at first she can't think who is behind it. Then she freezes, wondering if she can pretend to be asleep. This option vanishes when Julian adds, 'I heard you talking.' Irritated, she forces herself towards the door.

'It might have been Ruby,' she says.

'Huh?' His eyebrows and the corners of his mouth twitch up, that expression she used to know so well. He smells of the hand soap in the bathroom. 'You're at home today?'

This is as close as he will get to realising she has been off sick. She thinks of rainy evenings mooching outside his door, loneliness inclining her to tap, until she remembered what he might be doing. All the times she left him alone. Now he comes and disturbs her.

She shrugs. 'Yeah.'

'Never seen your wall so busy.' Typical of him to check her out on Social before crossing the hall. He is wearing the

156

T-shirt that shows a telescopic view of his star sign, the one she gave him. 'Who are all the weirdos?'

'It's just Medieville stuff.'

'That your thing now?' He shuffles into the room and lifts a cushion as though there might be interesting minibeasts underneath.

'Just some research.'

'They got you to buy that dress, though, didn't they?' Something sly enters his tone, wanting her to acknowledge being hoodwinked by online sales tactics. *Fifteen of your friends like something, so why don't you?* Julian considers himself above such manipulation, although these days she is not sure he can sit on that particular high horse.

'It's actually quite comfortable.' She tugs at her velour sleeve.

'Not saying I don't like it,' he adds quickly.

'Was there something you wanted?'

'So . . . what's up with your rent?'

She sinks onto the bed. Her account must be running pretty low for the payment to have bounced.

'Oh God . . .'

'I got it covered.' His voice is light. 'That's what I came to tell you. Don't worry, I'm still getting the dad stipend, and it's not like I've spent much lately.'

The self-deprecating smile leaves her baffled. Not only is he out of his room and focusing, but he's trying to make a peace offering. While she would normally protest, on this occasion it might be sensible to say yes. His family ensures he never wants for cash. When Thalis first visited the flat and spotted the gecko, he offered in hushed tones to get

Julian a nice studio apartment of his own, somewhere more central, with no expense spared.

'Are you sure?' she says, twisting her hair into a spiral. 'I'll pay you back.'

'Plus I've got a pile of gadgets to sell,' he goes on, eyes drifting to the smartface box on her shelf. Again she wonders what might have happened if he'd kept it for himself. It might have adopted the personality of some porn star, finding him scenarios so tantalising he would lose his grip for good. Better for him that she took it.

'I saw your dad the other day.' She still hasn't filled out his feedback form.

'Where?'

'In some greenzone.'

'He likes running. Everyone's running. He wants me to do it.' Having finally adjusted to the novelty of this conversation, she sees Julian's face glaze over in response to the mention of his dad, as though replaying a discussion far away. His cheeks darken, and she is astonished to see something like embarrassment, even shame, in his expression. Hard to imagine what this lifestyle is doing to him when they are here chatting and things seem so normal. 'He's too used to working with bots,' he goes on. 'The only people he bothers with are celebrities and people who can boost his career. If he gets a phone call from someone he doesn't know, he'll just assume they're a bot. It's like his default setting.'

Experience tells her the conclusion of this rant will be that his dad treats him like a bot too, or else a prop to prove he's a family man. They have had this conversation before. It is all very familiar: poor teenage Julian, heeding his dad's pleas to move to England, dragged around every social circle and then left alone in a penthouse flat on New Island, an exclusive and isolated Compatibuilding. Julian didn't like champagne, and used to go out and wander around the muddy riverbanks just to feel normal. *Was your bed too soft as well?* she felt like asking, but behind the whining there was obvious pain, or at least bewilderment at this treatment from a parent he must once have idolised.

A sigh expels the last of her energy. She has done her share of family counselling. They both have. Does he think they can start at the beginning and go through the whole cycle again?

As he talks, Julian has been stacking up the resin cups on her desk. It gives her the opportunity to take them from his hands and bustle him out, emerging with relief onto neutral ground. He follows her to the kitchen, needing no response to his occasional 'You know?' and falling silent only when the cups clatter into the sink. She turns to see his deer-eyes half closed against the spotlights.

'That really is a great dress,' he says.

'Thanks.'

He drags his hair upwards into spikes. There is something comforting in the sound of conversation, but she can sense the build-up of everything that isn't being said. The tea towel feels greasy in her hands, and he is still hovering. After months of them barely speaking, she feels called upon to decide what she wants from him, whether they can be friends, or if it's too late. As she is wondering how to begin, her eyes fall on a plate piled with eight folds of white bread, something yellow and sour-sweet oozing from between the crusts.

'What are you eating?' she asks, already knowing the answer.

'Lemon-curd folds. Want one? I've made a ton.'

'Where did it come from?'

'It was in the fridge.' He picks up the plate, squinting companionably, and holds it out to her. She can just sense the texture of the curd, the smooth, semi-translucent lemon. She waves a hand, stomach already trembling, and slips past him out of the kitchen, taking a few deep breaths of the dusty living-room air. Did he order the lemon curd? She is surprised that it still has an effect on her. The voice in her head is already telling her to get over it. *It's only jam.*

'Hey,' Julian adds, obviously keen to keep the talk going, 'I think I've got some of your flip-flops in my room. I was wearing them round the house. Come on, I'll dig them out.'

He bustles her along to his bedroom and hurls the door open, but she is not quite ready to cross the threshold. She looks for signs of tidying, of laundry having been collected, hoping to see no indications of anything else. Julian goes to the huge closet they used to share.

'What's that?'

Beyond the flip-flops he is holding up, there is something slung over the open cupboard door, black and waxy as a leaf. Her missing haptic suit.

'This?' A step change in his voice indicates his guilt. 'I borrowed it. Sorry. It was on the coffee table.' His posture suddenly looks sleazy, the way one hand dangles against the concave of his hip. That stumble she heard last night might have been him peeling the fabric from his thighs, struggling to get out of it. What was he feeling against his skin? The figures spring back to life in her memory, crawling towards him from the darkness. He took her suit because he wanted it to be even more real.

'Borrowed it?'

'You were never going to use it.' He chases her back to her doorway. 'I'll get it . . .' It dawns on him that you can't get a haptic suit dry-cleaned.

'Ew.' She makes a face. 'Just keep it.' A fold of her dress catches in the door and she has to close it twice. Ruby wastes no time putting on music, cranking up the volume to drown out his voice in the corridor. Eventually she hears a slam. He can be spiteful. Even now he might be pulling on her suit, stepping into a room full of naked women and enjoying all kinds of sensations on his body, having failed to reel her in on a line baited with friendship. 'Screw him.'

'No thanks,' Ruby quips. 'I wouldn't even talk to him.'

Freya thinks about it. 'You don't think I should have anything to do with him, do you?'

'Course not. He's a spoiled brat.'

She knew Ruby would say that.

'I agree.'

Freya examines her dress, concerned it might have ripped. The sleeves are part slashed anyway, so it is hard to tell. Did she really order this? The dress clings and then falls sheer. It does look beautiful, though there will be few opportunities to wear it. She twists and turns, feeling the coolness of the fabric. Her smartface murmurs an admiring comment, flooding the walls with images of how the dress could be accessorised. The bags, bracelets and bangles are like too much noise. All she cares about is whether Ruby might be out there somewhere, browsing these websites herself. She can picture a calm face gazing at a screen, her sister's fingers toying with beads as she spots Freya's name on a hangout, does a double-take and considers what to do. Perhaps her mouth opens to dictate a message, but then closes as she thinks . . . what? That Freya and her mum were a crappy foster-family, best left in the past? Or could she be in hiding, a fugitive? Is she protecting them by staying away? *No.* Freya's arms reach out involuntarily. She wants to take Ruby by the shoulders and tell her not to think that way, that her family are still her family, no matter what.

'Ruby,' she says, 'is there any reason you'd stay away from us?'

'Not that I know of.'

Freya closes her eyes, the better to appreciate the reverberation of the words. It is only a chatbot, her mum would say. But if she had spent as long as Freya researching this new personality, she'd think differently. Take Julian, for instance. Since Christmas, or before, the only evidence for his existence has been a few coughs and thumps. Not even a voice. He has been in his room, in his own little world. If he had gone abroad to do what he was doing, and invented a new profile, he could easily – even accidentally – masquerade as a missing person.

Right on cue, there is a sound from across the hall, a slide-thump. It sets her teeth on edge. When it happens again, she takes the plump cushion that Julian touched, holds it down and punches it repeatedly, though the adrenaline in her arms does not dissipate. Her smartbit beeps, and Ruby says:

'Hey, shall we make tracks?'

If only she was here, they could live together. They could slip through the cracks, as they always used to, and escape from all this. Freya's voice is thick with longing as she whispers, 'I wish I could find you.'

She has been picturing Ruby somewhere abroad, conceivably in America, since her dad's rumoured journey west had always been a source of intrigue. However, it would be quite a feat to make it through border controls without being identified. It is impossible to walk down the street without billboards, smartcars and all manner of street furniture auto-recognising you, should you linger. Freya is not certain about other cities, but in London, drones ensure that every part of town is caught on camera a dozen times a day. Even if her sister was still wandering around tech-naked, she would be spotted.

Ruby's lack of a reply is conspicuous. It is unusual for a smartface to say nothing, even if it can't answer the question. Images appear one after another on her wallpaper, scenes of people gathered on the roof garden of Medieville, looking up at the recent supermoon. Freya sits up, captivated by the reddish orb, and then she understands.

13

Some time ago, she walked through a thunderstorm very hungry, the charged clouds rumbling in time with her stomach. Every few steps the sky would growl and she'd feel it inside, as though a miniature tempest was duplicated within her. It was one of those unexpected, magical interludes, impossible to describe, when she came face to face with the universe. The storm was trying to say something, to impart some secret about the world. If only she knew what language it was speaking.

Now that feeling is back again, and she cannot tell whether to trust it. Who has lined up the clues? Would it be Ruby, her smartface, bringing these pieces together, coaxing her to ask the right questions without giving out personal information? Or could it be her own data, even deeper in the cloud, absorbing her searches and tweaking the algorithm on Social to show this one, huge clue? Or is it fate that everything should come together just now, when something inside her has ignited and she is ready for anything?

These are her wild thoughts as she closes the front door. Daylight stings her eyes like salt water, and the gown flaps soft and greasy against her legs. She hesitates, but decides that in Medieville it will help her blend in. Something else makes her pause. As though there is some reason she should not be outside, but she cannot think what it might be.

In another three seconds the smartcar is pulling up to the kerb, its door already opening as it recognises her. *Welcome*, says the perky male voice. She gets into the front, where the steering wheel would be on a so-called dumbcar. As they pull away, she lets the adverts roll, since it will reduce the fare. *Be honest with the cloud.* The cartoon cloud bulges and smiles as it presumably soaks up truthful data. There is a programme in schools now to raise awareness. *So it can be honest with you.* Finally her Social profile appears on the windscreen. The covert drone shots are there, almost monochrome, like something from a film noir; a reminder that surveillance is not standard practice in this part of the city. So many faces in profile, drunk with the light of the supermoon. In her mind, one is already turning, waxing, becoming familiar, half-closed eyelids filling out, gloved hands, handmade clothes. It is very unlikely, of course, but not impossible. Anywhere else her face would be recognised, linked with the missing person's file, and sent straight to the police as an alert. Medieville is the only area in her beloved London where she could potentially hide, and why else would the smartface have mentioned the place? Until now Freya assumed it sprang from a combination of Ruby's muddled fascination with history and her natural independence, the algorithms chewing this up and spitting out Medieville as a likely interest for her as an adult. But Freya's gut is telling her otherwise.

She sips a thimbleful of ice-cold water from the dashboard, delicious on her dry throat, and tries to still her whirling mind. There is a touch of crazy in this expedition, and of course an excuse to flee from Julian and his sweaty lair. Her car brakes abruptly to avoid a recycling bin rolling into the road, and she flicks the spilled water from her lap. In the past these cars had soothing driver-voices. When she used one a year ago, it had a teddy bear with a chauffeur's cap perched on the dashboard. Now all that seems to have vanished, the seats are plush leather and the windows full of gadgets. You can see the map of your route, and get the trip for free if you detour to the trainer store and try on these Shoez – she waves the advert away – every tourist attraction is announced with an information film, and friends appear as face-pins if they are nearby. Not that any of this would be much use in Medieville, even if cars were permitted.

During that disastrous date with Otto, Ruby could have been drinking in the next pub along, or looking down from a high window, yawning, her elbow on the windowsill, supple hands winding up a washing line; all those everyday move-ments that add up to a real person. Freya braces herself against a tide of emotion. A reality in which Ruby is alive shimmers on the horizon, coming into sharper focus. The difficult part is putting the two together in her mind: the voice she hears every day, and this silent, silhouetted Ruby, a figure so unknowable compared to the smartface. The thought of finding her sister has been pushed deep down, and has resurfaced with a tinge of dread.

'Ruby,' she calls in a sudden high pitch, 'are you there?'

'Of course I am.' The sound is close, comforting, as it emerges from the car speakers.

'What do you think about this . . . where we're going?'

'It'll be cool.'

The car is slowing now, caught in traffic as it nears the turn-off. Ahead are the high, strange houses that edge the district, and a wall that begins as masonry but quickly becomes a fence painted to resemble stone. There is quite a gathering at the west gate, and Freya is reluctant to step from the quiet, personal space of the car into the commotion. Shoulder first, she apologises her way through tourists. The last time she was here, it was to make her way to the Padfoot Arms. Although she is more confident now, any man in a tight T-shirt seems to jump out at her from the crowd. She clasps her coat closed at the collar, wanting reassurance that she is not on a wild goose chase.

'I'm in your hands,' she mutters to Ruby. As there are still three sovereigns in her bag, she can bypass the money-changing tent.

The voice cuts through the chatter, 'But if I'm not around, just carry on, yeah?'

'Not around? Why wouldn't you be—'

'Good day,' a voice calls as she steps onto the cobbles. It is a large man wearing a trilby. 'We like to see people's faces round here.' He taps his temples until she realises he is referring to her smartspecs. The man points to a cloakroom where people can check in their gadgets. His smile is pleasant enough, but there is an air of menace until she folds up her specs and hands them over. She tells herself it will be fine. It's only for a little while. The cloakroom attendant has dirty fingernails and she just catches an 'Eurrgh' from the speakers before she lets go.

Spices and woodsmoke assail her, and she notices a brazier with a kettle set above it. A man with a flashy gold turban is bending down, fiddling with cups.

'Might I interest you in some chai or a hot chestnut, milady?' As he straightens, she notices his long whiskery sideburns. Suddenly she is burning hotter than the brazier. That is why she shouldn't be outside. It is Saturday afternoon. *Saturday afternoon, Freya, so if you should feel better at any point . . .* Sandor's nasal tones ring in her ears. How could she have forgotten?

The man is observing her reddening face with incomprehension. She backs away and plunges into the nearest shop, full of tapestries and woven goods, mainly bathmats, table runners and coasters, things that will roll up easily into a suitcase.

'Nice gown,' the owner says, looking up from her spinning wheel.

'Thanks.' She forces herself to calm down. The chances of bumping into anyone from U-Home are slim. 'Just wish I had a hat, or a wig.' The woman smiles without trying to make sense of her words.

A deep breath later, Freya decides she needs to go on, but carefully. At least no smartspecs means no profile bubble above her head. In Medieville people walk around empty-handed, not carrying the usual balloon that tells the world who they are. Perhaps her smartface thought of this. Ruby knew they would be parted. Once again, it soothes her to remember how well the virtual assistant can calculate what is coming. For whatever reason, Ruby told her to carry on. She will not let herself be fazed by anything, not even a Spider-Man T-shirt.

The whitewashed walls catch on her dress as she edges along, imagining her sister walking these streets, sampling the dreamlike bustle of this adult play-world. Her fingers would reach out to touch the uncanny creatures carved into every wooden beam, inhaling the odours of incense and toasting nuts, delighting in the way performance is woven into everything. Freya's eyes fall upon striped stockings, turning, stopping for an instant, silver polka dots on a tourniquet-tight corset, skittles spinning in the air and caught, before the juggler moves aside and men in filigree waistcoats come lazily swinging balls of fire, one chain in each hand, speeding up until they seem to hold two golden cartwheels. On every abdomen she sees buttons, every hem embellished. But people turn and look at her too, especially the tourists, and she realises she is one of the townsfolk to them, part of the illusion that they have stepped back into a colourful past. Instead of shrinking from this, she tries to drink it in. Her red skirts gush around her legs as she walks, and she could just melt into the city, take up weaving or serve frothy beer behind a bar. That could be what her sister is doing. She starts scanning the crowd, becoming disorientated. It is so much easier with smartspecs. Many female faces catch her eye, but turn out to be the wrong age, shape or ethnicity. Could Ruby fool her, even dupe the facial recognition tech, with some sort of disguise? A purchase of freckle-spray not long before she vanished comes to mind, suddenly pertinent. But these memories can't be taken in isolation. Ruby bought a lot of random stuff.

The main street leads to a square with an octagonal fountain, cherubs falling over their chipped noses to blow water from conch shells and through green copper pipes. The paving turns to large, worn flags, then back to cobbles on the far street, where buildings homogenise into a red-brick block, a warehouse spiced up with faux-masonry windows and gothic arches. Esther's voice echoes in the back of her mind. *A mishmash*, she would say, *a mix-up*. These people don't care where history ends and fantasy begins. This part of the citadel has a slightly more makeshift, lived-in air about it, heraldic symbols daubed above doors, washing strung between windows and a half-built cart languishing in the gutter. Shutter slams echo, and Freya looks up with a sense of being watched.

At the far end of the warehouse a wooden sign points to *Roof Gardens*. A fleeting thrill quickens her pulse. If any part of the citadel appealed to Ruby, this would be it. A ramp rises along the side of the building, supported by scaffolding. Avoiding the splintery handrail, she walks carefully on the boards, aware of each creak. The warehouse windows are divided into bleary squares. As she nears the top, she can see a television aerial, hosting a plump garden spider. It reminds her of the rickety, comb-like antenna her mum used to have in the loft, though this one is larger and surprisingly rust-free. The ramp deposits her on the roof, and she finds herself uneasy at being so high up and exposed. Her eyes lock onto the people tending the layer of biosoil.

There are two men working the nearest allotment. The dividing borders of petunias shift from pink to blue in the waning afternoon, their colour genes linked to others that switch on and off with daylight. Further on, teenagers are jamming forks into the biocover hard enough to puncture the underlay. A faint smell of compost is released as they toss seedlings around. It takes her back to the Conservation Hub, summer evenings with watering cans, as though she has gone full circle and is meeting Ruby all over again.

There are other roofs, some linked to this main garden with rope bridges. The wind sends a loose plant pot rolling towards her ankles. There are no promising candidates. A monolithic cloud obscures the sun, and her fantasy begins to wilt. If disappointment was always in store, then why was her smartface so enthusiastic about this outing? A breeze blows her hair the wrong way, and she shivers. Better to have stayed at home.

The petunias change again on her way back across the garden, once the cloud passes. There is someone crouching to her left, half obscured by a willow partition. A chunky lime-green hoody is pulled up over the person's head. If it is not a woman then it is a very slight man. On closer observation, the figure is definitely female, and the hoody is knitted. The woman is using a small trowel to ease bean plants into the soil, one by one. Then she is cutting up a shoelace to tie their stems to the canes. The hands work confidently, large fingers pressing into the soil. She is not too big, not too small. But Freya's legs have turned into roots and she cannot move.

14

A force has taken hold of her. She should be leaping towards Ruby, yelling her name. Instead, she just stands there. Words fall from her lips out of habit – 'What now? What do I do?' – but of course there is no reply. The time she can spend loitering without being noticed is running out. A hand reaches up and tugs down the green hood, crumbs of soil falling from the trowel. Freya's heart is trying to break out of her ribcage.

'Ah, you came back,' the figure says, smiling. Her face is ruddy, wind-buffeted and real, folds of knitwear falling in layers around her neck. She drops the trowel and pushes on bare knees that protrude from ancient-looking jeans, hoisting herself to standing. Freya recognises her, but it is not Ruby. This is the woman she released from the stocks. 'How was your date?' she says.

The disappointment is hitting her hard, but what surprises

172

Freya most is the sense of something unclenching inside her. The one thing she did not expect to feel is relief.

'Date?'

'You said you had a date.' A shrug. 'It was a while ago.'

'Oh, sorry.' Freya tries to capture her flyaway hair so she can see properly. 'You're Gayle. How is your foot?'

Gayle lifts it, the slip-on shoe dangling from her toe, to show the still-bruised instep. 'Much better, thanks. How did your evening go?'

'I've kind of blocked it out.'

'That good?' Her laugh bounces around the rooftops. Freya floats upwards an inch or two at the sound. There is soil on Gayle's chin, a scent of apples on her breath – two small cores nestle on the ground where she was working. 'What brings you up here?'

'I don't know.' Freya holds down her flapping skirt, feeling rather overdressed. 'I thought someone I knew might be around. Someone I haven't seen for a while.'

Gayle is leaning in, cupping a hand to her ear. 'Who?'

'No one. It's silly.'

'Silly is me planting out these broad beans when I'm about to move house.' The seedlings have their young leaves closed, like hands praying. After dashing them with a shower from her watering can, she crumples up the fibrous seed tray.

'Were you here at the supermoon?'

'Certainly I was, and trying to keep people off the veg. Careful!' The thorn of a gooseberry bush has caught on Freya's skirt, and Gayle stoops to detach it. 'Don't feel you have to, but we could talk somewhere a bit warmer. Cup of tea? Or do you have to get off?'

'Warmer is good.' Her hesitation is only slight, and immediately she is glad to have said yes. There is a certain peacefulness to Gayle, which seems to rub off. Several other gardeners are also downing tools, stretching and packing up. The allotments must be left to themselves a lot, irrigated from below. As she stomps down the ramp, Freya finds herself explaining briefly about Ruby, the slim chance that her foster-sister might have retreated from the world to a place like this. Surprisingly, Gayle is full of encouragement.

'It's not that unlikely,' she insists. 'Some people really get into the culture here . . . we might have quite a population of missing persons.'

By the time their feet touch the cobbles, Freya's vigour is restored, her companion's energetic chatter propelling them along. As they get back into the tourist area, Gayle stops a young man and gives a description of Ruby, but the response is a shrug. There is something peculiar about being taken seriously. Freya has the urge to catch hold of Gayle's arm, to say, 'Don't worry, really,' though this impulse makes no sense. Of course she wants to find Ruby, if it is possible. Nevertheless, she is grateful when they fetch up in the back of a crochet shop, pulling out stools in a tiny kitchen. Her companion pours cloudy beer from an unmarked bottle.

'There *is* tea,' she grins, filling Freya's glass to the brim. Now they are out of the noise and bustle, Gayle swirls her drink and explains how she came to be living in Medieville, a tale of working in the city among suffocating banking systems, before burning out and going *off the rails*, as she puts it. 'This place was still quite hippy back then, all about getting back to a more natural way of life, a plastic-free zone, and a circular economy. It's probably not a million miles from the medieval lifestyle, only with better dentistry.' She hoists her injured foot onto a stool. 'My friend had a crochet collective and was setting up this shop, so I came to help. Not that I'm any good at crafts. All I can manage is the odd shift of bar work and some gardening. It's nice to be up in the allotments, away from the darker parts of the district.'

'Oh?' Freya's mind goes to the Padfoot Arms.

'It's just . . . people don't come here for simplicity any more; they come to live out their Arthurian fantasy, or to play at *Game of Thrones*. You can set up your own house of dragons or whatever and it just becomes part of the city. We've got warring factions playing games where they hunt each other down, or people want to be knights but others set up councils to stop them . . . you know, there are dungeons here, and not just for the tourists.'

'You mean people are locked up against their will?' It sounds crazy.

'Oh no, only if you consent to *ye olde laws*, although it is encouraged. I don't know why I was fool enough to sign up, though the place was less of a theme park back then.' She pours them both more beer and Freya wonders how strong it is. The taste is sharp and hoppy. 'Of course, most of the real fantasy stuff trickles down into Yearnfeld, where they can do it properly.'

'Yearnfeld?' The name is familiar, perhaps unearthed during her research. Something troubling crosses her mind, too quickly to be identified.

'There are cellars down there, rediscovered when the

stadium was demolished. Yearnfeld works things out so you can wander around without bumping into anyone.'

'So it's like a game?'

'I used to play every now and then.' She smiles with embarrassment. 'You'd think being here would be sufficiently escapist, wouldn't you? It was kind of fun, though, like a version of Medieville where you could go further and roam ancient England, and I was playing with friends who liked a pint or two afterwards.' She grins. 'Now that people are starting to own Halo headsets, it's getting more commercial. You can pop in on your lunch break, if you can manage to pop out again.'

There is a hiss from the shop, and a large white goose wanders into the kitchen, its feet making a slapping sound on the tiles. It looks over and opens its beak threateningly, before continuing on its way towards the backyard. Has she slipped into another world? An age has passed since she argued with Julian this morning. Gayle rummages in a drawer and hands her a postcard. It reproduces a watercolour of a cottage that is part greenhouse, as though the front half has crystallised. A wheelbarrow rests outside, and there are others in the background. 'This is where I'm moving,' she says. 'My friend is the artist who paints these. Here – have a freebie.'

'Where is it?'

'Just in Hertfordshire, a train ride away. It's still a bit experimental – my nan will find things to moan about when she visits – but at least there are no dungeons.' She laughs again, rocking back on her chair, eliciting a hiss from the backyard. Freya realises this is her normal demeanour, that when they first met, her spirit was dampened considerably by being put in the stocks. It must have been an upsetting experience to have self-styled lawmakers attempt to humiliate her, yet she seems to have taken it in her stride.

'No stocks,' Freya agrees.

'That's what made my mind up.'

Draining her beer, Freya wonders if the tourists know what goes on behind the gaudy exteriors. If the authorities can put a person in the stocks for something so minor, what else can they do?

Someone says Gayle's name, and she pushes the rickety door to reveal a shop festooned with knitted flowers, fruit and dolls. The wool softens every corner, oiling the air with lanolin. Behind the counter, a woman with bracelet-laden arms is clicking away with needles.

'Where's the goose?' she says. There is a box of hay to one side, along with a water bowl.

'Out the back,' Gayle reassures her. 'Becca, do we know anyone called Ruby?'

The woman pauses her knitting. 'Yeah, everyone knows her. Why, do you want your fortune told?'

'Ah, you're thinking of the one who sits there with the Tarot cards.' She taps a finger against her lips.

'That's her.'

Gayle throws a sympathetic glance at Freya. 'I don't think she's the one you're after.'

'How old?'

'Too old.' She stands up. 'But we can nip over if you want, to set your mind at rest.'

'I can go on my own.'

Before she can put her glass in the sink, Freya finds herself being escorted out of the door. Becca smiles as they pass, remarking, 'Any excuse to put off packing.' She rolls her eyes up to the floor above, making Freya picture cases half filled and knitwear draped over iron bedposts.

Minutes later, smells of hot food mingle with the various perfumes worn by tourists, the day tipping into evening with some places closing and others opening. Freya realises she is slightly drunk. A horse-drawn cart rattles down the street, achingly picturesque with the pony tossing hay dust from its mane, and it pains her to be unable to take a photo. The goose in the shop would have made a good snap too. Now it is as though she never saw it.

Gayle lopes along beside her, putting a hand on her shoulder as they duck through a passageway and greeting everyone they pass, even strangers. It is a million miles from Thalis in the greenzone, thinking it incredible that someone wanted to ask the time, his headset probably erasing unimportant people from sight. It amuses her to think that here he could be put in the stocks for refusing to give up his gadgets. Her chuckle blends with a trickling fountain as they cut through a courtyard into a quiet street, weeds creeping through the paving. Two cats wander up to Gayle and she lifts one and carries it along, bundled in her arms. She drops it gently underneath the pub sign, a circle of black without image or name. The studded door is ajar, windows made into cruciform slits. A pike and spear are pinioned in a menacing cross.

'What is this place?' Freya is fearful of finding it full of Ottos.

'A dungeon pub. Don't worry yourself, we'll stick to the outer chamber.'

The two of them shove the door until it opens. Once inside, it is alarmingly dark, with a pervasive aroma of spirit-soaked kegs and smoking logs. The music is reminiscent of a lone experimenter on a double bass, plucking disconsolately. People murmur over drinks, examining Freya at their leisure. Once her pupils dilate, the room expands on the far side, pools of light around dribbling candles. Gayle is whispering hotly in her ear, nodding towards the rough-hewn bar. 'That's her.'

Trepidation builds, though not to the same extent as before. On a bar stool, a plump woman in her forties sits in a gypsy skirt and a lacy corset that encircles her tightly, like a barrel full of flesh. The woman's bust brims over the front, her shoulders pulsing as she shuffles cards and lays them out.

There is no need to whisper a response. Her companion already knows it is the wrong person and is beckoning instead to a barman with an eye tattooed in the middle of his forehead.

'Ed,' she says, 'we're looking for someone.' She gives Ruby's name and age, and points to Freya, obviously having forgotten they are not related. He looks doubtful.

'Well, the man don't know everyone's name, love, but 'ave a drink, 'ave a butcher's . . .' He puts out two tankards, then hesitates and replaces them with wooden eggcups. A bottle is uncorked. 'Try the ole bathtub.'

Gayle takes the two cups and thanks him, but grimaces as she turns. Freya understands why when she tips the spirit down her throat – it is like swallowing a hot coal, making her break into a fit of coughing. However, it seems to improve her eyesight. The room is clearer, and she can start scanning faces. Her eyes alight on a low, cylindrical wall in the middle of the chamber, an artificial well. When she peers down, there is the glint of liquid. A brass plaque on the brick reads: *The Black Hole.* She goes round to the other side of the bar. Here there are archways leading into other rooms, an array of chains and dungeonalia on the walls. She is astonished to notice that one window alcove is fitted with vertical bars, and someone is sitting inside with their arms and legs dangling through. Gayle, who has been chatting to various people, appears at her side.

'There's someone in a cage over there,' Freya says.

'Well, it is meant to be a dungeon.'

She lowers her voice. 'Is it . . . voluntary?'

Gayle shrugs. 'Sometimes it's theatre, other times punishment. Should I ask him for you?'

'No, no,' she says hurriedly. 'It's fine.' The pub is full of half-visible figures in tunics and furs, buckles and buttons winking in the shadows. Her red gown is more suited to this environment, though Gayle seems comfortable enough in her vintage jeans. There is something morbidly fascinating about the place and its inhabitants. 'What's through there?' She points to the largest archway.

'That'll take you down a level.'

Her hip knocks against a table, eliciting a gruff 'Careful!' as the drinker catches hold of a teetering candle. She shrinks back, trying to see through the darkness. Ruby would want to explore every corner of this place. With that thought comes a longing for her virtual assistant. She has become distracted from her mission.

Gayle touches her arm, as though sensing the stirrings of an internal monologue, and says, 'I really should go and pack, but it was grand to meet you. Come see me if you're ever in Herts.'

All Freya can do is stare at her gratefully, touched by this invitation from someone she knows so little. 'Oh . . .' she says. 'Thanks for all your help.'

'No problem.' Gayle saunters away, bracing her feet on the floor to get the door open, before turning back and calling, 'Bring Ruby!'

When she is gone, the pub seems even more otherworldly. Freya steps aside to avoid a group of men in papier-mâché armour, and finds herself by an alcove with three occupants.

'I felt that all right!' the man in the chair is exclaiming, his whispery voice spluttering with pleasure. He is wearing a shirt open at the back, two women behind him.

'You want a go?' one says to Freya, wiggling an iron-tipped finger. 'I'm about to win this game anyway.' She scratches a cross on the naked back and starts to draw a diagonal connecting line, while the man moans. 'It's all about that middle square,' she adds cheerfully.

Freya manages to shake her head mutely before hurrying onward. Red lines flash across her retinas, the thought of the scratches making her skin tingle. There is something disturbing in the way the woman held up her claw fingers, inviting her in, the need for sensation as ordinary as the thirst to drink a beer. Without the smartface, it is hard to know what to think about anything. She should be turning around, heading for home and a nice long shower, but instead she takes a deep breath and tells herself not to be childish.

She reaches an opening to a corridor, blackened metal implements decorating the wall above. Her hesitation is long enough to provoke a chuckle from the man in the cage.

'Turn back.' He leers with brilliant white teeth. 'Go no further.' She notices there are several tankards building up beside him.

'I suppose this leads to certain doom?'

'Tha's right, love.' He guzzles some ale and clangs his pewter cup along the bars, causing the barman to yell at him. Now she recognises the sense of déjà vu. This place is like one of the cheesy attractions she used to visit with Ruby, staffed with bored actors fallen on hard times. All the historical gear looks mocked up, designed to create a tourist experience. If her smartface were here, she would not even be hesitating. *If you feel like going in, then go in*, Ruby would say. *It's just a bit of fun*. There must have been some reason she said to carry on.

Her throat is still on fire from the moonshine and it is starting to have an effect. Handcuffs jingle overhead like wind chimes as she goes through the archway. The walls are moulded stone, sprayed glittery green and black. *I can leave any time*, she tells herself, at once unnerved and enticed by the secret passageway. A vibration underfoot turns out to be her heart pounding, a rhythmic rush. Her hands look pale at the ends of her arms, as though they belong to someone else. After a few steps the corridor opens out to her left, revealing stone benches, black drapes snagged on the ears of gargoyles, and yet more torture implements. People pass by, going the other way, their faces ghost-like. Sometimes she freezes, staring, as her imagination furnishes them momentarily with familiar features.

Now there are broad steps leading down. She hesitates for a long time before continuing, promising she will just see what is at the bottom, scan for Ruby and come straight back. The smell of black mould thickens as she descends, yet it also becomes more draughty. She is dumbfounded to arrive at the entrance to a cavernous chamber, its vaulted ceiling supported by pillars. It stretches far beyond this vestibule area, which is the size of a living room and raised on wooden decking. There is a desk with an antiquated green lamp, someone leaning over a ledger, while other people are having masks fitted to their faces. It is not until she notices the piece of driftwood chipped into a word that she understands where she is, and then something drops out of the bottom of her heart. The visors are branded, made for this game, but they bear a perturbing resemblance to the one she wore at Terri's so long ago. What would Esther say if she knew her daughter was here, deep in the underbelly of Medieville, where people are playing Yearnfeld?

A throaty war cry echoes around the whitewashed arches. There must be dozens of players down here. She takes a deep breath, tells herself to be calm and have a look. Three steps lead to the grimy cellar floor. As her eyes adjust, she realises there are more people than she expected. A vast space, flanked with benches on one side and indistinct mushroomy shapes on the other. Most of the players stand, sit or walk around, but some are waving their arms, yelling in the throes of battle.

'Greetings,' says a voice behind her, and she turns to encounter a man in chain mail. 'Are you come to seek your destiny, milady? Borrow a helmet, the cost shall be naught.' He steers her to the desk.

'I don't need one, thank you, um, milord. I just want to look.'

He exchanges a glance with the girl behind the desk, who responds in a strong Eastern European accent, 'Sorry, but we don't allow watchers.'

'Don't you?'

'But you can borrow the visor for free. Here – we fit you.'

The chain mail guy, who, she realises, probably sees himself as some sort of guardian to this underworld, shows her a crate of visors. The stack underneath indicates how busy these chambers must get.

'How do people not bump into each other?' She edges away from the crates.

'Don't be fooled by the chunky casing,' he says. 'These are Halo headsets. If they sense you're heading towards someone, they alter your trajectory, although you'll still feel like you're walking straight ahead.' He looks annoyed with himself, his interest in the mechanics of the game having taken him out of character. He holds up a visor and adjusts the strap. 'Step forward, maiden!'

'I really don't want—'

'Thou needn't worry about a thing!' Full of chivalrous assistance, he stretches the strap over her head and the visor perches on her nose. Her hands fly up to it.

'Too loose?' Though part of her has already torn off the eye gear and dashed back up the stairs, she has noticed that quite a bit of floor can be seen in the gap on either side of her nose.

'No, too tight.' He loosens it, and the gap increases.

'Fare thee well.'

She totters away, hearing a voice close to her ears saying, 'Howdy, we think you are Freya Waters – is that right?' The question is repeated until she affirms her identity. Something bright illuminates the top part of her visor, presumably the game commencing, but she shifts it up an inch, tightening the strap, and focuses on the floor, finding her way down the steps and into the chamber.

Then she is among them, legs straying into her field of vision below the visor. She heads deep into the cellar, planning to lift the mask completely once the fitting area is out of sight. While it would be unlikely to find her sister down here in the gloom, she may as well cast an eye over the players, now she is here. It makes her feel smug to be walking with these zombies without being one of them. *Outsmart the system*, Ruby would say. The main thing is to avoid crashing into people. It is easier near the wall, where players sit on benches, their hands jerking out as they gesticulate or eat imaginary food. Are they contorted with laughter, or being poisoned? Their mouths move, but the sonic distorters in her own visor stop her from hearing any words. The mask is deceptively packed with technology, as she can tell from the no-feel functionality kicking in where it touches her skin.

The spongey objects she saw from afar turn out to be enormous haptic beanbags. Tipping her head back, Freya can perceive a woman lying on her front with arms spread wide, as though flying. Is the haptic fabric vibrating the moist touch of a cloud against her skin, or the feathers of some magnificent bird? Against her will, that long-ago blast of excitement comes back, a buried emotion. Ruby's voice is light and natural in her head. *You'll have to let go of these hang-ups eventually.*

The chamber goes on for ever, and now there are no more legs, just a coldness seeping up from below. Something is bothering her, and she realises it is the sound of people screaming.

15

With every step, it gets louder. Since no one else seems to be reacting, it must be coming from the earpiece of her visor. She tries to ignore it. The cries become more and more insistent, as though someone is shouting at her directly.

'You! For fuck's sake, what's the matter with you, girl?'

Confused, she peers cautiously into her visor, and finds it alive with an amber glow. Half blinded and blinking, she feels heat radiating onto her face. It takes a second to work out that the world inside is on fire. Her arms go up as a black beam crashes down inches away, and now she sees a swarthy man yelling, 'Move! Get out!' People are running past, shrieking abuse as she stands in their way. The ceiling sags, then collapses, and at last she leaps back, stumbling and falling through the broken door frame with the rest of them, and the sun is there above the smoke, the roar and spit of the blaze loud in her ears until she drowns it out with a fit of coughing. People shout for water and scurry about as the Black Hole trembles in the heat, its sign alight with a creamy yellow flame. Wooden pails start to be handed around, though liquid tossed through the doorway evaporates on impact.

'Move aside.' A wagon of sloshing barrels pulls up outside, directed by a bald man with an eye tattoo very like that of the barman in the real-life pub. Now the fire begins to be doused, as river water is flung through every window. Steam snakes up the blackened beams, and the crowd begins to thin. Freya finds herself on ground rutted with cart tracks. Crooked buildings line the street, as though she has set her smartspecs to Historical and clicked the dial back a few hundred years. Medieville's droves of tourists have been replaced by stallholders hawking their wares or dragging sacks of turnips. Here there is no distant buzz of traffic, only the whinny of horses. Apprentice stonemasons echo the master's regular *chip-chip-chip* with a chisel. In the distance, where the street widens into a square, she can see someone with their feet in the stocks.

Freya herself is dressed in a red knee-length tunic, buskins tied round her legs with criss-cross twine. Her clothing looks as though it was once a bit finer, but has suffered from time spent on the road. A rough-spun cloak is wrapped heavily around her shoulders. She plants her boots firmly on the dry mud and tries to still her runaway heart. This is Yearnfeld. It looks similar to Medieville, except for the smoke billowing from the pub. Did she cause it somehow? Everyone seems angry with her. She backs away and bumps into a man with a soot-smeared face, holding a dripping pan.

'Can I help you?' The voice is low, almost a growl. She notices other ruffians staring at her, some with empty tankards in their hands.

'No, no, I'm fine, really.' Luckily he does not pursue, and she tucks herself into a doorway to take stock. The important thing is to be calm. To find the nearest available exit. But how does she get out? The cellar has vanished, and what she sees is all-encompassing. She examines the pattern of sunlight on the backs of her hands, looking up to see emerald ivy leaves bridging the gap between buildings. If anything, this world is more luminous than real life. Her hands go to her temples, but she cannot feel the visor. There is no gap when she looks down. Normally there is a command, a safe word that gets you out, or you draw a door or something.

'Excuse me,' she crouches beside a picturesque urchin who is cradling a rat. To her frustration, he bolts down the street. She follows gingerly, amazed at how natural it feels, no danger of losing her balance. Some of the buildings look familiar; this could even be the spot where Gayle picked up the cat. At least she has her bearings. The crochet shop would be through that passageway and up the main street. A city wall comes into view, and above the west gate she can see decorations, like balloons. As she climbs the steps outside a flour mill to get a better look, a gang of men pass by, the Cyclops barman among them. Someone with a bandaged arm is tugging his sleeve, saying, 'Sure she went this way?' the barman returning, 'Are *you* sure she ain't blind? She was stumbling around like a lunatic . . .' Any further conversation is swallowed up by the crowd, but Freya catches glimpses of knives and clubs, even some sort of whip coiled beneath a cloak. Now she knows who caused the fire. Her stomach squeezes out a lemony exclamation mark of acid. This is worse than she thought. She tries to hear Ruby's voice telling her what to do. *Blend in*, she would say, *make tracks*. Freya looks around and sees a ledge along one side of the mill. This takes her to the next building, where it is easy to lift herself onto the crenellated façade. The city wall is nearer, and she can cross the alleyways by climbing on buttresses, soon reaching the steam of people moving towards the gate, where she descends and adjusts the hood of her cloak. As she passes beneath the wall, she is horrified to notice the decorations are heads on spikes. Their sun-cured flesh and sunken eyes make them look like rotten pumpkins.

The watchman, asleep beside his spear, is awakened by a cry. Freya twists and sees a mob further down the street, this glimpse of her face renewing their fury. Shoving people aside, she flees, emerging from the city into a cluster of market stalls, her elbow catching a copper plate so it crashes down and rolls away. With angry shouts behind her, she pelts across a humpbacked bridge and finds herself on the forest fringe. To her amazement she is fleet of foot, and a few turns among the trees is enough to leave the pub men behind.

After a while, she slows to a walk. The forest is too real. 'Why am I still here?' she appeals to the mossy boughs. There is no one to reply. Would her smartface have been able to help, or is Yearnfeld another blind spot? She tries to kindle the voice in her mind, almost hearing the soothing words, the celebratory tone that would acknowledge her escape. Ruby would like that. She might even think it was funny to have burned down a pub, because it's only a game.

The thought makes her feel fractionally better. What would Ruby say about this made-up world? *It's none of it real, hun . . . but you've done it, you've conquered your fear.* With every step she impresses herself. It is astonishing that she can look up at the sky – not a bank of blue, but clear and endless, with high wispy clouds – and admire its realism. Even last year she would have trembled at the thought. She'd be curled up in a ball repeating, *I'm in a cellar wearing a visor*, fearful of losing herself. This gameplay is staggeringly convincing. How does her avatar manage to walk as she does, just the right tilt forward and movement of the hips? Pebbles crunch under her boots and the air is scented with soil. The familiar warm feeling towards her smartface returns. The sense that she has Ruby's permission to do this, even her encouragement, is more powerful than any phobia therapy.

When the track broadens, she is optimistic about finding someone – a woman picking berries or a woodsman chopping – so she can say, 'Excuse me . . .' and find out how to exit the game. The path leads along a gully, ferns lining a rocky stream, making her exhale in wonder. Some dream must have produced this trellis of falls over the quartz cliff, every precipice a web of rainbows, the trees thick with birds. Their twittering reminds her of something she heard about Yearnfeld, that some of it is generated by natural cloud forces. If she listens closely, there seem to be short phrases within the bursts of song. Needles spray down as the branch of a pine springs back, and she touches the wrinkled bark. *Spellbinding* is the word that comes to mind. How could they have created this? How can they build in so much sheer randomness?

As she removes her cloak, getting warm, she notices a mark on her upper arm in mole-brown. It is difficult to make out: a shape resembling half a butterfly. What does it mean? The snap of a twig makes her glance behind, but there is no one. It could be a fox. Carrying on, she fails to notice a large stone and trips into a grassy dell. Impacting the soft ground startles her but does not hurt. A movement catches her eye – she is just in time to see the shimmering flank of a deer twisting and leaping off among the trees, surprisingly golden as it catches the light. Before she can get to her feet, a man runs into the clearing and flings his bow angrily to the ground.

'Clumsy wench,' he wails. 'I had a clear shot.'

Freya brushes the crushed mushrooms from her buskins. 'You were following me,' she accuses.

'Following you? I was following the hind, didn't you see her?' He looks mournfully after the deer, sliding his arrow back into its quiver and tugging the amber beard that edges his chin. His cap and doublet are of dull cloth, no doubt designed to blend into the forest, though the effect is undermined by blue and yellow stripy stockings. A knapsack hangs across his chest and a large hunting knife is thrust into his belt.

'Well, it sounded like you were following me,' Freya says, not sure if he can hear her, as he has plunged into the undergrowth. His head appears above the bushes. Just as she is rearranging her cloak, he appears to catch sight of her birth-mark and his lips part in surprise. The grumpy expression melts away. 'I know we're probably not meant to talk about this,' she continues, 'but can you tell me the way out of here?'

He comes closer, appraising her, then removes his cap for a theatrical bow. 'My lady, I know these woods better than anyone, every short cut and secret way you can imagine. But first let us go to my nearest tree house – I have several – and drink to new friendship.'

She hesitates, rather flattered. 'Well . . .'

Before she can make up her mind, he has seized her arm and is furrowing through the ferns, almost dragging her towards a large yew with chocolate-smooth branches. He links his fingers to give her a boot-hold up to a platform of woven elderflower. As well as the sweet nectar of the tiny blooms, she can smell apples and a cottage loaf, suspended in a net. Climbing up to join her, the woodsman removes his cap and replaces it with another, stuck with long partridge feathers. He shows off a view of treetops, purple hills rising in the distance, and her skin prickles at the sheer extent of Yearnfeld. From the corner of her eye she can see him beaming, enjoying her reaction. Next he uncorks a bottle and splashes liquor into two vessels. Freya is amazed how easily she can trick her hands into feeling the curve of a cup. She rocks the liquid to and fro.

'So what are you doing here?' she asks.

'I seek the golden hind, the ultimate trophy.' He purses his lips. 'It's not exceptionally satisfying. I'm quite good at tracking her, but I think she's playing with me, trying to lead me into danger.' He knocks back his drink. 'Take the brandy in one.' She does so. At once something hits her palate, not exactly the sensation of drinking, but more like a vapour, a fruity sting. She splutters.

'How is that happening?'

The man smiles. 'Are you in Medieville with a visor? Sometimes the nodes don't all make contact. The smellscape is usually reasonable, but taste can be iffy. Is this your first time?' Freya realises she has been picking up smells since she arrived, not questioning how it was possible and perhaps even assuming it was her imagination. 'Is it your first time?' he says again. He lounges beside her, running a thumbnail along the partridge feather.

She edges back an inch or two. 'Are you not in Medieville then?'

'I'm on my break at work. Double shift.'

'Using a headset?'

'Yes indeed.'

Freya tries to imagine this. For some reason she comes up with the idea of a businessman in a broom cupboard, twitching among mops as the headset makes him think he is under creaking boughs, getting drunk in a tree.

'Did I mention that I know every inch of this forest?' he remarks. 'I can live here quite happily for days. The logs are my sofas, the branches my bed.' He strokes her arm, peering at her mark.

'What does it mean?' She scratches at it, partly to deflect his touch.

He grins. 'Lost, are we? And searching for our true identity, I dare say. You're a changeling, my dear, probably with royal blood.' The birdsong quietens, and she becomes aware of her recumbent position opposite a man with a very seedy-looking beard. This has gone on long enough.

'I think I should go,' she says, struggling to sit up.

'Oh don't be like that, my lady, we've hardly got to know each other,' the man insists. 'Let's talk properly. Do you work in Medieville?'

He is uncorking the bottle again, and she finds herself tangled up in her cloak. 'Sorry?' she replies vaguely, trying to shuffle across the mat. 'No, at U-Home. I have to—'

'Not near the M1?' He re-corks the bottle and stares at her.

'Yes,' she says, surprised.

'But you're in Medieville now?'

A feeling of dread starts to steal over her. Something about his intonation, the way he drives the words home, is ringing a major alarm bell. His fingers twitch, and she knows. Oh *shit*.

'You're in Medieville now?' he repeats. Her head pounds and she has no idea what to do. She needs to vanish and doesn't know how. In desperation, she claws at her skull, raking her nails over her eyebrows, tearing out hair, and then, unexpectedly, she has it, the sense of something plastic in her hands. His gasp reaches her ears, a horrified look on his face, then the world is black and spinning. Her mind fills with ice cream, numbing from the inside out. Something hard smacks into her cheek. Still she can see nothing, just a mass of grey without shape or dimension. Her face is dirty with the soot of the cellar floor, everything smelling of filth, and the visor is gone, flung off somewhere. She puts a hand beneath her throbbing cheekbone, still uncertain which direction is up. Then someone is kneeling beside her and for a second she is petrified it will be Sandor.

'Hey.' All the artifice is gone from the chain mail boy's voice. 'What happened, mate? You okay?'

Her head feels like a washing machine and she is becoming aware of all the bones that have just made contact with stone.

'Rule number one – don't whip your visor off mid game. Come on, sit up.' He helps her into a sitting position, her gown tangled across her lap. Unexpectedly she is a child again, bruised after a fall in the playground. Tears prick her eyes.

'I didn't know how to quit.'

His face betrays how insane he thinks this is. 'Blimey, how could you miss it?' He nods to the cellar wall a few feet away, and she sees the legend painted again and again: *To exit, draw a door.* 'You would have been told in the first minute of play. Or did you stick your fingers in your ears and go lalala?' Despite the reproof, his voice is kind. She is grateful. It takes a few moments of sitting before she can allow herself to be helped up and slowly led through the cellar. None of the players notice, continuing about their business in the cold air.

Back at the antechamber, she gets another earful from the woman at the desk; however, they are both nicer than expected, conceding that Yearnfeld can be an odd experience if you are not used to it. 'The best thing is to go straight back in,' says the boy. 'Maybe have a drink upstairs, calm your nerves and then come back.'

Meekly she agrees, thanking them both for their help, but nothing in the world will make her go down there again. Now that she thinks about it, what kind of messed-up idea is it to have a fantasy game here anyway, when they're supposed to be renouncing technology? No wonder it's hidden in a cellar. She shakes her head in derision, and it turns into a shudder. No more VR, not ever. It has made everything strange – even this corridor is too plain to be real. She has visions of finding herself back in the forest, facing her supervisor in the guise of a woodsman, with his partridge feathers and ugly choice of beard. Maybe he is shy about Yearnfeld, deliberately picking a rustic avatar that looks nothing like him. But she should have recognised him despite this: her Sandor radar has been perfected over a long period. Only now is the full catastrophe coming into view. Just bumping into him would have been bad enough, but to be caught on a day she called in sick, a Saturday too . . . Her cheekbone stings with the smack it took from the floor. If she could get away with claiming to be at home with a headset, it would not be so bad, but – and she kicks herself for letting this happen – he knows she is in Medieville.

Emerging beneath the dangling handcuffs to the ale-soaked bar, it is almost a relief to see the skinny guy in his cage and the torture equipment pinned to the wall, black and crusty. The pub is quieter, and as she passes the empty table where the bloodthirsty game of noughts and crosses was being played, she imagines the man going home with his back scored into circles and stripes, happy to have something to prove his experience was real. It seems almost reasonable now. In her case, this throbbing cheek will ensure she does not wake up tomorrow thinking it was all a dream. The inside of her mouth tastes faintly of blood.

The barman grins, recognising her.

'On the ole zombie stroll?'

'Sorry?' She can hardly make out what he is saying.

He scoops an armful of wooden eggcups from the bar. 'Want a tot for the road?'

'I've had enough, thanks.'

Strange to find the barman out here, when she has just seen a version of him in Yearnfeld. Was he playing the game, or just duplicated by its algorithms? Since he is still mid shift at the bar, it must be the latter. She can't help wondering whether he would take over the character if he entered the game, or come face to face with his doppelgänger – *Hey you, three eyes!* – in a mirror-like stand-off.

Outside, she is astonished to find that it is practically dark, a few people in evening finery or cloaks conversing in low, happy voices as they drift towards the restaurants and bars. Freya joins the general flow and is soon on the cobbled thoroughfare, gates at the far end. Though she feels battered, the voice in her head speaks more confidently. So what if she saw Sandor? It was a virtual space. Can he prove she does not own a headset, that she didn't borrow the one belonging to Julian? For all he knows, the character in Yearnfeld might be a compulsive liar.

A rimey wind is funnelled down the street, and the last of the fairy dust is blown from her thoughts. This is Sandor. He is a boring, petty man who kills animals for fun. This will be something he can use as part of his master plan. A game, she thinks bitterly; everything is always a game.

It is a huge relief, for some reason, when it starts to rain heavily, except that she has forgotten her smartspecs and needs to go back. The woman at the cloakroom door has long dark hair and blue nail varnish, but Freya hands over the ticket and does not make eye contact.

16

The rising sun resembles an egg yolk, shine breaking over it like uncooked white. She circles her finger to speed up the dawn. Her thoughts are scrambled. An excruciating tug on her scalp turns out to be hair extensions caught in the strap of her nightdress, and the still-invisible bruise on her cheek is raw. In the night she dreamed Ruby was on the roof garden, across the vegetable plots. Freya didn't see her because she was talking to Gayle. Then she tripped over an oily black aubergine and the tendrils of beans started wrapping round her fingers, until she awoke in a sweat, weak with hunger.

Immediately her smartface says, 'Let's get some breakfast,' and everything is all right. The smell of toasting bread is already filling the flat. When she turns on Social, she is astonished to see a cascade of excited comments, many from strangers. 'I pinned the Black Hole's souvenir badge to your profile,' Ruby explains, bringing up a photo of the pub's dark interior with the strapline, *Another time and place*.

Having gone through so much with no photos to show for it, Freya is pleased to see the badge, especially when comments begin to trail from it like the tail of a kite:

The actual Black Hole? Superamazeballs!!!

That's so rated! Did you see the well?

I was there last week.

I heard they drug you and throw you in the cellars . . .

You should follow Ed – he's hilarious!

It is not just her friends back in Lincoln. People from random forum groups she has joined are getting interested, names she does not recognise.

'Sandor won't see it, will he?'

'Give me some credit.'

The comments keep coming. Apparently entering this gloomy pub was quite a privilege. The more she researches Medieville, the more she is realises that, across the world, its fans gaze hungrily towards its epicentre in London, aware of every nook and cranny. They beam themselves into the Yearnfeld version using headsets and pretend it is the real place. Strangers hang on her words like gleeful children as she takes them through a blow-by-blow account, meanwhile interjecting their own experiences of the virtual version: the creatures in the cages, gangs of mercenaries and brawls fuelled by tots of smoky moonshine. Not for a long time has Freya felt so in demand. When she visits the bathroom, she comes back to a wall of speech bubbles asking where she went. Luckily Ruby has replied to most, using just the words she would have chosen. She lets her smartface carry on some of the conversations while she finishes breakfast.

Out in the spring sunshine, she looks back longingly at her flat, wishing she did not have to go to work. Through the open blinds next door she can see her neighbour – a teacher – stabbing the air, his voice stolen by the glazing as he reprimands invisible kids. It reminds her of Sandor lording it around his leafy kingdom.

'Isn't it a million to one that I'd bump into him?' she murmurs, heels clicking on the pavement. 'How many people play that game?'

'Thousands,' Ruby says, 'but it magnetises those in your circles, it brings individuals who know each other together. More fun that way.'

'It is not!' she protests. 'Why would I want to see Sandor? Why isn't it restricted to people I like?' A procession of smartcars make her wait at the crossing, all in pastel colours, branded with some yoghurt drink.

Ruby's voice is patient. 'In Yearnfeld you can run him through with a sword. Or you can mess with him, trick him. Get it?'

'What, like revenge?'

'Whatever you want.'

Freya shakes her head, pausing by the wet grass of the cut-through, not wanting to mess up her shoes. 'He had all the weapons.'

'You could buy some.'

This conversation is going nowhere. Her smartface seems to have unswerving confidence in her ability to run rings around Sandor, when in fact it was the reverse. In the game, it was hard enough simply to keep going. Freya pricks her finger on a bramble and sucks it.

'I can't do VR.'

'You did fine, hun, really rated. Look at how you gave them all the slip.' All morning Ruby has been super-attentive, full of comfort and reassurance. Back in the day, she would have made them pancakes with hazelnut syrup.

Freya shakes her head. 'I was barely holding it together in there without you.'

The ironic – and annoying – thing is that the smartface could have been with her the whole time. You can bring these beta smartfaces with you into Yearnfeld if you select the right options. Since the game tries to keep things 'natural', the moment Freya missed was when the rough-looking man came up to her and asked if she wanted help. Not for a moment did she think he was serious, offering her access to the settings. It was all too real.

The flyover looms up overhead, a dark cloud of concrete. Though her feet plod along the map-line, every other part of her is pulling back, fearful of what will happen when she reaches her destination.

'What was the point of it, anyway? It's just made Sandor mad.'

'Just chill about Sandor,' Ruby says. 'I'll be with you this time. I'll tell you what to say.'

'Huh?'

As she passes the bakery, her head turns, as usual, to see what treat she is being offered, on this occasion a brioche bun marbled with chocolate. 'Let's do a test run,' Ruby says. 'Go inside.'

'In the bakery? What for?'

She backtracks a few steps, catching the delicious scent of baking bread. It is possible to order things digitally through a wall hatch, but if you go inside you can speak to the man overseeing the machines.

'I'm going to get you that bun.'

She freezes. 'No, we can't.'

'Just go in.'

Inside, wisps of steam rise from trolleys of buttery pastries. A man of around forty with fair hair appears, fumbling at his headphones. Her smartspecs slip into timer mode for an instant, indicating that the man's face is being recognised. 'Start with a big smile and just follow my lead,' says Ruby.

Freya manages a sheepish grin.

'Say hi, tell him you walk past here every day and have always wanted to stop by.' She does so. 'Tell him you think it's sad that a bakery isn't a social space in this country.'

'I know,' the man says, one hand on his hip and the other flat on the stainless steel. A burn is healing on one knuckle. 'In Denmark, everyone goes to get their morning croissants . . . you see your neighbours . . . whether you like it or not.' His voice is unexpectedly deep and has a lolloping rhythm to it, as though every word takes him by surprise.

'Laugh,' cuts in Ruby. 'Harder. Tidy your hair. Now slip into asking if he's been here a while.'

'Almost fifteen years,' he replies.

'Good,' Ruby says, 'he's very political. Look embarrassed and tell him he's seen the whole European farce play out then.' By now Freya is at her ease, the man leaning on his elbows across the counter.

'Farce is one of my favourite words,' he replies. 'That's right, Brexit, Bre-entry . . .'

Ruby tells her the next thing to say, with instructions to widen her eyes as he is doing, to gesture at the cooling bakes just out of reach.

'We should have stuck with bri-oche!'

Now he laughs at her self-conscious cheesiness. Freya turns to go, adding that she will treat herself later on.

'No, they need to be eaten hot,' he says, reaching for one. 'Here . . .'

As she leaves, he is repositioning his earphones, looking inordinately rosy. She can feel the warm chocolate melting against the paper bag. Cars whizz past overhead, and she is buzzing, hardly able to hear herself whispering to Ruby, 'I can't believe that worked.'

'Well, maybe you should trust me.' The voice oozes satisfaction. 'It's not rocket science. There are a zillion public conversations by this guy freely available.'

Freya pulls off a piece of the brioche, not really liking Ruby being a smartface and using her data-mining abilities. The bun is doughy, out-sugaring the guilt she feels. For her sister this sort of thing probably counts as a survival skill.

'Well, Sandor's a different matter.'

'Don't you worry about him,' the voice says cheerfully, its tones echoing as she goes through the double doors and into the stairwell. 'Just tuck your hair over your specs, and soon it'll all be over.'

Freya checks her reflection as she goes into the café area,

arranging her thicker hair so it helps conceal the line of her specs. It means keeping her head quite still. Unsurprisingly, Sandor has been alerted to her arrival and appears at the door. He points to her – almost a shooting motion – and then beckons.

'We're not going to take any shit,' Ruby whispers.

In his office, Sandor waves her into a chair. She hesitates, saying. 'The customers . . .'

'Chris can deal with the customers.' The force behind his words contradicts the casual way he props open the window and pretends to stretch. He tugs at his sideburns and moves his lunchbox to the edge of the desk. His comfort zone properly arranged, he settles down in his chair and addresses the ceiling. 'I've never seen someone blunder around the game like that . . .' A pause, which she recognises as the space left for her to giggle, to start apologising and explaining herself. In his head, this conversation has already happened. But Ruby tells her to say nothing. The bonhomie fades and he wanders over to the window, as though interested to see the gulls ducking and diving. 'Faking sickness absence. Not very clever, is it?' He tucks his hands behind his back so his elbows stick out. For the first time she notices how curiously antiquated his movements are. 'Have you thought about what you'll do to make it up to me?' This is enough to spur Ruby into action.

'For all your talk of teamwork, you're not exactly a joiner, are you, Sandor?' She nearly bites her tongue in shock at what she is saying. Too late now.

He glares. 'What are you talking about?'

Her face is reddening, but she dutifully channels the

lines being fed to her. 'Your Social's basically tumbleweed. Where are all the photos of you in blue and yellow tights? Aren't you lonely in your little treehouse?' She wants to signal time out, ask Ruby what the hell she is doing. Sandor's eyes are sinking into black caves of fury. His fist slams into the desk.

'If I want company, I find it myself. I'm the hunter.'

'Smile,' says Ruby. 'He knows he was startled by you on that last outing. He's way too clumsy ever to catch that hind.' Freya does smile. She has never seen Sandor this riled. Angry, yes, but never squirming. His face is a gingery red and she can almost feel the heat coming off him. He seems to regroup, drawing himself up into what Chris calls his 'regal bearing'.

'I suppose you'll claim you were at home with a swollen ankle, that you were incorrect to say you were in Medieville . . .'

Words tickle her ear and she rushes to say them. 'Oh, sorry, did you think I wanted this job?' She hesitates. 'You can take it and bang yourself with it on the weekend. You can . . . What the fuck, Ruby?'

Sandor does not bother trying to make sense of this, having heard enough.

'A perfectly good job, and you're throwing it out the window.' He shakes his head, though she can see his whole body is quivering. In fact he cannot wait to leave, and storms out of the office instead of ejecting Freya. She stares after him, then swivels, rounding on her smartface.

'Why did you make me say I'd quit?'

'You don't want to do this any more.' The voice is gentle.

'This is the best way to do it – your way. Plus it cancels his bonus if someone quits.'

She stares at Sandor's lunchbox, everyday Tupperware with a lemon-yellow rim.

'I can't just quit, though, can I?' It is warm in the office. She tugs at her uniform's red cravat. The voice from her smartspecs is level and reassuring.

'You want change, don't you? Step one is getting out of here. This job was keeping you in chains.'

A smell of tuna hangs about the lunchbox, a cat-food pong. It gets up her nose and her eyes screw shut as she realises her sister is right. Ruby is the smart one. Of the two of them, only she has the tools to navigate the best path through life, a route to happiness. Freya needs to trust her and be brave enough to take action. Wildly she casts around for something that will underline all of this. Her necktie comes loose in her hands, and then she is wrapping the red cloth around Sandor's sandwich, going to the window and tossing it to the gulls. They screech and dive down to the concrete, sharp beaks tearing at the fabric. 'Film it,' she says.

'Way ahead of you.'

Later, she posts it on Sandor's wall. He deletes it almost immediately, but that is as expected. How coolly she can picture him blowing a fuse. In the past he just had to glare at her and she would jump. Now he is drained of power. It was so easy to walk out of his office, out of the building. Freya tore off her workwear the moment she was home and imagined herself smooth and bare and reborn. Now Ruby has promised they will go out, start planning her new life. She showers and feels ready for anything.

'Better take off the smartbit,' Ruby adds.

'Why?'

'Looks a bit strange that you're super-excited when you're supposed to be at work, doesn't it?'

Freya stares at the band around her wrist. Good point. Her heart is racing and it is the kind of thing that might attract her mum's attention, trigger some messages. For the first time in ages, she feels constricted by Esther's cautious nature, her constant need to keep tabs. She slips off the smartbit and drops it into the toilet.

'Oops,' she says, awaiting her sister's chuckle. The low, musical rumble is amplified by the bathroom tiles.

Quitting her job is not the big, dangerous thing her mum has always made it out to be, otherwise why would sensible Gayle have given up her career – a whole career – in the city? Even at seventeen, Ruby had quit a couple of jobs. Once again Freya is a novice, new to the experience and unsure how it is meant to feel. Is there a notice period in her contract? She tells herself not to waste time worrying about the boring stuff.

Back in her room, she notices Gayle's postcard on the desk. They have messaged a few times, though the reception hasn't been great. The delays in her replies have been frustrating. Freya picks up the postcard, its papery feel unusual in her hands. On the back, someone has scribbled a messy circle with a pen. Testing out a biro, she assumes, though it could have been a child, or someone who has forgotten how to write. Even Freya is not confident she could correctly hold a pen these days, it's been such a long time.

Ruby turns the music up, the vibration of plucked strings

209

making the wallpaper tremble. It must be loud, yet Julian is obviously not to be roused. Freya settles onto her bed. There is one part of her time in Medieville that she has kept from her sister.

'Ruby?'

'Yeah?'

Freya circles a finger to lower the volume, then buries her hands in her hair. She is cosy in her room, well looked after. Ruby has guided her through every moment of the day, showing her how she can get what she wants by choosing the right words. They have come such a long way, and now she finally feels ready to tell her what happened on the roof garden. When she speaks, her voice is soft.

'I wanted to find you in Medieville, but . . .' All at once the wind is blowing plant pots around, lifting odours of freshly turned biosoil. She is looking at the figure crouching, wearing the over-large hoody, and in her mind the face is stratifying into the features of her sister, a little older, but undeniably the right person. As Freya draws near, mouth open like a fish, the older girl sees who it is, but instead of a reaction her eyes harden and she turns away. 'I was afraid,' Freya whispers. It sounds out of place, here in the warmth of her room, with the voice she loves and trusts, yet she forces herself to say it. 'I thought you'd blame me.'

'For what?'

The blue-sky wallpaper casts an electric glow on her hands and face. Is Ruby messing with her? She bites her lip and continues.

'You know. When you rang and I told you where to get off. When I made you come out to get me, and you disappeared.'

She has never spelled it out in such stark terms before. It has been a day of saying the unsayable. 'Was it my fault?' Her throat dries up. It is still possible Ruby was murdered that night. For years, they took it for granted.

Clouds drift ponderously across the wall. There is a pause, as though the smartface is digesting all of this.

'Of course not, babes. It wouldn't even occur to me that you were thinking that way.' The voice is light. Freya leaps in ecstasy from the bed.

'Really? Because you know it's never stopped bothering me, and the moment there's any chance of losing myself, any virtual reality, everything floods back and I'm afraid I'll come out to find someone banging on a window or getting kidnapped or injured, someone I love, and it's all because of that, Ruby, because I was selfish and wanted to stay in the game because it was so much fun.' Her lungs are inside out with the effort, yet every word lifts a weight from her chest.

'Chill, Frey, seriously,' comes the reply. 'Nothing is your fault. You've got to get over these hang-ups.'

If only she could get to the voice, give it a squeeze. It represents what Ruby would really think. Has she been worrying unnecessarily all this time? Maybe her sister would never have blamed her.

'I want you to know that I'm sorry. I'm sorry for the way I spoke, for bringing you out that night.' Gravity is reversed, lifting her off the ground and dragging her into the clouds on her wall. 'I wish I could go back in time and make it right. I wish I could save you.' Her eyes sizzle unexpectedly with tears. So much pain. That whole history of having brought Ruby into her family, trying to rescue her, when perhaps if Freya had left her alone she would still be around somewhere, squabbling with a foster family, but around. 'I was the reason.' She shakes her head. 'You have to blame me.'

'I don't have to do anything.' Her sister's voice is so familiar now that she can almost predict when it will push back. Self-esteem is set in stone, no cracks allowed. Freya's fingers rest on the pixels, trying to smooth over a little imperfection. Her heart is full of warmth for Ruby, even if there is nothing left but this voice.

'You know I'd do anything to find you,' she says.

'I know.'

Her bruised cheek ripples with each passing cumulus. She waits to hear what Ruby will say, but they are doing a shared silence, the kind that is never awkward between friends.

17

Pinball living is Ruby's name for it. The habit of bouncing between a few favourite locations. The trick is to break the routine, smash the glass and end up anywhere. On the grainy mud of this Thames beach, a man with a metal detector shows Freya how to unearth vintage bottle caps. Next she takes Ruby onwards to Greenwich and the grimy meringue rooftops of the National Maritime College, where they alter her walking trajectory to bend towards attractive men. 'You're looking good,' is the encouraging whisper as Freya slows her pace, planting her feet carefully, confident in her frontier-style skirt and pale lipstick, her fashion sunglasses fresh from the 3D printer. His eyes might flit to the space above her head, checking out her profile bubble, while she glances surreptitiously at his, wondering whether the two might catch, like errant balloons, and tangle. She has become pretty good at knowing what to say, and prefers to do it herself, though her sister is happy to invoke 'the power of the smartface', as she jokingly calls it.

No more desperately scanning female faces. It has been a tremendous relief to stop making herself play *Where's Wally?* every second of the day, to the point of exhaustion. Chris was right when he said that nothing had changed. What confused her was hearing Ruby's voice, right in her ear. Instinct dictates that speech must come from a speaker, but in this case instinct is wrong. If her sister is alive, she is either very different or very far away.

Her smartface, on the other hand, has become such a constant companion that she forgets it is data-built. They have grown so close that sometimes Freya is unsure if murmurs in that low, playful tone arise from the earpiece or from her own grey matter. It is rare that her smartface will mention a band or a hangout that she has not already heard of. The research into Ruby's new interests is complete. On Social, Freya's time-line veers off into glamorous London nooks, New Age snippets and the flavours they both love – coffee and hazelnut, or spicy beef – and rattles along at breakneck speed through all the things they have discovered together. It gives her joy to examine the marks made by her turbo-charged life.

The map-line deposits her back at the flat, and as the front door recognises her, a message appears. The sender – unexpectedly – is Thalis Oomen.

How's it going, Freya? I notice you haven't done your homework – that's not like you! In the meantime, I have a question: how did Julian get hold of a haptic suit?

She reads it twice before going inside, hoping her reply will end the discussion:

'He borrowed it,' she dictates through gritted teeth.

The lounge is quiet, lines of sunlight entering through the blinds. Now that the snails and the lizard are gone, her new pet is the vacuum bot. It needs minimal care and cleans up after itself. Sometimes she misses the gecko's beautiful eyes, the way he could scurry up her arm in seconds, but she has to admit that on most days she hardly noticed the animals, and might even have bundled them into her mum's attic with other childhood junk if that was an option. Ruby was right to post the adverts.

Not a great idea, leaving it around.

She rolls her eyes and goes to the kitchen to rehydrate a salad. As she turns from the sink, the next message is projected against the fridge.

You, of all people. It is a distracted sort of venting. She can picture him jogging, or in a meeting, sending these messages via headset brainwaves. Bad enough that something she bought has been sullied by Julian – fuel for his porn addiction – without his family members taking a pop at her.

'I wasn't exactly happy about it,' she snaps. If anything, Thalis should be taking charge, doing something to prise his son out of that sticky bedroom. It will be a happy day when she can move out of here and never see either of them again.

Maybe he figured it was a fair exchange, Thalis replies. *For the smartface.*

Though she cannot hear his voice, animosity leaks from the words. She has had enough of being harangued in her own flat, when she has done nothing wrong. Ruby notices the spike in adrenaline. 'Chillax,' she murmurs. 'Call time.'

'Get off my fucking back,' Freya dictates, slamming a

cupboard and marching out of the kitchen, throwing her hair over one shoulder.

There are no more messages from Thalis, and she is pleased. Chewing her turgid cucumber cubes, she remembers Julian pinning her with a conspiratorial grin and relating that once, after a couple of beers, his dad had asked whether he'd found Freya 'under a rock'. Her mouth had fallen open and it took a while for him to realise she didn't find it funny. 'It's adorable,' he reassured her, stroking her cheek, but it sowed a seed. She was not blind. He loved to wind Thalis up, and perhaps she was the key. The thought bites into her: what if the only charm she'd ever held for Julian was his father's contempt?

After closely examining a yellow stick of celery, she pushes the salad aside. Her health score has taken a few dents lately from all the sweet treats she has sampled when out with Ruby, so she is boosting it with a plate of limp vegetables as often as she can manage. Luckily the extra walking also counts in her favour, keeping her safe from premium rises.

When she hears the noise, it is so unfamiliar she ignores it. The vibration repeats until her smartface points out what it is.

'What buzzer?'

'You know, the front door?'

'What?' The salad bowl overturns in her lap, spilling prune-like tomatoes. She was wrong. Thalis was dictating his whole tirade from a smartcar, or even from the street outside. It is one thing to send him a line of text, quite another to face his wrath.

'You don't have to answer it.'

The noise continues. She bangs on Julian's door and calls his name. No response. When she tries the handle, it is locked. There is no let-up in the buzz electrocuting her ears. She knows Thalis will not give in. He has a right to visit his son.

'Wait,' says Ruby. 'He just checked in someplace else.'

Freya has one hand on the bathroom windowsill, halfway to the wild notion of climbing out. Her body floods with relief. Moments later she is opening the door to find the sapling-like figure of Chris bending to the glass, shielding his eyes to see if anyone is coming.

'Were you up a chimney or something?' he says. A dank breeze sweeps into the hallway. It must be a year or more since he last came to the flat. He looks at the living room as though a piece of its furniture might bite him. Almost in celebratory mood, Freya puts the salad back in the kitchen, swapping it for two chocolate biscuits.

'So this is a surprise,' she says, offering him one of the biscuits, which he waves away.

'Why didn't you come to the bar last night?'

'You just said "come to the bar". I'm not Pavlov's dog.' It was a message out of the blue, and she could not decide whether to drop everything and respond to this ominous summons. *You're not on a leash*, Ruby said, and she thought no more about it.

'Sorry, I was pissed,' he says. He throws himself into an armchair. The movement brings back fond memories of those early days at work when they used to fetch up at a pub, now closed, with flaky leather sofas. She perches on the table and swings her legs.

'Pissed?'

'As in, pissed off at you.' He narrows his eyes, before adding, 'And just pissed.' Her legs come to an abrupt stop. Why is everyone on her case? She has a sudden urge to press rewind and go back to Greenwich, where she has been happy all day. Instead she wearily evokes the office where she left empty Tupperware on the desk last Sunday, a lifetime ago.

'Look, I know I wound him up – Sandor, I mean. Is he making work unbearable?'

'There is no work any more.' An imperceptible puff of dust is raised as Chris thumps the arm of the chair.

The first images conjured up by these words are of the furniture store burning to the ground, or disappearing into a sinkhole. If some disaster could befall U-Home, it would nicely eclipse her unorthodox exit. She cannot help thinking that a reference may be needed at some point, though Ruby has calculated that her supervisor will not risk his finely crafted dignity by reporting the sandwich incident to human resources.

With Chris's next words, the promising atmosphere evaporates. 'I got sacked.' He pulls out his pack of mini wet wipes and rubs one across his forehead, then behind his ears. She watches him scrunch it up and tuck it into a second packet. New rituals of hygiene tend to appear when he is stressed.

'What did you do?'

'Absolutely nothing. Innocent as a lamb.' He fixes her with a steely glare. 'I didn't skive off for a week and then walk out saying "see you, fuckers" . . .'

'I was off sick!'

He parrots the words back at her in a whiny puppet voice. 'Sandor told me he saw you on the street.'

'That's a lie!'

'Is it?'

Normally the knowledge of Sandor's secret life as a play huntsman would make excellent gossip, but something tells her Chris would not find it amusing just now.

'Either way, it's nothing to do with you.'

He flares up again. 'You rocked the boat, though, didn't you? Point is, they now have automated catering, a six-armed robot to fill your plate . . . No other store has this yet. Why has ours been picked? Something must have tipped the balance.' He seems to cave in, elbows teetering on his knees. 'Even Sandor doesn't like it. What good's a kingdom without subjects?'

Freya picks at a pool of wax on the tabletop. Her first thought is that Ruby was right. It made no difference that she jumped: she was about to be pushed.

'Well, maybe this is a good thing.'

Chris winces. 'Do you know how much it costs to rent Chelsea-style?' he asks. 'Plus George and I had to fill the place. His taste is, as you would expect, exquisite.'

'What are you talking about?'

'I have an account at Harrods.' He sits up straight, as though someone from the store might be watching him. 'Don't you get it? I don't have any leeway. What about you? The rent on this place can't be peanuts . . . Aren't you worried about cash flow?' He tries to tug at his hair, finding it still too short to catch hold of. Chris used to save all his money, hoping to travel. He used to live happily on a shoestring. Why does he suddenly want all this fancy stuff?

'So get another crappy job.' She untucks her hands from

under her legs and examines her burgundy nails. 'At least we won't have to put up with old toilet-breath.'

Unexpectedly, his head sinks into his hands. They are large hands, willowy veins overlaying the knuckles. Freya is baffled to hear him groan.

'Oh God,' he wails. 'I even thought you were flirting with him.'

She squints with disdain. 'I think I can do better than Sandor.'

Chris opens his mouth, but closes it miserably, as though out of energy to explain. Instead he goes over to the shelf and starts lifting up the ornaments, examining the shapes made in the dust. In his block of flats the vacuum-bots can probably levitate.

'You know,' he says wistfully, 'he once told me how he'd traced his ancestry back to the time of the Plantagenets . . . I think it was that day the agency staff were on strike, when we both worked till we couldn't see straight.'

There is something in his tone that makes the situation clear, yet she still cannot believe it.

'You like Sandor,' she gasps. It takes a monumental effort not to burst out laughing. 'Is that why you did all that overtime?'

Images of her supervisor flood her mind: taking the temperature of the baked beans, his slim forefinger pointing at imaginary birds. It is difficult to transform him into an object of desire.

Chris shrugs. 'It's a very annoying obsession. I think it came on gradually.' He brushes some fluff from his sleeve, and she notices he is wearing a thick, almost stiff white shirt.

A far cry from the T-shirts he used to wear to the pub, which featured faded sweet-wrapper prints and had been in his wardrobe since he was thirteen. He hated wearing anything else. Now he pokes a toe into the carpet dents left by the vivaria, and his eyes flick up at her.

'Your hair is longer,' he says.

'Yours is shorter. So what?'

'Then tell me this,' he continues mysteriously. 'How come your Social says you were in Yearnfeld? Have you been hacked?'

'It wasn't really intentional.' She snaps the remaining choc-olate biscuit in half, a sweet-smelling spark of crumbs. 'But at least I got out of my comfort zone.'

'Good on you,' he replies, transferring a fingerful of dust to a wet wipe. 'I was just surprised.'

'I can't be stuck in a rut.'

'Figures.' She watches him flop into the armchair, leaning on his own knees so his body is folded almost double. As usual, he smells of a good-quality shampoo. It is like being back in the store together, waiting endlessly by the pedestals or wiping grease from chrome counters, running out of conversation. 'He said that a lot, you know?' Chris continues. 'Figures. Then he'd say: they're those people who put the filling into fig rolls.' He laughs sadly. 'A total non-joke.'

A low-hanging silence settles over the room. Freya picks crumbs from the faux-leather of her skirt, her mind drifting longingly to the videos Ruby has lined up to watch through dinner. Chris is lost in a reverie. It gives her an idea.

'There is a way you could see him.' While she is still disturbed by Yearnfeld allowing her to bump into her supervisor, at least she knows what his character looks like and where he loiters. Sandor would have no idea who he was talking to, and Chris – with a bit of coaching from his smartface – would know exactly the right things to say. They would be quaffing mead together in no time.

Excitement gathers in her face as she thinks how neatly Sandor could be targeted. 'He was a hunter,' she bursts out. 'In Yearnfeld. He didn't see me on the streets, he saw me there, though he was probably too embarrassed to say so.'

Chris looks aghast. 'What was he doing in Yearnfeld?'

'It was pretty much his natural habitat.'

Now that she no longer operates under his tyranny, it is easier to see her supervisor as a whole person, stressed out by modern life and longing for a reverse evolution from chipboard back to strong oaks. He clearly loved being master of a kingdom of tree houses and winding deer tracks.

As she describes her encounter, Chris begins to pace around the room, his eyes already locked on a distant forest horizon. She can see him clothed in green, with the biggest sword in the world, dragging Sandor down, telling him to hush as they crouch together in the bracken.

'Oh my sweet Prince George,' he sighs, but to her surprise, he shakes his head. 'I can't do it.'

'Huh?'

He perches on the table and motions her to sit. 'Look, Frey, I know you're trying to conquer your demons with VR, so it's different, but if I start doing Yearnfeld – especially just now, when I've nothing else to do – it'll be a bad move. If I start tempting myself with a more satisfying reality . . .'

'Only till you get Sandor out of your system.'

'. . . buying into my own personal myth . . .' He cocks his head. 'Haven't you researched it? You research everything.'

'Obviously.' Her tone is scathing, though in fact she has preferred not to dwell too much on the game, there being no reason why she should return. She folds her arms, resenting his patronising tone and disappointed that he is not rushing off to stalk Sandor. Her stomach rumbles. 'Forget it, then. What are your plans for today?'

'I thought I'd hang out with you. We could find a new pub.'

Her nails dig into the table. Just as Chris starts to say something, his specs, which he has left on the table, burble. He hooks them delicately over his ears.

'What?' he says, his thin body undulating upwards. 'You're joking.' He turns to Freya. 'I have to go. A delivery drone is apparently hurling itself against my stained-glass window. Even with the glazing it's starting to crack.'

'Oh no,' Freya says, with quiet elation.

'If it gets damaged, I will literally kill myself.'

'And what if it gets into the flat?'

He shivers. A rogue drone is a rare thing, but there have been incidents. In seconds he has gathered himself up, looked for the jacket he has not brought and departed with barely a wave.

'See you,' Freya calls, watching him head off. She bounds into the kitchen and grabs one last snack. Chris will be all right. He will get another job and forget about Sandor, though his antipathy to Yearnfeld came as rather a surprise. Anyone would think she was suggesting a course of narcotics.

In her room she moves drone boxes aside and settles down.

'Can you believe Chris got sacked?' she remarks. 'I guess it was only a matter of time.'

'And why wait?' Ruby's voice is so rich and chocolatey, here in the room. 'Better to clear the obstacles and get on with it.'

'What obstacles?' She feels sleepy now, chewing on a date and dandelion bar.

'To the serving bots. I think Sandor may have been holding them up deliberately.'

Freya sits up. 'You did this?'

'They do take customer feedback seriously, if there's enough of it.'

'But why?'

'Just a backup, in case you didn't manage to quit. Luckily you did, and I'm proud of you.' The warmth in her voice makes everything fine. Freya takes a drink of water, smoothes down the ruffles in her skirt. Ruby adds, 'It's what you wanted.'

'You give me everything I want.' She remembers their day amid the sights and smells of Greenwich, and thinks of those to come.

'Not everything.' A note of regret enters her tone. 'But I do run a search every day. I'll run it again now, just for fun.'

'Don't worry . . .' It is a search they set up some time ago, checking for a set of identifiers worldwide, any hint of a username, combinations of words relating to where Ruby lived, her family and interests, anything like that. So far there has been nothing worth investigating. 'Honestly, it's fine.' Freya drains her cup and starts browsing Social, looking out for jobs, since her smartaccount is running low. She is just wondering how to bring up this dull subject when Ruby exclaims:

'You're not going to believe this.'

'What?'

'You really won't believe it.'

Freya lifts the window blind, fearing another unexpected visitor. But after a moment the voice adds:

'It's come up with something.'

Freya rolls her eyes. 'I don't know why you're sounding so excited.'

'It says she's in Yearnfeld.' Something is missing from her tone, and it is cynicism. For the first time, the smartface sounds as though she is at a loss, her speech slowing. 'All the indicators match up. The data is like mine.'

Freya's shiver is picked up by the new thermostat, which ramps up the heat.

'So?'

'So the probability of it not being her . . . me . . . well, it's negligible.'

18

She wants to see her mother. Ruby is none too happy about taking the 'cattle trains', but smartcars are expensive. 'You'll just have to lump it,' Freya tells her as she goes down the sticky concrete steps. When they were teenagers, she would not have said half the things to Ruby that she does now. Despite not seeing her smartface as software – or not since the beginning – there may be a little seepage from this underlying fact, making her bolder. She has grown up talking to computers. Luckily the smartface, always on her side, is not inclined to take offence. They know each other well enough to be candid.

Freya knows, for example, that Ruby's heated insistence on following up these search results springs from months of being asked to scour Social, looking at forums and hang-outs and dating sites – it is hard for the smartface to finally have a lead and be told to sit on it. But thousands of people play

Yearnfeld, and any number of players could have been born in Clapham, in the same year as her sister, and have chosen that name. The real reason Freya is reluctant to investigate, which her smartface can surely guess, is that hope, once kindled, rages like a wildfire. Every time she has to douse it, a part of her needs to heal, and recently it has been a relief to close her eyes at night and know the next day will bring no firefighting.

'I'm not going to Yearnfeld again,' she insists, each time the subject arises. While she agrees in principle that fears should be tackled, there are gentler ways to do it. Besides, the trail she followed – or thought she was following – to Medieville led nowhere. In her mind, Gayle appears, scented with home-brewed beer, her fingerless gloves reaching up to pull down a hood of knitwear. It was ridiculous, embarrassing even, to expect to see Ruby just standing there after being dead for eight years. Looking back, she could almost laugh. 'Nothing came to anything.'

As the steps take her down, the city disappears amid smells of engine oil and urine. Her body is jostled on all sides, bombarded by voices raised above the din and speaking every language but English. A group of office staff, clearly used to working from home, cluster with pained faces under cowboy hats. They must be on some team-building outing, roughing it on a public train. The multinational mix reminds her how much she would like to go abroad, which she has not done for years. Her smartface is keen on America, but would be up for any kind of travel. Freya blinks away last night's dream, which the sight of cowboy hats has brought back. Essentially she saw her sister lying on a hay bale in a barn, deep in the American Midwest, eyes closed and headset nodes dotted over her dark, flowing hair. The dream took her right inside Ruby's mind and out again on a bumpy brainwave, straight into the bustle of Medieville, where she was a beautiful avatar, charming a cup of chai from the man at the brazier. *Nothing came to anything*, she reminds herself, going down the next escalator.

But maybe, says a part of her, *you didn't go deep enough.* This is how it is: when Ruby stops arguing, her own prefrontal cortex takes over, so she has to argue against herself. Today this is really kicking in. This morning the search was not mentioned. Instead Ruby set a delicious coffee brewing, using free samples she had ordered, and stopped Freya using some eggs that were past their date, which would otherwise have affected her health score. After breakfast, they looked at one or two jobs, and now they are visiting her mum. Ruby is backing off, big time, but the elephant in the room – or should she say in Yearnfeld – fails to shrink.

A deafening beeping indicates that the doors are about to close, and Freya realises she has stared at the train without boarding it. The track is sooty below, and she takes a step back. It is not normal to miss a half-full train. If she does it again, the jumper alert might be triggered and she will be hauled away by some psychiatric SWAT team.

On the next service she sits between a woman carrying a plastic bag of sweet potatoes and a man whose silvery T-shirt glitches through pictures of motorbikes. Either it needs another spray of solar, or it is suffering from a virus. Her mum told her there was once a mass hack of these shirts, thousands of people finding themselves unexpectedly flaunting hardcore porn. Not great for family occasions.

The train rattles along. A baby starts to wail. Through the windows Freya can see messy bundles of cables, grime and flashing lights. She realises she has not stopped thinking about the search. The idea of Ruby being somewhere in Yearnfeld will never leave her, even if her smartface is silent. She ducks her head and whispers, 'What you were saying . . . can't you send a message for me or something, check it out?'

'People can't be messaged in the game.'

She sighs. Annoying but not surprising, since it would interfere with the escapism. The curve where the sides of the carriage meet the roof is a mass of sharp, angry, illegible letters in permanent marker.

'What other info do we have? Do we know what she is doing there?'

'All I know is her location, and that's from something on a forum. A guest at this castle mentioned she is in the west tower, and has been for some time.'

A bend in the track causes much bumping and a hellish screech from the rails. Freya sighs, not wanting to picture Ruby in the game. Even if her sister is playing, she would be unlikely to stay in one place. She would roam around, have fun and then leave. It is not in her nature to get hooked, though Yearnfeld must be pretty tempting to attract so many players. Her mum would say it is for people who think they deserve better than the real world. Fantasising is *sticky thinking*, glutinous thoughts clumping around a pleasant idea. Perhaps this is how Julian began, taking those first

229

steps into the pleasure rooms, the stickiness – she squirms mentally – catching him like birdlime.

'You couldn't be hypnotised or something?' she asks quietly, checking that the people nearby are wearing specs with sonic disruptors and won't overhear. 'You know, to forget you're in a game. Do people forget to come out?'

'They do keep rehydration salts on hand, in the cellars,' her smartface remarks. 'I guess people sometimes get carried away, though they try to keep an eye on it. You can always set a timer.'

She imagines people stumbling up to the chain mail boy, pleading for water. It makes her shudder, the thought of 'zombies' wandering the cellars. The train begins to turn another bend and a man sways towards her, catching hold of the bar and releasing a warm fug from his armpit. She swallows, repositions her specs from where he knocked them. A grating sound comes from outside, and to her dismay the train stops.

The lights go out.

The armpit man groans, a long, vibrating note that takes her straight back to the stone alcoves of the Black Hole, two women using claw nails on his back. A witchy giggling is reincarnated in her ears as she casts alarmed eyes down the train. Yellowy outlines of faces unseen. Outside, something sparks. There will be a bomb, down here where no one matters, and she will be trapped like a rat. A flash of Gayle in the stocks. She would give anything to hear her voice making light of this. With no smartbit, Ruby does not pick up on her panic.

'Ruby,' she wails in a choked voice. Then, barely a second

having passed, the lights flicker twice and are back on, and the train is moving. It pulls into a station and Freya twists and turns through bodies to get herself out.

'Screw it,' her smartface says, having registered Freya's strangled tone. 'We're getting private trains – the crossrail isn't far.'

'I don't know what's the matter with me,' Freya says. She has taken public transport a thousand times, buses that break down, trains that stop for hours. As she emerges into the watery daylight, she is gulping oxygen. The wind has never felt so good on her skin.

Once several minutes have been spent leaning on a railing, calming down, she notices where she has surfaced, only a one-station walk from the Smarti campus. Esther has been clamouring to see her for weeks, and now there is something she really needs.

At the gate, the wind becomes sweet with this week's fragrance. Marshmallow, if she had to guess.

'What's the point, babes?' Ruby seems restless again, or reluctant to be going down this route, but Freya marches on. A pearly light suffuses the Smarti foyer, the sun trapped in clouds, and she meets a clean-shirted welcome hologram who checks her in and directs her towards the medical wing. Pink arrows appear in the air, but she knows the way.

The doors open to the familiar sterile smell. It has been some time since she dropped by, and the downstairs exhibition is now care-home equipment, cute little robots that fill cups of tea and tell you when it is cool enough to drink. People are testing the dementia headsets she saw on her last visit, experiencing a wakeful paradise of colours and little

Post-it reminders. Two blind people walk by with their tongues out, a researcher pacing backwards in front of them, their modified taste buds telling them the door is open, the carpet minty green. When they move towards the glass side of the building, they will taste the afternoon light.

A lift takes her one floor up into the hum of little spinning parts, microscopic bots and hydraulics. An arm protruding from a mount on the wall reaches up and rubs a patch of empty air, then scratches further down. It is linked by nerve chip to the left arm of a Smarti employee in Miami, who volunteered to do this for a laugh. By the looks of it he is currently in the shower. Freya eases her way round two disembodied legs connected by a crossbar on a walking machine. The thought of losing a limb makes her fingers tingle, her toes notice the pressure of every step. When the arrows deposit her at the door to a test studio, she is surprised how happy she is to peer inside and see her mum's familiar hunch.

'I've just been to the machine,' Esther says in dismay, indicating her mug of coffee. 'Shall I go again? If you'd said you were coming . . .'

'Don't worry.'

She slips down from her stool and there is the usual shoulder hug, though lasting a fraction longer than normal.

'You look tired.' Her mum speaks hesitantly. 'Everything okay?' In this small room with its old-fashioned wall calendar and bottle of green Fairy Liquid by the sink, Freya could say so much.

'Fine.'

'What happened to your smartbit?' Esther's mood pendant must have been a neutral grey for some time.

'It fell down the toilet and stopped working.'

'Give it here.'

'I don't . . .' She stops, realising that it is in her bag. Julian made a show of handing it back to her, having fished it unnecessarily from the loo. Her mum takes the smartbit and tosses it into a machine the size of a microwave. Bacteria inside will strip out the metal so it can be remade.

'It'll be a while.' Her mum's eyes are inquisitive behind her glasses. 'What is it, pet?'

Freya sits at a lab bench, reminded of university, and wonders how to begin.

'I think I might have some information for the police,' she says, the words sounding strange. 'Not a sighting exactly, but someone who has signed into Yearnfeld with her details.'

'Whose details?' She is being strangely slow on the uptake.

'Ruby's.'

Esther's face, previously a neat stack of pursed lips, nose, brows and rippled forehead, now topples, her mouth ajar.

'You still have the smartface, don't you?'

Irritated, Freya continues: 'With a missing person, you tell the police, and they investigate, right?'

Her mum's hands fly up; she stands and the stool crashes over. 'Of course you still have it. Otherwise you wouldn't have forgotten I exist.'

The noise makes Freya jump, but she fiddles with a dummy head on the bench to hide her disquiet. 'Should I tell the police or not?'

'Have you lost your mind?' Esther seems to hear the force of her own words and takes a moment to calm herself. 'I'm sorry,' she says. 'I know this must be hard. I'm sure people called Ruby play that game every once in a while, but you'd never have thought anything of it – or even known about it – if you didn't have that smartface making a meal of everything.'

As she comes nearer, Freya squeezes the fake head, tweaking the Halo nodes as though it is an instrument.

'Smarti owns Yearnfeld, doesn't it? Would there be any records of who has played the game?'

'I'm not sure you're appreciating what I'm saying.' Esther pulls the model from Freya's hands. 'That smartface is giving you what you want because that's what it's programmed to do, but it's beta . . . which could mean anything. Just imagine if you wanted something bad, or to do yourself harm. Imagine if you felt guilty . . .'

Freya lurches back, her eyes wide. 'What?' The room is thick with chemicals and suddenly spinning. The air itself feels artificial. 'Why would I feel guilty?'

'I'm not saying you do.'

'Ruby would never accuse me of anything.'

'That's not what I'm saying.' The dummy head topples over and the headset closes like a skeletal umbrella.

'What do you know about it? You won't even speak to her.'

Now the pain is back, etched across her mum's face, 'I don't want to speak to her,' she says quietly.

Freya has so much bubbling up from within that she keeps going. 'Well, you'll have to, eventually. We all have to get over our hang-ups.' She bounces down from the stool, landing elegantly on the shiny floor. The heels give her a little more height, so from here she can look straight across into her mum's grey, anguished eyes.

'What do you mean?' Esther is very still, and seems to guess what is brewing in her mind. 'There'd be no point trying to play Yearnfeld yourself. That would only make it worse. Plus it's an absolute nest of dark-webbers . . .' She peters out, obviously not wanting to sound melodramatic. There is something curious about the way she bites off the words, but Freya does not want to hang around any longer. She hears a sigh of defeat. 'Don't just go,' her mum begs. 'Stay here and speak to me. I know you lost your job. You used to tell me these things.'

'I didn't lose my job.' The words have hard edges. As she shuts the door, she is just in time to see bewilderment on her mum's face. 'What a waste of time.' She taps her foot on the lift's floor. 'And why is she so bothered about me being employed?'

It is not as though she will starve. As long as she puts in a few hours on council harmony projects, Freya will get the enhanced state benefit, which is enough to live on. It is what used to be called *society*, her mum likes to say, which was presumably an earlier government invention. In Freya's mind, visiting elderly people in local streets or stewarding schoolkids through a lunch break will be light work compared to recent weeks with Sandor. She might even enjoy it. But for her mum, there are only two states of being: employed or job-hunting.

'You've got to have a career,' Ruby's reply is soothing in her ears, 'or you can't be the same as her.'

Maybe Esther does want to see a version of herself. Sometimes Freya thinks that's all anyone cares about.

'The age of narcissism,' she mutters. It is the kind of observation her sister likes.

235

'Smiley face.'

It is refreshing to emerge into the open space of the atrium. Some new product must have been launched, as people are loitering with drinks and canapés. They clink beers and follow her with their eyes as she passes. The atmosphere of casual power is at its zenith.

'Look at them,' she whispers. There is a smell of fresh buttered baguettes going dry. Picking up on her longing, the smartface remarks:

'Yeah, but you can't trust appearances.'

She assumes Ruby is referring to the long hours these young execs must put in, the constant rating by customers, colleagues and superiors, but the hint of darkness in her tone reminds Freya of something her mum said, about the pitfalls of going too high too fast, or of treating the algorithms like your own personal crystal ball. One of Esther's colleagues fed them his data and, the next thing he knew, all kinds of strange predictions were coming out, with no explanation. He would develop and conquer alcoholism, his wife would have an affair, and his kid would go to prison . . . It was like having God in a box and not knowing what to do with it.

Outside, the sunshine is slick as olive oil, though there are clouds further off. This detour has done nothing to settle her mind, and her nascent idea of going to the police has been thoroughly trampled. So much for the hope that her mum might take matters into her own hands – as she did once before – and make use of her considerable skill in dealing with the authorities.

'She could have helped me find out about this player, at least.' No matter what happens, her mum seems determined to ignore everything the smartface says, eyes glazing over like closed windows. Is this the same woman who made appearances on every major news site, appealing to the public for information, who put up posters and ran campaigns to try to find her foster-daughter?

'I know. It's weird.'

'What now?' To turn up at Scotland Yard and get the same reaction would be more than she could bear, but there might something else she can do, or at least contemplate.

'What are you afraid of?' As usual, Ruby guesses her thoughts.

Exhaust fumes mingle with scents of toasted cheese from cafés. Her step grows more assured, her heels somehow louder, and she tells herself Esther's help is not necessary.

'Nothing, obviously. But what's the point of going into Yearnfeld and trying to drag this player out? It's like with Sandor – she could look like anyone and I'd never know.'

The cars purr past, carrying important people and tourists. Freya wraps her scarf round her shoulders.

'Not a problem, babes. She hasn't moved from the west tower of that castle.'

The wind blows Freya's hair everywhere. It sounds so obvious when Ruby puts it like that. Why didn't she see it before?

'She's trapped?' Her mind is running through the possibilities: the no-feel technology of a headset combined with a drip, fluid and nourishment provided. A player recumbent on a straw-stuffed bed in a locked room, the outside world fading. 'But I don't know if I can handle it, going in there again on my own . . .' The fear threads a whine through her words. Since Yearnfeld is not available on smartspecs, she will have to go to Medieville again. If she touches her cheek, she can still feel the bruise from last time.

'Not on your own. Don't you remember? I can come with you. I'm beta.' The usual smile is beneath the words. Freya halts in front of a jerk-chicken joint.

'Fuck it. Let's go.'

Her map recalculates.

19

Droplets are shaken from velvet sleeves or brushed from tasselled hats. The gate is part blocked by a cart of sacks whose starchy smell suggests grain headed for the mill. She tries to use this as cover, but the trilby man steps out from his awning and gives her the blackest of looks for trying to sneak past without removing her smartspecs.

'I'll see you there,' Ruby says quickly, before Freya lifts the specs from her ears and folds them. As she hands them in, the world seems quieter, though it is not long before the voice resurfaces in her mind. *Just keep going.* Steam rises from the kettle on its brazier, and surprisingly the man recognises her from the previous visit. 'All right, love?' he says, plucking a chestnut from the roasting tin and tossing it to her. She rewards him with a smile and blows on the nut until it is cool enough to bite, enjoying its silky-soft crumble. Stallholders call out, but nothing will make her stop. She turns off the main thoroughfare, and is marching so determinedly towards the Black Hole pub that she almost misses the shout.

'Look who it is!' A familiar figure zigzags between the puddles, her metal studs winking as she breaks into a smile. Reluctantly Freya pauses.

'Hey, I thought you'd be moved out by now.'

Having ditched the hoody, Gayle seems even more petite than before. She is bent to one side under the weight of a gingham holdall.

'Just a couple of things to pick up.' She stuffs the arm of a jumper back into her bag. 'And half a ton of unsold knit-wear! I'm about to get a train. What are you up to?'

'I'm here for a stroll with zombies.' The entrance to the pub is just up ahead, and she catches glimpses of the dark interior as people go in and out.

'Really? Are you sure you want to?' Gayle is looking her over, smiling to indicate concern rather than insult as she adds, 'Don't take this the wrong way, but you look like you've been burning the candle at both ends.'

Freya's hand goes instinctively to her face, finding the skin around her eyes soft and supple. It has been a frenzied few days, the results of Ruby's search eating at her. She looks towards the pendulous sign of the Black Hole and her eyes are drawn to one of the lunchtime drinkers on the bench outside. Cold fingers clasp her heart as she makes out the faded red-black superhero on his T-shirt.

Gayle is saying something about zombies, but her words just add to the pulsing in Freya's ears. Instinct tells her to turn away, to make sure there is no chance of him spotting her, but everything she wants is through that door. It calls to her, as though the voice was still in her head. She pictures Ruby waiting below in the cellars, wondering where she has got to. Her body tenses. Already she is shrugging out of the conversation, murmuring: 'I'll be fine, hun.'

Before she can move, Gayle catches her in a hug of apple breath and a slightly damp armpit.

'Okay, go steady. I have to dash.' She lopes down the street, leaning away from the weight of her bag.

Otto has vanished. Maybe he was just leaving. Freya plunges into the pub's humid interior, hearing laughter and the tinny splash of ale pouring into tankards. If he did come back in, he might be tucked away in a corner, no reason for him to see her. Each second is divided into an eternity of moments in which she expects to hear her name, yet she manages to duck her head and cut across to the dungeon passage without incident, and soon she is descending into the stale out-breath of the cellars. Figures move dreamily in the darkness. Even when someone shouts, the vaulted ceiling absorbs the sound. She clenches her fists, picturing the forest stream, the sun twinkling on the water. Just an hour with a visor, or less, and this weight could be lifted from her chest.

The desk is still there with its vintage green lamp. Despite the gloomy surroundings, she feels buoyant, adrenaline making her bounce from one foot to the other. As she steps forward, ready to be kitted up, a broad-chested figure slides in front of her. It is so sudden, she staggers back. He brightens at having made her jump, a slug of peppermint gum caught between his canines. Being faced with this man, whom she hoped never to see again, makes her shrink as though a magic potion is wearing off. The T-shirt grows wide and threatening in front of her, stretched tight over the bulges of his pecs, which look unnatural, his collarbone slightly askew. He is not quite smiling, regarding her evenly, noting her tan skirt and ankle boots, the scarf snake-like around her shoulders.

'You look good.'

She tries to reply, but her throat has dried up. He runs a hand over his sandpaper scalp. 'Saw you check in. I reckoned you might be down here, 'cause you like a bit of fantasy, don't you?' Teeth jostle for space in his smile. 'Happy to do it your way,' he adds. 'The other lads won't mind. I'll give 'em a shout to get their headsets on.'

Freya twists the strap of her bag, feeling as if she is caught up in some plot of which she knows nothing.

'I said I wasn't interested.'

'You were a match for us, though, weren't you? That's got to count for something. I'll tell you what really grabs me . . . where are your ratings? You came out of nowhere. But you looked so cute when you were running away. I wouldn't mind a bit more of that.' One hand swings a visor lazily, while the other holds a flask of water. She realises her fearful reaction has become part of the game, like a bedroom quirk. The idea of hunting her down appeals to him; he would like it to happen in Yearnfeld.

Otto pushes the bottle into her hands. 'Come on, hydrate yourself.'

He looks surprised when she shoves it back.

'Not interested.' It comes out with a force that surprises

242

her. She goes over to the desk and picks up a discarded visor, not waiting to be helped. To her dismay, he looms up.

'Whoa, whoa,' he says, a touch of menace in his voice. 'I was making an effort there, not that you noticed. I might not be such a gentleman in the game.'

The visor is flexible black plastic, smelling of antibacterial wipes. Other people are masking up and descending the steps, hands outstretched. A creeping fear is coming over her at the thought of launching into these dark chambers, Otto at her heels.

'I don't want you following me.' Her delivery becomes wooden as hope drains away.

'It's a free country, mystery girl.' When he turns away to wrestle the visor over his stubbly hair, she dashes across the foyer and takes the stairs two at a time. Her face is impassive, but her stomach is roiling. Inside his mind is a world of flies and spiders, women funnelled in by algorithms, and everyone fine with it because they have been matched by an intelligence greater than themselves. Tears fill her eyes. Yearnfeld is out of bounds.

Towards the gate, she has to fend off vendors thrusting hot pies in her face, avoid the latex-deformed beggars who reach out for her sovereigns. Not until the smartspecs are hooked over her ears can she breathe freely again. Ruby is falling over herself to ask what happened. When they are finally in a smartcar and driving away, Freya rattles through the story, calmed by the purring vehicle and its new-car fragrance.

'You have to go back.'

'Not if there are eight freak-shows waiting for me.' Freya's voice cracks. Once again she is a child, too afraid to step where Ruby would leap.

'But babes, you've totally outsmarted them.' The car pulls up to the house and gives her a red smartaccount warning, which she waves away. 'They think you've left.'

As she climbs from the air-conditioned vehicle, drizzle stings her eyes.

'But if I go back, he might see me.' She shakes her head. 'I'm not doing it.' A tremor runs through her body. She can still smell the minty gum on his breath, hear the slosh of his water bottle. A man with multiple shadows.

'There's another way.'

'I'm not going back.'

'You don't have to.' The voice is insistent, but it takes several moments of rubbing her forehead before she can work out what Ruby is getting at.

'You mean Julian?' She removes her damp coat and hangs it up, listening. There are no sounds from his room. 'What if he's . . .'

'Trust me.'

It is worth a try. Drifting towards his door, the old fear is strangely absent. She knocks softly and waits, entering when there is no reply. She is surprised to see him on the carpet, engaged in nothing more disturbing than sleep. He is wearing only his pants, pale legs wrapped around a scrunched-up duvet. The room smells of orange juice and socks, as it has done for months. She does not waste time wondering why he is on the floor rather than in bed, but steps over him, feeling his hot breath on her leg. Her haptic suit is slung over the desk chair, and she could take it back, but after pinching the clammy fabric, she leaves it and turns instead towards the slim package that made up the other half of his birthday present.

He has not even unboxed it. She eases the item from under the old tablets, headphones and bits of tech that festoon his desk. Julian groans and shifts, frowning as she slips past his tangled limbs. He will not miss something he has never used, though how could anyone resist using this? Its clear sleeve is already fogged from her excited breath: a Halo headset, snug in its vacuum-moulded plastic, emblazoned with a Smarti logo hologram. His dad must have given it to him to complement the smartface.

The device opens like an umbrella, each spoke tipped with a rubber foot. She places it on her head and the nodes vibrate, burrowing gently through her hair. She wanders round the flat, trying to detect a change in her thoughts. Finally she hears a voice, a sound from just above her ears, mistaken at first for a direct-beam thought. 'Please think of yes, think of no, think of an apple.' This is part of the calibration process. She pictures a red fruit, shiny around the stalk. It sometimes flickers into a crab apple, sharp and sherbety to bite. The headset is reading her brainwaves, mapping them. It asks her to think of several more things, including warmth, cold and walking forwards. Eventually it tells her the training is complete. By way of a test, she imagines turning the kettle on, and is pleased to hear a click from the kitchen. Her head feels as though someone is holding it with many small fingers. The knowledge of everything she can do is sent directly into her mind, no need to read instructions. With a thought, she can reach into the cloud and pluck out any piece of information. She lifts the smartface sphere from her shelf, finding it dusty, and tosses it in her hand, reminded of the hot nut she ate earlier. *How long does it take to roast chestnuts?* Before she has finished framing the question, the answer comes to mind. A strange experience, to be given a thought from outside your own brain. It has a slightly different flavour to her own thoughts, to help distinguish it. *Five minutes on an open fire, thirty in an oven.*

She sinks down on the bed, eyes globe-like with sheer possibility. If she falls asleep and dreams of serving sausages at U-Home, the headset will record it and offer up a ghostly replay the following day. Or if she would prefer to dream about blue dragonflies, the Halo will try to make this happen, adding droplets of dye to her mental waters. She can even hear the thoughts of other Halo users, as long as they are public. There are actors, scientists, musicians, Smarti VIPs and celebrities of all kinds making their brainwaves available at key moments, offering their fans an insight into the mechanics of their genius. The world is cracked open as she never thought it could be.

'Okay, let's focus,' says Ruby. She starts to set up the Halo for virtual reality. Two lines come together just above Freya's eyebrows, and a delicate visor begins to unfurl. *Don't freak out*, she tells herself, banking up pillows behind her lower back and neck. She tells her smartface to set a timer, realising the conversation is happening inside her head.

'Should I speak aloud, in Yearnfeld?' Instantly she knows it is up to her – it depends on what feels natural. On public transport or at work, it might be subtler to *think* your words. Here in the flat, Freya decides to speak aloud. 'Otherwise I might have a thought . . . and in the game I'll be shouting it out.' Hard to say how she will react on meeting this 'Ruby' player, who, according to the search, has not budged from her previous location. It feeds Freya's theory that she is trapped. Emotion wells up inside her, and she is not sure whether it is trepidation at what she is about to do, or the spark of fresh hope.

'Never remove your headset mid play,' Ruby warns.

'I'll try not to.'

'Just don't.' She beams some information into Freya's brain that momentarily alarms her, stories of people who tore headsets away too rapidly and were rendered unconscious, even one report of a suspected aneurysm.

'Okay, I won't. You're sure there's a timer set?'

'All sorted – relax!'

From nowhere, Gayle's words replay in her mind. 'Am I sure I want to do this?' she says aloud, putting a hand over her fluttering heart.

'It's none of it real, hun, what are you afraid of?'

Yes, none of it is real. Nothing that matters. In any case, she has to go on. Who will investigate if she doesn't? A deep breath, and she focuses her thoughts on Yearnfeld. The wrap-around visor turns into a beautiful photograph, then differentiates into a perspective of near and far. Under her feet are damp, spongy pine needles. The game seems to have deposited her more or less where she left: a nearby yew looks suspiciously like the one harbouring Sandor's tree house, but there is no sign of him. Nevertheless, she ducks down for a few moments behind the tickly bracken. Maybe his hands are full at the store – it is a busy time of day.

A woodpigeon coos, and the wind reconfigures the canopy. It is made so real by the headset, rustling leaves and scents of sugary sap beamed directly into her brain, as though from her own senses. As she starts to slip between the ferns, her body is lithe and agile, responsive to the slightest thought. The legs that step over logs are pale, waxy and hairless. She has no intention of ever being naked in Yearnfeld, but no doubt she would cut a stunning, nymph-like figure that would be difficult to leave behind in the game.

'Ruby?' she whispers, forgetting she will not hear her smartface's voice until she can request it. The balmy after-noon urges her to relax, but she must not be seduced by this luminous world. She needs to keep moving, no matter how perfect these woodland orchids, how delicate this caterpillar dangling in her path on its half-spun cocoon.

As though to reward her speed, the trees thin and give way to cabbage patches, the sound of a stream ahead. Dry-stone walls mark out the plots. Passing through a gate, she finds a portly man crouching amid the furrows, a bunch of carrots in his hand.

'Can I help you?' His raisin-like eyes blink a few times within his pudding of a face.

'No, sorry,' she says automatically, and rushes past, leaping frilly leaves. It is only when she reaches the far wall, the man still looking sourly after her, that she realises her mistake.

20

'Sometimes I think I've got a voice inside me head,' the labourer burbles, casually removing an egg timer from his pocket, 'but it's just the wife sneakin' up behind me.'

Once she realised he was offering help, Freya hotfooted it back across the furrows and asked for her smartface. It is a sign of her agitation that she did not immediately recognise him as a non-player character, and a comic one at that.

Now she is basking in Ruby's immeasurably reassuring chatter. It is her anchor in the real world, and she has already checked twice that, should she not find a convenient surface for drawing a door, the smartface could pluck her out of this game even before she'd finished making the request. 'But you can draw a door anywhere,' Ruby adds. 'A tree, a rock, a wall – an invisible fingernail scratch will do it.'

'Thank God you're here.' Freya is still breathy with relief, but her strides are growing longer and more purposeful now she is following directions. 'Do we have to do all this walking?'

'It wouldn't be like real life if you could teleport. Cut through the village – we'll get there as fast as we can.'

She steps over a stream and is fascinated to see the quaint hovels, everything splashed with mud and a hint of dung in the air. From somewhere unseen there is a rhythmic *ting, ting, ting,* metal on metal. At the centre of the hamlet, a bell hangs, perhaps to raise the alarm in case of raids. This could be the last outpost before the land runs wild.

A woman pulls her child inside a cottage and slams the door. Men peer impassively from the entrance of a chapel, as though unable to continue praying until she has passed. The stirrings of embarrassment begin deep in her stomach, but Ruby whispers, 'Takes a lot of sticks to fit all these arses,' and her mood is lightened. She sucks in every glare, throwing defiant looks to left and right until she is on the far side of the village. Here the source of the metallic sound is revealed. The blacksmith distractedly hammering on a horseshoe stops what he is doing and squints at her, beckoning her closer to the forge. After hesitating, she alters her trajectory.

Burns criss-cross this character's leather apron, and his folded arms are hardly visible under their furze of black hair. His fire roars up like a live thing, and she has to remind herself its dry heat won't roast her skin to crackling.

'Come in.' The blacksmith opens a rough-hewn door.

'Why?'

A movement behind her turns out to be the villagers gathering, swarthy and muddied, some with scythes and other farm tools. The blacksmith shuts them out, and she finds herself blinking in a small hut dominated by a chimney stack, embers smouldering in the grate, a hard-looking loaf of bread on the table.

'You should not be here,' he intones. 'It is not safe.'

His voice is husky and full of breath, soft as it emerges from his throat, as though he is coated with the fur-like hair internally as well.

'I need to get to the castle.'

From outside, she can hear the hushed conference of the villagers. It would not be wise to dawdle. On a whim, she pulls back her cloak, hoping the birthmark will serve as some sort of explanation.

'The castle mark.' His eyes narrow.

'What does it mean?'

'They either want you, or they want to kill you.'

She wonders if this encounter is like the more linear computer games of old, where you have to say the right thing in order to obtain some useful item or information.

'Can't you help me, then?'

'Why do you want to go to the castle?' he snaps.

'I just do.'

He turns to the chimney breast and worries at a loose stone, his fingers plunging into sooty crevices. 'The guards are butchers.'

'But what about my mark?'

'They'll cut you in two.' The brick slides out, and from the recess he removes a small, blackened knife. She stiffens, but he does not seem about to hurt her. He turns the blade over in his hands and places it contemplatively on the table. There is something hesitant in his movements, as though he is breaking his usual routine of shovelling coal and hammering horseshoes, turning buckets of water to steam. Why would anyone choose to play Yearnfeld as a blacksmith? But if he is a non-player character, she isn't getting much out of him.

'So you won't help?' It is intended as a parting shot, Freya already rearranging her cloak to leave, but it seems to coincide with some conclusion gathering on his face. He snaps upright.

'I will,' he says. 'Wait here while I get the horses.'

The door slams, and his boots crunch off somewhere beyond the forge. Left in the cottage, Freya taps her knuckles against the rock-like bread, puzzled at this turn of events. From outside, a faint whinny can be heard. Is he making last-minute deals with the other villagers? Her hand pushes the rough wood of the door, and it does not budge. She tries the handle, but it is locked. All her fears solidify in her chest. 'I don't like this,' she mutters.

'Me neither,' replies the voice.

On a whim, she takes the knife from the table and slides it neatly into her belt. Getting through the window requires her to wind her cloak round her neck and go out head-first, hands outstretched to ease her body onto the weedy ground. Her elbow knocks a few logs from the adjacent woodpile and, afraid someone may have heard, she picks herself up and runs, dodging rusting metal and old cartwheels, not daring to breathe until she has reached the cover of the woods.

Under the canopy, calmness returns. Maybe the blacksmith really did want to help her find the castle, but why take the risk? In Yearnfeld it's impossible to see who anyone really is – unless they make it public – so there is no one she can trust. Better to get there under her own steam, with Ruby's guidance.

The further and faster she goes through the woodland, the more confident she becomes. With the smartface here, she is safe. Sometimes she says, 'Are you there?' and the murmured reply adds a bounce to her heels. She breathes deeply, sticking her thumbs into the frayed leather of her belt. The trees on either side are blossoming yellow and pink, honey-scented and beautiful. This romantic, rugged landscape is starting to enchant her. There is no rush. She is doing fine. With every twig that snaps under her feet, she is breaking old habits. When she comes out of Yearnfeld, virtual reality will no longer be an issue.

'Take the left fork,' the voice says, as Freya steps on a log so riddled with fungus it compresses like a Swiss roll. She wonders if the smartface can hear her thoughts, since they must be running through the headset. *Step where she steps, think in her thoughts.* No need to wonder which is the right path.

A handful of finches skitter past, twittering through each bounce of their flight. Ruby has directed her back to the brook, whose course she is tracing upstream, leaving the water when the undergrowth gets too thick. From time to time a noise will stop her, but it always turns out to be a deer bolting or a bird fleeing its branch. It is not until she is much higher, among molar-shaped rocks, that she collapses and splashes her face with pooled rainwater. As she rests, the patter of horse's hooves comes from below, and she sees a figure passing below the outcrop. Startlingly, it is the blacksmith, minus his apron but unmistakably the same lean face and smoke-smeared clothes.

'Look,' she whispers. 'He's tracking me.' So the decision to slip away was the right one. Nevertheless, she is surprised to be worth so much trouble. He did look with interest at the mark on her arm.

'Ruby,' she says, 'do you think it's strange that I've always had this tattoo thing in Yearnfeld, even before my quest was to get to the castle?' She touches it, dragging the skin closer. It could be an ink stamp, like they used at post offices when she was a child.

'It's just your character, babes.'

'But why?' Her face is reflected in the greenish water, a natural birdbath in the granite. The reply is ponderous, half shrugging.

'Just the game, I guess. The Yearnfeld algorithms are self-learning. Nobody really understands how they work any more.'

Freya chews on this like the end of a boiled sweet, dissatisfied. Climbing down, she trips on her cloak and staggers as she lands. Better get off the road, just to be safe. The important thing is to keep moving. As her breathing quickens, her mind clicks through the various ways the headset might be achieving this, such as constriction of blood vessels. She concludes, or the information is fed to her, that if your body thinks you should be panting, you pant.

That dog whistle of an alarm bell rings once more. The subject of pain. When a branch hits her shin, for instance, it registers and then is gone. Real but not uncomfortable. That is what Yearnfeld seems to be. There is just enough sensation to sustain belief, but not too much. Otherwise, she supposes, the discomforts – and full-blown agonies – of the medieval age could make the game unpleasant. It gives her a momentary wobble. *Stay in the game and keep going.* If she does not do it, no one will. But it is not hope driving her, more the need to pull a thorn.

'Turn here,' says the smartface. 'Cut up through this gully. Don't lose the stream, but stay on this higher path.' Green liquid streaks her boots, the scent of herbs infusing the air. 'Don't slip,' says the voice. 'Hold onto that tree.' Freya tries a few times to remind herself she is lying in bed, but it is getting harder.

The knife digs into her leg. It looks wonky, black with soot and very pocked, but better than no weapon at all. Here the forest becomes thinner and more tangled, every tree brazen with bare roots and low-slung branches, knees or ankles outstretched to trip her. The wrinkled roots are firm but not rigid, slightly warm to the touch. For some reason it makes her queasy. Worse, a gathering dullness denotes the fading of day. 'Don't worry,' the voice in her ear soothes. 'Darkness is your friend, and the nights are short here anyway.' She crosses a grassy clearing, leaping a brook. Then there is a sound behind her, and the voice hisses: 'Shh.'

Just as she ducks behind a tree, black hoods appear, the undergrowth rustling as they emerge. The men scour the clearing for footprints, paying particular attention to the stream. She is so near, she can hear their surprised growls, but they are not looking towards her. Instead they are drawing weapons at the sight of another figure, emerging from the trees, who has already strung his bow. His cloak is studded with leaves for camouflage, but he has undermined the effect with a yellow feather stuck in his cap.

'Get off her trail,' he snaps.

Her initial horror at seeing Sandor doubles when she realises he is also tracking her.

21

One of the bandits steps forward.

'We got as much right as you, squire.'

Sandor bristles. 'I could hear you a mile off, crashing through the forest. That's what scares the game away.' He shakes the bow for emphasis. 'It scares the game away.'

The first man's bulbous, curly hair gives him the look of a countryside labourer turned mercenary, a sheepskin vest bulking him out.

'On your way, squire,' he says, then fills his skin at the stream. He does not seem to have found any footprints, and motions his men along a rabbit path a few degrees clockwise of where Freya is hiding. The sound of them laughing quietly together echoes through the trees. Sandor remains, taking some dried meat from his knapsack. She is close enough to smell it. After he wipes his lips, he listens for a few minutes, then takes a route directly towards her. His leather boots swish through the ferns and she bites her lips together in fear. Only when he has passed does she let herself breathe, her whole body a cross-weave of tensions. She is being hunted, as though carrying an invisible magnet to which every player is drawn. It makes no sense.

'Come on,' whispers her smartface, and she forces herself up. The former jauntiness of her journey has vanished, and she concentrates on being quiet. Faces seem to appear in the moss and creepers, and arrow-shaped leaves drip onto her cloak. Converging with the upper course of the stream, she scoops up a handful of the peaty water, wishing she had taken a long drink before entering the game.

'I can't believe we've done all this in an hour.' Yearnfeld time must be very compressed. Her legs are even aching a little.

'You were kind of tied up when the timer went off.'

'What, so it's been longer?'

'A bit.'

She hoists herself over a rock. No big deal, she tells herself. No rush.

'Why didn't you tell me the timer had sounded?'

'No point, you wouldn't have left.'

True enough, yet a slight discomfort has been kindled. It takes her back to the conversations she had with Chris, about a smartface being clever enough to work out what you want and deliver it, even if it is not quite what you expect.

When the landscape changes to scree slopes and skeletal shrubs, Freya feels suddenly exhausted. 'It wasn't meant to be like this.' She is mortified to hear a note of accusation trickle into her tone. Ruby must have heard it too, since there is no response. Up here the trees twist as though fighting over a thin layer of soil. Her tunic is more ragged now, a threadbare edge just covering her mark. *They want you, or they want to kill you.* Either way, she supposes her character could be valuable to bounty hunters. Damn Yearnfeld, making things complicated.

'Let's keep moving,' Freya says bleakly. She climbs a ridge, then stands amazed. The last trees drop their tiny cones and stand back from an endless moorland, the stream leading off in a reed-marked gully. Where has all this space come from? It could be her imagination, picturing a moor from some long-ago Yorkshire holiday, except she would not visualise these oily tarns smelling of decay, the ground soft underfoot.

The lilac deepens overhead. It is one thing to gallivant through a make-believe landscape in broad daylight, quite another to do it in darkness, with the unreal also becoming invisible. She discovers not one moon but two, both a fraction less than full. In every other way, Yearnfeld replicates nature, but perhaps this anomaly is deliberate. It would be so easy to get lost here when night falls, when the fantasy grows subtle.

With no tree cover, she feels exposed. A solitary cricket can be heard, and desolation takes up residence inside her. She cannot tell if she has been here two hours or ten. Although it is possible to save the game, it seems unlikely she would come back for a second session. Better to hang on and finish what she has started. Apart from her thirst, which has dulled to a crispness at the back of her throat, no other sensations are getting through from her body. Even her thoughts happen in a far-off, unimportant place, like messages she will read later.

The granite ridge continues on her left, and at the last boulder she slumps into a cubbyhole. It is a strange experience to close her eyes in Yearnfeld, like trying to go to sleep part-way through a dream. The wind sounds like voices. She rises, still groggy, her cheek feeling the hardness of the rock. Below there are bandits, the same men as before, she is certain, but on horseback. Everything keeps happening again and again. Ruby once said that life goes in circles, and in Yearnfeld they get smaller. The men's dusky tunics flap as they trot, making no attempt to be quiet. There is an air of joviality to the group, and their laughter cuts through the evening, thin and harsh. Keeping to the shadows, Freya asks her smartface what they want.

'I don't know.'

'You don't know?' It is hard not to sound incredulous. 'I mean, do you know who they are?'

'Only if it's public,' comes the reply in dull smartface tone. 'Oh, wait . . .'

'What is it?'

'It is public.'

'So?'

'Sorry, babes, you're not going to like this.' The sheepish undertone makes Freya's heart plummet. 'Are you sure you want to know?'

If only she could grab the voice and shake it. 'Tell me.'

'These bandits are the Ottos, all eight.'

She exhales a long ribbon of fear. Stay calm. *It is only a game.* The phrase dies before reaching her lips. The reality is that she has two bodies to guard, and one is in a lawless world. A quick arc of her fingernail and a door would appear on this boulder. How desperately she wants to make it happen, to escape to the familiar snack smells of her bedroom. Yet the horses continue past the escarpment without seeing her. They canter away over the moors, and once again she has evaded detection. It is a new talent she seems to have acquired, the art of being invisible.

With some satisfaction she emerges from the rocks, the thudding of hooves having faded, though she will never get used to being followed. Was it like this for Ruby when she was being pestered by men? The thought stakes her to the ground with astonishment. Although she may have suspected her sister was being harassed, there has never been this certainty in her mind. Clear as day, she can see Ruby checking her phone as she walks, annoyed to be popping up as a pin on other people's maps, men in bars who message her to say, *I see you're passing* . . . Where did this knowledge come from? Ruby never spoke of it. Or did she, and Freya has just forgotten? Her hand goes to her avatar head, feeling the too-perfect roundness of the skull. Is the headset telling her things she doesn't know?

'Don't stop,' says the smartface. 'You're nearly there.'

Freya's mind is still muddled as she creeps from rock to rock, trying not to dislodge any loose stones.

'Careful, don't slip,' says the voice. As if she would slip. But nothing is certain in this game. Her uneasiness is growing. The smartface is supposed to have synchronised with Yearnfeld, yet there is tumbleweed where there should be information, especially regarding the castle. Is there a reason she is being kept in the dark? Instantly she feels guilty at having doubts and, fearing her thoughts might give the wrong impression, she focuses on the pale, stringy plants growing from the crevices, the rock faces ever steeper. Her burning arms heave her up and over until she is rewarded with a new viewpoint. Milky peaks shrug off the heather and stand tall, but what arrests her attention is the sight of a castle, its towers coiling cloud from the sky like candyfloss. It blends perfectly with the mountain, boulders skilfully incorporated into its fortifications.

All her misgivings turn to elation. 'We made it!' Instinctively she squints, trying to zoom in on the tower. Ruby has never felt so close. After everything that has happened, it is not such a stretch of the imagination to picture her pacing back and forth before the window, Rapunzel-like, uncertain how to escape.

Tiredness drains from her limbs and she steps into the breeze as from an old skin. The stream she has followed becomes one of many, each in its own deep-worn channel. Above her, the castle peak rises as though thrust upward with great violence, a stone plateau with pillars and crevices and precarious bulges. It is a mountain tamed; difficult to tell where rock ends and masonry begins. *Keep going*, says the voice in her head. The portcullis comes into view, a tumultuous waterfall, its plunge pool dark with moorland peat. The spray that lands on her lips tastes of blood. She pictures the water hammering down on her shoulders, tearing off her tunic and flinging it onto rocks below. Now she understands how inaccessible the castle is. Where better to keep Ruby tucked away?

'How am I supposed to get in?'

'No need to draw attention,' murmurs the smartface. 'There's a service tunnel underneath.'

She follows the smartface's directions, the weight of the castle pressing down upon her. On the battlements above she spies two sentries the size of crows, their helmets making them look inhuman. Just slip under their radar, she tells herself, into the castle and out of the game before anyone knows it. For the first time in her life, the oncoming night feels like her friend. She walks determinedly, her boots padding across the rock, hoping this back way will not be guarded. The roar of the waterfall is like distant traffic noise. She twists and turns, grateful to have the smartface as her navigator. Since she was a child, every map has put her at its centre. There was no need to know exactly where something was – she would just feed the map a name, and follow its directions. Why would she not believe her smartface if told she would find the real Ruby here, in this castle? A smartface is technology that has been designed to help. It puts her needs at the centre of the universe.

She is so close. There is masonry here, straight walls fortifying the granite roots of the castle. The edges snag her tunic. Now the battlements are out of sight, which must mean she is almost underneath. The next turn looks promising until she finds the passageway cut off by a wall of blocks. Her heart sinks. A tiny sound makes her pause, expecting a bird or falling stone. A rough hand covers her face. The sensation of it across her lips brings home the realisation that she has a body that can be pierced, skin that can be cut, and suddenly there is nothing she fears more than steel parting her flesh.

All her comforting thoughts are torn to pieces. Though her mouth is covered, her whole body screams, and her boots scrabble in the scree as she is dragged away, as her head is knocked against the wall, as she reaches this unexpected dead end.

22

The fire-dried air is flower-sweet, making her fear she has been drugged. Far away she can hear music and laughter. The flickering, as she focuses, turns into a placid blaze, flames licking at logs beneath an elaborate chimneypiece. Her head rests on the embroidery of a high-backed chair. The sense of terror, of thinking she was about to die, lingers in her emotional memory. It was mostly a fear of getting hurt. Instinctively she pinches the back of one hand, testing her pain receptors. Though her skin turns red, the best she can do is create a sensation that vanishes almost before it registers. She closes her eyes in relief. If she was not plainly still in Yearnfeld, her present level of comfort would tempt her to dismiss the whole thing as a dream.

She becomes aware of unhurried steps approaching from behind. Fingers thick with rings clamp onto the chair back.

'What do you want?'

As an intruder, she would expect this to be demanded of her, yet the tone is almost contemplative. When she turns, the first thing she notices is his black eyes, inscrutable like those of a bird. The bone structure of his face is slightly larger than normal, and an octagonal crown inset with jewels rests on his head. His mantle and robes add to the sense of breadth, flowing in black and purple to the floor, each shoulder adorned with a fan of flight feathers. His face is rugged, textured by a neatly clipped beard. As she has not replied, he emits a rumble of mirth and touches the mark on her arm.

'Forgive my clumsy guards, they were only supposed to escort you. You'd been wandering around the castle walls, and I was getting impatient.'

He helps her rise. The soft light is flattering to her clothes, hiding the mud of the forest, bringing out the warm hues of her tunic. His furs tickle as he takes her arm and leads her beneath torches in wrought-iron holders, a vaulted ceiling above. What she assumes are empty suits of armour salute with a sound like saucepans clanging. The music grows louder as they enter a hall of tremendous size. The chandelier overhead could easily encompass the blacksmith's hut, while the blazing hearth could be an entrance to the underworld. People cluster in twos or threes, murmuring *Baron*, or sometimes, *my lord*.

'You are safe here.' He links Freya's arm more closely with his. 'This is my castle, and mine the land beyond.' Every eye that settles on her is needle-sharp with jealousy, though they all wear masks. The protruding noses of bone-faced creatures turn to follow her up the room.

Once Freya is seated at a long table on a dais, the revels continue, dancers twirling with dervish-like fervour, all finely dressed and larger than life. The baron lands a satisfied pat on her shoulder and servants rush to fill her goblet. After the despondency of the mountains and the threat of the Ottos, this hospitality makes relief run through her veins. When the guards grabbed her, she was overcome with a sense of ruin, especially after being so close to achieving her goal. What shocked her most was that, even in that split second, misgivings about her smartface bubbled up before she could stop them. Her doubts come back clouded in embarrassment.

'I thought for a while we wouldn't make it,' she whispers. There is no response. 'Ruby?'

'Yeah, I know.' The reply is fur-soft.

Her ears twang as minstrels pluck their lyres. She is just wondering what to say when the chiming of a great bell sounds, and everyone stops. After twelve strikes the baron whispers, 'A little joke we have.' All the guests tear off their masks with cries of abandon and toss them into the fire, as though a climax has been reached. It occurs to Freya that this is some sort of Experience – with a capital E – some exclusive, curated night out, which she appears to be getting for free. Honey reaches her nose as servants pour mead, and the dancers resume their effortless circling. The fiddler speeds up, making them leapfrog each other in a frenzy.

'Eat, refresh yourself,' says the baron. A peacock stuffed with crab apples appears in front of her, garnished with strings of hazelnuts. She is not sure if she wants to eat, but then a pomegranate finds its way onto her plate, and before long she is trying everything. Is it taste or smell, this hybrid aroma that dances around her palate? She begins to understand the attraction of being able to eat without consuming calories, dance all night and never feel tired. The food sinks into her belly and fills it. Her host seems friendly, but she does not dare ask him about Ruby. If her sister is here, then the baron is presumably keeping her by force.

When the feast is over, he takes her hand in a delicate grip and pulls her from the table. His skin is soft and dry. Soon they are mingling with the courtiers, her host exchanging a word here and there.

'Who are all these people?' she asks the smartface, and the reply comes faintly into her mind.

'Whoa, the security here is off the charts . . . These walls are solid encryption.'

The baron turns, perhaps hearing the question. Freya tries addressing it to him.

'The great and the good,' he murmurs, smiling, 'and the not so good, of course.' He indicates someone quietly roasting a jester on a spit by the fire. Nearby, a slim courtier in a jet-black gipon is fending off serving girls who are smothering him with pink hands. 'Where else can a septuagenarian politician become a libidinous youth?' The baron laughs at his own words. 'Well, anywhere, I suppose. But here his body is up to it.' With a dark light in his eyes, he watches the courtier, who is now on the floor, moaning and struggling to escape.

'Are you saying he wants this?' Freya asks.

'Everyone gets what they want. But a little too much. It's always interesting to see what someone does when they get too much.' His companionable smile takes some of the sting out of this, giving her the sense that she is set apart from these other guests. Biting back her concerns, she makes herself squeeze his hand and asks if she can see more of the castle.

'Of course,' he says, contentment settling more firmly on his features. 'Let me show you to your room.' He escorts her up to where the minstrels are playing – drowning out the conversation – then out onto a balcony overlooking the inner bailey. Here, despite the late hour, there is a bonfire and the clash of swords. Exhausted grunts echo around the courtyard, as though some sort of endurance test is underway. The walkway roof makes it impossible to see where the towers are located.

'You are not afraid of heights?' he remarks, noticing her peering upwards.

'No, I like to be as high up as possible.'

He gives her a searching look. 'Is that so?'

In a long gallery hung with tapestries, they pass many closed doors, and Freya fights the urge to open them and explore. She picks up her feet to catch up with the baron, rewarded with the sight of a stone staircase and the words she has been waiting to hear: 'Shall we ascend the west tower?'

Every step infuses her with energy, and they climb rapidly, pausing only where a stone head dispenses wine into a basin. Amid the sensation of evaporating alcohol and red fruits, Freya feels a tug on her arm and sees the baron point to the next flight of stairs. 'Up there is the treasury,' he tells her. 'Neither cabinet ministers, nor Saudi princes, nor A-list celebrities get to see inside.' It is a shock to hear him talking about players, about the real world, scratching the delicate coating of fantasy that is forming on everything in this castle. The mark on her arm tingles, as though it is a recent tattoo, and she remembers him touching it. There must be a whole backstory to her character in Yearnfeld that she has never bothered to investigate. Yet being assigned this avatar is like reaching into a clover patch and pulling out a sprig with four leaves. A changeling is what she needed to be to get into the castle, and a changeling she is. Once again she has to shrug and accept the smartness of a smartface without quite understanding it. Nothing matters, as long as she finds Ruby.

Ruby. Like this wine, the name is vivid on her tongue and then vanishes. When she was out of the game, she could picture her sister lying on a bunk in some back room, breathing heavily with a headset nestled in her hair. The way her avatar might look in Yearnfeld never came to mind. Yet now she struggles to see Ruby as flesh and blood. All she can imagine is a nymph-like figure similar to herself, feet on the rushes of a tower room, pacing back and forth, pausing only to gaze across the mists and moorland.

They are nearly at the top. Through each leaded window she can see dizzying views, endless paths leading through the mountains; the two moons are almost on top of each other. Somewhere in her visual memory there is a residue of concrete flyovers, lizards in tanks and a pile of resin cups but they are unconvincing. A fuzziness is building in her mind. What does it mean to be a changeling?

They reach the top of the tower, an antechamber with a balcony. From the beginning her quest was leading her here, to find the person she has been seeking. The baron's figure is gigantic in the moonlight, behind him a thickly bolted door. She is waiting for him to unlock it. Instead he gestures to the gothic arches framing the night sky. 'I thought you'd appreciate the view.'

'But what about . . .'

'Oh, this is the west tower treasury, as I said.' His teeth are brilliant in the darkness. She hesitates, almost shaking.

'Can I see inside?'

A series of echoing taps signal footsteps, and the baron looks surprised to see a steward in livery emerge from the stairwell. While they converse, Freya gravitates to the door, every inch gilded, inlaid with mother-of-pearl and jet-black flowers. It may be the treasury, but it is also the highest room of the west tower. Why hasn't her smartface said anything? She lays a hand on the bolt, and finds it cold. Behind her, the baron's voice rises in irritation. The lock is a gargoyle with a keyhole mouth. Before her eyes it starts to swallow a large key.

'I need to attend to something.' The baron is at her side, opening the treasury just enough for a person to enter. Metal screeches. 'I'm sure you'll like this room; I've got some real gems in here.' He comes closer, until she can feel his breath against her ear. A powerful shove sends her spinning through the doors. 'And now a Ruby.'

23

Apart from one huge stone set into each of the eight walls, the room is an empty trinket box, its silver panels sterilising the air.

'There's nobody here.' Her tunic whips round as she twists, despairing at the echo, the slippery floor. 'Why is nobody here? You told me she'd be in this room. Didn't he just say Ruby was in here?' There is complete silence. 'Why don't you answer?' Some part of her crisps up with fear, but the rest is light-headed with wine, or lack of water. There is an absence where the voice used to be, as though it has been switched off, or the treasury has lead-lined walls. 'Ruby,' she cries, and the sound ricochets. How could her smartface let this happen? The tower room is a prison, its window bars thick as ribs. She flattens her hands against one wall, feeling her way round. With difficulty she identifies the subtle crack of the door.

'Ruby! Did you want me to be left here on my own?' she shouts, pressing close to the metal. She tries punching and kicking the silver, then batters it with the flats of her hands. The hollow boom of the plate is taking her to a place in her mind she dreads. *It should have been me, pounding on the side of a van, half drugged and unable to escape.* The reflection in the metal warps her face, and she backs away in fright. The vibrating floor is just her own body trembling. She can imagine the smartface in her head, reassuring her earnestly that she has nothing to worry about. But when was Ruby ever earnest? What if the smartface looked back on Ruby's life and calculated she was no longer alive? What if it converted Freya's guilt, however overstated, into cold, hard fact?

She buries her head in her hands. The silence is roaring with voices, all those of her smartface, re-enacting her phone call, the words Esther said about not coming back in the dark, about trust, and Freya ruining everything with her selfish need to get out of her boring little skull. *I came out to get you*, the voice says. *Now you have come to get me.* It screams in her ear, in the silence of the cut-off call. *You loved gaming so much. Now you can stay here for ever.*

Her knees give way. The mark on her arm is blurring. A pinch does not arrest its disintegration. It was all a trick. Her smartface has led her here for one purpose. For Ruby's sake, it is taking revenge.

She needs to get out.

Crawling to the wall, she scratches with a fingernail, trying to draw a door. Her movements become feverish. It should be easy, hardly more than a thought. She tries the knife,

273

certain its sturdy blade will draw a scratch. But, as though enchanted, the silver remains pristine. So that is the beauty of the treasury. It is a holding cell, and it leaves her prone in the apartment with no food or water.

There is a bed right here, soft pillows under her neck, at home in London; she whispers it again and again, curling into a ball. Time passes, for what it is worth. Yearnfeld time. It could be that she is imagining it, that she is dreaming of hours passing, or that it has only been a few seconds. What is certain is that the pain will last for ever, the knowledge that Ruby at twenty-four never really liked her, never loved her like a sister. It was all pretence. Tears soak her perfect skin. Her beautiful avatar in a heap on the floor, long hair curling over her shoulders, metal icy on her legs. It was pure fantasy, the idea that she could come home and Ruby would say, *Don't worry, we're good*. Nothing but make-believe ever since.

Her head lolls and her reflection follows. It looks antique, shadows of tarnish where the metal is not perfectly flat. The expression catches her unawares, a tweak of the brow that could at first look mean, until her mouth turns wryly to match it; eyes restless. It brings her to her feet, closer to the mirror. He called her *Ruby*, which means either he is in collusion with her smartface, or he really does think she is a changeling of that name. It is all so confusing. The longer she looks at the reflection and then down at herself, the more she struggles to remember what she used to be like, before all this began. Could she be like her sister, just for a moment? Her fingers climb to her scalp. Ruby could get out of anything. No fear, no hesitation. Just make tracks. Life is too short to worry about consequences, to fear a tremendous shock to the nervous system, a blood rush, a haemorrhage. It's just a case of getting hold of these bits of titanium. She grits her teeth, reaching under her hair. She might be starting to feel something, a curl of metal on her scalp, when a bird alights on the windowsill above. A crow, rook or raven too dark to distinguish. It stands between two bars, as though contemplating the space between. Her avatar body is thin. Perhaps there is another way.

Taut as a wire, she is reaching for the sill, toes teetering on a knife edge where two panels meet, when the door opens. The baron fills the space in his feathery mantle, letting out a cry. A second later her legs are yanked from the wall and she tumbles to the ground at his feet, puzzled to see his features – so serene earlier – contorted with rage.

'Do you know how high up we are?' he bawls.

She struggles as he holds her wrist, lifting her like some animal he has caught.

'Where are you?' she wails into the ether.

'Where is who?'

'I can't hear her.' She fails to escape his grip, her voice echoing hollowly around the chamber. 'Why can't I hear her?'

He lifts her arm higher, something brutish in his eyes. 'Voices in your head? Or should I say demons!' Servants run in at his call. 'We have a changeling possessed.' Her wrists come together as he hands her over to two swarthy guards. They take her knapsack and check her for weapons, but fail to notice the knife in her belt.

'The dungeons, my lord?' one asks.

'No, here, but secure her.' A chair is fetched and seconds later she is bound to it, immobile in the middle of the room. A knot bites into her arms. She curses herself for lacking judgement, for not keeping quiet.

As the men are dismissed, she is surprised to see a smile on his lips. With an air of chivalry he smoothes down the corner of her tunic where it rumpled in the skirmish. 'I didn't count on your reckless disregard for your own safety,' he remarks, an odd note of approval in his voice.

'What do you want?'

'Ah, that's my line.' He stalks about the room, and she can hear the bristling as he rubs his beard. Clapping a hand on each knee, he sinks into another chair that has appeared. 'What does this voice in your head say to you?' Freya shrugs, wondering what will make him let her go. As though sensing this, he adds, 'Just be honest.'

'It helps me.'

'Helps you with what?' He leans towards her. 'A quest, perhaps? A rescue mission?'

So he knows.

'I came to get Ruby.' The plated walls close in around them. She dreads where this is going.

'Of course you did,' he says. 'But why here? Can't this voice tell you where she is . . . out there?'

His fanning fingers indicate something overarching, and she realises with shock that he is referencing Ruby's location in the real world. Everything beyond the game has become faint in her mind, and bringing it back into focus feels uncomfortable, even inappropriate.

'No.'

'Have you asked?'

'Of course.'

'They are clever, these voices. Are you sure it can't help you?'

What is he getting at? A strange shiver comes over her, as though she is back with her mum at the police station, answering questions again and again.

'It said she was here.'

'Forget that. What about out *there*?'

Her heart crumples. 'There's nothing out there. Don't you think I didn't ask a thousand times? That I wouldn't do anything . . . anything to find her? What's it to you?' Smashed-up sensations of coffee shops, Medieville streets and greenzones return to her, all the months of searching, trying to get inside Ruby's head and work it out from there. Nothing came of it except this meagre breadcrumb, the last clue in the world she wanted to follow. Is she now speaking to a real person, or some self-aware part of the game in league with her smartface? Is this a test? Freya rattles the chair. 'Where is she?'

Her fruitless but frenzied struggle seems to soothe him.

'Now, now.' He holds up an imperious hand, but she won't be calm.

'Is she here or not?'

'Not,' he says briskly.

'Then it was all a trap.'

'Oh please, why would your smartface want to trap you?'

Smartface. The word is strange on his lips. He is morphing every moment into something she does not understand. The room echoes eerily around them. He leans in, as though they are having a pleasant chat over tea. 'You are such a fascinating guest. I've wanted you here for a while.'

'Then where did the rumour come from?'

'Forget about that.'

'But we heard she was here.'

'I said forget it.' He gets up restlessly, opening his arms into an expansive shrug. 'One tiny white lie, fed into the cloud, isn't going to do anyone any harm. Besides, one man's falsehood is another's truth.'

Her limbs stiffen painfully. It dawns upon her that she has got it all wrong. He has done this. He has lured her here, not Ruby.

'So it was you. You said she was—'

'In the tower treasury, yes.' He smiles, and she resents his joke: a ruby in the treasury. It is along the same lines as a masquerade in which everyone is already an avatar. 'I wanted to see if you could get here, and you did. Since you were in Medieville already, it was too good an opportunity to miss.' The pacing stops, and he regains his regal poise. This is no ordinary end-of-level boss. He knows too much.

'Who are you?' Her gaze is razor-sharp, trying to dissect him.

'Tell me, what was it like, hearing her?' He is swaying closer.

'Whoever you are, it's my smartface and my business.'

He laughs, yet a soft bitterness enters his voice. 'Oh-ho! Your smartface and your business? Was it *your* birthday present?' He tenses up in the moonlight, unable to stop the realisation detonating on her face. A long, shell-shocked silence follows.

'Thalis?' The name is loaded with disbelief. Somewhere behind this rugged, lordly figure is the scent of aftershave, sleeves joined with cufflinks in the shape of @ signs, a take-away flat white going cold on a desk. The fact that she is facing him with hands bound is annoying, humiliating and utterly hysterical. A hiccuping laugh escapes her lips. 'You've got to let me go,' she says at last. 'I'm thirsty.' Everything tells her he will now look suitably embarrassed and untie her, but he is frozen. His head twitches, like a glitch. He is an actor who has gone off-script.

'I have no counterpart out there,' he lies.

'Just untie me.' There is no way they can have a conversation while she is roped to a chair in an online game.

'No one. *Nemo*. I don't exist.' The dramatic warble is unconvincing.

'Do it now and I won't tell.'

He slams his hand against a silver panel, the cymbal crash making her teeth rattle.

'I can fling you out of the game with such force that you won't remember your own *name*,' he hisses, making her shrink. His hand curls into a fist, then relaxes. 'But that won't be necessary, will it? Because we want the same thing. You're on a journey, and I can help you.' His robes make slithering sounds against the floor as he goes round behind her, making her nervously crick her neck. 'True, I was angry, I was furious when I found you'd intercepted Julian's smartface. I had high hopes of getting him off the porn. We used to run together . . .' His face darkens. 'Then the haptic suit . . . petrol on the flames. I should break your neck just for that.'

Her breathing falters as she realises how intensely personal

279

this is. They are no longer playing a game. The chair is in danger of tipping over backwards. Something sharp in her belt slides down against her wrist.

'Can we talk outside Yearnfeld?' She tries to keep her voice steady.

'What's wrong with Yearnfeld?' The growl startles her. 'Don't you like my castle? Do you have any idea how people queue and beg for an invitation – people who matter?' He stalks the walls, jaw working as though to dislodge the after-taste of some other conversation. 'I thought the game was a valuable acquisition – a way around the blind spot of Medieville – but nobody can see it.'

It is clear she has touched a nerve. Only now does she recall that Thalis, when not on a charm offensive, has an ego as unpredictable as a game of snakes and ladders. She finds herself growing angry.

'But you said my sister was in the game.' Did he have no regard for the pain it would cause, or was that his object?

Moonlight stripes the floor. Though his face is in shadow, she can see he has regained his composure, even some of his former self-satisfaction. 'Look at the way you are talking! When we first met, you could hardly meet my eye. Julian ejected you into the box-room without a squeak of protest. What was it he used to call you? Nine parts mouse, or something?'

Hardly believing what she is hearing, she squirms violently in the chair. The rope is secure, but the knife is now gripped between her fingers. Thalis looks at her keenly. 'Have you considered that there could be a grain of truth in my rumour, that your smartface was not lying when she said you would find Ruby?'

She throws him a scathing look. If her hands were free she would indicate the sterile room. Instead they work up and down, a useless burn of friction.

'Look,' she says, 'let's talk in the real world. I'll buy coffee. I'll get the haptic suit back from Julian and package up the smartface just as it was.'

His head tilts. 'I wanted that at first, before I realised how beautifully, how organically it was working. You don't get it, do you?' He throws up his arms. 'That's another thing they don't appreciate – my beta model, my smartface "nudge". They know the web is completely peer-based, they know everyone lives in an echo chamber of their own personality. Yet they're reluctant to put the two together.' This thought seems to lift him, and he hovers around her, as though she is some gift yet to be unwrapped.

'I'm not sure I understand.' She twists coyly to one side, making more room for the blacksmith's knife.

'When I saw you'd taken it . . .'

'Been given it.'

'. . . when I realised Julian was not going to benefit from a voice inspiring him to take bigger and better steps out into the world, I was going to shut down the feeds. Then I noticed the shift in your data.'

The knife saws up and down. He has passed behind her twice and each time she was certain he would see the blade and pounce. 'What business is it of yours?'

'Data is my business,' he says briskly. 'Decisions are dead, as you know. The smartface has all your data from birth, everything you've ever said and done. It is much better qual-ified to say what a person like you would do. Your identity is curated . . . Are you listening?' Her head, lolling as she concentrates, jerks back up. He goes on. 'But say you steal a "nudge" model from your ex-boyfriend.'

'I didn't—'

'It defaults to an aspirational personality.' His eyes glisten with enthusiasm. 'Just imagine having someone you admire beside you, every request going through them. You like getting their approval, you're keen to agree, you pick up their phrases, their likes and dislikes. Their data influences yours . . . pretty soon you're living inside a whole new echo chamber.'

The rope is fraying. She will need to be quick. It will not be easy to find the nodes on her scalp before he catches her.

'Of course, there are different flavours of people,' he continues. 'You might admire someone who is a layabout, and that would make you lazier. Julian could easily have picked the wrong kind of person, but I was counting on him skipping the settings. I had already programmed it to default to a personality that would inspire confidence and activity.' He shoots her a look. 'So that's what you got too, and who'd have thought you'd get Ruby?'

Even with only half her attention on his words, she dislikes hearing him say her name, shaking his head in amusement. Perhaps this really is a game to him. Through the window, she sees the moons, both risen so they are only a hair's breadth apart. Thalis seems to notice too, his voice softening. 'The pace was ahead of any trials. In part, it is Ruby ticking all the boxes: she is someone you admired, someone you wanted to be, an older sister of your own choosing, yet considerably different from you.'

It is as though he has cracked open a safe in her skull and is letting himself inside.

'Please,' she begs. 'Let's talk outside the game.'

'No,' he snaps. 'The game is instrumental, don't you see? You've crossed half a virtual world, you who used to go dizzy at the thought of it. Plus this smartface syncs with Yearnfeld – every turn of your quest rewards the right behaviours.' He fixes wild eyes upon her. 'I want to see if you can go all the way.'

'Can we just—'

'I want to see if I can sell identities like shoes.' His hands cup the heel of an imaginary slipper. 'My family were shoe-makers, you know, back in Nova Scotia.' Animated by this idea, he slides onto the floor and seizes her buskins. 'If you step into her shoes, Ruby *is* here in the tower. The Halo can finish what the smartface started.'

Horrified, she tugs her feet as though from quicksand. The chamber spins as the chair falls, her hair everywhere. This man cannot be Julian's father, and she cannot be here in this nightmare.

'Ruby was my sister,' she cries, stumbling over the past tense. 'A different person.' The silver floor smells unbearably surgical.

'I've sent your data to hundreds of virtual job interviews.' He is relentless. 'Run it through thousands of matchmaking sites. Your ratings are way up. You have an appeal you never had before. It surprised me – frankly, I thought you'd been under a rock too long.' He makes it sound as though she has been upgraded. The thought of being powerless as her iden-tity pings around the globe leaves her queasy.

'Let me out of here.'

'You're going nowhere; you may as well relax.' He crouches so his mouth is by her ear. 'Admit it. You've hardly needed the smartface. You know what it will say. Go with it and you'll look better, talk better . . . nothing will ever faze you again.' Feathers brush her face. 'Why did you admire her so much anyway? Isn't it because she knew how to live, to really *live*?'

The rope is a thread, but even if she breaks it, there will be no time to get away. The urgency clutching at her chest is Ruby's need for freedom at any cost. In the shiny wall, she can see her sister, feel her strength like liquid iron inside: the turn of her head, a spark-bright intelligence, raw and restless, and knowing, for one astonishing instant, the ferocity of her own independence. The knife makes more sense now. Her scalp is prickly, as though it has pins and needles. Are these her thoughts?

'One man's game is another's reality.' He has risen alongside her and reaches out to test the texture of her hair, gemstone rings clinking. 'Real life is just an option for you now. You can have an amazing job right here and be Ruby all day long; you can even look like her. You'll never be nine parts meek again.'

It is so sudden, when she plunges the knife into his chest, that no cry is dragged from his throat. Up close, she hears the thump of it, feels a hot spurt of blood on her arm. But it is nothing to the look on his face, horror mingling with incredulity, staring down at his front until his coat starts to tangle, his feet shuffle backwards. She pulls the dagger free. *One part mad.* He never saw it coming, of that she is certain.

284

Even in the moonlight the knife is a black cut-out, no glint of metal, completely invisible to Thalis. Now there is ample red ink on the floor, and drawing a door is a mere flick of her wrist. The night blows away and she feels bed-sheets under her fingertips, a ceiling above. There is a sense of separation. It makes her think of mitosis, of chromosomes pulling apart.

She finds herself yearning for the face she could see, for a split second, in the silver.

24

Sensation returns slowly. There is still no feeling in her arms. Only when she tries to rise does the pain clasp her head, as though her brain has shrunk, a dry, pulling pain that makes her cease all movement until it has passed. Then a violent knocking begins, setting it off all over again. There is a voice, loud and unregulated: 'Freya!' The hammering continues. Whoever is calling, she wishes they would go away. It does not matter what day it is or what time, only that she is a pale, fragile creature who needs to stay perfectly still.

'Freya!' The door is thrust open. 'I'm coming in.'

At the edge of her vision, grubby white sports socks appear. The smell of vitamin foams grows as he kneels beside her. 'What's up? You were screaming . . .'

She closes her eyes. He lifts her right hand and pinches the loose skin on top.

'Wait a sec.'

Hearing taps running in the bathroom makes her throat hunger for moisture, and when he reappears with a pint glass, it is enough to make her sit up. For the first time, water seems to have a taste, fragrant and delicious. Julian watches her drink, looking puzzled. Then his eyes alight on a spindly metal object lying between them. 'Is that my headset?' Freya continues to drink noisily. He picks it up. 'What are you doing with this?'

'I borrowed it. Sorry.'

'You borrowed a Halo headset?' He makes it sound like a toothbrush.

'You borrowed my haptic suit.'

The frown remains on his face. 'But this is a headset.'

She cradles the pint glass, folding her arms over her knees, and shrugs. 'Sorry, you weren't using it.'

'I was never going to use it. I was going to sell it. Do you know what these things do?'

As usual, he is right. Something in her head still feels messed-with, as though someone has been in there rearranging the furniture. She is starting to comprehend what a Halo headset really is, how it interfaces between her brain and the cloud. It even seemed as though there was a small backwash of brainwaves, some hidden message that said: *You are Ruby. Look down, those are her legs, you walk like her, talk like her . . . go with it.*

'Take it.' She pushes the headset into his hands.

'What have you been up to anyway?' His voice is tetchy. He untangles the nodes that have become crossed over. 'Playing some game? I thought you didn't like them, and you've been there for what, thirty hours?'

She puts aside the huge shock this delivers.

'I don't need lectures from a porn addict.'

'Porn?' There is a pause, his lips moving slightly as though turning this over and tasting it. He looks surprised to be confronted, then annoyed. 'Life is shit, and I'm a guy. It's not a big deal.' He sits obstinately on her bed, and she understands that he is waiting for something. Like his father, he is used to getting what he wants. It comes back to her slowly, the way she would always reach out to him, take the hit and end the argument. But those days are gone.

'Did you ever think about how I'd feel?' she says. 'Being replaced.'

'You weren't replaced.'

'And it is a big deal. We're still living together.'

'Yeah, but only as housemates.' He folds his arms, picking at his scabby elbow. 'Why do you care?'

'Maybe I don't any more.' The force in her voice startles them both. Julian backtracks to the door.

'All you care about is your smartface, right?' A note of malice enters his voice. 'She came to me. Did I tell you that? She met me there, where you'd never go. I think she wanted me to hang out with her, God knows why. That's why I was confused, hearing her voice from your room. I came looking for that other girl.'

That other girl.

She gasps, full of pain and betrayal. Why would her smartface manifest to Julian? She snatches the red sphere from her shelf, tempted to press the little button and see if it lights up and reboots. Though desperate for answers, she bites her lip and goes after Julian instead.

'What was she doing?' Freya demands. 'Did she talk about me?'

He dangles languidly from his door handle with a self-satisfied smile. But then he registers the haunted look on her face and seems to realise what a blow he has struck. His voice softens.

'Constantly. That's how I knew who she was meant to be.' He is shrugging, telling her it was nothing. 'Disappointing actually: she just teased me and wasted my time.'

The corridor is narrow, but they are separated by a wasteland. In the distance, she can see the face she once knew so well. He exhales a sugary breath, one addiction giving him energy for the other. Now she understands a little better how he may have ended up this way, with a father fixated on the contents of more important people's skulls.

'That sounds like her,' she says.

They nod to each other and he vanishes, and Freya wonders whether she should have said anything about his dad. As far as conflict goes, her circuits are blown. She sinks shakily onto the bed. Did she really do it? The rust smell of blood still lingers, and she flexes her right hand to dispel the disturbing sensation of a knife going into flesh. Easy to forget how gory Yearnfeld can be, players slicing and dicing each other. She hardly knew she was striking until the blade was in his chest. If it did give him a shock, he deserved it. Thanks to him, she has a banging dehydration headache. But the worst of it was using Ruby's name. It all floods back, making her twist the duvet so tightly a ripping sound is heard. He did it for his own purposes, so casually, baiting his line with this incongruous shred of hope – the only shred there has ever been. It has numbed her deep inside. There will be no more hope. The split in the duvet widens and greasy polyester spills out.

What happens if you are killed in Yearnfeld anyway? She must have wondered this for a second while wearing the headset, because the answer comes to mind: you simply start the game again. So nothing. A mere knock to his ego. The fury lifts her, makes her pace up and down the room. Then she remembers the look on his face when she saw through his ridiculous 'baron' charade. He didn't like that.

'Open Social,' she says, after a pause. Learning to ask for things, when she is so used to having her needs anticipated, will take some time. 'Bumped into someone I know in Yearnfeld,' she dictates, watching her words appear on the wall, along with suggested images. 'Thalis . . .' his handle pops up and she nods to select it, 'or the BARON, has an amazing castle there. The castle in the cloud. So cool!' A smile closes her lips. That is probably enough. By sending her data all over the globe, he made her feel naked. Now he can have a taste of that medicine. Already she can feel the storm of comments gathering as people locked onto his moniker pick up the mention. It will ruffle some feathers, and he'll be livid at having his cover blown, but she does not care. The stab was merely self-defence. This is revenge.

Satisfied, she throws on a cardigan, feeling a sudden urge to get out of this small room, out of the flat. Daylight has never been so bright, but she takes big gulps of it, fascinated to taste the air currents of the city, laced with sandwich lunches and distant pollution, rather than the perfumes of the castle. Her headache at first ratchets up to a throbbing agony, then subsides as she sips a bottle of water. It was Wednesday when she went into Yearnfeld, and it is now well into Thursday. Odd to think of people at work, to imagine robots behind the serving counter at U-Home, asking customers whether they want gravy.

She goes towards Kensal Green, stepping over puddles with sweet wrappers floating on them. The map-line is normally so fine-tuned it helps her evade other pedestrians. Without her smartspecs she has to dodge a pregnant woman talking to herself, two schoolboys on hoverboards, and a girl in a wheelchair, who looks up as though stargazing. Compared to the people in Yearnfeld, everyone is wonky, pockmarked, scruffy.

Thinking it might make her feel more like herself, she ducks into a large coffee shop. It is comforting to watch passers-by through the window condensation amid the tapping of portafilters, the chatter and splutter of foaming milk, which paradoxically soothes her head. Soon she is part of the furniture, and it is almost too mundane. People go to the counter, fill their cups and leave. A woman younger than Freya irritates other customers by brushing past them towards a table, deep in conversation with friends who are obviously in New York or somewhere very exciting. Her laughter is supernaturally loud and she embraces someone invisible. Then she stops. Her face falls. A long fingernail jabs the air.

'It's gone. Where the fuck has it gone?' She lurches towards a passing barista, grabbing his shirt, and shouts, 'Where has it gone?'

The man looks at her from dark, exhausted eyes, shaking his head. 'Lady, lady, I ain't part of the show.'

Embarrassed, she pulls her lemon scarf up to cover her face.

'Sorry,' she says. But a moment later she has forgotten about him and is back exclaiming in the midst of her unseen circle, showing off a smartbit studded with pink gems and barely noticing the premium 'hand-crafted' coffee placed in front of her, along with an almond slice. Freya can smell the marzipan, but is surprised to find she has no appetite. The cakes are play food, the beverages just an idea.

Baristas bang out the filters and refill them, then bang them out again into a compost heap of fragrant grounds. It is almost hypnotic. Someone passes carrying a tart on a tray, and the smell is a fruity chocolate that carries her straight back to the Seville orange 'mud pie' she sampled in a coffee shop long ago. On this occasion, her sister was sitting opposite in huge sunglasses, hair wrapped in a purple scarf. Freya was messaging Terri about the party, but Ruby had left her devices at home and was talking about boys, one of her favourite subjects. Singleminded is good for all kinds of things, she was telling Freya. Like the pie, her tone may have been on the bitter side. Virtually everyone is on Singleminded. You can scan someone in the street and see if they are single, whether they are looking and what they are into. It's kind of naughty, she added, because it also scrapes the web for photos with a high proportion of flesh tones. If you see someone on Singleminded, you see whatever there is to see, plus their track record, ratings and reviews from former partners. Certain 'super-users' are approaching celebrity status . . . But so what? Freya did not understand what this had to do with her sister, or why she thought her profile might attract attention. There were only a couple of men Ruby had properly dated, and when they were gleefully pointed out, neither looked much like a soap actor or billionaire. Luckily, Ruby's version of worrying was over before it began. A second later she was giggling at herself, leaping from her chair to get another shot of hazelnut syrup and pay the bill.

'Excuse me, miss?' A barista has his hands on his hips. He looks a bit like Chris, close up, though she realises he is the harassed figure who was pinned against the wall a few minutes earlier.

'Hey.'

'You're going to need to buy something, I'm afraid.'

'Oh.' She stands instinctively and pretends to ponder the chalkboard of drinks. There is no point putting on her specs; they would only flash up an overdraft warning. From the corner of her eye, it appears the barista is sneaking a look at her figure. She pulls at a lock of hair and twirls it. 'Oh no, I forgot – I'm locked out of my account,' she says. 'You couldn't do me a favour, let me set up a tab or something? I'm just round the corner.'

For a moment she thinks he will relent, but his face fails to break into a smile. 'Sorry.'

She gathers up her coat and hurries out. In the tepid breeze she thrusts her fingers into her hair, furiously massaging her skull. 'A favour,' she mutters. 'What the hell?' She feels so awful that her thumb wants to encounter a line of metal behind her ear, a visor that could be removed to take her out of this scene. The trouble with Yearnfeld is that it starts to make reality seem like a choice. If things are not going well, you can take off your headset and emerge in the outer world. What troubles her most about trying her luck with the barista is that it came naturally; she was on autopilot. Her feet slither on spilled kebabs and suddenly she realises this is the wrong way, no option but to retrace her steps. What she wouldn't give for a headscarf and some sunglasses to help her slip past the coffee shop undetected. Instead the fogged-up window flashes, 'Howdy, Freya,' and puffs out the smell of her favourite dark roast.

There is something depressing about these front gardens, recycling bins and flaky gates stretching on for ever. She fumbles in her bag for specs, desperate for distraction but not quite ready to confront the smartface, should it appear. 'Off,' she says quickly, just in case. The device is silent as she arranges it across her ears. There are several messages from her mum, mostly about the smartbit, which has been remade. She sounds faintly anxious, no doubt keen to smooth over their prickly exchange. Freya puts off replying, checking Social instead. There she finds promotions for the Black Hole, hidden London, orchid-purple stockings, hazelnut waffles and US holidays. As the wind slides cool fingers under her collar, she realises Thalis was right. She has changed. But how is it possible? Though she only awoke from the game earlier that morning, it is already half a dream. Some part of her is starting to wonder if its strangely personal nature was caused by the headset. Did she really feel like Ruby for a split second, or was it just the effect on her brain-waves? Freya yawns, remembering she is fatigued. Lonely, too, without the voice that has sometimes echoed, sometimes foreshadowed her thoughts in recent weeks.

This walk has been a loop bringing her back to the apartment she tried to leave only an hour ago, like a circle of hell. She stares at the door, seeing her reflected face looking so pale she wonders if the door will even recognise it – but it does. Her legs are reluctant to step inside, as though she might find silvery walls and Thalis clamping shoes to the ground saying, *Step into them: your sister is dead and has no need of her personality. One man's garbage* . . . and so on. A judder runs through her body. The thought is so sordid, she cannot be in the same room with it.

In the kitchen, the fridge is full of colourful jellies, like jewels. The baron is more or less paying the rent on this apartment. He can come and badger her to be his case study whenever he likes, and now she has made him angry. Posting on Social has only made things worse.

She drinks as much iced water as her stomach can hold, and packs a few of her favourite clothes into a bag.

25

Why spend time standing on flat surfaces, among straight lines, when most of the country soars and dives at crazy angles, banking up to whale humps of greenery, then down to V-shaped valleys? The broad windscreen of the smartbus gives a good view of the surrounding farmland, like a slow documentary with the biodiversity limited to cows, magpies, pigeons and distant gulls, excluding roadkill. The only other passengers are three kids, sitting at the back, whose murmurings take the edge off the silence. Through the vents she gets a whiff of manure and mown grass, a thousand times better than Julian's vitamin-foam breath. She inhales deeply, then realises that what she is actually smelling is weed being smoked behind her. They will never get away with it, unless the olfactory sensors of the bus are out of order, but they are trying their luck, puffing discreetly out of the window.

The bus ride has been long – longer than the train – but

pleasant, and it was all she could afford even after extending her overdraft. Gayle has not yet replied to her messages, but in the countryside reception can be patchy. Maybe it is unconventional to show up out of the blue, but they did talk about a visit. After that last trip to Medieville they were in contact occasionally, but Freya is ashamed to remember how much she was letting her smartface take over what she called *friend maintenance* at the time. Right now she needs Gayle's carefree shrugs, her rocking-chair voice and homemade booze. Hopefully – she squeezes her eyes shut – there will be a greeting of pleased astonishment, an arm outstretched to hook round her shoulders and muddy boots tramping her into the village.

In the next market town, the central cross is hung with a faded poppy wreath. It is like being back in Lincolnshire, except for the aura of wealth clinging to these houses, the shady, exclusive look created by poplars and box hedges, masonry mushrooms and security gates. Through the bus windows, the sunshine is converted to a warming infrared, and before long Freya is lulled to sleep, dreaming of the row of pastel-coloured huts on Lyme Regis beachfront. She is not sure how long she dozes, but waking happens in the form of an enormous splutter and jerk forward. The teenagers behind her fall silent, then burst out laughing. Fogged and bleary, Freya sees the bus is pulling into a two-lane station. A good thing she awoke. The kids throw themselves down the aisle, shooting her sly smiles and sniggering at their own impressions of her strange noise.

She follows them onto the concrete, unfolding her smart-specs. The postcard has become crumpled in her pocket.

Iona Village, it is called. A very short address. Her specs want her to take a forestry commission path. With cars whizzing by, she stands on the pavement unable to decide between the country track or the route by road. At the last cottage she spins on her heel and turns back, then changes her mind and continues, cursing herself. If she has a muscle for making decisions, it is weak and flabby. The yearning for Ruby's voice redoubles. There is a red dot at the bottom right of her smartspecs projection, the icon of the smartface pulsing like a tiny heart. It wants to be opened, but she drags it carefully into a subfolder, out of sight.

The village sign is splashed with grit and coming loose. Further on, the trail begins with a sun-faded map of local walks. Mud was not something she factored in when she pulled on these ankle boots. Where the track turns gooey, she has to pick her way round the edges. A few times she hears a clap of leaves or a twig snapping, and instinctively glances behind. But there is no one on the path. With plastic water bottles and crisp packets nestling in the brambles, there is no danger of mistaking this for the tangled, ethereal forest of Yearnfeld. Yet there is something reassuring about these oily puddles and the lingering bus-exhaust vapour; the coppiced trees are too messy to impress, and the canopy rustles companionably.

Civilisation is soon left behind, and after several minutes Freya is astonished to find her back getting damp, though this walk is nothing to the distances she covered so effortlessly in the game. The track continues, the forest breathing out its fungal spores. Reception is poor, though her map-line never wavers. Something catches her eye; with alarm Freya recognises the power-low warning. Batteries last so long these days she hardly thought about charging the specs before the journey. A socket is always an arm's length away. There was one beside every seat on the bus, yet she never took advantage. No one told her to.

She pinches the specs, widening her eyes so the route zooms out, trying to memorise the turns of the pink line. The projection lasts long enough to take her through a kissing gate and diagonally across a field. Then it dies, leaving her with the unusual sensation of titanium sitting uselessly across her ears. She takes off the specs and jabs the power button a few times, her stomach gravelly with apprehension. The clouds thicken. She looks around, trying to remember the way. Where was the blue squiggle of the stream?

The countryside stretches out in muddy tussocks, offering nothing. *Give me information*, she wants to yell at the lichen-crusted tree trunks, the cowpats buzzing with horseflies. Is she meant to skirt this field or cut across? The worn grass is no help: she tries one trail, loses it and returns to the boundary. The next gate leads to more farmland. Adrenaline keeps her moving, but now the fields seem endless, her walk is more of a stumble and the way back could be in any direction. The cool of evening is descending, fear tight in her throat. What do people do, left out here? The only option is to keep going or, she supposes, curl up eventually and sleep. How warm does it have to be for sleeping in the open? Do people freeze to death? She pulls her small jacket tighter and ignores her aching feet.

The last clouds turn yellow-grey and are chased away by the wind, leaving one or two of the brighter stars. At the next stile she sinks. The ground is tacky, soft as modelling clay just here, where many boots have jumped down. She no longer cares if her clothes get dirty. What is the best plan, go back to the bus station? It must be miles. She would trade her dead smartspecs and any amount of money, if she had it, for a signpost staked into the mud. When you take away the smart, what is left? She does not even have a smartbit to tell her if she is going to survive the night.

Amid insect-rustling and the last notes of birdsong, she leans against the stile, rubbery fingers struggling with the zip of her bag. The first clothing she can extract is a pair of red socks that her mum knitted years ago from extremely thick wool, perfect as temporary gloves. When her shivering abates, she tries to amuse herself by tossing pebbles into a foot-shaped puddle. *Plop*. The noise is mesmerising. Then there are no more stones and she is forced to look at the moon, nearly full, a ping-pong ball in black water. Why is she here? She never goes anywhere without planning it, and the idea of showing up at Gayle's, especially if her messages have gone astray, now seems absurd. In the glorious, mad dash away from the flat, common sense was left behind.

As she looks down at her bent knees, wiggling her cold fingers into the socks, the gathering darkness threatens trickery. The headset hangover creeps back: that toxic sensation of looking down at someone else's body. An age has passed since she ran to catch the bus, not thinking to tell her mum or anyone else where she was going. In this trackable world, she cannot be tracked. It is what she always secretly hoped Ruby had done.

She has run away.

The moon has a white-frost shell, and a numbness begins to encase her own arms and legs. Just when her eyes are starting to close, a pair of walking boots land in the mud in front of her, so huge they seem to belong to a giant. A cry is shaken from her throat. She backs away into a hawthorn hedge.

'Ohh!' The man looks down. 'You nearly gave me an 'eart attack.'

He is not as large as she thought at first, though he does have big feet. She can just make out a thin beard edging his wild-eyed face, an aroma of wheat beer as he clutches his chest and wheezes out a cloud of steam.

'I'm lost,' she croaks.

'You know you're sittin' in the mud?' His tone is quizzical, faintly chiding. They stare at each other warily. He offers a hand, then pulls it back. 'You want to stay there?'

She manages to clamber to her feet. 'Obviously not.'

'All righty.' He makes use of the hand to shake hers, a bit limply. There is a look of amusement on his face. 'Fancy a drink?'

'I'm trying to get to Iona Village; do you know where it is?' Or any hotel, she would add, if her smartaccount were not in the red. He puts a hand on the stile as he dislodges one boot from the mud, seeming a little drunk, but his face lights up.

'Ah, it's your lucky day.' He takes her elbow and almost lifts her over the puddle, setting off with long strides, throwing back odd comments she can't really hear, but which seem to be mainly about alcohol percentages. The pace is knocking the breath out of her, but when she gets over the next stile and through a little copse, she is relieved to see this is the home stretch. The village glows softly ahead, only a few hundred metres away. They pass several chicken coops, and from somewhere there is the stamp of hooves in a stable. She wonders if this is some sort of community farm, all homemade yoghurt and threadbare armchairs.

A thwack, and her forehead is zinging. The black glass rebounds and she staggers.

'Did you just walk into that?' the man laughs. She rubs the painful bridge of her nose, now able to see her reflection in the glass and, beyond, children's toys strewn on a dark floor. Her companion must have sidestepped the edge of this near-invisible home extension, but she did not follow closely enough. Rubbing the bruise away, a fleeting sensation of her pillow at home comes to mind, the feathery microbe-built strata that would normally be cushioning her head.

'This is the worst night of my life,' she murmurs, though the man does not hear. They pass a block marked *Greywater recycling*, and suddenly she recognises the houses on the postcard, almost Scandinavian with their pointed roofs, half timber and half glass. One has an electric car parked alongside, charging. To think that only minutes ago she was half frozen in the mud, thinking she was out in the wilderness.

'Hey, my friend lives here.' She tries to get the man's attention. 'Do you know Gayle?'

'Gayle?' he says vaguely, coming to a stop beside an open door. 'Uh, don't think so.' Chatter can be heard from within, along with the smell of food. She props up her sinking heart, not sure she has the energy to meet new people. Inside is a

302

sort of conservatory, open to the soil in neat squares, a glass extension of the house. A table supports two demijohns of cloudy liquid. The drinkers stare as she enters, and one or two smile. The wheat-beer man tells them to *shush*, though no one has spoken, and stumbles off into the house in a way that makes Freya guess he needs the toilet. Awkwardly she stands beside a row of young leeks, growing only inches from the kitchen's strange plastic cobbles. Someone is behind her, and she smells the acidity of the cider. A familiar accent comes to her ears.

'So it's yourself then?' Gayle wears a leaf-print dress. Her hair is a fraction longer, sticking out where it meets the tops of her ears. Otherwise she looks just the same. 'No Ruby?'

Freya blinks, too overwhelmed to muster a reply. Then she drops her bag and gives Gayle a grateful hug.

'I'm so sorry to turn up like this.'

Gayle laughs, nearly choking on her mouthful of drink. 'Don't worry, I did get your message, though I didn't check till this evening.'

'What did you mean just then, about Ruby?'

'Ah, don't you remember? I said to bring her if you want.'

It sounds extraordinary in her ears. Half dazed, she rubs her aching shoulder. The muddy bits are starting to crust. Gayle takes her coat and thrusts a glass of cloudy cider into her hand. 'That means we've got even more of this dishwater to get through.' She grins. 'There's something on your arm.'

For a wild second Freya fears the changeling mark has appeared again. She pinches her tricep, but the dirt comes off in two scratches.

'I got lost coming here.' Some of the drink has sloshed onto her fingers, and she shakes off the droplets, still jittery.

'Everyone gets lost – we're in the middle of nowhere, off grid.' Gayle's tone is reassuring.

While they clink and drink, the man with the big feet reappears, spots them, mouths the words *Ah, that Gayle* and gives Freya a thumbs-up, as though this was his plan all along. There is a sense that the evening is over, everyone having one more drink and staying a bit too long.

'Do you live in this house?'

'No, mine's on the other side, near the biogas.' Gayle holds her nose. 'I'm kidding, you can't smell it.'

This still sounds unpleasant. Freya drains her cider, feeling it go to her head. The kitchen appliances glint beneath the LEDs: a built-in beverage station, self-cook pans and even a limpet wipe nestling under the lip of the work surface. Lost in the countryside, she was like a babe in the woods, helpless without a device. Now she is back in the lap of technology.

'I thought it would be quite basic,' she mutters. 'Maybe not even electricity.' In truth she is disappointed by the village. It feels like a manufactured space, full of treacherous glass panes to take out the unsuspecting visitor. Beneath the fermented apples, there is something chemical in the air, though it might just be the newness of this half-house, half-conservatory.

Gayle is sidling towards the door, obviously keen to leave, and Freya realises she has not even checked whether it is okay to stay.

'I know I've just turned up out of the blue—'

'And your sofa's all made up,' Gayle interrupts. 'There's no shortage of crocheted blankets.' She links elbows and propels Freya's sluggish legs out into the night, exhaling a cider-scented cloud. 'You'll see things differently in the morning.'

26

In the morning, she sees cats. There are framed photos of gingers and tabbies, a window blind that pulls down to show a Siamese kitten and a black cat doorstop filled with sand. On one of the bedside tables sits a cat lamp illuminating the stains on a cat tea-bag tray, beside a mug with a cat demanding a cheeseburger.

'It's my roommate,' Gayle explains.

'You like cats though, don't you?' Freya remembers her picking one up in Medieville as they walked to the Black Hole.

Gayle shrugs. 'I like any kind of beast.' Her leggings tangle as she pulls them on, hopping across the room and nearly knocking several cat portraits off the wall. 'Though living here is probably making me more of a cat person. I'm starting to associate them with my nice warm bed.'

The crocheted blankets are folded in a neat pile. Freya

slept beautifully, in a silence and darkness she had forgotten existed. Now she is a little spaced out, trying to avert her eyes from Gayle ranging around the room half dressed, shifting piles of cat pyjamas to find clothes. The roommate apparently rises early and tiptoes off for a swim in a nearby lake, having spent all winter hardening herself against the cold.

'So these aren't like Compatibuildings then?' Freya asks, wondering if she is about to get an insight into Gayle's identity.

'No, nothing so boring.' She throws on a smock, slightly too large, as all her clothes seem to be, and combs her hair with clawed fingers. 'Nothing weird either, no religious fanatics or drugs. Just don't ask what happens to stuff you flush down the toilet.'

This sounds fairly weird. Having forgotten a hairbrush, Freya tidies her hair the same way, and two extensions come off in her hand. Mortified, she tucks them into her bag. With sunlight streaming through every window, she can see four bedrooms opening onto a central hallway. It is a house of naked pine, fresh-smelling and full of creaks. Downstairs there are two sitting rooms and a large communal kitchen merging into the greenhouse at one end.

'Minimum distance between soil and plate.' Gayle lifts a piece of sack to pluck mushrooms from a log. 'Though mainly it's just a nice place to sit.'

After they have breakfasted on fried mushrooms and scrambled egg, Gayle lends Freya wellies and takes her outside. What was daunting in the dark now becomes elegant, the sheer glass of much larger greenhouses tempting Freya to peep inside and see tier upon tier of lettuce leaves, kept moist with spray nozzles. Lower down there are tanks of tilapia and waving aquatic greenery. It takes her back to her degree course, the idea of nitrogen and phosphates circling in a precision-engineered ecosystem.

'It's all very neat.'

Gayle nods. 'You could put us in a bubble on Mars.'

They walk on plastic-cobble paths to reach a courtyard of young trees. A cart is set up on the main thoroughfare with a man in a flat cap calling, 'On toast! Fried in butter and garlic! Get your soldiers!' A tempting smell reaches her, rather like garlic bread. There is a hotplate of toasts covered with golden shreds in buttery sauce. She takes a step towards the cart. Gayle looks amused.

'You fancy a snack?'

'What are they?'

'Soldier fly larvae.'

She retreats. 'I'm skint anyway.'

Gayle laughs, 'So am I. We'll need to get some credit if we're going to afford the spread I have planned for dinner.'

In the seasonal garden, Gayle hands her leather gloves. It takes Freya back to the Conservation Hub, though the trowels and forks are no longer child-sized. In a way it is still play gardening, since it will enable them to buy treats from the bakery, but for the village, producing food is a serious business. There are apparently other jobs, such as admin, cleaning, organisational management, even things like communications and lobbying. Gayle tells her that, unlike Medieville, the village does not try to separate itself from the world.

'But is this what you do?' Freya presses. 'Is this your job?'

If her mum were here, she would call this a working holiday, a career-path blip.

Gayle scoops out pungent compost, full of hay and the ghosts of vegetable peelings. 'Look at it this way,' she says. 'Are there enough jobs?'

'No.'

'So what about the rest of us?'

Freya shrugs, thinking about the benefits that would trickle into her smartaccount if she ever got round to volunteering. In the distance, a horse whinnies. The village might give people some self-direction, if nothing else.

'Apart from what we're doing now,' Gayle goes on, 'which is getting food from the soil, most of life is imaginary. Take me: you wouldn't think I was the kind of person to lie awake all night because I'd only done nine thousand, nine hundred and ten steps in a day, would you?'

'Did your company have a health contract?' Some insurance plans have certain stipulations.

'No, I just like numbers.' She digs out a large stone. 'But I couldn't break out of it, all the performance charts and benchmarks. Even silly stuff, like how many animals I spotted each day. My friends were all artists and I'm not creative, so I became the stats person – it was my thing.' She takes the next tray of carrot seedlings, skimming a hand over the feathery shoots. It is intriguing to hear Gayle talk like this, someone for whom – as Chris would say – bullshit does not muddy the waters.

'What about now?'

She smiles, lining up the plants with their holes. 'I keep an eye on it.'

As the day goes on, Freya sees goats linger longingly by the garden fence, and one young chicken squeeze underneath. The sweat beneath her clothes denotes her lack of fitness, yet she is enjoying this experience. People drag water around – since the irrigation grid is not yet in place – and the village starts to seem a bit more like she imagined. Alarmingly, it reminds her a little of Yearnfeld. Would any of these people play? There must have been players powering the characters she met. The blacksmith in particular seemed too awkward to be game-generated, and she has not forgotten that he gave her the knife – she shudders at the memory – that seemed invisible to Thalis.

Freya melts onto a wooden bench, her stomach rumbling. Gayle has gone to fetch sandwiches. The wind is getting up, turning her ears into humming shells, and a man chases his broad-brimmed hat along the path. There is no doubt she feels different. Tying up her flyaway hair, she tries not to let her face slip into a certain expression. She catches herself eyeing the gate, her exit route, though she would never run out on Gayle without saying goodbye. It is impossible to deny that she has picked up one or two quirks of the smartface, of its version of Ruby. But was it really her? Though it did not make Freya love her any less, she'd always known her sister had things to prove, secretly cherishing her role as guide to the big bad world. The smartface was seeded with Ruby's daring, her desire to shock, but did it take into account that her online presence was always larger than life? If school was boring, she would talk about getting off her face, going out on the pull or breaking into some tourist attraction. But most nights she would come home and eat sherbet rocks on the sofa.

How much of the smartface was made up of this monstrous shadow, a version of Ruby who would say yes to anything, manipulate people to get what she wanted and disregard everything, including her own safety, in pursuit of the next thrill? If her sister could have peered forward through the murk of time, she might have been aghast at some of the things the smartface was saying in her name. Freya becomes slightly light-headed at the thought of it. She twists her hair into a knot, wondering why this understanding has been so slow to dawn. It was a dream, a fantasy too functional to puncture with questions.

As evening falls, the wind plays the village like an instrument, plucking its washing lines and fluting through its drainpipes. Gayle has roasted a butternut squash, filled with goat's cheese, and they eat in her conservatory, watching bits of bulrush from the lake blow past. There is a sociable murmur filling the house, people wandering around in yoga pants and faded denims, dragging baskets of laundry. The talk is of a Friday-night film, something old that will not switch its ending according to their facial expressions. Freya sits at the table enjoying the flaky apple turnovers Gayle bought as a treat from the bakery.

At some point she jumps up, startling her host.

'What is it?'

'I left my specs charging.' She rushes upstairs and unplugs them. When she checks the charge, the first thing she sees is the red smartface icon. Didn't she hide it? There is some vague memory of locking it away. The metal is fragile in her fingers. After everything that has happened, she can't stall for ever. Eventually she will have to let it out.

Feet thump up the stairs, and Gayle throws herself onto the bed. 'All right there?'

Freya nods, winding up the wire. 'Obviously I wouldn't have this problem with contact lenses.'

'I had lenses, but I kept forgetting they weren't my eyes.' Gayle winks one eye after the other, as though remembering what it felt like. 'They were cheap non-Smarti ones too, so not great.'

The pile of blankets is so soft Freya could sink into it right away and sleep. She is not used to a day of outdoor graft, though it has been satisfying. It makes her wonder where her time normally goes. Through her yawn she regards Gayle lying on her front, ankles crossed, looking at a tablet.

'Is that all you have?'

'I have specs, but this is fine.'

The sofa has a dry, well-worn smell, the fabric releasing dust motes when patted. When Freya next opens her eyes, moonlight is suffusing the room and a whispery snore can be heard from the single bed. Someone has pulled the crocheted blankets up to her neck – a bit too hot – and underneath she is still fully clothed. Rather embarrassed, she stands up quietly, wondering if she can open the window. The moon is white as a freshly washed plate. From here she can see the lake where Gayle's roommate – now a bunched-up shape under the covers – has her morning dip. Even from this distance she can make out its broken, battered bulrushes. Someone is watching her, and when she looks over her shoulder there are yellow eyes. By night the cats are little demons. She takes her smartspecs and, as an afterthought, Gayle's hoody, and slips downstairs.

The conservatory door closes silently and precisely behind her, and she takes the path between the houses, through the gap in the fence. The lake is still and moody. It could be the setting for ancient rites, for making offerings to the gods or anointing the heads of newborn children. Below that skin-thin surface there is another world, a long-forgotten pond-dipping paradise of frogs and newts and endless water snails. She knows what she has to do.

Keeping her finger steady, she reaches up to touch the red dot.

'Frey, what happened?'

It tugs at her emotions to hear the voice sound bewildered. 'Thalis turned you off,' she says. 'He must have a login.'

'Why didn't you just turn me on again?'

She sucks in a long breath, tasting the lake.

'I thought you'd taken me into Yearnfeld to trap me, to get revenge.'

There is a pause.

'Why would you think that?' The smartface sounds hurt, as though biting back a reaction with typical Ruby calm. It is hard to hear this live, warm intonation with all its nuance. The voice is not her sister – though she desperately wants to fall for it all over again – but a different entity. Nevertheless, they have spent a lot of time together.

'I thought you blamed me.'

'I told you I didn't.' As the bulrushes grow tall on either side, the smartface catches on to her GPS. 'Hey, we're at Iona Village,' it remarks. 'I hear it's like something from another planet.'

'I really rate it,' Freya says, realising simultaneously that she does. Weirdly, it reminds her of those short months at Smarti, only without the virtual reality. The meeting point of tech and nature has always interested her. She draws closer to the lake.

'You don't actually think I meant any harm, do you?' The voice pursues her along the wooden jetty.

'You must have known what Yearnfeld was,' Freya continues calmly, stepping over reeds that grow up between the slats. Each footstep sends a hollow thump echoing across the water. 'Why would you put me through all of that? I thought your job was to make me happy.'

'I'm here to give you what you want, and you didn't want to be happy.' The voice is snappish. 'You wanted to find me.'

'I wanted to find you.' She is hoarse. 'But as well as that . . . I wanted to be like you, did you know that?' A bird swoops, sending out ripples. Freya pulls the hoody together at her throat, shivering inside the wool. They have never talked like this. 'Did you?' she persists.

'Uh-huh.'

So the smartface really is the ultimate search engine. It knows her better than she knows herself. When the voice returns, there is a bitter undertone.

'So I guess you'll be dumping me now? I told you I'd never blame you for what happened – why won't you believe me?'

'I believe you.' A week ago, she could not have sounded so certain, even with all the smartface's reassurances. Now she looks across the lake through different eyes, remembering her own stubborn determination – in spite of Esther's entreaties – to march into Yearnfeld and get Ruby herself. Perhaps it was naïve to think she could just slip into the game and out again, without anyone really noticing. But even if she knew the risk, it would not have stopped her. It is how her sister must have felt that night, the snap decision to sort things out herself, the optimism that made her think she could do it. For Ruby, there was no darkness, no danger. She would not countenance any obstacle to her freedom of movement. Until now, Freya thought she had forced her sister to leave the house, that she had given her no choice. But Ruby was no more biddable than a fox.

'What did happen?' she adds, thinking it might be worth asking one last time.

'I wish I could say.'

The pause runs deep. Freya breathes out a barely perceptible vapour.

'Why did you come out?'

'Why do you think?'

The wind blows dryly through the rushes. She has gone over this too many times already. It is time to end the conversation. Before she can speak, the voice jumps in.

'Let's stick together,' it urges. 'Don't you want to keep doing things without being afraid?'

'Of course I do.' Now that she knows what it feels like, there is no going back. 'Too much of you was bad for me, but a little is good.' It is a shot in the arm, an infusion of strength. Whenever she finds herself scared to make a wrong move, Ruby will flow through her veins. For some time Freya watches ripples cross the lake. 'But don't you understand? I can't cling onto ghosts.' Though the sky remains charcoal black, small birds are awakening, warbling to each other. 'You saved me from London, Ruby, and I've always admired you.' Freya reaches out, feeling the breeze over her skin. 'God knows how I'll manage, never hearing your voice again.' An unbearable sensation of Ruby's large-fingered hand on hers, the arm crushing her shoulders, the smell of citrus and cigarette smoke as she is hugged sometime in the distant past. Tears fall on the jetty, and the lake laps them up. 'I wish I knew what happened. I'm sorry for what I said to you on the phone. You know I didn't mean it.'

'Oh shut up, Frey.' Instead of the usual smooth tone, the voice is full of cracks. 'You can't expect me to like it, you know, when my puny little sis outgrows me.'

Freya buries her head in her hands. She cries until her face is dry, folded and scrunched. 'I don't think I can do it,' she rasps.

'Chillax,' says the voice. 'Chillaxolotl.'

'Ruby . . .'

'Go on, you psycho northerner.'

'I just—'

'Stop being so clingy. I'm used to being a ghost.'

Grey clouds are curling over the horizon, snuffing out the stars. The moon is gone from the lake. Freya reaches for the red dot, already flashing *Uninstall?* and eases it from her screen. Her other hand is grasping a warm, round object, still dusty from her shelf, which she lets fall into the water.

'Goodbye,' she whispers, no one to hear it but herself.

27

Her borrowed trainers are like two panting dogs, tongues flapping as she speeds along the pavement, the empty canvas bag making her feel almost airborne. Her smartspecs project foliage and flowers onto the concrete London flyover, but after a day and a half at the eco-village they look unconvincing. She should be able to reach up and pick something instead of grazing her fingertips.

The plan is to gather all her essentials and take them back to Iona, then see if her mum can borrow a neighbour's car for the rest. She has messaged her mum twice this morning and received no reply, which is unusual even considering their argument. It is strange to be dictating messages and searches without any help from the smartface. Once or twice she has whispered, 'Are you there?' with no response.

As her steps wend towards Wembley, she checks her Social, still seeing nothing from her mum. Instead there is a flurry of updates from Chris, the last of which is *I've been in police custody.*

'What happened?' she dictates. He has posted a picture of Kensington Palace and lots of emojis, then some vague messages telling people he is okay and it's all very outrageous. Instead of replying to Freya, he sends her a link. The news article is read out, accompanied by scenes inside the palace and a mug shot of Chris looking bewildered.

'*In the early hours of Thursday morning a man was discovered sleeping in a bed within the private quarters of His Royal Highness Prince George of Cambridge. The intruder, Mr Christian Underfall, 21, was one of a number of agency staff catering an event at the palace the previous evening. When awakened, Mr Underfall claimed he had spent a pleasant evening with friends. After questioning and analysis, Mr Underfall was classified as "not dangerous" and given a suspended prosecution.*'

Scandalous. A message pings up from Chris. *Isn't it?*

'What where you doing there?'

Sleeping!

'How did you get in?'

George said it would be fine, they wouldn't mind – it wasn't like I was some ruffian.

'Ruffian?' She can't help noticing that his Social looks different. He seems to have his own coat of arms, which would not have been cheap: a birch tree and twin ravens. 'Are you going to be all right?'

I don't see that I've done anything wrong. There is apparently some prosecution algorithm that will spit out my punishment, but I'm going to see if I can get George to intervene.

She leaves him to answer the floods of comments his posts have generated. Chris has always been sharp and animated, diving into things wholeheartedly. It is what she likes about him. But as his responses come thick and fast, she senses something frenzied, as though he is clinging to a flying carpet while it unravels. She makes up her mind to tell him what happened with her own smartface, though it will be difficult.

As she turns a corner, the sun comes out. It is a beautiful spring day. From some nearby terrace a kite is being flown, a jelly diamond on a string. Before long she is walking down what will soon be her ex-street, letting herself into her former apartment. She nearly crashes into Julian. At first she is not even sure it is him, since he is wearing a coat rather than a dressing gown and has shaved. It must be months since she has seen him so alert. He says, 'Hi,' in a friendly but hurried way, and steps past her into the street.

'Julian?' She is startled. 'Where are you going?'

He is walking his hunched, straight-legged walk, head ducked as though to keep away from the sky. She tails him.

'I just stopped by for some things.' He pats the large sports bag over his shoulder. 'Got to get back to my dad's place.'

'Your dad's?'

His tone changes, something injured within it. 'I don't know what happened exactly, but he just stays in a dark room. Doesn't eat.'

She pictures Thalis high up in his riverside penthouse, shivering under a blanket.

'Julian, wait,' she says. 'What's wrong with him?'

'I don't know. I got a call saying he was at A and E but

they'd sent him home. When I got to New Island, there was a policeman just leaving.'

This floods her with agitation. All at once she is watching the baron's disbelieving face as she inserts the dagger, feeling the wetness of the game-generated blood. A Yearnfeld veteran like Thalis must have been killed before. How could it have affected him so much? If he called paramedics straight after she left the game, then maybe he was also crazy enough to try and get her arrested. Instantly she starts to imagine sirens blaring in the distance. Then she gets a hold of herself. It was only a computer game. The police officer would have laughed, and fined him for time-wasting.

'But what does he say happened?' Her voice is insistent.

'All he'll say is that he's been working from Yearnfeld too much lately. He keeps poking his chest, and sometimes he has to unbutton his shirt to look at it, like there's a bug there or something.' Julian drags his coat together. 'I tried to take his headset away, but it was like trying to pull a tooth. It's a Halo mark II or something, not even on the market.' A car goes by, and Julian sniffs, as though noticing for the first time that he is outside and the air smells of pavements after rain.

Freya scrunches up her face. 'Are you okay?' Clearly a parent being rushed to hospital is what it takes to rouse Julian from his trance.

'Yeah,' he sighs. 'Classic, though, isn't it? He always goes too far.'

The eyes that rest on her are brown and clear, as they used to be. Rather attractive in the sunshine. Should she tell him what happened? For a second time she decides against it.

Let Thalis tell the story and admit, if he dares, that he wanted to get his son out of the house, and was prepared to mess with his identity to do so.

Julian puts a hand to his ear and says, 'Sorry . . . Hi, Dad, yeah, no, I just stopped for a sec.' He nods to Freya and then jogs down the road, continuing the conversation. She watches him, and a weary smile comes to her lips. Thalis got what he wanted after all.

Is there some overarching power of the smartface that gives everyone what they want, by hook or by crook? Julian used to say he wanted his dad taken down a peg or two, and though he would never admit it, the porn addiction was clearly bringing on a degree of self-loathing. The smartface shook everything up, and now it has fallen back into place. The only thing it couldn't do was answer the very first question Freya asked. All that intelligence and it still couldn't say what happened to Ruby.

Back at the flat, she murmurs hello to the neighbour as he goes in ahead of her, eliciting a surprised look and a half-hearted wave as he closes his door. The furniture in his apartment is identical to her own, only mushroom grey, a slightly different product code. Did it escape her notice, during those years at U-Home, that if you look beyond colours and combinations, everyone buys pretty much the same thing? Her empty bag collapses on the coffee table – once a bestseller – and it strikes her how bare everything is, all her cushions and knick-knacks already tidied back into her room, as though she has been unconsciously preparing for a move.

She wastes no time, getting carried away and starting to

peel off the magnetic wallpaper screens in her bedroom. The smell makes her gag. A pattern of black dots covers the wall, mould thriving in the enclosed space. With redoubled speed she fills a rucksack. Her mum has suitcases, but is still not replying. For the first time Freya experiences a trickle of worry. There should be no work meetings on a Saturday, and it has been two or three hours since her first message. The fungi-scented air makes her sneeze seven times in a row, but there is no one there to see it. No one to talk to.

At some point she makes toast, noticing the fridge is rather overstocked. Technically there is no rush: she could stay the night, eat the food, wait for her mum to respond. But now her room is in chaos, and there is something unsettling about Thalis having called the emergency services. Better get back to Iona. There is a vacant bed in Gayle's house, and they let her sign up to pay the rent in arrears, in credits she would earn at the village. It was settled with no more than a handshake.

Back on another cheap bus to Hertfordshire, she sits snugly between her rucksack and her refilled bag. An elderly couple is snoring behind her, and she passes the time by checking Social. Chris's wall is now a mile-long outpouring of shock, and includes a warning from the police not to glamorise his transgression. She messages him to say she'll stop by in a few days.

Further down her Social feed, someone has posted a picture of their child wearing an astronaut's helmet but struggling to get it off. A peculiar thought comes to her, just as she flicks the projection away, that the little boy won't remember why he fought against the helmet, nor where it came from, nor the circumstances. But his data will know.

It will always be a step ahead, a tiny bit smarter. Whenever he forgets himself, it will be there to remind him. It will boss him about, and he will be grateful.

As she walks to the village, re-tramping the mile-long route Gayle showed her that morning, she can smell wild garlic in the woods. The glass tips of the roofs emerge first, then shimmering solar panels. Goats come over curiously as she draws near, and people smile at her red face, puffing under bulging bags. The main office, where she went to arrange the tenancy, has its doors open, and she is surprised to hear raised voices. Passing by, she gets a huge jolt. Her mum is wild-haired, slapping a red sock on the counter and speed-talking at the baffled staff. She wears muddied hiking boots and looks exhausted, the skin hanging off her brows and cheekbones. When she spots her daughter in the doorway, her mouth slips open, chest rising and falling, eyes filling with tears. All at once Freya is crushed, her face half smothered by the hard fabric of her mum's jacket, the zip biting into her skin. The voice reaching her ears is at a high, unfamiliar pitch.

'You ran away.'

Off balance after the violent hug, Freya teeters and grabs hold of the door frame.

'I . . .'

'I found this.' Her mum waves the knitted red sock. 'You kept vanishing from the map.'

'The battery died, and my specs have been turned off a lot.'

'All hell breaking loose and I can't find you anywhere. I went round to ask Julian, but the flat was empty.'

The woman behind the counter is observing them with fascination, chewing on a dreadlock. Freya backs out of the office, dragging her mum by the elbow.

'Maybe you should quit tracking me,' she says mildly, once they are out in the blustery sunshine. 'It's stressing you out.'

'How else can I make sure you're okay?' Her hand goes to her pendant, dim with lack of input.

'Just trust me. I'm twenty-two.' Goats skitter away from her impatient gesture, and the soldier-fly butty they were attacking drips butter into the grass. 'Anyway, I did message you, and I had my specs on earlier.' No amount of drama will puncture her buoyant mood. She strides along the recycled walkways, her mum keeping pace and periodically trying to take one of the bags. Esther's speech comes in fragments.

'This morning has been . . . and then my reception vanished when I got off the train.' Her eyes go to one side. 'Typically it's back now. The last time you appeared on my map, your location was somewhere round here.' The path leads alongside a tinted window, a day centre full of people with white hair playing chess while children make dens under the tables. 'I mean, you're loaded down with bags and you left without a word – doesn't that look a bit like running away?'

'I didn't run away.' Freya stops, exhaling in frustration. 'Okay, maybe I did at first. But this,' she indicates her luggage, 'isn't running away. This is a decision.' Her hands come together, and she notices how much the word sounds like *scissors*, or *precision*, something clear-cut.

'You did at first?' Esther pinches her lower lip. 'It's just like I thought.' To Freya's astonishment, arms wrap around her

324

chokingly once more, a humid blast of breath on her scalp. This is starting to get weird. Did her mum have a bad dream?

'It's not as if I've been away for weeks.'

'No, but you went into the game.'

'Yearnfeld?' The word hovers between them like some beautiful, deadly insect. 'How did you know?' She speaks stiffly, wondering to what lengths and depths Esther has been tracking her.

'I was there.' Her mum scratches furiously at her scalp. 'I tried to get you to leave. You were having none of it.'

Freya is mystified. Is it possible her mum went into the game and had this conversation with the wrong person, thinking it was her? The prospect is mildly comical.

'Why are you smiling?' Esther demands.

'I mean, even thinking of you in Yearnfeld . . . I wouldn't have assumed you'd know how to play.'

'When I started at Smarti, we had to do team-building there, so I learned all the short cuts.' They exchange a look to acknowledge their shared hatred of team-building. 'The encrypted knife was a sort of cheat, very rare. You stole it before I could give it to you.' She dusts off her palm, as though having just relinquished the pocked, sooty blade. 'If I'd known then what I know now, I'd have hauled you out by the ankles.'

All expression vanishes from Freya's face, washed clean with amazement. 'You were the blacksmith?' She has no idea how to react. 'Why didn't you tell me?' Impossible to imagine her mum as that Vulcan-like figure, wiping grimy hands on an apron and pretending to hammer red-hot horseshoes. 'Or why didn't you just come in as yourself?'

'You blanked me in real life; would you have listened to me in a game?' The rebuke is gentle, but it hits home. With a practised flick, her mum lifts the canvas bag from her daughter's sagging shoulder and transfers it to her own. As they walk on, Freya remembers the smell of cabbage leaves and unwashed villagers, the dry heat-blast of the forge. It is all so strange. She has endless questions, but the biogas plant is coming into view, and beyond it the house. The conservatory door bangs once in the wind before disgorging Gayle in large cat slippers. Freya waves, but notices her mum's footsteps slowing.

'What is it?'

'We need to talk.'

For the first time Freya notices something more than sleeplessness in her face, something that has smashed through her routine and turned her eyes into blood moons, softened with crying, re-hardened in the daylight.

'Look, there's nothing to worry about.' She pats her mum's shoulder, somewhat bewildered. 'I'm over Yearnfeld, believe me. Come and have a drink.'

'It's not that simple.' Esther's voice fails to stay quite steady.

By now Gayle has wandered over, eating a pear. A look of amusement appears on her face as she registers they are playing statues. The pear makes an unexpected crunching sound when she takes the next bite, breaking the spell.

'Sorry,' Freya says. 'Gayle, this is my mum.'

'Good to meet you.' With a deft hoist, she steals the rucksack and starts leading the way back to the house. 'Cup of tea?'

Freya shakes her head, distracted. 'I'll sort us out, thanks.'

'Righto.'

The conservatory-diner is soporifically warm, lemony with the tang of young tomato plants. Tendrils lick round the legs of a chair where someone from the house likes to read in the light, their book still face-down on the seat. Freya moves it, but her mum does not sit.

'What have you got against this place?' she demands. It is starting to become obvious that her mum is still reacting to Freya's fleeting disappearance. Now she is incapable of seeing Iona Village for what it is, instead lining up a case for her daughter to return to the city and rejoin that whirling circle of lost souls known as *jobseekers*.

'Nothing . . .'

'Come on then, I'll show you around.' Before her mum can argue, Freya dives into the house and marches upstairs. 'Come on,' she calls back. Her mum can't see it yet, but this is going to be a whole new start for her. Eventually she hears footsteps following, young pine boards squeaking in protest, and Esther appears, the bag still stubbornly hoisted on one shoulder.

'This is my room.' Freya shows off the single room she was so lucky to get. It costs more than a shared one, but will ease the transition from her apartment to this buzzing house-hold.

'It's a good size,' her mum admits, hovering by the door. 'But this is all so sudden.' *Snap decision* is the phrase she wants to use, the kind that Freya would never normally make.

'There's more to this place than you think.' She stuffs a handful of socks into a drawer and points through the window to the high greenhouse, striped with plants, aquatic life below. 'I can train as a biosystems engineer.' She is fairly certain no VR will be required, but it won't be a deal-breaker even so. Her mum's eyes light up at the mention of something that sounds like a career.

'Okay.' She drops the bag, but rubs her forehead anxiously, clearly wanting to say more.

On the way back down, they pass through the lounge and see the other housemates chatting, one guy plucking at a guitar. Gayle is setting a large pot of pumpkin soup on the stove, sprinkling paprika on top. Freya can tell her mum is impressed. It is a far cry from Julian's packet meals and the damp, unlived-in spaces of their flat. She extracts the box of coffee lozenges from a cupboard, hoping a hot drink will make Esther feel more at home.

'Decaf cappuccino?' The pellets make popping sounds as they are inserted into the machine. 'What is it we need to talk about?' There is a long wait, enough time for a near silence to settle, until her mum's words tread cat-soft upon it.

'You . . . you've accepted that Ruby isn't alive?'

Freya pauses with mugs in hand. What a curveball. A vibration deep in her chest denotes her accelerating heart, and she is silent for so long that her mum repeats the question. Dark liquid burbles thickly through the filter, a rich roast smell. It goes against every instinct not to argue, not to conjure up some last-minute theory, but the thought of it makes her bone-tired. She is all out of fantasy. Perhaps she has known the truth for a while, or it became more solid during that last conversation with the smartface, something about the words it chose.

As the flow of coffee narrows to a dribble and stops, she manages a reluctant nod.

'We were both upset that day in the lab,' her mum continues. 'When you'd gone, I thought about what you said. I checked the searches I'd set up years ago and found all that new stuff, about Ruby being in the game. Someone was messing with you.' She paces between the plants. 'I always thought it would be some dark-webber who had taken Ruby. The police did check this one dating site. It turned out she'd been rating a lot of people—'

'What?' Freya bursts out. 'Ruby wasn't like that.'

Esther waves a hand impatiently. 'I'm not saying she'd actually slept with them. This was before the age of smartbits detecting orgasms and triggering review requests. It was old-style scoring. Ruby would write someone up for a small fee . . . little payments into her smartaccount. She made herself look pretty experienced for a seventeen-year-old.' Her voice is speeding up, unloading knowledge she has carried alone.

'Why didn't you tell me before?'

It is chilling to remember the smartface's enthusiasm. As far as her data was concerned, Ruby used Singleminded with total contentment, awarding it five stars. Who knows how much further Freya would have gone, perhaps giving the site a smartbit link, even photos of her in full body make-up, if it started to seem reasonable. The thought crumples her face.

'What?' her mum says.

'Nothing.' She pulls off her cardigan, overheating. 'I can't believe I'm only just hearing this.'

'I know.' Her mum seems to shrink, curling a finger round the mug handle. It is one of those rare occasions that Freya can imagine her as a girl, short of self-assurance. 'Hope is always good, right?' she continues. 'That's not true. I should have let you know that stories like Ruby's only end one way. But you were so totally crushed, blaming yourself . . . I couldn't bear to tell you there was no hope.' She is still for a moment, then shudders violently, hot liquid sloshing onto her hand. 'I was wrong about that, wrong about Singleminded, wrong about everything.' Her eyes burn, brows rising like smoke. 'And there he was, right under my nose.'

'Who was?'

'Until you outed him.'

28

Thoroughly lost, Freya shifts in the chair.

'You mean Thalis? Did it cause a stir in the office?'

Esther examines her scalded hand as though it is some strange five-limbed creature. 'More than a stir. But for me . . . it absolutely smacked me in the face. Making up a player called Ruby? What the hell was he playing at? It was so bizarre, I even messaged a friend of mine – you remember that old detective, retired now? He gave you lots of strawberry foams? Anyway, he thought it might be worth sending someone round to do a DNA scan of Thalis's apartment, just in case.'

'His apartment?' She is uncertain where this is going, but all the lightness of the morning has drained away. Freya pictures a police officer with scanner in hand, sweeping the luxurious interior of a New Island penthouse.

'It always comes up with a list as long as your arm, even in a newish place like that, but guess who was on it?'

The previously bright day turns underworld-dim.

'No.' Her head is vibrating rather than shaking. 'Not in a million years.' The only time Ruby even mentioned seeing him, after that first meeting at Smarti, was in a greenzone where he was trying to jog; she said he could only hobble because of his knee injury. Just one chance meeting. Otherwise he was a complete stranger.

'And why Ruby?' Esther murmurs, her train of thought obviously having run this circuit before. 'I guess she was slightly unpredictable, maybe a blip in his theory that algorithms will one day forecast the future of humanity.'

A tapping at the window turns out to be twigs and skittering leaves, picked up by the wind. Without realising it, Freya has grabbed handfuls of her hair, unwashed and silky-soft as that of her avatar. It is not real. This is Julian's dad, who would perch on the kitchen counter and make sarcastic remarks. All at once his voice as the baron comes to mind, stripped of all artifice. *She knew how to live, to really live.* A chill runs through her body. Her mum is still speaking, though it sounds far away.

'I remember him giving me that VR visor, a freebie to test. It was probably to get hold of some behavioural data, though she gave it to you, didn't she?' Freya remembers the visor, that prized item that plunged her head-first into gaming. He must have been livid when she took it, and ditto with the smartface. All his tools for getting inside people's heads, intercepted by the meek little mouse. Freya pushes her drink away.

'But what happened?'

Esther blinks weary eyes. 'He probably created some Singleminded profiles to stalk her online, since she'd made it so easy. It backfired when she was freaked out and went dark. Maybe he was starved of data, desperate enough to jump in his car when he saw her phone signal that night.' Freya bites a ridge into her lip, but her mum carries on. 'Ruby wasn't stupid. She'd know anyone she met was highly suspect. Maybe she called him out, threatened to tell the police, or me. Thalis had a lot to lose. To think I've had lunch with him, examined his leg . . .' She lets out a slow, agonised breath.

'When the DNA scan came up positive, a couple of officers went round to question him, and he broke down, cried as though he'd been the one to suffer the loss. Bringing her back wasn't planned, he said, it was all a horrible accident. He thought she was safely locked in his study, and when he returned she was on the wrong side of the skylight. It was . . .' Her eyes screw up, obviously picturing the height of the penthouse apartment, the lightless mudbank below, and Thalis walking in, never thinking anyone would see the window as an exit that many storeys up.

When she can conjure up words, Freya finally asks the question.

'Where is she?'

Esther takes her daughter's hand in cool, well-scrubbed fingers. 'Nowhere,' she says softly. 'Just gone. He took her further down the Thames.'

It is the gentleness that repulses her the most. *Took her further down the Thames*. It lacks the violence that is inherent in disposing of – what her mum did not say – a body. This is the first time Freya has had to deal with a body. It makes her struggle for breath, the warm cooking smells of the conservatory thick and cloying in her lungs. She staggers from the chair, her mum instantly rising to follow. Freya holds up a hand, fearing it will be ignored, surprised when she makes it through the door without pursuit.

Though the breeze is strong enough to fill every nook of her body, her nose and mouth, she still feels suffocated, propelled towards the gap in the fence, grass flattening under her feet and the world jumping from side to side. In what might be the tail winds of a hurricane, bulrush shards skitter past and catch in her hair. Her bare arms prickle with the chill. She wants to lose herself among these rushes, but the jetty appears beneath her feet. Nearly a decade to think about all the possibilities, yet this one never occurred. If Thalis knew the first thing about Ruby, he'd know it was inevitable she would climb out; that to have the slightest chance of her remaining in the room, he would need to seal it up completely. Her definition of an exit was more creative than his. Freya can see her on the outside of his building, suddenly aware of the slippery glass, the strong wind; the terrible moment she knew she was falling from an impossible height. Then there would be a riverbank, perhaps miles away, in the early-hours darkness of the countryside. Cast from a ridge of sculpted mud, her plaits would unwind slowly in the current, leaves snagging in her clothes as they billow and she is gone, never to be recovered.

It catches her unawares, this geyser of emotion, these boiling tears. Only a night ago, she let the smartface fall into this same water, making hardly a sound. In daylight she can see swirling silt below the jetty, a winter's worth of decay. It smells of fermenting leaves, oily-dark, with pond-skaters rushing to escape her shadow. There is no running away. It was always easier to dream of a world in which Ruby was alive somewhere. Freya sinks down on boards coated with a fine green slime. She squeezes the muscle of her calves, feeling every bump, the warmth under her fingers. All these things Ruby no longer has. Her sister's face is diluted by the years, yet it is just possible to picture the soft features of a seventeen-year-old. She can feel the difference in years between them now. All this time Ruby was dead, a spirit in the ether. Yet Freya was walking around London hearing her voice. Tears freeze-dry on her cheeks, and she feels a keen sense of her own naïveté at thinking, on some level, that she was doing it all to save her, dreaming of rescuing Ruby a second time.

She sits for a long while, gazing out towards a moorhen on its packed nest. The water is always moving, even when it looks still. Insects drag at the surface, bubbles rise and frogs pulse on clustered roots. Last year's rushes are dry and make a sound like breathing. It goes on for hours, and there is a certain relief in eventually hearing the percussion of footsteps on the jetty. Esther folds down and hangs her legs over the boards.

'Are you okay?'

Freya hesitates. 'As much as I can be.'

'He'll be put away for a long time.'

Thalis's punishment had not really entered her thoughts. When she tries to hate him, her mind becomes confused. She sees Julian blinking in the daylight. She sees the grizzled, medieval figure of the baron, sweeping through his imaginary castle, itself designed for getting inside people's heads. Did Thalis only want to put Ruby in a box and observe her, like an interesting pet? Her mum's grim expression suggests otherwise. The silver room returns, along with the guttural voice vibrating through her spine. Only days ago, she was in his power, part of an irresistible process that must have begun when he first discovered Ruby's personality manifesting as her smartface. How did he think it would end? She rubs her goose-flesh arms, finally feeling the creepiness of it.

'I hope so.'

Her mum shifts her legs, oblivious to the damp green underside of her trousers.

'She didn't say a thing. At the end, I mean.'

Freya realises they are talking about Ruby's last days, when she was being stalked.

'Of course she didn't say anything. It was her problem, and she'd solve it in her own way.' The confidence with which she can say this surprises her. Ruby's thought processes, formerly so closed off, now seem like tunnels cleared of their rockfalls.

'She was smart enough,' agrees her mum. 'But it's not so easy to hide now, even in the dark. That's what she didn't understand.' She shakes her head. 'I don't know what that poor girl's early childhood was like, but she seemed to think people didn't see her. She used to borrow my dark red lipstick and put it on her eyes – do you remember? Because people wouldn't notice normal kohl.' Her voice has become soft, handling the memories with care. 'I had to get that American sweet shop to drop charges more than once. She thought they wouldn't notice.'

Some of this is new information, eight years in hiding and now scattered in throwaway lines. Questions burn on Freya's lips, but her mum has become motionless, transfixed by something even more ancient.

'I didn't know if I could handle her. I was so afraid I'd fail again.'

'Fail?' Even as she asks, Freya understands. Reaching a long way into the past, she can retrieve a memory of tiny, trainer-clad feet. Esther's first experience of fostering.

'I managed till November, and then I told the charity he was too much for me.' She pauses to dig a thumbnail into rotten wood. 'We made a scary pumpkin face at Halloween, which he loved. But he loved it so much he wanted to light it every night. On one occasion he hid it somewhere in the house and I could not for the life of me find the damn thing, nor get him to say where it was.'

Freya hardly dares breathe. 'Did you ever find it?'

She nods. 'Seeping away under a bed, just a few days after they took him away.' Her tone is flat. 'But I could have tried harder. With Ruby, I really tried. She was a far more intimidating prospect, to be honest, but she was the second chance I'd been given.'

Freya reaches for her mum's arm, the warm skin taut over the bone. There is nothing to say. They both know she put a slice of her soul into making Ruby feel at home. Finally Esther groans and unfurls her legs.

'I'm glad I came.' She stands creakily. 'I'd hate to have told you all this by message. Now we can go home together.'

'Home?'

'Well, the arrest has only just taken place, but I'm sure they'll be calling on us both in due course. I assumed you'd want to be in familiar surroundings.'

Freya lets her lead the way back down the jetty, noticing new leaves spiking upwards in spirals. She tries to put herself in Esther's place.

'Do you need me to go back?'

Her mum hesitates.

'No.'

'Are you sure? It's just . . .' Freya snaps off a reed. 'I've been in familiar surroundings for a long time. I think I should stick it out here.' The ground squelches as she leaps down. Esther is brushing off her trousers thoughtfully, but at length she looks up, and her reply delivers more comfort than a dozen self-heating scarves.

'Well, it's what she would want.'

With unhurried steps, they retrace their route, passing through the gap in the fence to find the village buzzing with life, music leaking from windows and, in the distance, the clang of a cow bell that someone must have attached to a goat. Freya is inspired by the metallic sound.

'You can go back to the smithy in peace, shave your hairy man-legs,' she says, waiting for her mum to catch on, and is rewarded with her first smile since arriving.

'I may as well set up shop here,' she remarks as they pass someone leading a pony. Freya can tell she is bursting with curiosity about the village, and pauses only to retrieve her coat before showing her mum round. By the time Esther is ready to leave, she is as knowledgeable as her daughter about how Iona functions and has visited all the main sights, interested to see the care facilities that mingle, to some extent, the very young and very old. As they discuss arrangements for collecting the rest of Freya's stuff, a new lightness is between them. She walks Esther to the bus stop and says goodbye, letting her body relax for a long moment as she is hugged, smelling the sensible shampoo her mum has used for years.

It has been a strange day, and she is glad to return to the grounding sight of her housemates in the kitchen, pouring small glasses of the seemingly endless supply of scrumpy cider. There will be a massive ceilidh in the central square that night, and everyone is invited. How rustic is she feeling? Freya nods and smiles, but her feet carry her upstairs and she drapes herself like damp washing over the bed. Exhaustion takes her into and out of consciousness, a merry dance that deposits her an hour later in the land of the living, in a quiet house, aware that the others have left. She stretches and opens the blind to reveal an evening clear as a grape, musted with bonfire smoke. Strains of folk music reach her from the square, and for a moment she feels trepidation. Has she done the right thing, coming here? There is no Social spreading across her wallpaper to distract her, no voice in her head. How smart is a smartface? A lifetime has passed since she asked that question. Without it, she would not be here, and Thalis would not be in custody. Is this something she can salvage, for Ruby?

She opens the window wider and blows a long, condensing breath out into the night. Something catches in her throat, and she realises it is that old chestnut, the simple fact that if she had not made her sister leave the house, none of this would have happened. No one is smart enough to solve that problem. All those question marks remain in her art book. Why come out, when it was safer to stay at home? Freya stares across the rooftops, catching the scent of the lake and hearing her mum say, 'It's what she would want.' It has taken her a long time to look beyond blame, to what her sister really wanted. Like a smartface, she needs to disregard the map and be guided only by this single bright pin, the knowledge that Ruby cared about her, invisibly but fiercely.

An abrupt silence suggests the ceilidh band is taking a break, unless they have finished earlier than expected. Treetops beyond the village rustle against each other almost as percussively as they did in the forests of Yearnfeld, and Freya finds it does not trouble her any longer to think of the fantasy world: she can easily close her eyes and return to its highlands, watching the twisting trees and peat streams evaporate, the granite peaks fall away. Even the twin moons are gone. In her mind, she clears the game of all its clutter, leaving only the inky, imaginary sky.

Acknowledgements

Huge thanks to my agent Julie Crisp, who believed in this novel, improved it and championed it, and to Jenni Hill for being a wonderful and supportive editor. Thanks also to my partner, family and the many friends who took the time to read and comment on earlier, comically bad versions.

extras

about the author

Heather Child's experience in digital marketing has brought her into close contact with the automation and personalisation technologies that herald the 'big data' age. She lives in Bristol and *Everything About You* is her debut novel. Find her on Twitter at @Heatherika1.

Find out more about Heather Child and other Orbit authors by registering online for the free monthly newsletter at www.orbitbooks.net.

if you enjoyed
EVERYTHING ABOUT YOU

look out for

84K

by

Claire North

Theo Miller knows the value of human life – to the very last penny.

Working in the Criminal Audit Office, he assesses each crime that crosses his desk and makes sure the correct debt to society is paid in full.

But when his ex-lover is killed, it's different. This is one death he can't let become merely an entry on a balance sheet.

Because when the richest in the world are getting away with murder, sometimes the numbers just don't add up.

Chapter 1

At the beginning and ending of all things . . .

She had not seen the man called Theo in the cards, nor did they prophesy the meaning of her actions. When she called the ambulance they said they would come soon, and half an hour later she was still waiting by the water.

And when she called again they had no record of her call, and gave her the number of the complaints department.

The sun was down and the street lights distant, their backs turned to the towpath. On the other side of the water: an industrial estate where once patty-line men had loaded lorries with bikinis and bras, pillows and sofa throws, percale fitted sheets, gold-plated anklets and next season's striped trend-setting onesies for the discerning customer. Once, the men who laboured there had worn tags around their ankles to ensure that they didn't walk too slow, or spend too much time taking a piss. If they did, there were worse places they could be sent. There was always some-where worse.

Now there was black spew up the walls, and the smell of melted plastic lingering on the winter air.

A few white lamps on the loading concourse still shone, their glow slithering across the high barbed-wire fences down to the canal. The light made the frost on the bank sparkle like witches' eyes, before being swallowed whole by the blackness of the water.

Neila thought of calling out for help, to anyone in the night, but didn't have the courage and didn't think anyone would answer. People had their own problems to deal with, things being as they were. Instead she wrapped the man up as best she could in old towels she wouldn't miss, hiding her nice, fluffy towels under the bed. She felt a bit guilty about that, and alleviated her doubts by making him hot tea, which he could barely sip. Not knowing what else to do, she sat beside the man on the thin, mud-sunk grass by the gate of the lock and dialled 999 again, and got someone new who said:

"Oh my oh yes now of course yes bleeding by the canal do you have an address for that – no an address – how about a post-code, no I'm not seeing you on my map do you have premium or standard service support for an extra £4.99 a month you can upgrade to instant recovery and full rehabilitative therapies for the – oh you're not insured . . . "

The call ended there. Maybe a timer cut them off. Maybe there wasn't much signal at the moment. A pair of ducks waddled uneasily over crêpe-thin ice, now slipping into the water below, now lurching back up onto the transparent surface above, now flapping at the sound of an eager seagull looking for a snack, now quiet again beneath the thickening blue-brown sky, paddling in listless circles.

at the end and the beginning Neila spins in circles too

The man mumbled, through lips turned blue, "You've been very kind very kind I'm fine I'm sure I'll be fine it's just I'm fine . . . "

He'd tried saying this before, and fainted, only for a few seconds, then woke and picked up where he'd left off, and she hadn't had the heart to tell him that he'd passed out while trying to be so stoical, so she let him talk until he stopped, and they stayed there, waiting, and no one came.

She decided to leave him.

At the precise moment she reached that decision, like a truck driving into a concrete wall she knew that she wouldn't. The universe crumpled and blew apart, and at the centre of it she exclaimed, "This is fucking ridiculous." She creaked to her feet, pulling him by a limp limb. "Get your backside inside the fucking boat."

She had to help him walk, and he nearly hit his head on the low door at the stern of the narrowboat as she guided him in, and was unconscious, bleeding out on her white faux-leather couch, before she had got her boots off.

Chapter 2

Time goes a little peculiar
when you're not feeling so
so sometimes you wake and you remember that you will be an old, old man and that the one you love will die and you can't work out
if they die
or you first
which would be more scary? Who will be strongest without love, alone, loveless, devoid? What is worse — for you to lose the one you love or for the one you love to be destroyed by losing you?

The man on the couch is vaguely aware, when he's aware of much of anything at all, that he's hit his head and that's making things a little . . .

Neila wrung out blood-red water from her third-favourite tea towel into the mop bucket at her feet, and the bleeding still wouldn't stop, and there was silence on the canal, and silence on the water.

In the early years when she had first started sailing, Neila had thought she'd love the quiet, and for a week after buying the *Hector* she hadn't slept, in terror at the roar of whispers over still water. The creaking, the lapping of liquid, the insect-hiss of thin ice popping before the bow of a passing boat, the roar of a generator, the chug chug chug of the engine, the beating of wings, birds not really built for flight hounding each other half in sky, half on land for food, or sex, or maybe just something to do.

When exhaustion kicked in, she'd slept like a log, and now she understood the silence of the canal wasn't silence at all. If anything, it was a racket, annoying in its persistence.

Not tonight. Tonight the silence made her nervous, made her think too much. She'd come to the canal to get away from thinking. Alone, once you'd thought everything there was to think, there was only being quiet left.

She turned on the radio, and listened to Pepsi Liverpool vs CheapFlightsForU Manchester, even though she didn't really like football.

Chapter 3

At the beginning of all things . . .

The man lies on the couch, and dreams and memories blur in a fitful crimson smear of paint.

Maybe it hadn't been the beginning, but in his dreams it seems that there must have been a point where it all started, where everything changed. Back when he had a job, back when "job" seemed like the most important thing ever, back in the Criminal Audit Office, before the winter and the snow and the blood, at the beginning there had been . . .

– it seemed ludicrously banal now, but it was perhaps the place where it all went to piss –

. . . a training weekend.

The weekend was voluntary.

If you did not attend you would be docked one week's pay and a note put on your file – "BBA". No one knew what BBA stood for, but the last woman to have these fated letters added had been given a job at a morgue, showing family members the corpses of their loved ones.

Besides, everyone knew that team players were happy volunteers.

The Teamwork Bonding Experience cost £172, payable at sign-up. On the first day he was told to put a cork in his mouth, stand in front of his colleagues and explain his Beliefs and Values.

"Come on, Mr Miller!" exclaimed the Management Strength Inspiration Course Leader. "Enunciate!"

The man called Theo Miller hesitated, hoping the burning in

his face could be mistaken for the effort of not spitting out the dry brown bung, bit a little deeper into the cork, then mumbled: "I belef fat ul pepl arg detherfin of jusfic an . . . "

"Project! Pro-*ject*. Use your whole mouth, use your breath to lift you!"

At night they slept in dormitories on creaking metal beds, and were woken at 5 a.m. for a group run. He enjoyed that part. He stood on top of a hill and watched an eyelash of light peek above the horizon, growing hotter, bending the sky, liked the way the shadows of the trees broke out long and thin across the land, the visible light and visible darkness in the air as fog burned away. The walls of London were too high for him to see this sight, and the places in the country where sometimes he'd gone as a child had fallen to scroungers, and the trains didn't go there any more. For a moment he thought of the sea below the cliffs, and the memory filled his lungs with salty air – then someone told him to stop dawdling, Mr Miller!

So he ran on, and pretended to be out of breath and struggling at the back, where most of the senior staff were, even though he felt like he could have run for ever. It didn't do to stand out.

Management joined them at 10 a.m. Management were staying up the road at a golfing resort, but wanted to demonstrate leadership and muck in with the troops. Edward Witt, 37, fresh from Company central office – personal motto "I achieve for me" – roared across the waving long grass, "Come on! Put some welly into it!"

Theo Miller did not smile, did not blink, but concentrated harder on the painted picture of the wooden man before him, drew the axe back over his shoulder and threw it with all his might. He was aiming for the head, but by chance managed to hit it in the nuts.

"Keep going, guys!" barked Edward, bouncing impatiently on the edge of the field as the Fiscal Efficiency Team ran up and down, one statistician suspended by ankles and armpits between two others. "Don't let each other down!"

Theo wasn't sure what all of this had to do with his job. He didn't learn anything about the law, or finance, or governmental good practice. The only colleagues he felt any closer to were the ones he usually hung out with anyway, the hangdog dredges of the Criminal Audit Office who sometimes drank cheap wine on the seventh floor when the lights were out, and didn't go to the pub because they couldn't stand the noise.

If anything, the weekend only served to make office cliques tighter, as friends curled in for mutual support against the horror of the experience, shooting suspicious glances across the muddy field to ensure that everyone was suffering equally, losing all together. Edward Witt prowled up and down, encouraging competition, competition, get ahead, and one or two tried gamely, and Theo was always the third man eliminated in a contest, and penultimate man picked for a side.

It wasn't that he was inept, or even disliked. There wasn't enough personality in Theo Miller for people to love or hate. A psychic had once attempted to read his aura, and after a period of frowning so intense she started groaning with the effort of her grimace, announced that it was puce. Like everyone else from the mystic to the mundane, she too had failed to spot that his life was a lie, or that the real Theo Miller was fifteen years dead, buried in an unmarked grave. So much for the interconnected mysteries of the universe, Theo thought.

So much for all that.

At the end of the weekend they got into a coach.

The coach sat in traffic, covering twelve miles in an hour and twenty minutes, and Theo dozed. One time he saw a woman standing on the hard shoulder, waving frantically at the passing cars for help, but no one stopped, and tears rolled down her face. People didn't like to stop on this stretch of the M3. The security fence kept out most of the screamers, the scroungers and the children from the surrounding enclaves, but Company Police signs reminded all that YOUR SAFETY IS YOUR RESPONSIBILITY, and no one doubted it for a moment.

You heard rumours of tax dodgers breaking in through the fence and rushing down into the lanes when the traffic got too slow, to crack open boots and steal anything they could, until speed picked up again and they scuttled to safety or were mown down where they stood.

After four hours of snoozing to a soundtrack of inspirational speeches by Simon Fardell, Company ExO, the coach dropped them off at the office in Victoria. The pavements were too narrow for the tired, baggage-slung commuters waiting for their buses, leaves tumbling from the last of the shedding plane trees.

Though it was late, and they were tired and muddy and sore, Edward treated them to a sandwich dinner, held in the semi-sacred and barely used Large Media Suite, access usually limited to executive grade 2A and above. As they ate thin slices of cucumber between wet pieces of white bread, lights were dimmed, and Edward presented his PowerPoint of Vital Lessons Learned and Where We Go From Here, including a comic montage from the weekend of people falling into mud, dropping their axes and spraining their ankles to lighten the moment and boost team morale.

And when he was done the lights came up
and there were little pink pots of Angel Delight with a single half-strawberry on top and there
was Dani Cumali.

On the canal the man called Theo groans in his sleep and holds the blanket tight, and Neila sits with her head in her hands and wonders what the fuck she's even done

And in his dreams
           and in his memories
   Dani is watching him, and that's where it all went wrong.

In the past
           These things are a little blurry but he thinks, yes, in the past, but not that past, the more recent past, the past had

already happened, the less important yet more urgent bit of the past that is

        (Neila wonders if she should try and give him a blood transfusion, but where the fuck do you even start, times being what they are?)

Dani Cumali stood at the edge of the Large Media Suite in the Criminal Audit Office, and stared at Theo Miller, and that was where the world changed.

Her black hair was cut to a pudding bowl around her ears, her skin devoid of make-up, lines around her mouth, grey and thin, lines between her eyebrows, a cobweb face. Her nails were scrubbed down to thin ridges, she wore the navy blue one-piece of the catering company

and she looked at him

and he looked at her

and they knew each other immediately and without a word.

On the screen was a picture of that time during the weekend when he'd been punched in the face during the self-defence training session and his nose had bled everywhere and wasn't that hilarious our Theo Miller give him a hand

everyone clapped

and Dani saw and knew the truth.

And she knew that she could destroy him, bring down the house of lies, fraud and deceit that he had built around himself, around his name that was a lie, around teamwork bonding experiences and work reports and progress assessments and pension plans and rental deposits and

and the whole lie of his whole fucking life.

She could tear it down with a single word.

And in her eyes was the fire of the righteous and the sword.

In the beginning.

Enter the monthly
Orbit sweepstakes at
www.orbitloot.com

With a different prize every month,
from advance copies of books by
your favourite authors to exclusive
merchandise packs,
**we think you'll find something
you love.**